# BE CAREFUL WHAT YOU *Wish For*

### A NOVEL

## CHERYL FAYE

A
**SBI**
PUBLICATION

A STREBOR BOOKS INTERNATIONAL LLC PUBLICATION
DISTRIBUTED BY SIMON & SCHUSTER, INC.

Published by

Strebor Books International LLC
P.O. Box 6505
Largo, MD 20792
http://www.streborbooks.com

LCCN 2004117498
ISBN 1-59309-034-X          ISBN 978-1-59309-034-0

This book is a work of fiction. Names, characters, places and incidents are products of the author's imagination or are used fictitiously. Any resemblance to actual events or locales or persons, living or dead, is entirely coincidental.

Distributed by Simon & Schuster, Inc.
1230 Avenue of the Americas
New York, NY 10020
1-800-223-2336

Cover design: Marion Designs

First Printing December 2004
Manufactured and Printed in the United States

10   9   8   7   6   5   4   3   2

# DEDICATION

*For Michael and Douglas II*

# ACKNOWLEDGMENTS

First and foremost, I give all honor and glory to God. "I can do all things through [my Lord and Savior, Jesus] Christ, who strengthens me"—Philippians 4:13 (emphasis added). It is only by the grace of God that I have been blessed with the gift of writing stories that touch the lives of others. Thank you, Father.

To Zane—Thank you for being the incredible person you are. What you are doing for your writers will go down in history. You are truly the essence of the Black Woman—proud, beautiful, confident, generous, positive, and unpretentious. I greatly admire you.

To Everyone at Strebor Books—What an amazing group of people. I am honored to be a part of the family.

I must give heartfelt thanks to William Fredrick Cooper. Although I penned "Be Careful..." it was your poetic spirit that added just the right zing to my words, making for a more interesting, colorful and enjoyable read. William, I know that God put you in my life for a special purpose. Keep giving it to God, and He'll keep giving it to you.

Unlike blood relatives, real friends are the family that we choose. I have to give a special THANK YOU to My Girls, who have supported me through it all. Some of you I've known just a little while, some I've known a lifetime, but all of you are the real deal and I am blessed to have each of you in my life. You each have the patience of a saint; you've taken the time to listen to my ranting; you've dried my tears over the years when my heart's been broken; you've given me your honest opinion whether I liked it or not; you've encouraged me; you've laughed with me and cried with me; you've kept my secrets; you are many and varied, and I love you all, especially Rhonda, Charisse, Shari, Sheryl, Tina, Peggy, Michele, Edwina, Dawn, Dianne, Sonia, Velda, Yvonne and Xoli. Hope I've been as good a friend to each of you, as you've been to me.

To my immediate family (blood). My sons, Michael and Douglas—I am so proud of you both. You are the joy of my life and giving birth to each of you was the greatest gift I have ever received. I love you with all my heart. Mommy and Daddy—Barbara and James Smith, Sr.—what can I say? I love you both so much. I love you both so much. I love you both so much. You are the best parents any kid could ever have. To my siblings, Jackie, Mamie, Jimmy and Stephanie, we've been through it all together and together we will always be. I'm so grateful that you are my blood. I love you all and thank you for your constant support and encouragement. To my beautiful granddaughter, Mikayla—I love you, sweetheart. I've finally got my little girl. Thank you, Michael. To my nephews, Torian, Jimmy III, Jovonnie II, Avery (great-nephew)—I love you. To my nieces, Stacey and Breóne—I love you.

To everyone who's ever bought or read and enjoyed any of my books, thank you from the bottom of my heart. You are what it's all about.

# Chapter 1

Sitting comfortably on the plush gray leather living room sofa with her stockinged feet tucked under her ample bottom and wearing an old pair of sweatpants with a hole in the knee and a paint-splattered sweatshirt, Jamilah Parsons cradled a bowl of her favorite ice cream, Häagen-Dazs® Vanilla Swiss Almond, in her lap, despite the chill in the apartment on that cold February night.

Jamilah's roommate and childhood friend, Sabrina Richardson, accompanied by her latest conquest, Darius Thornton, had just entered the apartment that Friday evening looking glamorous as always.

Wearing a full-length fox coat which draped her long, slender frame as if she had been born in it, Sabrina's long, luxurious black hair fell down her back and, combined with the fur, gave her a regal air she carried all too well. Jamilah had always believed Sabrina could have been a high-paid super-model who traveled the globe showcasing world-renowned designers' clothing while her picture graced fashion magazine covers worldwide. Possessing stunning looks with a figure to match, in addition to the exaggerated air of sophistication she had learned from her mother, Sabrina, nevertheless, was determined to fulfill her childhood dream of marrying a wealthy man so she would not have to work for a living.

"Hey, J," Sabrina chirped.

"Hi."

Immediately noticing what Jamilah was watching on television, Sabrina frowned. "Not again, Jamilah."

Ignoring Sabrina's comment, Jamilah continued watching Robert Townsend's

*The Five Heartbeats*, one of her all-time favorite movies. Since there was no special man in her life right now, and being the movie buff she was, Jamilah frequently passed her time in front of the television or at the theater, if she was not curled up with a good book or working.

"You remember Darius, don't you?" Sabrina inquired.

"Yeah. Hi."

Believing him to be one of the most handsome men Sabrina had ever brought home, Darius reminded Jamilah of Denzel Washington, although she thought he was much better-looking. Wearing his dark brown hair in a stylish fade, his smooth, cocoa-brown face was clean shaven, allowing his true masculine allure to shine. Although not unbecoming, his nose was somewhat flat, but his lips looked soft, sensuous and ripe for kissing. Despite his finely polished *GQ* cover model look, Darius' warm, welcoming personality shone through as did his sincerity when he smiled at Jamilah and greeted her in that smooth baritone voice she remembered. "Hello, Jamilah. How are you?"

"Fine, thanks."

Having a substantial title or position as a prerequisite to dating Sabrina, Darius was a senior associate at a major New York City law firm. She had been seeing him for a little over a month and often bragged that he would bend over backwards to do anything she asked. Beauty aside, Sabrina was quite pretentious, and it amazed Jamilah somewhat that Darius, who exuded humility, would be so taken with her. The old adage "opposites attract" sprang to mind whenever Jamilah thought of the obvious contrasts in their personalities, but truth be told, the same could be said of her and Sabrina's friendship.

Peeling off her fur coat and tossing it carelessly across the arm of their rose-floral silk upholstered easy-chair, Sabrina said, "Sit down, Darius. I'll be right back."

Beneath the luxurious coat, Sabrina wore an ecru angora turtleneck sweater over ecru wool gabardine slacks. High-heeled leather boots of the same hue completed her ensemble. Standing five feet, eight inches in her stocking feet, even in her four-inch heels she was still dwarfed by her handsome friend who stood close to six inches taller.

Giving further direction as Darius took a seat at the opposite end of the sofa, Sabrina intoned, "Jamilah, keep Darius company for me while I go change."

Sarcastically, Jamilah responded, "Yes, ma'am." Smiling apologetically at Darius when she realized that Sabrina had not even taken his coat, she added, "Let me hang up your coat, Darius."

"Oh, thank you." Rising to remove his tan cashmere overcoat, he handed the garment to Jamilah, who immediately noticed how elegantly his brown tweed suit covered his tall frame. When he unbuttoned his suit jacket, she could see that his white shirt was crisp, as if freshly ironed. A beige and brown "power" tie was knotted expertly at his neck.

After hanging his coat in the closet near the front door, Jamilah then picked up Sabrina's fur coat from the chair and hung it up, as well. Before taking her seat again, Jamilah asked, "Can I get you anything? Something to drink? Some ice cream maybe?"

"Oh, no, thank you, Jamilah. I'm fine," was his reply.

*You most certainly are, you gorgeous hunk of...* Secretly ashamed of her lustful thoughts, she asked, "Is it really very cold out?"

"Yeah, the hawk is out in full effect tonight."

Chivalrously, he waited for her to sit back down before he did the same. *Mmm, Mama raised him right*, she thought. Seated again, Jamilah picked up her bowl of ice cream, assumed her former position and resumed eating. Silence ensued for the next few minutes until she spoke.

"Do you want to watch something else? I've already seen it a dozen times, as I'm sure you've guessed from Brie's remark. I can turn this off."

"No. Actually, this is one of my favorite movies," Darius commented.

"Really?"

"Yeah. I've seen it about five times myself. It kind of takes me back. Me and a couple of my college buddies used to sing together. We did a few talent shows while we were in school," Darius admitted.

"Really?" Sitting up straight on the couch, she placed her bowl on the glass-topped coffee table and turned toward him. "You know, I used to sing with my cousins when we were little. We never did any talent shows, but we put on plenty of shows at family gatherings."

Laughing, Darius guessed, "The Supremes, huh?"

"The Parsonettes."

Puzzlement covered his face.

"Our last name is Parsons."

Nodding with understanding, he responded, "Oh."

"Hey, what are you two talking about?" Sabrina inquired as she returned to the living room. Dressed now in red silk lounging pajamas, wearing red satin stiletto mules with her hair pulled over one shoulder and fresh make-up, Sabrina looked stunning.

Jamilah noticed that Darius was immediately taken in by her friend's appearance.

Sitting next to him and draping one of her long slender legs across his lap, Sabrina listened as Jamilah said, "Darius was just telling me that he used to be in a singing group when he was in college."

Cooing in his ear with slight envy, she remarked, "Is that right? You've never sung for me."

Jamilah blushed, but not as deeply as Darius did, she noticed. Suddenly feeling like a third wheel, she grabbed the remote control and turned off the television before picking up her bowl and heading out of the room.

No one noticed her departure.

Entering her spacious bedroom and turning on her bedside lamp, Jamilah sat on top of the multicolored goose-down comforter that covered her queen-sized bed and finished what was left of her ice cream.

"How come I can't meet a man as fine as that," she murmured in her solitude.

Placing the bowl on the nightstand and rising from the bed, she walked over to the full-length mirror that hung on the closet door and gazed at her reflection. *I'm no beauty like Sabrina, but I look good enough.*

Two inches taller than Sabrina and full-figured, Jamilah, however, was by no means fat. *Healthy,* that's what her mother called her. Her size sixteen hips had turned plenty of men's heads and her ample bosom had captured many men's undivided attention. Beautiful, blemish-free, pumpernickel brown skin was her covering. Her nose and mouth were small and more European-looking than African in their structure. Many times had she been told that the slant of her eyes was very sexy. Shoulder-length culture locks were worn like an Afrocentric crown.

*Maybe if I was a little slimmer...* She suddenly frowned. "What am I thinking about? There is nothing wrong with me." Turning in a huff and walking back to her bed, Jamilah picked up the book she was currently reading from the night-stand and propped herself up against her fluffy throw pillows to read.

# Chapter 2

Hot, horny and hard, Darius turned to Sabrina immediately upon Jamilah's departure. Her red silk pajamas—despite completely covering her body—afforded him a delicious view of her perfectly formed breasts, and the imprint of her erect nipples against the fine fabric had a titillating effect on him.

Strong arms enveloped her as he pulled her closer before finding her lips with his. Sabrina accepted his kiss, and relished the power she knew she had over him.

Having just dined at Morton's on Fifth Avenue, Sabrina was impressed that Darius had not batted an eye when he was handed the one hundred and seventy-dollar check. She liked that. *At least he isn't cheap.*

As she let his lips touch hers, Sabrina decided that she would keep him around for a while, but at arms' length. Expert in the art of teasing, she knew his libido was inflamed because his breathing had become somewhat irregular, but she also knew how far she could let him go before she would have to stop him.

*Good*, she thought, *let him set his heart on me. That way I'll be sure to get exactly what I want.*

Deciding to enhance his arousal just a bit more, she slowly slid her hand along the length of his thigh, until she was just inches from his crotch.

He moaned a breathless "yes."

Reaching for her breasts, he gently but firmly squeezed one erect nipple before cupping the entire mound in his large hand. Aroused by his touch, Sabrina sighed involuntarily. Nevertheless, she would only let him go so far.

Her soft caress continued along his thigh, moving now to the inner side of his muscular limb. Removing his hand from her mound for just a moment, he reached for hers and guided it to the masculine evidence of his desire.

Impressed by his length and mass, Sabrina moaned, "Mmm."

"Oh, Sabrina, I want you so bad."

*I know you do*, she said to herself. *But not yet.*

"Let me make love to you, baby."

Feeling Sabrina begin to pull away from him, Darius urged, "Come on, baby. Let's go back to your room," as he gently kissed her neck.

"No."

"Aw, baby."

Still pulling away, she declared, "No, Darius! It's too soon for that."

"Sabrina, you can't tell me you don't want me just a little. I can feel how much you do."

"That's not the point. I need to get to know you better." Completely disengaging herself from his embrace, she rose from the sofa.

Disillusioned, dejected and dissatisfied, Darius remained where he was. His fierce arousal showed clearly in his pants. "What do you want to know about me?"

Shooting him a cutting glance, she sneered, "Don't be funny. I'm not one of those girls you can take to dinner a couple of times and expect to fall into bed with you."

"That's not what I expect at all. I care about you, Sabrina."

"Well, if you really care, you'll wait until *I'm* ready," she stated from across the room. Arms folded across her bosom, she wore a pout reminiscent of a spoiled child.

Rising from the sofa, Darius adjusted his pants before he stepped in front of her. *Damn, she's beautiful*, he thought. *She knows how much she's turning me on, and I know she's trying to play me, but try as I might, I can't resist her.*

Gazing into her lovely brown eyes, he was immediately reminded of the first time that he had laid eyes on her. It was about five or six weeks ago and he had just left the office of one of his firm's biggest clients. Standing directly in his line of sight when the elevator doors opened, he was momentarily awestruck by the long-haired beauty in the fox coat; the same one she had worn tonight. Stepping into the elevator, he noticed her right eyebrow rise just slightly, as though her curiosity was piqued by his appearance, but she masked it almost immediately, her face becoming that of a statue before he turned his back to her. Five other men occupied the elevator with them, but the silence in the car was deafening.

The sweet fragrance of her perfume filled the air, without being overpowering. Looking over at the brother who stood to his left, Darius was slightly amused when he noticed that he was watching her out of the corner of his eye.

When the elevator reached the lobby, Darius stepped aside to allow her to exit first. He noticed that none of the other men made a move to leave the elevator before her, either. Once she had cleared the car, it seemed that they had all breathed a collective sigh of relief. He overheard one of the men murmur, "What a fox!"; knowing all too well that he was not speaking of her coat.

Lingering a moment once she had cleared the elevator bank, she'd glanced back at him with seeming indifference. *She certainly is beautiful,* he'd thought, knowing that she had expected at least one of the men who had exited the elevator behind her to say something to her, as was probably the usual case. But although each of them had made a point of getting one last look before continuing on their way, no one had said a word.

He had walked past her at the same moment she had turned and looked at him. He'd acted as if he hadn't noticed her presence.

"Excuse me."

Still remembering a chill that had run down his spine at the sound of her voice, he'd turned to her. "Yes?"

"Don't I know you?"

*Damn, that's the line we fellas usually use,* he'd thought. "I don't think so. But that can be easily rectified," he'd quipped.

Blushing, she'd said, "You look so familiar, I was sure we had met before."

"No, I would definitely have remembered *you.* My name is Darius Thornton, though, so if we happen to run into each other again, I'll be able to say we did meet before." He then extended his hand.

She lightly took the hand he had offered. "Sabrina Richardson."

"My pleasure." Recalling how soft her hands had been at their first touch, he also remembered wondering how they would feel on his body—actually, he still did.

"Do you work in this building?" she'd asked.

"No, I was just meeting with a client."

"Oh, I see. Would I be nosy to ask what line of business you're in?" she had asked sweetly, but without pretense.

"Not at all. I'm an attorney." He suddenly realized, *she'd sized me up right there.*

"Really? What area of law do you specialize in?" she had next asked.

"Banking."

"That sounds interesting."

"It can be."

They had stood together in silence for the next few seconds. Darius had been waiting for her to make the next move since she had started it all.

"Well, I don't want to take up any more of your time. I'm sure you're a very busy man. It was nice meeting you," she had said while extending her hand.

She'd snagged him at that point. "I would be honored if you'd take up more of my time. Is there any chance that I might be able to take you to dinner one evening?"

"Are you married?"

"No, I'm not. Never have been. And no kids, either."

"Well, then, I think that can be arranged," she had said with the sweetest, sexiest smile he had ever seen.

Standing in front of her now, Darius acknowledged that he was crazy about her and unwilling to do anything to jeopardize what he was sure they could have together. *I'll do damn near anything she asks.* He couldn't help himself. Not only was she beautiful, but she possessed such confidence and poise that he was proud to have her at his side. Being genuinely modest and not believing he was as handsome as he actually was, Darius felt privileged that a woman as fine as Sabrina would want to be with him.

Taking one of her hands in his, he softly said, "I'll wait, Sabrina, for as long as you want me to. But I want you to know that you do something to me that no one has ever done before, and I can't help how I feel, so if at times I get a little... excited, don't hold it against me, okay?"

Smiling, she took a step closer to him, eating up the inches between them. "I just don't want to go too fast."

"I won't rush you, Sabrina. I'll never rush you."

While allowing him to pull her into his arms and tenderly press his lips to hers, Sabrina thought, *I've hit the jackpot.*

# Chapter 3

Employed as a graphic artist by a large insurance company for the past six years, Jamilah had a hand in developing brochures and other literature used by the company to assist orientating new employees. This year, for the first time, she had played a major role in designing the company's annual report. On a few occasions, she was afforded the opportunity to work on the company's advertising brochures. Working with the advertising team was what she really loved, but those opportunities only arose when one of the team members was out of the office. Artistic and ambitious, Jamilah often worked on a freelance basis out of her home. A computer with all of the latest software was perched atop a large antique cherry desk in one corner of her bedroom/office. The four-drawer, imitation cherry credenza that held hard copies of all her business records and jobs had a fax machine, color printer and scanner atop it, and was positioned between the desk and a drafting table.

Currently working on obtaining a full-time position with a major advertising agency as the second in command of its art department, she had interviewed with the head of the agency last week after speaking with the vice presidents of the art and marketing departments. Fairly certain that she had the job locked up, she was still on pins and needles awaiting their call.

Meanwhile, she dragged herself to work every day at the insurance company she'd been with for six years. Bored out of her mind with this position, she was feeling inexplicably and inconsolably melancholy on this particular Monday.

Currently in the throes of a severe case of PMS, the last thing she'd wanted to do was sit in the cramped little workroom she shared with three other artists, so she'd gone home early and was surprised to find Sabrina and Darius in the apartment when she walked in that afternoon at four twenty-five.

"Hi, J," Sabrina greeted her cheerfully when she opened the door.

Wondering briefly what Sabrina and Darius were doing there so early in the afternoon, Jamilah's curiosity about them waned just as quickly as she grumbled, "Hi, Brie. Hi, Darius."

With a warm smile, Darius asked, "How you doing, Jamilah?"

"I've been better."

Genuinely concerned, Sabrina asked, "What's the matter?"

"I don't know. I'm PMS-ing." Dropping her pocketbook and portfolio on the floor without removing her coat, Jamilah flopped down into the plush cushions of the easy-chair she and Sabrina had purchased together when they first moved into the apartment.

Sabrina walked over to the console table that held their telephone and answering machine. Smiling brightly as she picked up the notepaper lying there, she said, "Well, I know what might cheer you up." Sauntering back to Jamilah, Sabrina stopped in front of her. "Ellen Stengle from the Harper Agency called. She asked that you get back to her as soon as you can."

Lighting up like she'd been jolted by electricity, Jamilah snatched the paper out of Sabrina's hand as she hurriedly rose, almost knocking Sabrina over. "She did? When'd she call?"

Grabbing Jamilah to steady herself, Sabrina said, "Whoa! Take it easy." Glancing at the clock on the wall above the dining table, she answered, "She called about fifteen minutes ago."

Quickly checking her own watch, Jamilah nearly ran across the room to the telephone, immediately picking up the receiver and dialing Ellen Stengle's number, which she knew by heart. "Oh my God, please let them tell me I've got this job. Cross your fingers, y'all."

Holding up his two large hands, Darius crossed his fingers on each. Sabrina did the same.

The call was answered after the first ring. "Good afternoon. My name is Jamilah Parsons. May I please speak with Ellen Stengle? Thank you." Turning toward Sabrina and Darius, Jamilah crossed her fingers as well. "Hello, Ellen?

Hi, how are you? This is Jamilah Parsons returning your call...I'm fine, thank you...Yes...I accept." Nodding her head vigorously and smiling broadly at Sabrina and Darius to show her delight, she continued, "Yes, that's wonderful... Yes, I can start on the eighth...Oh, thank you. I'm really looking forward to working with you, too, Ellen. Thank you very much...Okay. Good-bye." Screaming, "I got it! I got it!" Jamilah hung up the phone.

Elated and excited about her best friend's good fortune, Sabrina rushed over and hugged her. "Congratulations, Jamilah! I knew you would get it. Oh, I'm so happy for you."

"Thanks, Sabrina. Oh, my gosh, I got the job! I'm so excited!" Jamilah screamed once again.

Walking over to Sabrina and Jamilah, Darius leaned in and kissed her cheek. "Congratulations, Jamilah."

"Thank you, Darius." Sighing with pure satisfaction, Jamilah cried, "Oh boy, oh boy."

"We have to celebrate, you know," Sabrina said.

Chuckling to herself as she strolled back to the easy-chair, Jamilah flopped back into it. "I'm so happy, I could croak."

"Come on, J, we've got to celebrate. We'll take you to dinner," Sabrina said as she moved back across the room to stand in front of Jamilah.

Finally shrugging off her coat, she said, "Oh, no, that's okay, guys. I'm okay."

"No! We're going to take you to dinner, right, Darius?" Sabrina turned to him.

"Yeah, come on, Jamilah. This definitely calls for a celebration."

"I don't want to impose on you two."

"How would you be imposing? You'd do the same for me," Sabrina pointed out. "As a matter of fact, you did. When I got this job with Bryce, you took me out to celebrate."

Sabrina was the personal assistant to the president of a large brokerage house on Wall Street.

Darius added, "Yeah, Jamilah, you deserve this. Sabrina told me how much you wanted this spot. And the way you walked in that door a minute ago, with your head down, looking all dejected... I think this would be the perfect way to cap off this great news."

Looking over at him, she thought, *Damn, he's fine! Sabrina sure is lucky to have found such a sweet guy*. Then, speaking directly to him, she asked, "Are you sure you don't mind?"

"Do we mind?" Sabrina asked incredulously. "Girl, you know how we do. You're my girl, and I'd do anything for you and we're going out to toast your new job. Now come on."

Reaching out and pulling Jamilah up from the chair, Sabrina directed, "We'll go to Michaels in midtown. Darius knows the guy who owns the place."

"Oh, that place is so expensive," Jamilah grumbled.

Looking at Darius with a sugary, sweet smile, Sabrina stated, "Don't worry about it. Darius can afford it. Can't you, baby?"

Embarrassed by Sabrina's statement, Jamilah frowned, but Darius just smiled. "Don't worry about it, Jamilah."

"But don't we need a reservation?" she questioned.

"I told you he knows the guy who owns the place. We'll get a table. We always do," Sabrina stated confidently.

Looking at Darius questioningly, Jamilah watched him nod his head before she sighed.

"Come on," Sabrina urged.

"Well, if we're going to go there, I need to change. Do you guys mind waiting?" Jamilah humbly asked.

"Of course not," Sabrina answered for Darius. "Sit down, baby," she said, waving her hand in his direction. "Come on, J. Let's see what you're gonna wear." Grabbing Jamilah by the hand like an anxious little girl, Sabrina led her back to her bedroom.

Once they were behind closed doors, Jamilah turned to her. "Sabrina, I've got to call Mommy and let her know I got the job. I'll just be a second."

"Go 'head."

A registered nurse by profession, Jamilah's mother, Alexia Witherspoon, lived outside of Atlanta, Georgia with her husband of nine months, Frank Witherspoon, Jr. She and Frank had moved there five months earlier. Before their relocation, Alexia and Jamilah would talk on the telephone nearly every day, and when Alexia first moved away, they had continued their frequent phone calls until they both came to realize it was too expensive, so they now conversed via the Internet, mostly.

Growing up, Jamilah had been the only child of her previously unmarried mother with no knowledge of, or contact from, her father. Abandoning the scene when Alexia told him of his impending fatherhood, at twenty years old and in her third year of college, and although crushed by his abandonment, Alexia knew she would do neither herself nor her child any good by harboring ill feelings for him, so she put him out of her mind before Jamilah's arrival into the world. With her family's unwavering love and support, Alexia was able to graduate from college and obtain her R.N. status, thereby affording her a means of earning a comfortable salary so she could care for herself and her young daughter.

As a little girl, Jamilah had inquired about her father only once. Alexia, having made a point of always been being honest with her daughter, had told her the truth, but without antagonism. Refusing to beat the man down about his irresponsibility, Alexia's thinking was that it was truly his loss alone.

With the help of her father, Alexia was able to buy a modest three-bedroom house across the street from Sabrina's family when Jamilah was four years old. Alexia and Dolly Richardson had never really become good friends, but the girls had taken an instant liking to one another despite their widely contrasted upbringings. Sabrina was the only daughter and youngest child of Dr. Martin Richardson and his socialite wife, Dolly. Whereas Jamilah's mother often had to penny-pinch to make ends meet, Sabrina's family was relatively well off. While Alexia was busy at the hospital sometimes working double shifts, Dolly Richardson split her days between carpooling kids, sharing gossip at afternoon teas with the other housewives in the neighborhood and planning dinner parties for her husband's colleagues.

When Jamilah was thirteen years old, Alexia began dating Frank Witherspoon, Jr., a retired Army captain. He was, in fact, the only father Jamilah had ever known and she loved him dearly. He and Alexia met when he was hospitalized after a car accident and she was his attending nurse. When he had first asked Alexia to move back to his home in Georgia after their marriage, she had been totally against it. Not wanting to leave her only child alone in New York City, Jamilah had finally convinced Alexia that she should go, telling her, "I'm not a baby anymore, Mommy, and you've sacrificed enough of your life for me. Now I want you to have your own happiness," knowing she would never have to worry about her mother as long as Frank was around. She missed not being able to just pick up and go by their house, but every time she spoke to Alexia, Jamilah could hear how happy she was now that she was living her life for herself; that was enough for Jamilah.

Frank answered her call. "Hi, Frank," Jamilah said happily.

"Hey, sweetheart. How you doin' up there?"

"I'm doing great! I got the job. I was just calling to give you guys the good news."

"That's beautiful, baby. I knew you'd get it."

"Hi, Frank," Sabrina yelled in the background.

"Tell the glamour girl I said, hi."

Jamilah relayed, "Hi, glamour girl." Sabrina laughed. "So, how're you doing?" Jamilah then asked Frank.

"I'm pretty good. Just got back in from a day of fishing a little while ago. You should see these catfish I caught. Lexi's gonna make us some fritters tonight. Too bad you're not here to have some."

"That's okay; y'all better save me some. I'll be down in a few months." Jamilah laughed.

Laughing with her, Frank replied, "Yeah, okay. I'll put some in the freezer for you."

"Is Mommy there?"

"Yeah, hold on, baby. Here she comes with her fine self."

Jamilah heard her mother say, "Will you stop?" Then, "Hi, sweetie. How you doin'?"

"I got the job, Mommy!"

"Oh, congratulations, baby. I'm so proud of you. I knew you'd get it."

"Hi, Mommy!" Sabrina yelled over Jamilah's shoulder to Alexia.

"Is that Sabrina?"

"Yeah."

"Tell her I said, hi."

"Hi, Sabrina. I can't talk long, Mommy, 'cause Brie and her boyfriend are taking me out to dinner to celebrate, but I wanted to call you to let you know."

"Well, I'm glad you did. That's so wonderful. When do you start?"

"In two weeks."

With her mouth away from the phone Alexia scolded, "Will you stop, Frank?" Then to Jamilah, "This man is a mess."

"Sounds like I interrupted something," Jamilah teased.

"If he keeps messing with me, there's not going to be anything to interrupt."

With a chuckle, she responded, "Well, listen, Mommy, I've got to run, 'cause they're waiting for me to get dressed. I'll talk to you this weekend, okay?"

"Okay, sweetheart. I'm happy for you and I miss you."

"I miss you, too."

"I love you, baby."

"I love you, too, Mommy. Give Frank a hug for me. Bye." When Jamilah hung up the telephone she said to Sabrina, "Frank is something else. I think he's trying to get his swerve on."

Sabrina laughed. "I heard that!"

"Hey, Brie, you know, we can go somewhere else. That place Michaels is so expensive."

"I told you Darius can afford it. Stop worrying about it," Sabrina reiterated with an off-handed wave. Already at Jamilah's closet, she was going through her clothes looking for an outfit for her friend. "Ooh, wear this."

Pulling out a black and shimmering gold spandex dress with a low princess neckline and long sleeves, she held up one of Jamilah's favorite dresses.

"No, that's too dressy. I'll just put on my green velour pantsuit."

"Oh, yeah, that's cool."

With her high sense of style and keen eye for fashion, Jamilah had always felt that Sabrina could be the commissioner of the fashion police. She never hesitated to tell Jamilah when she thought her outfit was not appropriately chic. Although Jamilah's taste in clothes was perfectly fine, she did not spend time worrying about what the latest trend in clothing was or what other people would think about what she was wearing the way Sabrina did. Quality, comfort and how a garment looked on her full frame were what mattered to her.

"Why don't you pin your locks up?"

Jamilah often pinned her hair up in various styles, depending on where she was going and the mood she was in. Since they were celebrating and she was dressing up a bit, she agreed with Sabrina's suggestion.

Minutes later, as she stood in front of her bedroom mirror adjusting her clothes, Jamilah turned to Sabrina and said, "Hey, Brie, I hope you realize what a good man you've got in Darius. It's really nice of him to do this."

As she sat on Jamilah's bed touching up her nail polish, Sabrina dryly replied, "Chile, that man will do anything I tell him to. I've got him wrapped around my little finger."

"Don't you care about him, though?"

Offhandedly, "Yeah, he's all right. He's a little soft for my taste, but he'll do until something better comes along. Besides, he knows if he wants some, he'd better do the right thing."

Surprised, Jamilah asked, "You've never slept with him?"

"Nope."

"Doesn't he ask?"

"Oh, yeah. He's always trying, but I'm making him wait," Sabrina said with a wicked grin. "It's always better to make them beg for it."

"How long have you been seeing him?"

"A little over two months."

"You don't think he'll get tired of waiting, especially considering that he's so generous with you?" Jamilah asked.

"Hey, if he does, he can get lost. I'm not sleeping with anyone who doesn't do right by me, 'cause let me tell you, I know he can afford to do a whole lot more for me than he does, but since he's holding out, so am I," Sabrina said indignantly.

Jamilah chuckled. "You're something else, girl. I don't know if I could resist a man that sweet *and* that fine for too long."

"Honey, he ain't all that. I told you, he's a pushover. I like my men to have a little bit of backbone."

"Did you ever consider that maybe he has genuine feelings for you and he's waiting for you out of respect?" Jamilah posed.

"Of course, he has genuine feelings for me. I don't have time for anyone playing games. That's my department," Sabrina said with that same wicked grin.

Shaking her head, Jamilah said, "One day you're gonna run into the wrong man with that attitude. You'd better be careful whose feelings you play with."

"I'll worry about that when the time comes. So far, I'm batting a thousand, don't you think?"

# Chapter 4

Dinner that evening was an event. Although Jamilah was very impressed with the atmosphere and décor of the restaurant, as well as with the food and service, she initially felt like a "sixth" toe. Sensing her discomfort, Darius went out of his way to make her feel at ease. Jamilah was a little embarrassed at the way Sabrina seemed to fall all over him while they were out, though. She really thought Sabrina was overdoing the affection thing, especially since she knew Sabrina's real feelings for Darius.

When they arrived at Michaels, the maitre d' immediately inquired about their reservation. It was clear to see that the restaurant was very busy on this night. Before Darius could speak, however, Sabrina chimed, "We're friends of the owner. He told us to come in anytime and not to worry about reservations."

Clearly discomfited by Sabrina's brashness, Darius was the picture of humility, however, when he spoke. "If you don't have a table available right now, we'll wait at the bar."

"Well," looking at the reservations list briefly, then looking out into the busy restaurant, the maitre d' stated, "I believe I can accommodate you, sir. If you'll just give me a moment."

"Thank you. By the way, is Mr. Michaels here?" Darius asked.

"No, sir. He's gone for the evening."

"All right. We'll be at the bar."

They moved into the smoky sitting room where Darius immediately ordered cocktails for each of them. Fortunately, they only had to wait about ten minutes before they were seated.

Once seated, Darius ordered a bottle of Moët & Chandon to toast Jamilah's new job and, although Sabrina dominated most of the conversation throughout dinner, Jamilah tried to have a good time anyway. Looking across the table at her two hosts, she could see that Darius did, indeed, have very real feelings for Sabrina. That being the case, she felt a little sorry for him, especially knowing that Sabrina's feelings were superficial, if not completely a lie.

Suddenly, and to her surprise, Darius spoke directly to her. "Jamilah, what are you doing this weekend?"

"Me? Nothing," she quickly answered.

"Oh, good. You can come with us to this dance Saturday night," Sabrina interjected.

"What dance?"

"A friend of mine is a member of the Association of Black Accountants and they host a spring dance every year which includes a full-course dinner," Darius explained. "It would be great if you came. I'm sure you'd have a good time."

"No, that's okay. You know what they say, 'three's a crowd.'"

"Hey, there'll be so many people there, you won't even have to worry about that."

"Yeah, J. Besides, Darius has a friend I think you'll like," Sabrina added. "Darius, Mike'll be there, won't he?"

"Yeah, he'll be there, but I'm not into matchmaking."

"Oh, come on. All you have to do is introduce them. They'll do the rest."

Jamilah firmly stated, "I'm not into being match-made, either, and I don't like blind dates."

"It won't be a blind date. Like Darius said, there'll be plenty of people there so if you don't like Mike, don't worry about it."

"I don't know. How much are the tickets?" Jamilah asked.

"Darius'll get the tickets," Sabrina volunteered.

Rolling her eyes at Sabrina, Jamilah looked across the table and asked again, "Darius, how much are the tickets?"

"Don't worry about it. I've got it."

"No. You don't have to pay for mine."

"Jamilah, I've got it," he insisted.

Sighing, she shook her head, "You're too generous."

He smiled appreciatively.

"Is it a formal?"

"Semi-formal," Sabrina answered.

"Can I think about it? I'll let you know before Friday," Jamilah said to Darius. He responded, "Sure."

Sabrina, however, impatiently exclaimed, "Oh, come on, J! You need to get out. When's the last time you went dancing? Besides, you're not going to meet any men sitting up in that damn apartment all night."

Embittered and embarrassed by Sabrina's carping attack, Jamilah was thoroughly incensed. She needed no reminder that there was no man in her life; that there hadn't been one in her life in a damn long time. She certainly didn't need it broadcast in this restaurant.

With her head moving to emphasize each word, Jamilah stated, "I don't remember telling you I was trying to meet any," in an indignant tone as she stared icily at Sabrina.

Not at all put off by Jamilah's tone or the look on her face, Sabrina threw back, "Well, you obviously aren't."

Angrily, "And why the hell is that your concern?"

Knowing that if he did not intercede, this little spat could escalate into World War III, Darius quickly interjected, "Ladies." He glanced at Sabrina with a disapproving frown and an admonitory shake of his head, before he turned to Jamilah. "You can let me know by Friday, J. That's fine."

"Thank you." With her anger growing steadily, Jamilah had to get away from Sabrina because she was afraid she would cause a scene if she stayed there. Rising suddenly, "Excuse me. I'll be back." She started toward the ladies' lounge.

"Sabrina, you didn't have to say that to her," Darius gently scolded. "I think you embarrassed her."

"Good. Maybe she'll get up off her butt and do something about her situation."

"Did it ever occur to you that she might not want to date anyone right now?"

"Look, you don't know her, Darius. I do. I've known Jamilah for almost thirty years, long before either of us could spell our names. I live with her and I'm the one who has to listen to her whining about how she can never meet a nice man. How the hell is she ever going to meet anyone sitting at home?"

"Yeah, but you didn't have to embarrass her like that. Maybe she didn't want me to know that," Darius considerately suggested.

Sucking her teeth indifferently, "Yeah, well it's a little too late now."

# Chapter 5

After much consideration, Jamilah decided to attend the spring dance with Sabrina and Darius. Although she would never admit it to Sabrina, she *was* tired of sitting up in their apartment by herself. She'd grown weary of the solo movie runs, also. Besides that, how many times could she expect to go out with Sabrina and Darius without Sabrina eventually coming to resent her? Despite the fact that Sabrina didn't really care about him—at least not the way he cared about her—Jamilah also knew that she would not hesitate to tell her to get lost if she thought Jamilah was getting too comfortable in his presence.

Indeliberately, Jamilah was actually looking forward to meeting Darius' friend, Mike. Sabrina told her he was a doctor at St. Vincent's Hospital, and that he also had his own practice in Harlem. According to her, he was even better-looking than Darius. She said Mike was not as tall as Darius but was taller than her and had a great body with muscles everywhere.

After struggling to decide what to wear, Jamilah settled for the black and gold spandex dress that Sabrina had initially suggested the night they had taken her to dinner. She loved the way this dress clung to her body. Although she was not thin like Sabrina, she was quite shapely. Her stomach was flat and firm for the most part, and this dress exposed her cleavage without being too revealing, and hugged her round hips comfortably. Due to her height, Jamilah often wore longer dresses, but the just-above-the-knee length of this one exposed her long, shapely legs. Slipping her feet into the black and gold peau de soie pumps with the two-inch heels, she prayed they would behave. The last thing she wanted to worry about tonight was her feet hurting. It had been too long since she had been dancing and she was actually looking forward to doing so all night.

Jamilah pulled her locks up in a French roll but left a few loose in front to form a bang that hung down on the left side of her face. For an added touch she stuck a gold comb in her hair.

Reaching into the jewelry box that rested on top of her dresser, Jamilah decided on the one and a half-carat diamond solitaire necklace that her parents Alexia and Frank had given her when she graduated from college. It was small but elegant and did not detract too much from her natural beauty. She liked simple jewelry, nothing too large or flamboyant. Adding a pair of diamond studs to her ears, she next put the thin diamond tennis bracelet she had treated herself to when she got her Christmas bonus two years ago, on her right wrist. On her left wrist, she added her gold-tone and rhinestone watch-bracelet with the mother-of-pearl face.

Jamilah seldom wore make-up. She usually reserved such excesses for special occasions. This was one. With expert ability, despite the infrequency of it, she put on eyeliner and mascara and added a soft burgundy color to her lips. When her make-up application was completed, Jamilah stepped back and took a long, appraising look at herself. Noticing the seam of her dress was a little crooked, she corrected it. Turning left, then right, then completely away from the mirror but looking over her shoulder to check out the back, she thought with a smile, *You go, girl.*

She grabbed her everyday pocketbook from the bed and removed her wallet and keys. From her closet she pulled down her black and gold beaded dinner bag, and put her lipstick, wallet and keys inside, knowing that it would not hold much more than those few items.

"Okay, I'm ready," she said to herself.

She left her bedroom and headed straight to the living room. Unaware that anyone had entered the apartment, she was surprised to see Darius and his friend standing just inside the front door.

"Hey, Jamilah," Darius said brightly.

Sabrina turned to face her. A smile spread across her face when she saw Jamilah and an unspoken message passed between the two women with Sabrina's wink. Despite how angry Sabrina made her at times, Jamilah was always happy to get a nod of approval from her friend.

"Hi, Darius. I didn't hear the door."

"I ran downstairs to check the mail and they were coming in," Sabrina pointed out.

"Oh. Anything for me?"

"Nope. No mail. Mike, this is my roommate and best friend, Jamilah Parsons. Jamilah, this is Darius' friend, Mike Francis."

Jamilah stepped over to them and extended her hand with the introduction. "Hi, Mike. Nice to meet you."

Mike extended his hand but his handshake was weak. "How you doin'?" he stiffly asked.

Sabrina was right about one thing; Mike was fine, but Jamilah didn't think he looked better than Darius. His skin was fair and the reddish-brown hair on his head and face looked freshly trimmed. Sabrina had said he was taller than she was, but his stockiness made him look shorter, in her opinion. With a physique rivaling that of a weightlifter, he was generously built. Although Jamilah had heard on the radio that the temperature was close to freezing, Mike was not wearing a coat, and his suit—despite obviously being top of the line—made him look a little absurd. She thought to herself that he would probably look better in tight shorts and a muscle shirt.

Knowing immediately that he was not for her, especially after that handshake, Jamilah was polite nevertheless.

"Well, I must say you ladies are looking very lovely this evening," Darius said sincerely as he put a hand around Sabrina's waist.

"Thank you," Jamilah said with a shy smile.

"Thank you, baby."

Her usual glamorous self, Sabrina was wearing a long satin tuxedo jacket of shimmering bronze over a crinkled ankle-length bronze silk skirt. On her feet were t-strap peau de soie heels that were the exact same shade of bronze as the jacket and skirt. Her long black hair was curled and fell easily over her shoulders like a waterfall. As always, her face was expertly made up and her costume jewelry, although never ostentatious, quite noticeably matched her entire outfit perfectly.

"Do you guys want anything to drink before we leave?" Jamilah offered.

"No, thanks, Jamilah," Darius said.

"Mike?"

"No, thank you."

"Are we ready?" Jamilah asked, looking over at Sabrina.

"I am. Just let me get my purse."

Jamilah moved to the closet and removed her brown mouton coat. As she started to don the outer garment, Darius moved to help her.

"Thank you, Darius."

"You're welcome," he said with a warm smile.

Jamilah thought his friend could probably take some lessons in being a gentleman from Darius.

Reaching past her, he then removed Sabrina's coat from the closet. As she returned to the living room, he held it up so she could slip her arms inside.

"Thank you, baby."

He kissed her gently on her neck as he whispered, "You're welcome."

The 12th Annual Association of Black Accountants Spring Benefit was held at the Marriott Marquis Hotel in midtown Manhattan. While waiting to enter the hall, Jamilah noticed how elegant everyone looked. She noticed, too, the number of extremely handsome solitary men in attendance and hoped Mike would vanish like Copperfield as soon as they got inside. She already knew he was not interested in her, but that was perfect as far as she was concerned. *At least I don't have to worry about him getting in my way*, Jamilah thought.

Once they were inside, Darius escorted them to their assigned table. Mike sat down for all of five minutes, then did the first polite thing Jamilah had witnessed him do all night.

"Excuse me, ladies. I see some people I know," he said as he rose and quickly moved away from them.

Darius was at the bar getting them drinks when Mike walked away.

"Well, I'm glad he's gone. Hopefully, he'll stay with his friends," Jamilah said, as she leaned in closer to Sabrina.

"Yeah, I didn't realize he was such a jerk. Sorry, hon."

"Hey, that's okay. This is a big ocean, and I see plenty other fish," Jamilah joked.

Giving her a high-five, Sabrina laughed. "That's right, girl. Oh, yeah, I didn't tell you, but you look great, J."

"Thanks, Brie. So do you."

"Thanks."

Darius returned to the table then, carrying three glasses in his large hands. Sabrina reached out to grab the one closest to her, so he would not spill them while trying to set them down.

"Where's Mike?" he asked immediately, as he turned and looked around the large hall for his friend.

"He went to visit some friends," Sabrina volunteered with a sneer.

"And left y'all here alone?"

"That's all right, Darius. Everything happens for a reason," Jamilah said with a smile.

Looking embarrassed and quite uncomfortable, he shook his head. "I'm sorry, Jamilah."

"Don't apologize. He's not my type, anyway."

He tried a smile but Jamilah could see he still felt bad about his buddy.

Suddenly, Jamilah was approached from behind. "Excuse me, Miss. Would you like to dance?"

Turning, she looked up and into the eyes of a tall and very handsome brown-skinned man in a tuxedo. A smile of pure satisfaction creased her face. "I'd love to," she answered.

The gentleman pulled her seat back so she could rise with ease, and offered his hand. Taking it gently and graciously, she let him lead her to the dance floor. As she walked away, she looked back at Sabrina and Darius with a smile and winked.

It was almost five a.m. when Darius pulled up in front of Sabrina and Jamilah's apartment building. Jamilah moved to get out of the car as soon as he was parked.

"Oh, gosh," she grumbled.

"You okay, Jamilah?" Darius inquired as he turned to look at her in the backseat.

"Yeah, but my feet are killing me."

Smiling, "Well, you *were* on the floor all night. I guess they're protesting a bit, huh?"

"More than just a bit. But thanks, Darius. I really had a great time tonight."

"Hey, you're welcome. I'm sorry that Mike wasn't more hospitable."

Waving her hand, "Don't apologize for him. It was no skin off my teeth. To be perfectly honest with you, he did me a favor. I didn't have to sit there pretending to like him."

"Well, if I'd known he was going to be like that, I wouldn't have brought him along. I mean he was going to be there anyway, but I wouldn't have subjected you to him."

"No, biggie. I had a great time. It's been too long."

"Well, I'm glad you enjoyed yourself."

"I did. Thanks. I'll see you later."

"Okay, good night."

"Good night, Darius. Good night, Brie."

"I'm coming up," Sabrina said.

"Oh, okay, but I'll be asleep by then." Jamilah laughed.

Once Jamilah had closed the door and started toward the entrance, Darius looked after her and said to Sabrina, "She's cool. I like her."

Looking over at him antagonistically, she sneered, "Oh really?"

"Yeah. She's good people."

"And what am I?" she sniped.

Darius turned his attention to Sabrina. "What?"

"What am I?"

"What do you mean?"

"You said she's good people. What am I?"

"You're good people, too, baby. You're the best," he said sensuously as he reached over and caressed her face.

Jerking her face away from his touch, her simmering ire began to surface. "I've noticed that you two are becoming quite buddy-buddy." She could not hide the jealousy she felt in her heart.

"What?"

Yelling, "Have you suddenly lost your hearing? Why is it that I have to repeat everything I say to you?"

"Sabrina, I know you're not thinking that I'm interested in Jamilah? I know that's not what you're thinking, right?"

"What am I supposed to think?"

"What? Did I do something I wasn't supposed to?"

"It just seems to me like you've become quite friendly toward her. I mean, you paid for her ticket to this dance and you seemed to go out of your way to make sure she was comfortable tonight."

Darius responded in annoyance. "If I remember correctly, Sabrina, you were the one who *volunteered me* to get her ticket."

"Yeah, but you didn't put up much of a fight."

"What was I supposed to do when you put me on the spot like that? Besides, it wasn't a big deal. And as far as me going out of my way to make her comfortable, I felt kind of responsible for Mike's behavior. That's why I'm not into matchmaking people."

"Yeah, well, she didn't seem to be having too bad a time after Mike left us. You didn't have to fawn over her the way you did."

Becoming angry now, he spat, "I wasn't fawning over her."

"What do you call it?"

"I call it your imagination!" Briefly looking away from her due to his agitation over her unfounded assault, he turned back and said, "You know what, Sabrina, why don't you go on upstairs, because you're obviously tired, coming up with all this craziness about me and Jamilah. She's your best friend and I'm your man. Do you really think I would do something like that to you?"

"It's been done before," Sabrina stated calmly.

Banging the steering wheel in frustration, Darius didn't believe that Jamilah had ever done such a thing. Angrily, he pushed his door open and jumped out of the car, immediately walking around to Sabrina's side and sharply pulling her door open. He reached in to help her out of the car. When she was standing in front of him, he slammed the door shut and said, "When have I ever disrespected you, Sabrina? When have you ever seen me do anything sneaky and conniving like you're suggesting?"

Sabrina ignored him.

"Look at me!"

She still would not look at him nor would she speak.

Darius could not believe she was acting this way. Trying to think of a time that night when he had paid an undue amount of attention to Jamilah, he kept coming up blank because he hadn't. He had been courteous to a fault, but that was not unusual. He had an enormous amount of respect for women, black women, in particular. That was how he was raised. Besides, Jamilah was Sabrina's friend and since she had always been nice to him, he tried to reciprocate her kindness. He did not see the harm in that.

"Sabrina, look, I'm sorry if you think..." Darius sighed defeatedly. "I'm sorry, okay?"

He loved this woman, but he didn't know why. Aside from her beauty, he had learned that she was one of the most superficial and selfish people he had ever known. He felt, however, that she just needed someone to look after her, some-one who genuinely cared about her. He wanted to be that person. He was sure she had many redeeming qualities that would come to light with the right nurturing. After all, seeing the type of person that Jamilah was and knowing that they had been friends for so many years had to mean something. Sabrina had once told him that she was an only daughter and had two older brothers; she was simply spoiled, he decided. He was aware that he didn't help matters by giving in to her all the time, but his insecurity left him powerless in her presence.

"Sabrina?"

"Good night, Darius." Sabrina turned away from him without another word and started toward the building.

As he stood there in stunned silence, a feeling of despair slowly panged at his heart and spread throughout his body uncontrollably. *What did I do wrong?* He watched as she entered the building and stepped into the waiting elevator. When the door closed, he turned and walked back around to the driver's seat.

As he started home, he debated with himself about whether he should just forget about her. *Hell, if she's so sure that I would disrespect her like that already, what can I expect from a future with her?*

# Chapter 6

Jamilah was in the kitchen relatively early Sunday considering what time she had gone to bed. She had awakened feeling ravenous. She had just taken her pancakes off the skillet when the telephone rang. Reaching for the wall phone near the refrigerator, she answered, "Hello."

"Hey, Jamilah. It's Darius. How are you?"

"I'm fine, Darius. How you doin'?"

"I'm okay. How're your feet?"

Laughing out loud, Jamilah replied, "Much better, thank you."

"That's good. Is Sabrina there?"

"Yeah. Hold on a minute."

Jamilah placed the receiver on the counter that separated the kitchen from the dining area and walked back to Sabrina's bedroom. Knocking on the door once, she then eased it open.

"Hey, Brie, Darius is on the phone."

"What does he want?"

"I don't know; I didn't ask him. Why don't you pick up the phone and find out."

Sabrina rolled her eyes at Jamilah, then reached for the extension on her nightstand.

Jamilah closed the door when she heard Sabrina say, "Hello."

Immediately returning to the kitchen to hang up the phone, Jamilah wondered, *What's her problem?* Ever since she had gotten up that morning, she noticed that Sabrina was in one of her moods.

When she'd entered the kitchen upon rising, she'd been surprised to see Sabrina sitting at the dining table drinking a cup of coffee. Considering how tired she had been, Jamilah had greeted her as cheerfully as she could. Sabrina had barely responded. When Jamilah had inquired as to what was bothering her, Sabrina remained silent. She'd just taken her cup, walked to the kitchen sink and dumped the remainder of her coffee in the basin, then left the kitchen.

"Do you want breakfast?" Jamilah had called behind her. "I'm making pancakes."

"No."

Sabrina's bedroom door had slammed shut immediately after, and she hadn't left her room since then.

They had been best friends for most of their lives, and growing up, Sabrina had always been the more popular of the two, but in her heart she had always been envious of Jamilah.

When they were kids, Sabrina had been a beautiful little girl and, as she did now, even then she attracted all the boys. The girls had all wanted to be her friend because boys were always hovering around her. Being her mother's only daughter, she was always dressed in the finest clothes (she'd been selected Best Dressed Female three years in a row when they were in high school), and she was invited to all of the "in" parties.

As a child, Jamilah had always been big for her age and the smarter of the two girls. Having earned straight A's all through school, she had always been some teacher's pet, too. When they were kids, Jamilah wanted to be like Sabrina, to have boys fawning over her and girls looking at her with pure, unadulterated envy in their eyes. But when it didn't happen, she went on with her life. Due to the fact that her skin was dark and she was slightly overweight as a child, Jamilah was overlooked by most boys, unless she was the object of their teasing. Most of Jamilah's time had been spent either at the library—because she had always had a fierce love of books—or at home with her magic markers and construction paper creating one thing or another. Since Jamilah and her mother had lived across the street from Sabrina's family from the time the girls were four years old, they had become fast friends despite their differences. Jamilah had always been content simply being Sabrina's best friend; that had always been enough for her, and although she had never been a part of the "in" crowd, Sabrina had shared all of her confidences with Jamilah before anyone else.

Unbeknownst to Jamilah, Sabrina envied her brains and self-confidence. Jamilah never worried about what people thought about her; she was happy doing what she liked and to hell with whomever didn't like it. She never felt a need to impress anyone with exaggerated stories or expressions of affection. With Jamilah, it had always been "what you see is what you get." Sabrina didn't feel secure unless she was included in all the right cliques.

Although she hadn't been dating anyone for close to six months now, the relationships Jamilah had had in the past had been meaningful ones. The few men she had known had remained her friends even after their relationships ended and every so often she would get a call from one or another to see how she was. Sabrina knew plenty of men but she had never had a relationship that lasted much more than a year; most, not even that long. When she and her men broke up, it was for good; there was no communication and certainly no friendship. Sabrina had no friends who were men; with her it was always "what can you do for me?" and if the answer was nothing, she had nothing to do with you.

Despite her selfish ways, Jamilah loved Sabrina like a sister and, like sisters, they had their occasional fall-outs. Whenever Sabrina got in one of her moods though, like today, Jamilah steered clear of her. She did not know the origins of Sabrina's sour disposition and she would not ask. She knew when, or if, Sabrina wanted to talk to her about whatever was bothering her, she would. Jamilah figured, however, that it had something to do with Darius, although she could not imagine what it could be. As she took her plate to the dining table and sat down to eat, Jamilah wondered, *could they have had an argument after I left them last night, and if so, about what?* Sabrina could be so temperamental sometimes, that Jamilah knew it could have been the littlest thing that had set her off and poor Darius, not really knowing the "real" Sabrina, would be completely unprepared for her attack.

## Chapter 7

Darius had briefly considered not calling Sabrina at all the day before. Despite how tired he was, he lay awake that Sunday morning chiding himself for allowing her to get to him the way she did. Knowing he should forget about her, his heart would not listen to reason. Against his better judgment, he had reached for the telephone on his night table and dialed her number, needing to know if there was still a chance for them to be together.

When he had finally gotten out of bed Sunday afternoon, he was still somewhat shocked by her accusation that he had designs on Jamilah.

*Where could she have gotten an insane notion like that?* Jamilah was not even his type. Granted, she was pretty enough, but she was too laid-back for his taste. The only other time he had ever seen her dressed up was when they had taken her out to celebrate getting that new job earlier last week. Usually when he visited Sabrina, Jamilah was hanging around the house in jeans or sweatpants and an oversized shirt.

Still, it pained him that Sabrina had so quickly made such an asinine assumption about him when he had always made every effort to give her whatever she'd asked for. As he'd lazed around his apartment that afternoon watching basketball, Darius' mind kept coming back to her. Finally, he'd given in and called her.

They had talked for over an hour that morning and before hanging up, Sabrina had even apologized to him for her unfounded accusation. Although they'd made plans to have dinner Monday night after work, in his heart, he was still unsure about the sincerity of her apology.

It was important to him, however, that she know for certain how he felt about her, so upon arrival at his office that morning, he'd called the nearest florist and had a dozen long-stemmed white and yellow roses sent to her office with a note that read, *You're the only woman for me. Forever, Darius.*

He looked forward to seeing her that evening. He felt an overwhelming need to hold her and reassure her that he had eyes for only her.

**✱✱✱**

Having received the flowers just before lunch, Sabrina had shaken her head in disbelief when she opened the envelope and read his note. *He's an even bigger sucker than I imagined. Why do men make it so easy for me? Isn't there at least one man out there who's not afraid to tell me no?* It actually got boring for her sometimes, knowing that she could pretty much control the men in her life like mere puppets on a string.

As she prepared to leave her office that evening, Sabrina contemplated how much longer she was going to continue with this charade. Darius was no challenge. He had shown a bit of promise the other night when she had accused him of wanting Jamilah, though. Seeing the anger in his eyes when he'd pulled her out of the car, she had almost believed that he would call it quits, but then he'd gone soft again and apologized for something he hadn't even done. *Spineless!* She sucked her teeth in disgust at the memory.

One of the few things she genuinely liked about Darius, though, was that he moved in the right social circles. Well known and, from what she observed when attending various social functions with him, well liked and respected in the legal field, the ease with which Darius moved among his mostly white, strictly upper-class colleagues—as if he had been cavorting with them his entire life—impressed her to no end. His self-confidence was what had attracted her to him in the first place. *Where was that confidence when it came to dealing with women in his personal life?*

Upon reaching the lobby of her building that evening, Sabrina saw that Darius was waiting, but she had expected no less. Keeping her face devoid of any emotion, she slowly strolled over to him.

"Hi, Sabrina," he whispered as he reached for her and gently kissed her lips. "How are you?"

"I'm okay."

"Did you get the flowers?"

"Yes, I did. Thank you. They were beautiful."

"Not as beautiful as you are," he softly intoned as he gently caressed her cheek.

Cracking a reluctant smile, she could not deny how genuinely sweet he was, regardless of what she thought about him being a pushover. She decided to hang on to him a little longer. *Maybe he'll lead me to something better. Who knows?*

# Chapter 8

Ecstatic about the fact that she would have her very own office with plenty of space and a view of Central Park, Jamilah started her new job the following Monday with the glee and eagerness of a child. *I can create right here.* A personal secretary and five other artists would be her supporting staff; she would report directly to the Vice President of the department.

Still in a jubilant mood when she got home that evening, she found Sabrina on the telephone. Dressed in black spandex leggings, black patent leather ankle boots and a short pink sweater, Sabrina looked ready to party.

"Okay, girl, I'll meet you there." Hanging up the phone, Sabrina greeted Jamilah brightly. "Hi! So how'd it go?"

"Great! You should see my office. It's huge. I have my own secretary, too."

"Well, excuse me, Miss Thing."

As she hung her jacket in the closet, Jamilah asked, "Where you going?"

"I'm meeting Vera over at the Shark Bar. You wanna come?"

With a frown, Jamilah answered, "No, that place is always so crowded. I get claustrophobic in there. Besides, it's nothing but a meat market."

"And your point is?" Sabrina asked with a grin.

Jamilah laughed. "Why are you going? You don't have to look anymore. You've got quite a catch in Darius."

Sucking her teeth and waving her hand, Sabrina said, "Please, girl, I'm so tired of him. He's too damn easy. I told you that. It gets old after a while."

"I think he's in love with you. Don't you see that?" Jamilah admonished.

"And your point is?" Sabrina again asked, this time without the grin.

Sighing, Jamilah asked, "Are you going to break it off with him?"

"Eventually."

"Well, if you're so tired of him, what are you waiting for?"

"What difference does it make to you? What, do you want him for yourself?" Sabrina sniped.

Outraged that Sabrina would even suggest such a thing, Jamilah figured she must be hearing things. "What?"

"You heard what I said. You're so damn worried about him, you make me wonder."

Completely speechless, Jamilah just stared at Sabrina. *After all these years, she hasn't changed a single bit. She's still the same insecure little girl she always has been.* Unlike when they were children, however, Jamilah no longer felt sorry for Sabrina. It hurt Jamilah terribly that she would make such an accusation about her, but more than that, it angered her that after all they had been through together, Sabrina could believe something so terrible about her.

"Do you really think I want your leftovers, Sabrina?" Jamilah finally asked. "I don't want your man, Sabrina. I don't need anyone so bad that I would go behind you." Having said that, Jamilah turned and marched to her bedroom.

She called behind her, "What the hell is that supposed to mean?" Sabrina wondered.

Before slamming her bedroom door, Jamilah yelled, "Figure it out!"

✳✳✳

The next day Sabrina was extremely apologetic, but Jamilah was not quite ready to forgive her. As far as she was concerned, it was better if Sabrina said nothing to her at all.

Not wanting to be in Sabrina's presence any more than necessary, Jamilah stayed closed up in her room when she came home from work. Of all the cruel and thoughtless things Sabrina had said to her over the years during their arguments, accusing her of wanting Darius was the lowest she had ever gone, especially since there was no basis for her accusation outside of Sabrina's own insecurity.

It was not until that weekend that Jamilah had any conversation for Sabrina and even then, it was sparse, but Sabrina was happy that Jamilah was speaking to her again. Admitting that what she had said was uncalled for and unfounded, Sabrina was quite remorseful. Jamilah, who was probably the only *true* friend she'd ever had, hadn't deserved that. Jamilah's friendship was precious to Sabrina, and she did not want to lose it.

She offered to take Jamilah to dinner to make up for her assault, but Jamilah insisted that wasn't necessary. Instead, Sabrina stayed home and cooked up a batch of Jamilah's favorite food, New Orleans-style crab cakes, made with fresh crabmeat which she deboned herself. She also bought a bottle of Jamilah's favorite wine, and her favorite dessert, chocolate mousse. They rented a couple of movies and sat in front of the television, eating, drinking, laughing and reminiscing about the "old" days.

By midnight, they were drunk and crying on each other's shoulders, and Sabrina was again apologizing for what she had said. Assuring her that they were still friends and always would be, Jamilah promised Sabrina that she would never let a man come between them. She made Sabrina promise the same.

"We been friends too long for that, Brie," Jamilah slurred. "We go too far back."

"Thas right, J. Men come and go, but sistahs are always there. We all we got."

"Thas right."

At a little past one o'clock in the morning, they passed out on opposite ends of the sofa.

# Chapter 9

Ten days later, Sabrina burst into the apartment, the picture of jubilance. Although she was barely watching it, Jamilah was sitting in front of the television working on a layout for wedding invitations for one of her freelance clients. It was close to ten p.m.

With a smile so prominent it practically swallowed up her face, Sabrina cried, "Hi, J!"

Smiling, too, although with skepticism and curiosity about her roommate's mood, Jamilah replied, "Hi. What're you so happy about?"

"I just left the man I'm going to mar-ry," Sabrina sung.

Elated about her friend's change of heart, Jamilah's smile brightened. "Really? So you changed your mind about Darius. That's good."

Grimacing, Sabrina said, "Please! I'm not talking about Darius. I told you I was gonna cut him off." Not wanting to dwell on anything but her wonderful news, the bright smile of seconds earlier immediately reappeared. "I'm talking about someone else. Someone totally... Girlfriend, this brother's got it goin' on and on. Jamilah, this is the one."

The feeling of sorrow she felt for Darius at Sabrina's words was difficult to swallow, but Jamilah didn't let her feelings show. They had made a pact that they would not let any man come between them, and Jamilah felt certain that if she protested about Sabrina's disregard for Darius' feelings, Sabrina would attack, assuming she had been on the mark with regard to Jamilah's interest in him.

Trying to show genuine interest, Jamilah asked, "So what's his name and where'd you meet him?" She was definitely curious, but in all honesty, she did not want to know anything about this man right now.

Pulling off the lightweight brushed-suede jacket she was wearing over her mauve lavender silk sheath, Sabrina tossed it carelessly on the easy-chair, then plopped down on the sofa next to Jamilah and proceeded with the man's résumé. "His name is Quenten Blanchard III. You've heard of QB Associates, haven't you?"

"Yeah, I think so. That's a public relations firm, isn't it?"

"Right. They represent some of the highest-paid athletes in the NBA and the NFL. Well, Quenten owns QB Associates. He's also one of the founding partners of a brokerage house, Blanchard-Thomas Associates, Incorporated, down on Wall Street. I'm telling you, the man is loaded. He's got his hands in a lot of different pots."

"So, how'd you meet him?"

"He was in to see Bryce today."

"He picked you up in Bryce's office?" Jamilah asked incredulously.

"No, silly. I met him at lunchtime, really. I mean, we met when he came in to see Bryce, but we really met at lunchtime. I was having lunch at this new Chinese restaurant across the street from the office with Margo when he walked in. Of course, when he looked my way, I smiled and waved so he came over to our table. The man is very straightforward. I mean, he doesn't pull any punches. He said to me, 'I hope Bryce is treating you right, and if he's not, I hope you'll let me know.' I looked him dead in the eye and told him, 'I'm not looking for another job and Bryce is not my man, so it's not up to him to treat me right.' He stared into my eyes, girl, and I knew he understood my meaning. He asked me, 'Is your man treating you right?' I told him he wasn't giving me what I wanted. He asked me what it was I wanted. I told him, 'We don't have time for me to tell you what I want. I have to go back to work,' so we made plans to have dinner."

Jamilah interrupted, "Where was Margo?"

"Right there."

"What did she have to say about all this?"

"Chile, please." Sabrina grimaced. "Like I really care what she thinks. She just shook her head and said, 'Unh, unh, unh.' Anyway, he picked me up from work in a black Porsche Carrera and we drove up to White Plains to this beautiful little French restaurant for dinner. Jamilah, he's on the money and the man is fine. I mean p-h-i-n-e, *phine!* He's the one, J. He's the one!"

Trying to appear happy for Sabrina, Jamilah could not push aside the feeling that this was yet another man she planned to wrap around her finger and step on like she did all the rest. With a smile she didn't feel in her heart, Jamilah said, "Well, I hope it works out for you, Brie, but be careful, okay? Don't rush into anything with him."

"Oh honey, you don't have to worry. This man is top shelf. Twenty-four carat," Sabrina said assuredly as she rose from the sofa and grabbed her jacket off the chair. "You'll see." She winked at Jamilah as she headed toward the back of the apartment to her bedroom.

Jamilah called after her, "Oh yeah, Brie. Darius called."

"Oh yeah?"

**✳✳✳**

The next evening, Jamilah was in the kitchen preparing a light dinner of chicken salad on a bed of romaine lettuce with tomato slices, a boiled egg and Ritz crackers when Sabrina entered the apartment with Quenten Blanchard III.

Gripping his hand firmly, Sabrina led him toward the kitchen.

Jamilah could not help but notice as they walked toward her that Sabrina had not exaggerated a single iota when she said Quenten Blanchard was p-h-i-n-e, phine! A mature man of about fifty, Jamilah guessed, Quenten was a bronze god. His bald head gleamed and his handsome face was partially covered by a silver-streaked, short-haired beard and mustache. Dark eyes seemed to penetrate Jamilah's skin as he stared at her. Approximately six feet tall, the slight paunch at his middle took nothing away from his massive sex appeal. *Must be a Scorpio,* Jamilah thought. There was an air of confidence about him that was unmistakable, and Jamilah got the impression that he was very used to getting exactly what he wanted. *What a pair they should make.*

Although quite understated, she could tell that his clothes were expensive. He wore a navy blue ultra-suede blazer, gray wool slacks, a gray silk shirt opened at the collar to reveal a hint of the salt and pepper hair that covered his chest, and navy blue suede loafers. A thick but elegant gold link chain draped his neck.

"Quenten, this is my best friend, Jamilah Parsons. J, this is Quenten Blanchard."

"Hello, Jamilah," Quenten said warmly as he stepped over to her and extended his hand.

Immediately taking note of the firmness of his handshake, Jamilah said, "Hello, Quenten. Nice to meet you." She did not miss the large diamond ring he sported on his right pinkie when he shook her hand, either.

"A beautiful name for a beautiful sister. Jamilah is my daughter's name," Quenten said.

"Really?" Smiling, Jamilah's eyes darted toward Sabrina briefly. *What does she think of her new man paying me a compliment?*

Not seeming to mind Quenten's compliment at all, Sabrina added, "I've always loved the name Jamilah. It reminds me of Africa and the name totally suits you, J."

Cutting her eyes at Sabrina questioningly, Jamilah thought, *Africa? Where the hell did that come from?*

"Sabrina tells me you're a graphic artist. Are you a freelancer or are you with an agency?" Quenten then asked.

"Both. I manage the art department at the Harper Agency in midtown, but I have a number of independent clients, as well."

"Really? I have a couple of clients at the Harper Agency."

"Do you?

"Yes, and my daughter wants to be a graphic artist. She's currently enrolled at the School of Visual Arts."

"Really? That's quite a coincidence."

"Isn't it?" Sabrina chimed.

Trying to steer the conversation away from her, Jamilah asked, "So, what do you two have planned for this evening?"

"I'm going to go in here and change; then we're going to the game at the Garden," Sabrina chimed.

Knowing Sabrina hated all sports, Jamilah asked, "Are the Knicks playing tonight?"

"Yes, they're playing the Lakers," Quenten responded.

"Quenten has center-court season tickets on the floor," Sabrina bragged.

"Oh that's nice," Jamilah responded and continued to fix her dinner. "Do either of you want a sandwich before you go?"

With his penetrating stare that made her slightly uncomfortable, Quenten answered, "No, thank you, Jamilah,"

"No, thanks, J. I'm gonna run in here and change. Quenten, you want to help me out?" Sabrina purred.

"Yes, I think I can do that," he said with a seductive smile as he followed Sabrina to her room.

When Sabrina had told her about Quenten last night, Jamilah had been pretty sure that she was going to try to take advantage of him as she did most of the men she dated. After meeting him, however, she got the distinct impression that Quenten Blanchard was a man no one took advantage of. In all sincerity, she hoped that Sabrina would not try any of her tricks on this man because she was fairly certain he would probably have a trick or two of his own for her.

She already noticed that Sabrina would probably be the one doing the chasing this time, and that was an unfamiliar role for her. *I wonder how she's going to handle that,* Jamilah thought as she took her plate and glass of 7-Up to the dining table to eat.

As soon as she sat down, Sabrina appeared right behind her. "Jamilah," she said in a whisper, "if the phone rings and it's for me, I'm not here."

"What about Darius?"

"Especially Darius." Then she was gone again.

As if she had talked him up, the phone rang two minutes later with Darius on the other end. "Hey, Jamilah. How you doin'?" he asked pleasantly.

"I'm fine, Darius. How are you?"

"I'm pretty good. Is my girl in?"

"No, she's not here right now. I'll have her call you, okay?" She hated lying to him and wanted to get him off the line as quickly as possible.

"All right. Thanks a lot. I'll talk to you soon."

"Bye."

As she sat back down to finish her meal, Jamilah sighed. *Why is it that the women who always treat men like dogs get all the attention?* She couldn't understand. These were the type of women who could ruin a good man, make him bitter and resentful and cause him to look outside the race for a mate.

In the past couple of weeks, Jamilah had been out on two dates with two different guys, but they had both been everything she did not want. One was only interested in getting her into bed. The other was totally absorbed in himself. Jamilah wanted much, much more. She wanted a man she could talk to, whom she could trust, and who would be her friend before anything else. It seemed that none of the men she met had a similar agenda as hers and she did not want to, nor would she, settle for anything less. Despite that she occasionally yearned for male companionship, she was not lonely to the point where she was willing to settle. *I would rather be alone*, she philosophized. *Anything worth having is worth waiting for.*

Although she would never admit it to Sabrina, she would miss seeing Darius. In her past, Sabrina had been known to kick a man to the curb with no regard for his feelings, but Jamilah prayed she would let Darius down easy. She felt it a shame that someone as nice as he was would fall victim to Sabrina's selfishness, and feeling he would make some lucky woman a good husband one day, Jamilah hoped he would not become bitter behind what Sabrina had done.

# Chapter 10

It was six forty-five on Thursday evening of the following week and Jamilah had been home for all of twenty minutes. She had just changed from her work clothes to a pair of shorts and a midriff top and was about to prepare something for dinner when the doorbell rang.

"Who is it?"

"Darius."

*Obviously, Sabrina hasn't told him of her plans*, she thought. Not looking forward to facing him, she pursed her lips and unwillingly opened the door. For some reason, she felt he would know from her face that Sabrina planned to dump him. Knowing how deeply he cared for Sabrina, she felt genuinely sorry for him.

As she opened the door, however, her face gave away no trace of the sadness she felt in her heart for him, and before she could open her mouth to greet him, she was struck speechless by his appearance.

Darius was decked out in a black wool tuxedo with silk appointments that was accented by a deep brown and beige Kente-designed bow tie and cummerbund. Despite how handsome Jamilah had always thought him to be, seeing him this way nearly floored her.

"Hi, Jamilah," he greeted her in his usual cheerful tone.

Nearly drooling, she said, "Wow, Darius! You look great!"

He blushed. "Thank you."

The door was open wide enough for him to enter, but she was so taken in by his appearance that she completely forgot to invite him into the apartment.

"Wow," she repeated with a broad grin. "Where're you going all decked out like that?"

As he stepped into the apartment, he answered, "To a political fund-raising dinner one of my firm's clients is hosting. Is Sabrina ready?"

A frown creased her brow immediately and her stomach knotted anxiously as she pushed the door closed. She turned to him. "Sabrina's not here."

He had started toward the couch but with Jamilah's words, stopped in his tracks and turned back to her. The bright smile he had been wearing moments before fell from his face. "She's not?"

"No."

"Where is she?"

"I don't know," she answered with a shrug of her shoulders, but she was pretty sure that Sabrina was with Quenten Blanchard III.

"Has she called?"

"No."

"Oh no, Sabrina." He sighed. He lowered his head and covered his face with his hands. Anger and anxiety began to fill his heart as he stood shaking his head.

"What time is the dinner supposed to start?" Jamilah asked as she took a cautious step toward him.

"Seven-thirty."

"Oh no."

"Do you think she could still be at work?" he asked softly.

"I don't know. She may be." *I seriously doubt it, though.*

"Do you mind if I try her there?"

"No, of course not."

Immediately stepping over to the telephone, Darius picked up the receiver and began to dial.

Jamilah could not believe Sabrina would stoop so low as to stand Darius up for what, evidently, was a very important social function for him—career-wise.

Darius held the phone to his ear and listened to Sabrina's office phone ring repeatedly, but his face belied the true depth of the hurt he felt in his heart. He could not believe Sabrina would forget about this dinner. She knew the magnitude of the occasion, and she also knew that he had put in a special request for her to attend it with him. Usually, unless you were a partner, the firm made no provisions for guests. Knowing, however, that his boss often gave him liberties because he was such an excellent performer on the job, Darius had asked and even volunteered to pick up the extra tab so she could accompany him. He appreciated his boss's generosity in agreeing to his request because he was in line for a partnership and with that, his attendance at this fund-raiser, despite how much he truly hated these types of functions, was non-negotiable.

When her voice mail clicked on, he hung up, but he was momentarily paralyzed by the idea that Sabrina's absence could have a detrimental effect on his partnership chances.

Seeing his distress, Jamilah tried to think of a response. "Maybe she's on her way home."

Darius turned to her and murmured, "Yeah, maybe," but his gut feeling screamed contrasting volumes.

"How far do you have to go?" Jamilah asked.

Dragging himself over to the sofa, he sat down with his elbows on his knees and his head in his hands. "To midtown," she heard him utter.

Their apartment was approximately two miles away. She moved to the sofa and sat next to him. "Did you speak to her today?"

"No. I called her earlier but she wasn't available. I left her a message, though. She never got back to me, and I got so busy at work that I didn't have a chance to get back to her. But I just spoke to her about this yesterday," he lamented.

Not knowing what to say to him, they sat in silence for the next few minutes.

"I can't believe she'd do this. This is a two hundred and fifty-dollar-a-plate dinner that I asked my boss if she could come to. My firm is picking up the tab for this. If I come in there by myself after they've paid for her...after I asked them to pay for her..." Rising from the sofa suddenly, he began to pace the floor in front of the television set. "She knows how important this dinner is. How could she do this?"

Feeling empathy, an uncontrollable anger rolled in Jamilah's stomach. Her patience at its end, Jamilah was fed up with Sabrina's total disregard of everyone's feelings but her own. For years she had watched her step on people's hearts with not a bit of compunction for her actions. It mattered not how much she hurt someone or betrayed his or her trust; the only thing that mattered was that she came out on top.

As Jamilah watched Darius pace back and forth, she felt an overwhelming desire to give Sabrina a taste of her own medicine, but Jamilah did not have the capacity to do anything to intentionally hurt another human being, especially someone she loved. And she did love Sabrina, despite her shortcomings. Just lately, however, she was beginning to dislike her.

Darius had not said so, but Jamilah was certain that he was fearful of the ramifications of his not attending this fund-raiser or even showing up without his special guest. Knowing his firm would not suffer from a two hundred and fifty-dollar loss, it was the principle that mattered most. It angered her, too, that Sabrina would do something so heartless to this man—this sweet, sensitive, generous man who loved her unconditionally—when there were so many single women looking for a man like him and who would appreciate the kindness and generosity he so unselfishly showed Sabrina.

Suddenly she looked up at the clock on the living room wall. *Five minutes to seven. I wonder...* "Darius."

"Yeah?" he murmured, as he continued to pace.

"Look...I don't know how you might feel about what I'm going to suggest...I mean, I don't want you to get the wrong idea or anything, but...I know how important this is to you and I know how upset you are that Sabrina isn't here. I don't want you to think that I'm trying to..."

He stopped pacing and turned to face Jamilah. "What?" His face was a picture of sadness and trepidation.

"I was just wondering, if you want...I mean so that you won't get in trouble... I...I could go with you. I know you were looking forward to being with Sabrina but...you know...I figured, if it'll save you some grief, I'll go with you," she hesitantly offered.

Darius stared at Jamilah for a long moment before he answered. Interpreting his silence negatively, Jamilah lowered her head as she apologized, "I'm sorry. I...I shouldn't have even..."

Cutting her off in mid-sentence, he asked, "Would you do that for me?"

Her head snapped up. "Yeah, if you want."

Stepping over and taking her hands, he excitedly replied, "Oh man, Jamilah, that would be so great. I'd really appreciate it. If I go in there by myself, I know I'll never hear the end of it."

"Okay, let me go get dressed. I can be ready in fifteen minutes," she said a little brighter.

"Thanks, Jamilah." A tentative smile crossed his face.

Although genuinely hurt by Sabrina's forgetfulness, that had ceased to be Darius' major concern. Foremost, his main concern now was for his job. During his pacing, he had tried to think of a feasible excuse to tell his boss when he walked in there alone. Although the thought had crossed his mind, he was extremely grateful and relieved that Jamilah had offered to stand in for Sabrina because he knew he could have never asked her. After Sabrina's accusation, he knew if she found out that he had invited Jamilah to go with him, she would surely make it into an entirely different issue.

Hurrying back to her bedroom and straight to her closet to see what she should wear, Jamilah had no trouble deciding. Her red silk evening gown with the red and gold bugle-beads was selected from her closet and laid across her bed. Bending over in the closet, she then removed a box that contained red satin, beaded pumps and the matching dinner bag and placed them next to the dress. Moving to her dresser and removing a package of sheer panty hose, a red lace push-up bra and matching thong, she tossed the panty hose on the bed, grabbed her robe and headed straight to the bathroom for a quick shower.

Upon emerging from the stall, she quickly lotioned her body from head to toe and put on her underwear. Then, carelessly, albeit with the good fortune that sometimes comes from not trying too hard, she pinned her locks up in a manner that created an elegant crown. As quickly as she could, she lined her eyes with a dark pencil and brushed her lashes with mascara.

Hurrying back to her bedroom and pulling the panty hose from the package, she called out, "I'm almost ready, Darius."

He called back, "Okay."

Smiling, Jamilah felt a momentary twinge of guilt in her heart as she realized how easy it would be for her to fall in love with him. But she would never let any-one know that. Besides, he was in love with Sabrina.

Once she had donned the evening gown and stepped into her shoes, Jamilah moved to her jewelry box and started to reach for her diamond necklace, then quickly decided to leave her neck bare, but placed diamond studs in her ears and her tennis bracelet around her wrist. She opted not to wear a watch since she didn't own a real gold one nor one with diamonds. She was sure her rhinestone one would stand out like a cancerous growth on her arm amongst the wealthy people she figured would be in attendance.

The final touch was her lip color and once she had added that, she stepped back to survey her reflection in the mirror. *Good enough.*

"Okay, I'm ready," she called as she snatched her bag off the bed and grabbed her black velvet shawl from her closet. She rushed back to the living room. "Okay."

Having resumed his pacing, Darius turned to her when she entered the room behind him. Realizing immediately that he had never really looked at her, he was struck speechless by her beauty. The ankle-length gown she wore had a slit on the left seam that started just above her knee and exposed one very shapely dark brown leg. Only a hint of her ample cleavage peeked out from the neck of the long-sleeved gown, but it was enough to make any sane man want to see more. The dress fit her body like a glove, accentuating her full, curvaceous frame.

"Do I look okay?"

Smiling reverently, he replied in a soft tone, "You look fantastic."

Blushing, she responded, "Thank you."

As he reached for her hand, he asked, "Ready?"

"Uh-huh."

It was seven-twenty when they walked out of the apartment.

# Chapter 11

The fund-raiser was held at the Waldorf-Astoria. Arriving at seven-forty, miraculously, they were not hindered during their twenty-minute drive by the normal rush-hour traffic that usually clogged midtown streets of Manhattan. Besides that, Darius had driven pretty much like a bat out of hell. Fortunately, there was a parking garage just around the corner.

As they approached the entrance of the hotel, Darius said, "If anyone asks why we're late, we had car trouble."

"What kind?"

"I don't know. I'll think of something."

Upon entering the lobby of the hotel, Darius took Jamilah's hand and linked her arm in his. Looking around in awe as they started toward the ballroom where their function was located, Jamilah whispered, "Oh my goodness, Darius. I've never been inside the Waldorf before. This place is beautiful."

Smiling at her, he said, "Well, I'm sure you'll fit right in."

She looked over at him and smiled.

"Come on, we're in here."

Ornate crystal chandeliers hung from the ceiling of the atmospherically dim ballroom they entered. Circular tables, most of which seated ten and were already occupied, were set with the finest china and silver serving utensils. A podium and dais that seated twelve was at the front of the hall. Waiters and waitresses dashed about trying to serve the generally mature white patrons who were in attendance. As Jamilah perused her surroundings, she thought, *these people are probably filthy rich.*

Almost immediately upon entering, Darius heard his name. Turning in the direction of the voice, he whispered to Jamilah, "There's my boss."

"Darius! I was beginning to wonder if you were going to make it." The well-aged white gentleman approaching them reminded Jamilah of a penguin because he was short, bald and his portly physique was stuffed into a tuxedo that looked as if it barely fit.

"Hello, Bob. I had a flat on my way to pick up Jamilah," Darius quickly invented.

Surreptitiously eyeing Jamilah, Bob said, "Well, I'm glad you made it."

"No way I would miss this."

"So, are you going to introduce me to this beautiful lady on your arm, or do I have to do that myself?" Bob boldly turned to Jamilah and offered a broad smile that bared tobacco-stained teeth.

"No, of course not. Jamilah, this is one of the senior partners at my firm, Bob Fisher. Bob, this is my friend, Jamilah Parsons."

Taking her hand in both of his, Bob said, "Jamilah, what a beautiful name. It's a pleasure to meet you."

Surprised to hear that Darius remembered her last name, Jamilah smiled pleasantly. "It's nice to meet you, too, Mr. Fisher."

"Please, nothing so formal. It's Bob."

"Bob," she said sweetly.

"Well, come on, let's get you kids seated. They're about to start serving dinner."

Bob led them to a table a few feet away where his wife; two other partners from his firm and their wives; another senior associate; and a female client of the firm were already seated. Darius greeted everyone and introduced Jamilah before helping her into her seat between his and Bob's.

As soon as they were seated, a waiter came over and began to serve the first course of the meal. Almost immediately following, one of the members of the panel seated at the dais stepped to the microphone and the speeches began. By the time they began to serve dessert, all of the political diatribes had been delivered and the audience picked up their individual conversations at the tables.

Jamilah sat quietly, smiling at all the appropriate times as she listened to the mostly shop talk that went on around the table between Darius, his colleagues and their client. Although not really surprised, she was impressed by the professionalism that Darius displayed during their conversation. This was a side of him she had never seen and she felt tremendous pride at being there with him. Knowing how many large firms or organizations often looked upon black professionals as tokens or placed them in senior positions merely to fill quotas, Jamilah was positive that Darius had reached his level of success due entirely to his intelligence and self-assurance.

Cake and coffee had just been served at their table when one of the wives seated with them asked, "Jamilah, are you an attorney, also?"

Poised to put her fork in her mouth, she lowered it and answered with a smile, "Oh no. I'm a graphic artist."

"Really?" Bob questioned. "Are you self-employed?"

"Well, yes and no. I manage the art department for a major ad agency across town, but I also do freelance work."

"What types of things do you design?" another of her tablemates asked.

She turned to this man, one of Darius' partners, and answered, "Posters, flyers, invitations, business and greeting cards, that kind of thing. I also design brochures and do other types of desktop publishing."

"You design invitations?" one of the other wives asked.

"Yes."

"Wedding invitations, by any chance?"

"Yes."

"Oh, my daughter's getting married later this year and I was going to start looking around for a printer to do her invitations. Do you have any samples of your work?"

"Yes, I do."

"I'd love to see some. Do you think that's possible?"

"Of course. I'd be more than happy to show you some of my samples. Can I give you my card? You can call me and we can set up a time that I could bring them to you," Jamilah replied with a bright smile. Excitement had her bubbling inside at the prospect of gaining one of these wealthy old women as a client.

"Oh, that would be wonderful. Yes, please give me your card. When's a good time to call?"

Handing the woman one of her business cards, Jamilah answered, "Anytime.

My office and home numbers are both there. If you don't get an answer, leave a message and I'll get back to you."

"Excellent."

"Could I have one of your cards?" the female client asked. "I'll be giving my twins a birthday party in July. They're going to be five years old. Maybe you can design some party decorations for me."

"Certainly. I do that, too," Jamilah said, smiling broadly.

Before they were finished with dessert, Jamilah had given everyone at the table one of her business cards. Briefly glancing at Darius after she had handed out her cards, she blushed when she noticed his smile and wink. *Was that a nod of admiration?* she wondered.

Darius sat silently as his colleagues and their wives grilled Jamilah about her work. Somewhat tickled by their fascination, after the inquiries regarding her freelance work and the doling out of her business cards, when one of the wives questioned her about her hair, he, too, couldn't help but admire how exquisite her locks looked styled the way they were. Ordinarily, he was not particularly fond of the look, but on Jamilah it was very becoming.

Actually, she looked better tonight than he had ever seen her. Not that he didn't think she was attractive, but it had taken her less than twenty minutes to transform herself into the goddess that sat before appreciative eyes. *How come I never noticed how beautiful she is before?* Aside from that, the way she kept Bob and the others captivated for close to an hour with her witty conversation allowed another look at the person she was.

Her benevolence and warmth were no secret to him, but this was a side of her he had never seen. Not even when they had all gone to his friend's annual dance had he glimpsed this intelligently versatile creature.

Suddenly, Jamilah began to rise. Entranced by his own musings of her, it did not immediately register when she excused herself from the table. Rising quickly, Darius helped her with her chair.

"Thanks." She smiled at him. "I'll be right back."

"I'll be right here," he responded with a smile.

As soon as she was out of earshot, Bob leaned over and whispered, "Darius, that's some young lady you've got there. I hope you plan to hang on to her."

Fixing his mouth to explain that his relationship with Jamilah was not what they thought, Darius quickly decided to keep quiet. If he had done otherwise, he would have had to explain why it had been so important that he bring a guest who was not his significant other. Not about to admit that he had been stood up by the woman he loved, he simply said, "I'm no fool." He could understand Bob's sentiment, though. He had learned more about Jamilah in the past couple of hours than he had in the few months he'd dated Sabrina and she fascinated him, too. She was a rare specimen and any man with half a brain would be proud to call her his own.

Shortly thereafter, Darius excused himself from the table and headed toward the bar. Returning his thoughts to Sabrina and her whereabouts, he began to develop a headache.

"Can I have a shot of Dewar's on ice?" he solemnly asked the bartender.

He didn't notice Jamilah until she tapped him on his arm. "Hey."

Turning to her brought him back to the present. "Hey, J," he said with a weak smile.

Noticing the sadness in his eyes, she asked, "You okay?" She knew he had been thinking about Sabrina.

"Yeah, I'm fine," he lied.

Gently touching his arm as a show of understanding, she, nevertheless, remained silent.

"You want a drink?" he asked her.

"Sure. I'll have a glass of white Zinfandel."

Ordering for her, silence ensued until her drink was placed on the bar in front of her.

"You're certainly a big hit tonight."

Chuckling, she agreed, "Yeah, how 'bout that. Do you think any of them will actually call me?"

"Yes, I do. They were all very impressed with you," Darius said with a warm smile.

"Well, it'll be nice if I can make some money out of this."

He sipped his drink, then placed it back on the bar. "You know, Jamilah, I can't begin to tell you how much I appreciate you offering to come with me tonight. You really saved my butt. I'm in line for a partnership offer at my firm and missing one of these functions, especially when it involves a client as big as the one who hosted this, is greatly frowned upon. I don't want to do anything to blow my chances."

"Darius, it was no problem. I would've just been sitting in front of the television anyway."

"Yeah well, I owe you."

"No, you don't."

"Yes, I do and I always pay my debts. Anything I can ever do for you, you let me know. You've got it."

Shaking her head, she responded, "You don't owe me anything. If I've just won some new clients out of my coming here with you, I'd call that even."

"One thing has nothing to do with the other."

"Darius..."

He cut her off. "I'm not going to argue with you about this."

Although he was smiling, she could tell he was serious. She simply shook her head.

Shortly thereafter Darius admitted, "Oh yeah, Jamilah, Bob thinks we're...he thinks we're a couple. I didn't correct him because I figured I'd have to explain why you're here and Sabrina isn't. I hope you're not too upset about that."

Smiling, she stated, "No, it's okay. I won't tell." *If we were a couple, you can bet I would treat you better than Sabrina does; that's for sure.*

"I still can't believe she forgot about this."

"Do you want to try and call her, see if she's home?"

"No, not now. There's really no point."

"Yeah, I guess."

Darius finished off his drink, then glanced at his watch. Noticing his impatience, Jamilah asked, "How long do you have to stay?"

It was a quarter to ten.

"Well, I've done my obligatory two hours and we've listened to all the speeches, so we can cut out whenever you're ready."

Taking a final sip of her wine, Jamilah said, "I'm ready."

They returned to their table to say good night to their dinner companions. As they were about to leave the hall, they ran into Bob.

"You kids leaving?" he asked in a booming voice.

"Yeah, Bob, we're calling it a night."

"Well then, Jamilah," Bob said as he grasped her hand, "I must say it was truly a pleasure meeting you this evening. I hope I get to see you again."

"Likewise, Bob. It was a pleasure meeting you, too," she said with a bright smile.

Bringing her hand to his lips and gently kissing it, he remarked, "Lovely. Lovely. If I might, I must tell you, you are truly a beautiful woman. You remind me of an African queen."

Jamilah blushed. "Thank you."

Shaking his head in admiration, Bob uttered, "Darius, you take care of this lady."

"Yes, sir."

"I'll see you tomorrow," he said as he and Darius shook hands.

"Good night, Bob."

When they cleared the hall and were passing through the lobby, Jamilah began to laugh.

"What's so funny?" Darius wanted to know.

"An African queen?"

"I can see that," he said nonchalantly.

Smirking, she said, "Oh, come on."

"What? You do look like an African queen."

"Oh, please, Darius."

Chuckling softly, he unpretentiously asked, "Didn't you look at yourself in the mirror? You look beautiful."

Jamilah looked over at him and blushed when their eyes met. Suddenly feeling extremely shy, she murmured, "Thank you."

"Thank *you!*" he countered.

As they began their drive home, they shared a comfortable silence. When they were approximately a mile away from the girls' apartment, Jamilah inquired, "Darius, can I ask you a favor?"

Taking his eyes off the road for a split second, Darius quickly glanced over at her. "Anything."

She smiled and asked, "Would you mind stopping somewhere so I can get some ice cream?"

"Sure, no problem. You're an ice cream fiend, aren't you?"

"Yes, I guess so."

He laughed. "You know, I could go for some ice cream myself. That cake they served was pretty dry."

"Yes, it was."

Stopping at a neighborhood ice cream parlor, they decided to sit down and eat. Jamilah ordered a chocolate sundae, complete with syrup, whipped cream and a cherry; and Darius, a banana boat.

Before placing a generous helping of his dessert in his mouth, Darius said, "I still can't believe she stood me up."

"She probably just forgot," Jamilah said in Sabrina's defense as she, too, took a taste of her sundae.

"I don't know. I've been telling her about this for weeks and I spoke to her about it just yesterday."

Jamilah did not comment but she thought, *She's probably with Quenten.*

"You know something, though? I'm almost glad she wasn't there."

Jamilah's eyebrows arched as her eyes widened in surprise. "Why?"

"Because I really don't think she could have held her own with those folks the way you did."

"Oh, I don't know. Sabrina can be…" Jamilah paused, searching for the right word.

"Quite the phony," Darius jumped in.

She was even more surprised at this statement.

Upon noticing her expression, Darius laughed. "Come on, J. I love her madly, but you know our girl puts on quite a few airs."

Smiling, Jamilah was in total agreement as he continued. "I know she's smart and everything but it's not because of any great academic knowledge. Sabrina's got what you would call 'street smarts.' I mean she can hold her own in most instances, but after a while that will only get you so far. I don't think her airs would have gone over too well with our tablemates."

"You don't think so?"

"No, I don't. Those people have money coming out of their rear ends, but they're also book smart and Sabrina can be quite pretentious. Lord knows we didn't need any more of that tonight. Like when Bob's wife commented on your hair. We know that white folks are basically ignorant to the grooming needs of our hair. Sabrina would have probably asked, 'Don't you know anything about us?' But you were quite gracious and very patient with them. I think they appreciated that," Darius said. Then he added, "I'm sure they did."

"I always get a kick out of the comments I get from them about my hair."

"Well, I'll be honest with you, I've never been crazy about dreadlocks, but I think they look great on you. And the way you fixed them tonight, makes you look quite…regal," Darius said with a sincere smile. "Like an African queen."

Blushing, Jamilah thanked him for his compliment.

They ate their ice cream treats in silence for the next couple of minutes.

"She's seeing someone else, isn't she?" Darius asked suddenly.

Totally unprepared for his question, Jamilah's immediate reaction was one of shock. Before she could utter a sound, however, he added, "I don't expect you to answer that. I guess I'm just thinking out loud."

She began to feel uncomfortable.

"You know, I've had a feeling lately that she's lost interest in me. I don't know what it is about her. I mean, it's like…" He paused momentarily. "When I was in junior high school, there was this girl, Wilhemina Matthews. Wilhemina was the prettiest girl in school. She was smart *and* pretty. All the boys were crazy about her, but I had an enormous crush on her. I don't think she ever even knew I was alive. I wasn't down with the 'in' crowd like she was."

"Neither was I," Jamilah interjected.

"Yeah, so I could only admire her from a distance. But I used to dream about her. I mean I had fantasies about her being my wife one day and I was only thirteen years old. But she was untouchable as far as I was concerned." Taking a spoonful of his ice cream, he continued, "Sabrina is my Wilhemina Matthews. She's that untouchable girl I always wanted to have notice me. As much as I love her, I've always had a feeling deep down inside that we wouldn't last. And even though I know she's pretty much a gold digger, I'd still give her anything she asked for. I just can't tell her no."

"She has a good heart," Jamilah said, although she knew how truly selfish Sabrina could be.

"Yeah, I know it's in there somewhere." He laughed good-naturedly. "It amazes me sometimes, though, that the two of you are such good friends. You're so completely different."

Jamilah laughed and said, "Yeah, I know, but we've been friends...seems like forever. Of course, knowing each other the way we do, we have our occasional fall-outs, as you've seen. There have been times when we'd stop speaking to each other for days at a time, but she knows how far she can push me and vice versa, and we both know when to leave the other alone. We respect each other that way."

"That's good."

"Yeah. People are always amazed that we're such good friends, too. But I guess I can understand that; we really are on two completely different pages, but we have fun."

"Well, that's probably because you're such a personable individual. I bet you get along with anyone," Darius said with a smile.

"Well, I don't let people's idiosyncrasies get to me. We all have our moments and unlike some people, when I know a person doesn't want to be bothered, I don't bother them. I try not to aggravate anyone and I try even harder not to let anyone aggravate me," Jamilah said with a chuckle.

"That's good policy."

"Of course, living together that's not always possible, but we manage. We've been roomies for three years and we haven't managed to kill each other yet."

Thoroughly enjoying his conversation with Jamilah, Darius laughed heartily. When he thought about it, he realized that she transformed what could have been a totally disastrous night into a complete joy. "You know what, Jamilah? You're all right."

Laughing, she said, "Well, thank you."

"No, I mean..." He chuckled softly. "When you told me that Sabrina wasn't home, I didn't know what to think; I didn't know what I would do, but you saved the day. It's good to know I have someone like you in my corner."

Jamilah was moved by his appreciation. *Why can't I meet a man like this one?*

When Darius pulled up in front of her building twenty minutes later, Jamilah asked, "Do you want to come up and see if she's home?"

"No. I don't want to see her right now. I'm too angry at her," he said solemnly.

"Do you want me to tell her to call you?"

"No. You don't have to tell her anything. I'll call her tomorrow."

"Okay."

Opening his door, he stepped out of the car and made his way around to the passenger side as Jamilah opened her door and started to step out of the vehicle. Darius reached for her hand to help her out.

When she was standing before him, he said, "Thank you again, Jamilah, for coming tonight. I can't begin to tell you how much I appreciate what you did. I hope you'll let me return the favor one day."

"Darius, I had a great time and made some potential business contacts while I was at it. It was really no problem," she said with a smile.

He stared into her eyes for a long moment before he surprised her by pulling her into his arms and hugging her. He placed a tender kiss on her forehead and said, "Thank you."

Flushing in embarrassment, Jamilah was suddenly overcome by the mixture of joy and sadness, her eyes began to water, but she fought to control her emotions as she softly replied, "You're welcome."

She quickly moved away from him and started toward the entrance.

"Good night, Jamilah."

"Good night," she called back to him.

## *Chapter 12*

When Jamilah entered her apartment that night, she was not surprised to find that Sabrina was not yet home. Heading straight to her bedroom, she began making preparations for bed. As she hung her gown in the closet, she recalled the past few hours. *What a wonderful evening.* She couldn't think of a single moment all night that hadn't been perfect.

Darius had been the quintessential gentleman and although she thoroughly enjoyed the conversation and the company at the fund-raiser, the high point of her evening was the half-hour or so that they had spent in the ice cream parlor where she learned the true extent of his open-hearted sensitivity.

Her laughter rang out suddenly in the otherwise quiet apartment when she recalled his comment about Sabrina's superficial mannerisms. She had always felt sorry for him because she had been under the impression that Sabrina had pulled the wool over his eyes. However, that he was well aware of the basic nature of Sabrina's true self and that he, admittedly, still loved her despite that, proved that he was no one's fool; he was simply human.

He had really surprised her though, when he asked if Sabrina was seeing someone else. For a minute she was afraid that he'd seen something in her eyes which confirmed his thought.

After spending the evening with him, she now wished Sabrina would hurry up and break off her relationship with him, since it was obvious to Jamilah that he wouldn't. Knowing that the breakup would hurt him, she, nevertheless, felt the sooner it was done, the sooner he could overcome his impending grief and get on with his life. He was too good a man to have to deal with what Sabrina had put him through. Maybe after he got over Sabrina, he would meet a woman who would love and appreciate the warm and gentle person he was.

**\*\*\***

Waiting until Jamilah was safely on the elevator and the doors closed before he pulled off, Darius then headed for his duplex apartment in Brooklyn. Smiling while shaking his head in wonderment as he recounted the past few hours, he fondly thought, *Jamilah is some woman*. He found her to be smart, personable, and funny, and probably the most beautiful dark-skinned woman he had ever known.

He still could not get over that she had offered to stand in for Sabrina, thereby saving him from having to endure embarrassment and countless lectures from his superiors about the protocol regarding guests at firm-sponsored social functions.

She was such a down-to-earth and intelligent woman, and this only helped to make the evening that much more spectacular.

Genuinely enjoying her company, he found that she was easy to talk to. Although he would not ordinarily be so forthcoming with a woman he barely knew regarding a woman he was involved with, he felt comfortable talking to her about Sabrina, despite them being best friends. Having no fear that anything he revealed would get back to Sabrina—not that it really mattered—he felt as though he could trust Jamilah to keep their conversation strictly confidential.

The only other female besides his mother with whom he felt such a degree of trust was his sister, Brianne. Since Brianne lived in Detroit with her husband and their two kids, and he did not speak to her as often as he would like to, it was nice having that female counterpart to whom he could bare his soul again.

Beaming as he remembered Jamilah's reaction when he told her he agreed with Bob's comparison of her to an African queen, Darius pondered, *She would make a noble one at that*. She possessed a natural love of people, and she treated everyone with the same level of graciousness.

Jamilah was truly a rare gem. *She'll make some lucky man a wonderful companion one day*, he reflected. Darius greatly admired her unwillingness to settle for someone who did not appreciate her for the complete woman she, no doubt, was.

Halted at a traffic light while musing over his evening with his new and valued friend, his thoughts were rudely interrupted by four young thugs who had approached his car as it sat at the intersection. Pouncing on him quickly—two on each side of the vehicle—he had no opportunity to react.

His window was down halfway because the evening was relatively warm. Savoring the breeze that blew in as he drove turned out to be to his disadvantage because the window was open so far.

Seemingly, from out of thin air, a gun appeared at his temple at the same moment he heard the words, "The car or your life, muthafucka!"

Jamilah was sitting on her bed in her baby doll pajamas when Sabrina entered the apartment twenty minutes after she had gotten home. She stuck her head into Jamilah's room. "Hi, J. I'm home."

"Where've you been? Like I really need to ask," Jamilah added in a snide manner.

Immediately on the defensive, Sabrina stepped into the room and responded, "I was with Quenten, why? And what's the matter with you?"

Anger rose in the pit of Jamilah's stomach at a rate she could not even explain. "What's the matter with me? I'll tell you what's the matter with me. I'm just sick and damn tired of the way you treat everyone's feelings but your own with total disregard!"

"What? What the hell are you talking about?" Sabrina demanded, now angry with Jamilah for attacking her for no apparent reason.

"I'm talking about Darius!"

"Darius? What the hell has he got to do with this, and what do *you* have to do with my relationship with him?"

In answer to the first part of Sabrina's inquiry, Jamilah responded, "You were *supposed* to be attending a fund-raiser with him tonight that one of his clients was hosting. He made special arrangements for you to be there with him and you stood him up."

"That thing's not until tomorrow night."

"No, Sabrina. It was tonight. He came to get you but you were out with Quenten."

"Yeah, so what do you want me to do about that now? It's over, right? It's not like we can turn back the hands of time, now can we?"

Sucking her teeth, Jamilah sighed in exasperation. "How can you be so smug about this? You knew how important this dinner was to him."

"So what the hell are you so bent out of shape about? Are you his personal spokeswoman now? You act like I did something to you!"

"Doesn't it even matter to you that he's in love with you, Sabrina? Can't you at least have the decency to be honest with him if you don't want to be with him anymore? You know he would do anything for you. Doesn't that count for something?"

Sabrina stared at Jamilah for a long moment before it dawned on her. "You're in love with him, aren't you?" She laughed viciously. "You're in love with my man!"

"I am not!"

"Yes, you are. That's why you're so upset. He came here to get me, and you were pissed because I wasn't here and he wouldn't take you!" Sabrina charged.

"For your information, Miss Thing, I *went* with Darius, but not for the reason you think."

"You did what?"

"I went with him. He could have gotten in big trouble if he didn't go, and since he specifically asked them if he could bring you, I went with him to spare him the embarrassment of showing up there alone."

"I don't believe you," Sabrina said as she shook her head. "You're trying to screw him behind my back?"

"Oh get real, Sabrina!" Jamilah said in disgust. "I'm not interested in Darius and he's not interested in me. I told you why I went, but if you're so damn insecure that you actually believe the nonsense you're spouting, then that's your problem and I really don't give a damn what you think. But I'll tell you this. You don't deserve a man like Darius. He's far too good for you. Unfortunately for him, he doesn't know it yet."

Stepping past Sabrina to her bedroom door, Jamilah put her hand on the knob. "Now, if you'll excuse me, I'd like to go to bed. Good night!"

"You can't tell me you don't want him," Sabrina continued.

"Good night," Jamilah repeated, thoroughly dismissing Sabrina.

Sabrina paused a moment, giving Jamilah a sinister look. Sucking her teeth, she rolled her eyes before she turned and sauntered out of the room. Jamilah immediately slammed the door behind her.

"Same to you!" Sabrina yelled through the door.

Her bedroom was adjacent to Jamilah's so she stepped right into her own room and slammed her door, also.

"She's got a lot of damn nerve," Sabrina declared as she began to remove her clothing. "She's getting on my case about standing him up and the whole time, she's pushing up on him."

Yelling so Jamilah could hear, "I know you want him! You're just jealous 'cause you can't get a man, and I've got 'em knocking down my door!

"So what if I take my time cutting him off! What the hell difference should it make to you unless you're trying to snag him for yourself?" she continued to yell as she hung her outfit in the closet. "If you got up off your lazy ass and went out sometime instead of sitting up in this damn apartment in front of the TV, maybe you'd find a man of your own; then you could leave mine alone!"

Sabrina was furious. *Who the hell does she think she is, telling me anything about how I treat my man!* "If I want to keep him hanging on a string for the rest of my life, it ain't nobody's damn business but mine," she ranted.

As she put away her jewelry, literally throwing it into her jewelry box, she seethed. *Where does she get off, criticizing me? And what the hell does she mean, I'm not good enough for Darius? He ain't all that!* Sabrina sucked her teeth in disgust.

She was so angry that the jubilant mood she had been in as a result of her evening with Quenten was completely forgotten. He had taken her to a dinner party in Englewood Cliffs, New Jersey at the elegant home of one of his business partners. It was a casual affair but she made sure she was dressed to the teeth for the occasion. Having carried a change of clothes to work, she discarded her office "uniform" for a black velvet catsuit before he picked her up. She had accessorized the unitard with black patent leather ankle boots, a wide black patent leather belt with a gold buckle to accentuate her tiny waist and a red silk scarf for a splash of color.

When Quenten picked her up, his tongue almost fell to the floor at the sight of her. Immediately noticing the look of desire in his eyes as they traveled the length of her long, slender physique, she was tickled because he'd tried to be so nonchalant about her appearance. She knew she looked great, but he had simply responded, "Nice outfit." *That's okay*, she mused because there would be plenty of time for him to shower her with accolades about her appearance, she figured.

The party had been a blast. Sabrina loved schmoozing with the "black elite," which was all that was in attendance at this function. Quenten had left her to fend for herself a couple of times while he discussed business with his colleagues, giving her the opportunity to chat with some of the other women. The spouses of the men in attendance were all stay-at-home wives and belonged to social clubs that held afternoon teas and charity lunches. The other single women were high-powered executives themselves and basically had no conversation for the wives.

Sabrina made herself comfortable among the wives, since she had every intention of joining their little clique in the near future, if you let her tell it. She noticed, too, the way the other men there all stared at her when they thought she or their wives were not looking. She also caught Quenten ogling her quite a few times. *Good*, she had thought, *I don't want you to miss a thing.*

Her thoughts returning to the present, Jamilah's sudden attack had soured the entire evening for her. In truth, she had thought that Darius' affair was Friday night. She hadn't intentionally stood him up. When they spoke yesterday, she didn't remember him saying, specifically, that the dinner was Thursday. Knowing she would be seeing Quenten that evening was basically why she hadn't returned his call that afternoon. Unbeknownst to Jamilah, she had no intention of stringing Darius along any longer. Her plan had been to tell him that she couldn't see him anymore when he brought her home after the dinner, and she was fully prepared to tell him why.

Admittedly, Darius was a nice enough guy, but he just wasn't for her. He was too easy; he presented no challenge. She wanted a man who was not afraid to be a *man*.

As she climbed into bed and pulled the covers up under her chin, she sighed in resignation. It hurt that Jamilah would believe that she had left Darius hanging intentionally, especially since she knew how important the dinner was to him and that it directly reflected on his job. For that reason alone, she would not have stood him up on purpose. It also hurt that Jamilah seemed to think she was so completely heartless. *Why would she think that?*

Sabrina, however, did not believe Jamilah when she said she had no designs on Darius. She had noticed how Jamilah made a point of smiling up in his face every time he came to the house to see her. Of course, she wasn't worried that Jamilah could steal Darius away from her, that is, if she had planned to keep him around. Jamilah wasn't his type. Sabrina was secure in the assumption that the only reason Darius had taken her with him tonight was to save his own butt.

She turned over in the bed and closed her eyes as she felt sleep creeping up on her. Her last thought before slumber overcame her was that once she and Quenten were married (which she had decided was inevitable), she would not have to deal with Jamilah's self-righteous attitude at all.

# Chapter 13

Having endured a restless night, Sabrina was up early the next morning. When she stepped out of the shower, it was only six forty-five. She didn't usually get up for another half-hour, but since she was, she decided to get dressed and run down to the twenty-four-hour market to get some "fresh from the oven" croissants to have for breakfast. When she stepped out of the apartment, it was seven-ten.

The telephone rang five minutes later. After the third ring, Jamilah reached over and picked up the receiver. "Hello," she groaned sleepily.

"Hello, can I speak to Sabrina?"

"Hold on." Putting the receiver down on her night table, she called out, "Sabrina!"

When she got no answer, she grumbled and threw the covers off. Sitting up on the bed, she called to her once again. "Sabrina!" Still, there was no answer.

Jamilah sucked her teeth and rose completely from the bed then lumbered over to her door and pulled it open. She immediately noticed that Sabrina was not in her bedroom or the bathroom.

"Sabrina? Where the hell is she this early in the morning?" Jamilah said aloud.

Dragging her feet, she headed back to her bedroom and over to the night table, then picked up the receiver. "She's not here. Who's calling?"

"Do you know when she'll be back?"

"No, I don't. I don't know where she is. Who's this?"

"This is Mike Francis, Darius' friend. Is this Jamilah?"

"Yes. Hi."

"Hey," he said shortly. "Listen, tell her I'm down at St. Vincent's Hospital. Darius got shot."

Instantly wide-awake, Jamilah gasped, "What? Darius? What happened?"

"Some niggas jacked his car last night and the sonsabitches shot him. When I was driving home last night, I found him lying in the middle of the street down near Canal Street."

Her breath began to come in gasps as tears welled in her eyes. "Oh my God. Is he going to be okay?"

"He just got out of surgery and he's in critical condition, but I think he'll pull through," Mike answered solemnly.

"Oh God, oh no. Why did they do this to him?" she cried into the receiver, although she really was not expecting an answer from Mike.

"'Cause the muthafuckas are ignorant and can't stand to see a brother trying to do something positive for himself," Mike angrily stated.

With the exception of Jamilah's soft crying, they were silent on the line for the next few seconds. Finally, Mike said, "Tell Sabrina he's here. His visiting hours are from two to eight."

"Okay, Mike. I'll tell her," Jamilah said between her sobs. "We'll be there this afternoon."

"All right. See ya later."

When she hung up, her cries broke free as she could no longer contain them. "Oh God, why'd this happen to him? Why Darius? He'd never hurt anybody. Why him?"

Jamilah was still crying when Sabrina returned from the supermarket fifteen minutes later. Hearing the door, Jamilah rose from where she'd been sitting and hurried to the front of the apartment to tell her about Darius.

Immediately noticing the look of distress on Jamilah's tear-stained face, Sabrina asked, "What's the matter?"

"Darius has been shot."

"What?" Horror and disbelief were apparent on her face.

"His friend Mike just called. He said he found him lying in the street last night when he was driving home. Some guys jacked his car and shot him. He's in St. Vincent's Hospital. He just got out of surgery."

Sabrina slumped against the counter at hearing the awful news. "Is he all right?"

"Mike said he's in critical condition but he thinks he'll be okay."

"Oh God," Sabrina lamented as she shook her head slowly.

"He said his visiting hours are from two to eight."

"Thanks." Despite the delicious aroma that filled the air, Sabrina had lost her appetite upon hearing the dreadful news. She left the bag with the warm croissants she had just purchased on the counter and started out of the kitchen.

"Are you going to leave work early so you can go see him?" Jamilah asked as Sabrina walked away.

"I don't know."

Jamilah followed her. "You are going to see him, right?"

"I don't know," she answered without turning.

"What?"

"I said, I don't know."

"Sabrina, you have to go see him. You know he's going to want you there."

Turning to Jamilah, Sabrina testily replied, "Look, don't tell me what I have to do."

"But Sabrina…"

"Save it, Jamilah! I've had enough of you telling me what I should and shouldn't do!"

Jamilah stood where she was and watched as Sabrina entered her bedroom and closed the door. *She has to go see him. She can't be that indifferent to him.*

✱✱✱

Jamilah was at the hospital at four-thirty that afternoon. Although she had gone to work, she had been there in body alone; her mind was totally out of it because she couldn't stop worrying about Darius. When she finally told her boss what was bothering her, he insisted that she leave and go see about her friend.

She had been dying to call Sabrina before she left her office to see if she would be coming by the hospital, but each time she recalled Sabrina's earlier reaction, she cringed.

As she stepped out of the elevator on the fifth floor where Darius' room was, she pleaded inwardly, *please come and see him, Sabrina.* Ambling down the corridor in the direction of his room, her stomach was in knots. Mike had not said where or how badly Darius had been shot so she automatically thought the worst. "Please let him be okay," she prayed softly as she continued down the long hall.

Suddenly, the familiar figure of Mike Francis appeared in the corridor a few feet ahead of her. He stepped over to the nurse's station and began conversing with the nurse on duty. As she approached, Jamilah called to him, "Mike."

He turned to her. "Hello, Jamilah."

"How is he?" she anxiously asked.

"He's coming along. He's in and out, you know, because he's pretty drugged up, but you can go in and see him."

She needed to know, "How bad was he shot?"

"Lucky for him, the bastard that shot him was no great marksman and he wasn't right up on him. Darius was shot in the midsection. The bullet hit one of his ribs and broke it, but it also deflected it, so it passed out of his right side. There was some internal bleeding, but they were able to stop it during surgery."

Jamilah sighed. "Thank God."

"Where's Sabrina?" he then asked.

"She'll be here when she gets off," Jamilah said with a prayer that her words would become a reality. "I got off of work early."

"Well, you go on in and see him. He was awake a minute ago."

"Okay, thanks."

Taking a deep breath, she turned toward his room. An elderly man was asleep in the bed near the door and the green curtain between the beds was drawn, so she couldn't see Darius from the doorway. Stepping up to the partition and not knowing what to expect, she held her breath.

Jamilah was relieved to see that he didn't look too bad. His normally rich brown complexion was pale, but he looked comfortable as he lay slightly inclined with his eyes closed. Wondering if he had fallen back to sleep, she sighed as her eyes took in the scene. There was an I.V. pole with two bags of clear fluid draining into his arm on the curtain-side of the bed, so she went to stand near the window. Tiptoeing to his side, she sat in the chair next to his bed before reaching out and taking his hand. Darius slowly turned his head toward her and opened his eyes.

"Hi," she said with a nervous smile.

The painkillers they were giving him were doing their job, but kept him slightly incoherent, so it was a few seconds before he could respond. "Jamilah?" he inquired in a raspy whisper.

She could no longer control her tears. Squeezing his hand gently, she asked, "Are you okay, Darius?"

He tried to smile as he answered, "I'll live."

"I'm so sorry they did this to you," she cried.

Due to the drugs coursing through his system, Darius slurred when he said, "Don't cry. Jamilah, please don't cry. I'll be all right."

Rising from the chair, she leaned over to hold him. "I'm so glad you're okay. When Mike called this morning and told me what happened, I was so afraid." She tried to smile through her tears as she gently caressed his face. "I'm so glad you're okay."

He, too, tried to smile at her. "I'm glad you came."

"How could I not come? Do you know if they got the bastards who did this?"

Slowly shaking his head, "I don't know."

"You didn't try to fight them, did you?"

"No."

"Good."

As he gently squeezed her hand, the doubt in his eyes shone clearly and she knew what his next question would be before he voiced it. "Is Sabrina coming?"

She couldn't look him in the eye as she lied to him, "She said she'd be here when she gets off of work." *She had better bring her ass down here!*

"What time is it?" Darius suddenly asked.

Looking at her watch, she said, "A quarter to five."

"Friday?"

"Uh-huh."

"I thought it was still morning."

"No, it's evening. Mike said they have you pretty drugged up."

"I'm glad. I can't feel a thing," he said and cracked a weak smile.

Jamilah stayed at the hospital until six-thirty when his parents arrived from Norfolk, Virginia. Although he dozed off a couple of times during her visit, he kept a firm grip on her hand so she made no attempts to leave before then. To her chagrin, Sabrina didn't make an appearance while she was there.

Promising to come and see him the next day, Jamilah kissed him softly on his forehead before she left. He whispered, "Thank you for being such a good friend."

∗∗∗

Sabrina wasn't home when she got in that night, but she really hadn't expected her to be. Jamilah was past the point of being angry with her about her treatment of Darius at this crucial time in his life.

Deciding to not even discuss him with her anymore since Sabrina didn't want to hear anything she had to say about him, Jamilah figured, *why waste my time?* When Darius looked into her eyes earlier and asked about Sabrina though, the sadness she saw there gave Jamilah the impression that he knew she wouldn't be coming.

Jamilah felt it a shame that such a nice man would become so smitten with her. Sabrina needed a man who was as materialistic as she was. Darius had always been willing to give Sabrina whatever her heart desired, but Jamilah knew his feelings for Sabrina ran much deeper than the mere objects he bestowed on her. His concern was that Sabrina be happy with him, and if that meant spending his hard earned cash, then so be it.

Darius' love blinded him to what Sabrina really needed, which was a man who had no qualms about telling her "no." Used to getting whatever she wanted, Jamilah decided that the idea of someone actually refusing Sabrina anything was probably anathema to her.

# Chapter 14

At two-thirty Saturday afternoon, Jamilah arrived at the hospital and was delighted to find Darius looking much better than he had the day before. He was propped up in the bed and when he noticed her, his face came alive with a bright smile. "Jamilah!"

"Hi! Oh, I'm so happy to see you sitting up. You look so much better than yesterday." Stepping right over to the bed, she gave him a big hug and a kiss on his cheek.

"Yeah, I feel a little better, too, despite the fact that since they've cut back on my drugs, I can now feel this wound."

"Does it hurt a lot?" she asked as she winced in sympathy.

"Only when I breathe."

"Ouch."

"But I feel more alert than yesterday."

"Well, that's good."

Referring to the bouquet of colorful balloons Jamilah was still holding, Darius then asked, "Are those for me?"

"Yes, they are. I started to buy you some flowers, but figured these would probably last longer." She rearranged the few items that rested on the miniscule bed stand to make room for the balloons.

"Thank you, J. That was real sweet."

"Well, you know, that's just the kind of person I am," she said facetiously, but with a wide grin.

Smiling, he admitted, "I've never gotten a bouquet of any kind from a woman before."

"Well, that makes two of us. I've never given a bouquet of any kind to a man."

"You know, a couple of detectives were in to see me today. They found my car."

"Oh, good. Was it still intact?"

"Yeah. Of course they stole everything I had in it, my stereo system, a few CDs, my cell phone, and a few other little things, but at least it wasn't damaged."

"Well, that's good."

"I wasn't able to give the cops any information, though. It all happened so fast. Those guys just came out of nowhere."

"How many were there?"

"Four, I think. Two of them on each side. All of a sudden, there was this gun in my face, you know, 'cause I had my window open. I don't even know where they came from."

"Damn! You know, it's so disgusting that you can't have anything decent without some lowlife trying to take it from you," Jamilah said bitterly.

"Tell me about it. I'll tell you, too, I was never so happy to see Mike. I think I blacked out right after he got there. I don't remember anything from the time I saw him till I woke up in here."

"Yeah, that was really fortunate. When he called the house yesterday morning and told me he found you in the middle of the street, I almost passed out. I was like, 'I just left him.'"

"Yeah."

An uneasy silence crept upon them as they reflected on the events of Thursday night.

After a moment, "Bob came by last night after you left. He asked about my African queen," Darius said with a smile.

Laughing, Jamilah shook her head in wonderment.

"He said he was going to make sure that Ray's wife calls you about those invitations."

"Oh, yeah, I spoke to Suzanna Winston this morning. When I got home last night there was a message on the answering machine from her. We made an appointment to get together on Monday. She wants me to make some party decorations."

"Excellent! I told you you'd hear from them." Even in agony, Darius was happy for her.

"Yeah, I'm kind of psyched."

Staring into each other's eyes for a few seconds, the thought they both tried to keep at bay surfaced. Jamilah noticed the sudden difficulty Darius had in maintaining his smile. His eyes clouded over briefly, and he turned his face away from Jamilah and toward the window as his voice took on a softer tone. "Sabrina didn't make it by last night." He turned back to Jamilah. "Is she coming by today?"

Jamilah hated to lie to him but, truthfully, she was not sure what Sabrina would do. "I think so. She wasn't at home when I left."

"Did she say she was coming?"

"I didn't really talk to her this morning before she left. We had a bit of an argument the other night," Jamilah admitted. Getting up from her seat, she strolled to the window and looked out.

"Not about the fund-raiser, I hope," Darius said.

"No, it was something else."

"Are you sure?"

"Yes," Jamilah answered shortly.

Darius stared at her back for a few seconds because Jamilah would not face him. "Why am I having such a hard time believing you, J?" he quietly asked.

"It wasn't just about that, Darius. I had some things that I needed to say to her, so I said them." She still would not face him.

"I don't want to come between you two, Jamilah. You've been friends for a long time. Sabrina's… What goes on between Sabrina and me shouldn't concern you."

She turned to him then because he had just told her, basically, what Sabrina had the other night. Coming from him, however, the words really hurt. She was trying to protect him, but it was quite obvious that he did not want her protection.

Darius could see that she was surprised and a little hurt by his rebuff. Despite her good intentions though, his state of affairs with Sabrina was a very personal matter, one that was extremely sensitive, as well. Although he was not so naïve as to believe that their relationship wasn't in jeopardy, the last thing he felt he needed…the last thing he felt *they* needed, was outside interference, no matter how well intentioned it was.

***

Despite her reservations about visiting Darius after his reprimand Saturday, Jamilah could not stay away.

Darius was happy to see her, too, when she arrived Sunday afternoon. After the way he had hurt her, albeit unintentionally, he was happy that she had not written him off because her friendship was important to him.

When Jamilah arrived, there was a young woman sitting with Darius so he made the introductions. "This is my sister, Brianne. Brie, this is my good friend, Jamilah Parsons."

"Hi, Jamilah, it's nice to meet you," Brianne said sincerely, as she stood and reached across the bed to shake her hand.

"Hi, it's nice to meet you, too, Brianne."

Jamilah was surprised that Darius' sister was so tiny; she figured she couldn't be more than five feet tall, or bigger than a size one. Dark complexioned, like her brother, was where the similarity ended because they looked nothing alike. Brianne had close-set eyes that sparkled with confidence, a button nose and a small mouth, the lips of which were covered with a natural shade of brown. She had a bit of an overbite, but her smile was warm and genuine. She wore her hair in long, finely braided extensions which fell freely down her back, and reminded Jamilah of a little girl, but she liked her right off.

"Brianne just flew in this morning from Detroit," Darius informed her.

"Oh, how long will you be here?"

"I don't know. At least until Darius gets out of the hospital."

"They're talking about sending me home tomorrow or Tuesday," he said.

"That soon?" Jamilah asked in surprise.

"Yeah, you know they try to kick you out as soon as possible nowadays if you're breathing."

Frowning, Brianne agreed, "That's for sure."

Genuinely concerned, Jamilah asked, "Will you be up to going home that soon, though?"

"Yeah, probably. Besides, my mother and father are at my place and they won't be leaving anytime soon, so I don't have to worry about being taken care of. Also, this stuff they're trying to make me eat in here leaves much to be desired. I'm quite anxious to taste my mother's cooking again."

"The food's gross, huh?" Jamilah said with a grin.

"To put it kindly."

"Jamilah, how long have you and Darius been dating? He usually calls me and tells me about any new girlfriends. I guess he didn't get a chance to tell me about you," Brianne said frankly.

"Oh, no, we're…"

"Jamilah and I are not dating, Brianne. We're just friends," Darius cut in.

"Oh."

Without thinking, Jamilah volunteered, "Darius is dating my roommate, Sabrina."

"Oh. Well, how come she's not here?" Brianne asked, looking from Jamilah to Darius and back, awaiting an answer.

"Sh-she'll be here later," Jamilah stumbled, wanting to kick herself for her slip of the lip.

"Mommy told me you were here Friday night, Jamilah, when they came and yesterday, too. They didn't say anything about anyone else coming by. Did she come to see you yesterday?" Brianne asked, looking to Darius for an explanation.

He sighed. "Sabrina's… She couldn't make it by yesterday, Brie. She'll be here later."

"Why couldn't she come yesterday? What could have been so important that she couldn't come and see you yesterday?" Brianne wanted to know.

Furious with Sabrina because she didn't even have the decency to come and see if he was all right or not, Jamilah wanted to know the answer to that one, too. Sabrina hadn't even come home last night. Knowing she had spent the night with that Quenten Blanchard fellow, though not really caring one way or another who she'd slept with, Jamilah, nevertheless, felt that her indifference toward Darius now was inexcusable, regardless of what he said.

"Did she say what time she was coming today, Jamilah?" Darius asked in a solemn tone.

Unable to ignore the hurt or anxiety that showed in his eyes when he looked at her, Jamilah wanted to tell him not to waste his time pining over Sabrina, that he was too good for her, and that she didn't deserve his love, but she would never hurt him by telling him that. Besides, after yesterday, she was certain he would resent her if she did. "I didn't really speak to her this morning. I left the apartment pretty early today and she was still asleep," Jamilah lied.

"Did she at least call you?" Brianne asked Darius.

Becoming agitated, Darius asked, "What difference does it make?"

"What do you mean, what difference does it make? She's supposed to be your woman and she can't even come by here to see how you're doing, much less, call?" Brianne said in an annoyed tone.

Embarrassed for Darius, Jamilah didn't make a sound in response to Brianne's statement, because she was in total agreement with everything she'd said.

"I'd like to meet this witch who thinks she's too good to come and see my brother after he's been shot, when I *know* you've probably been treating her like royalty!"

*Boy, what I would do to be a fly on the wall when that happened*, Jamilah thought while admiring Brianne's call. Knowing the type of man her brother really was, she had Darius pegged. He had treated Sabrina like royalty; that had always been one of the things Sabrina bragged on him about. To be so heartless that she couldn't take thirty minutes out of her day to check in on him, greatly diminished Jamilah's already sinking opinion of her.

"Brianne, you don't know Sabrina, so you can't judge her for not being here. How do you know she hasn't had a crisis of her own?" Darius said in her defense.

Looking to Jamilah for confirmation, Brianne asked, "Is that the case?"

Startled, she hadn't expected Brianne's question but she was not about to lie for Sabrina, not anymore. "Not that I know of."

Embarrassed, impatient and incensed, Darius declared, "Brie, why don't you just mind your business. I don't want to hear any more talk about this. It's not your place to decide who I should be with or who I shouldn't be with."

"Darius…"

"Leave it alone, Brianne!"

Sucking her teeth in exasperation, she poked out her lips in defiance of him. After a few seconds of silence, Brianne rose from her chair and started from the room. "I'll be back."

Darius did not respond nor look her way when she walked out.

Jamilah felt like an intruder among them. She lowered her head slightly, afraid to meet Darius' questioning eyes. "She's not coming, is she?"

"I don't know."

"She probably thinks I'm angry with her about the other night."

Jamilah remained silent.

"Would you do me a favor, Jamilah?"

"Sure."

"Would you tell her I'm not angry with her."

She was slow in answering.

"Please."

Gazing into his eyes as she felt her own beginning to water, she nodded her head affirmatively.

After a few seconds, Darius softly explained, "I can't help how I feel about her. I know she doesn't feel the same way, but I still care about her." He paused momentarily before he continued reflectively. "She just needs somebody to take care of her."

Jamilah could not bring herself to say anything positive about Sabrina, so she abruptly changed the subject. "Margaret Rosenbaum called me this morning."

Darius was slow in comprehending.

"You know, another of your partners' wives. I'm going to see her tomorrow afternoon, too. She's interested in my wedding invitations," Jamilah said in an attempt to lighten the solemn mood that had pervaded the room moments earlier.

His eyes brightened at her news. "That's great, Jamilah. I knew she'd call. They were quite impressed with you, you know."

"I have a few different samples that I'm going to show her. I even have some ethnic and religious ones, if she wants to go that way."

"That's great. Make sure you cover all your bases."

"I will."

"Have you ever thought about going into business for yourself?"

"Yeah, I've thought about it, but I don't have a large enough client base just yet."

"Well, when you're ready, let me know. I can work up a business plan for you, if you like."

"Thanks, Darius. I'll keep that in mind."

Jamilah stayed with Darius until almost five p.m., sidestepping all conversation regarding Sabrina so everyone was in good spirits when she left. An hour after she had stormed out of his room, Brianne returned and apologized to Darius for upsetting him.

# Chapter 15

Jamilah was surprised when she called to speak to Darius on Monday and was informed that he had been discharged. Since she did not have his home phone number, she was unable to contact him there. Asking Sabrina for it was completely out of the question.

It was approximately eight o'clock Monday evening when Jamilah got home after her dinner meeting with Suzanna Winston. Earlier in the day, she'd had lunch with Margaret Rosenbaum and, happily, both women contracted for her services. Jamilah was excited about the new business and had every intention of starting on the wedding invitations for Margaret when she got home.

Her mood darkened immediately, however, when she opened the door of her apartment and noticed Quenten Blanchard sitting on her couch.

"Hello, Jamilah," he said brightly. "How've you been?"

"Fine, thank you," she replied colorlessly.

As usual, he was the picture of masculine elegance. He was wearing a pearl gray suit, and the French cuffs of his crisp white shirt peeked out from the sleeves of his jacket just enough to offer one a view of his gold/diamond cufflinks. His polished good looks made him the picture-perfect match for Sabrina. Besides, he seemed to be just as conceited as she was.

Sabrina emerged from the back of the apartment. "Hi."

As Jamilah gave her a cursory glance and mumbled, "What's up?" she removed her jacket and proceeded to hang it in the front closet.

Sabrina nearly floored her when she uncharacteristically asked, "Are you just coming from the hospital?"

Turning to face Sabrina, Jamilah's amazement left her momentarily speechless. Regaining her composure after a few seconds, she informed Sabrina, "No, I had a meeting with a new client."

"That's excellent, Jamilah. So your independent business is doing well, huh?" Quenten asked with seemingly genuine interest.

"Yes, it is."

"Who's in the hospital?" he asked.

Jumping in before Jamilah could respond, Sabrina answered, "A friend of Jamilah's got shot the other day."

Through blazing eyes that conveyed sheer malevolence, Jamilah stared at Sabrina in disbelief. *A friend of Jamilah's?*

"I'm sorry to hear that," Quenten said. "Is he...she...all right?"

"He's doing fine," Jamilah answered, although continuing to glare at Sabrina. "He went home today."

"Already?" Sabrina asked.

"Already," Jamilah sneered as she started past Sabrina and out of the room. *What gall she has*, Jamilah thought. Suddenly, remembering the promise she'd made to Darius the day before, she stopped in her tracks and turned back to the living room. With a smile as phony as a three dollar bill, Jamilah said, "Oh yeah, Sabrina, Darius said to tell you he's not angry about the other day." Her mischievous grin grew even more prominent when she noticed Sabrina's stunned expression. *Well, if Darius asks, I can at least be truthful that I gave Sabrina his message.*

"Who's Darius?" Jamilah heard Quenten ask before she entered her bedroom.

**✱✱✱**

Tuesday morning, when Jamilah stepped out of the bathroom after her morning shower, Sabrina was waiting for her. "Why did you do that?" she asked. Her face was a story in anger.

"Do what?" Jamilah asked innocently as she brushed past her.

Sabrina followed Jamilah into her bedroom. "If you think you can break Quenten and me up with that little stunt you pulled last night, you're in for a big letdown, sister."

"I couldn't care less about you or Quenten," Jamilah said nastily.

"Yeah, right. If you think I believe that, you're a bigger fool than I thought."

"Well, if that's not the pot calling the kettle black, I don't know what is. You're the fool, Sabrina. You think you've found your knight in shining armor in Quenten. Chile, that man will use you and throw you out when he's finished, just like yesterday's trash. I'm sure you've already noticed that you can't wrap him around your pretty little finger like you did Darius."

"Don't you worry about what I can or can't do with Quenten. I've got him exactly where I want him," Sabrina said smugly.

"Is that what you think?" Jamilah smiled. "I guess that's why he's got you spending the night with him already, huh? Or is that your way of trapping him? You made Darius wait for what, two, three months and you never gave him any, and he would have done anything for you. What has Quenten given you for your services? I remember you once said the price has to be right."

"Fuck you, Jamilah," Sabrina said in a caustic whisper.

With a deadpan expression and pointing her finger for emphasis, Jamilah replied, "No, Sabrina, that's what Quenten's doing to you, remember?"

"You know, it's really sad that you're so completely jealous of me."

"Jealous of you?" Jamilah laughed. "You've got to be kidding. What reason do I have to be jealous of you?"

"Look at me!" Spreading her arms wide to display her perfect thirty-six, twenty-four, thirty-six figure in her matching silk and lace bra and panty set, Sabrina continued, "Now, look at you!" Jamilah, in comparison, was wearing a tattered, but very comfortable, terrycloth bathrobe with an old scarf on her head. "I have men knocking each other over just to get next to me. What do you have? Nothing! You're so desperate for a man that you're trying to push up on mine. I know you've been at that hospital every day fawning over Darius, trying to be his sweet little nursemaid, hoping that he'd fall for you over me." Sabrina stopped and laughed for a few seconds before she sneered, "Darius doesn't want you. When are you going to open your eyes and see that? What was that you said last night? 'Tell Sabrina I'm not angry with her.' Look at that! Doesn't that tell you something? He still wants me! I haven't even visited him and he still wants me! I know that must be killing you."

"You know what kills me, Sabrina? It kills me to know that a man of Darius' caliber could be so blind and so hopelessly in love with a witch like you. You think you've got something in Quenten. With all the money he supposedly has, he will NEVER be the man Darius is and you'll never be good enough for a man like him. You think because you're beautiful on the outside, you're better than I am? You're the one who's jealous, Sabrina. I've never met anyone so completely insecure in my life. And you've always been, even when we were kids. If you thought someone didn't like you, you broke your neck to find out why and to do whatever you could to fall into his or her good graces. Unlike you, I don't need a man or anyone else to validate who I am. I know who I am and I like myself just fine. I'm doing what I want, when I want and I don't have to wait for any man to do anything for me. Who are you, Sabrina? Who would you be without a man to tell you?"

"I don't need a man to tell me who I am," Sabrina argued.

"How would you know that? How much time have you spent without one? Yeah, so what, you've got men falling over themselves to get next to you, but you know something, Sabrina? I don't want to be any man's trophy and that is all you are. A trophy. You're just too blind to see it. And if there's one thing I know, men like to collect trophies 'cause after a while, when one trophy gets old, it's time to get another one."

Jamilah's mood was sour the entire day as a result of her early-morning confrontation with Sabrina. She began to notice that lately, their arguments seemed to occur more frequently than ever before, and they were more intense than they had ever been. It bothered her that their friendship had become so unstable. *Is Darius at the root of our problem?* Jamilah hated to admit that there was some truth to what Sabrina said with respect to her feelings for Darius. She did care for him, but she knew she had as much chance as an ice cube in Hell that he would ever feel for her the way she felt for him.

She had never even been slightly attracted to any of Sabrina's male friends. They were all quite different from the type of man to whom she was attracted. Sabrina's suitors were usually "stuffed-shirts" who were more concerned with trying to impress than with being themselves. That was a complete turnoff for Jamilah.

# Chapter 16

A lthough he was still quite sore and not nearly as mobile as usual, Darius was glad to be home, especially since his parents and sister were there to take care of him. Despite his family's presence, though, he was quite sad because he still hadn't heard from Sabrina.

Nobly trying to be cheerful when he was up with his family, due to the soreness he still experienced, however, Darius stayed in bed for most of the day on Monday and also on this day. It was at times like this, when he was alone, that his thoughts would drift to Sabrina, and he would try to figure out what he had done wrong in her regard. Missing her terribly, it genuinely hurt to acknowledge that their relationship was, most likely, a thing of the past. *She's probably found someone else*, he figured. He could not imagine Sabrina without a man in her life for too long. She struck him as the type of woman who wanted a man around at all times to take care of all her needs. *Why couldn't she see that I wanted to be that man? She had to know there was nothing in this world I wouldn't have done for her.*

He wondered if Jamilah had given her his message. He had not missed the disapproval and disappointment in Jamilah's eyes each time he had mentioned Sabrina when she visited him. Darius knew that Jamilah had his best interests at heart. *She had probably lied each time she told me Sabrina was coming to the hospital.* He realized now that she had been trying to spare his feelings. After all, he figured she probably knew that Sabrina's seeing someone else.

Despite Sabrina's apparent indifference to his near-death experience, he still wanted to see her. Irritated about her lack of concern for him and wanting to tell her so, more than that, he was hurt. Although he was sure there was no chance of them being together anymore, he wanted to hear her tell him she had moved on. He would not let her off so easily that she could brush him aside with no explanation. Regardless of the hurt he knew would come from hearing the words from her lips, his heart could not let go of her without that solid closure.

As he lay across his king-sized bed with memories of Sabrina constantly invading his thoughts, he decided to go to her. Easing himself slowly to a sitting position, he winced as the pain from his wound shot straight to his brain. He moved his hand to his side and covered the area gently until he felt the pain slightly subside.

"Brianne!" he called out, minutes later, to his sister who was downstairs.

"Coming, Darius," he heard her call back.

A few seconds later, the door to his bedroom flew open and in breezed his precious baby sister. *She's going to flip when I tell her what I want.* She was a little thing but full of fire and seemingly fearless when it came to righting any wrong done to a member of her family.

"Hey, what's up, guy? What ya need?"

"Can you hand me my sneakers out of the closet?" Darius asked.

"Why, you planning on taking a jog around the block?" she asked with a devilish chuckle as she moved to the closet.

He laughed, too. "No, I'm going for a little walk."

"Do you think you should do that so soon? Shouldn't you be resting?" she asked with genuine concern as she placed a pair of sneakers on the floor at his feet.

"I'm tired of resting. That's all I've been doing for the last five days," Darius said testily.

"You just got shot!"

"Do you think I've forgotten that?"

She sat on the bed next to him and shook her head as she stared at him. He would not meet her gaze. "You're so damn stubborn."

"Look who's talking."

They sat in silence for the next couple of seconds. Knowing he wasn't strong enough to bend over and put his sneakers on without help, he dreaded having to ask her to do it, but what choice did he have? "Would you help me, please?" he asked softly.

She sighed but immediately squatted in front of him and put his sneakers on his feet.

"Thank you," he said with a smile when she had completed the task.

"You're welcome. Have you talked to Jamilah since you've been home?" Brianne asked as she stood in front of him.

"No. I don't think she has my number."

"Has your girlfriend, Sabrina, called you since you've been home?" Brianne asked with a sneer.

He lowered his head briefly and shook it.

"Why would you want to be bothered with someone who doesn't even visit you in the hospital after you've been shot?" Brianne asked.

He looked up at her for a moment, not able to form an answer that would make sense to anyone but him. Not about to try to make her understand what he felt, he knew he'd have a big enough fight on his hands when she found out where he really planned to go. "We've been having some problems lately, that's all," he answered.

"So what? Whatever problems y'all were having, she should have put them on the back burner once she found out what happened to you," Brianne insisted with her hand on her hip.

"She's pretty stubborn."

"She sounds pretty heartless to me."

"Whatever," he muttered.

He rose slowly from his bed and reached for the lightweight bomber jacket that was hung across the back of the chair next to his bed. Brianne helped him put on the garment. "Thanks, sis." He turned to face her. "You know, I'm really glad you guys are here."

"Where else would we be?" she answered as she looked up into his eyes.

He curled his lip into a half-smile before he turned and started out of the bedroom.

When Darius reached the top of the landing that led to the main floor of his duplex apartment, Brianne ran into the guest bedroom, where she was staying, to retrieve her own jacket. When Darius saw what she was doing, he asked, "Where are you going?"

"With you."

"No, that's all right. You don't have to. I'll be okay."

"Now, you know Mommy and Daddy are not going to let you go anywhere in your condition—alone. And since you're too stubborn to listen when we tell you that you need to have your butt in bed, I'm going with you to make sure you stay okay."

Darius started to take the first step down the stairs when he suddenly stopped and swore under his breath.

"What's the matter?" Brianne asked with slight alarm.

"I forgot my keys."

"You don't need your keys. Mommy and Daddy'll be here."

"My car keys."

"Why do you need your car keys? Where are you going?"

"Would you just get them for me, please? They're on top of my dresser."

"Where are you going, Darius?"

"Brianne, would you just get them for me?"

She regarded him suspiciously for a few seconds before she reentered his bedroom to retrieve his car keys.

Once they had made it downstairs, Darius explained to his parents that he needed to get out for a little while. Despite their objections, he insisted on going. Although they were not happy about it, they eased up a bit since Brianne was going with him.

Darius stepped alongside his car on the driver side and beckoned to Brianne to toss him his keys. She was at the passenger door. She looked at him like he was crazy. "You're not driving."

"Yes, I am."

"Where are you going, Darius?"

"Can I have my keys, Miss Marple?" Darius asked, referring to Agatha Christie's female sleuth.

"I'm not letting you drive. If you want, I'll drive you, but I'm not letting you drive."

Darius took a deep breath and counted to ten silently. "You're really starting to tick me off, Brianne."

"Do I care? Now if you want to go somewhere, you'd better hop in over here, 'cause I'm not giving you these keys."

He shook his head, then gave his sister a look that expressed just how much she was getting on his nerves, but he gave in and slowly made his way around to the passenger side. She helped him into the car, then hurried around to the driver's side and started it up.

"All right, where to?"

"Just drive. I'll show you."

During their drive Darius did not speak much except to give Brianne directions. After a half-hour, she asked once again, "Where are we going?"

"Make a right turn on the next block and start looking for a space."

Suddenly, it dawned on her. "You're going to see that witch, Sabrina, aren't you?"

"Stow it, Brianne. I don't want to hear it."

"Darius, how can you do this?"

"I said I don't want to hear it, Brianne. As a matter of fact, pull over."

"Right here?"

"Yes, right here."

She stopped the car and Darius immediately proceeded to exit the car, albeit quite slowly.

"Wait. Let me park."

"No, you wait here."

"Darius..."

"Wait here. I'll be right back."

Making no attempts to disguise the anger and disappointment she felt in her older brother, Brianne could not understand why he would let Sabrina get to him in such a manner that he would chase behind her after she had shown absolutely no concern for him, simply by not calling or coming to the hospital.

Darius made his way to the building slowly. He was actually in a lot of pain, not just physical, but emotional. It was almost as though the closer he got to the door of their apartment, the more the realization sunk in that she was truly out of his life. It hurt his heart, too, but he had to see her one more time.

✱✱✱

Jamilah and Sabrina were both in the apartment, but they barely spoke to one another. Jamilah was disgusted with Sabrina and Quenten and their affair, while Sabrina was fed up with what she called Jamilah's "holier than thou" attitude, so they pretty much just grunted at one another as they passed in the apartment.

When the doorbell rang, Sabrina was in her bedroom. Jamilah was in the kitchen fixing dinner. She walked to the door, looked through the peephole, and was stunned to see Darius standing on the other side. She hurriedly opened the door. "Darius! What are you doing here?"

"Hi, Jamilah. How you doin'?"

"Fine. How are you?"

"I'm okay. I'm making it. Is Sabrina home?"

"Darius," she pleaded with a look of unmistakable disappointment.

"Jamilah, please, I don't need to hear it from you, too, okay? Is she here?"

"Yeah, come on in," she said in resignation.

Jamilah was afraid for him. It hurt her that he loved Sabrina so much, that he still loved her after she had treated him so heartlessly. "Sit down. Are you okay?"

"Yeah, I'm okay." He moved slowly to the easy-chair.

"How did you get here?" Jamilah asked.

"Brianne drove me."

"Where is she?"

"She's downstairs. I didn't think she should come up."

Jamilah knew if Brianne had come upstairs, she would have lit into Sabrina like nobody's business.

"I'll go get her," Jamilah said in reference to Sabrina.

"Thank you."

Jamilah walked back to Sabrina's room. She was on the phone. Jamilah stuck her head in the room and said, "You have company."

"I gotta go. Talk to you later." Sabrina wasted no time with formalities before she hung up. She immediately sat up and put her feet in her slippers, then headed out of the room, certain it was Quenten at the door. She rushed out to the living room with a big smile on her face. She stopped dead in her tracks, however, and the smile fell from her face when she saw Darius.

"Hi, Sabrina."

"Darius. Hi. How are you?"

"I'm okay." He rose from the chair with difficulty. "How you doin'?"

"I'm…okay. I'm sorry I didn't make it to the hospital."

"That's all right. Don't worry about it," he said lightly.

"Shouldn't you be resting?"

"I wanted to see you." He took a couple of steps closer to her and he reached out to touch her face. "How've you been?" he asked softly.

Sabrina turned away from him. "Darius…Darius, I'm seeing someone else. I…I can't see you anymore."

Despite the fact that he had known she was going to tell him it was over, Darius felt the wind knocked out of him. He'd always known. He had not gone there with any illusions that she would run happily into his arms, but he was demoralized upon learning that she had found someone else already. Standing there bravely, he tried to accept what she had said, but it was difficult.

Sabrina then turned back to him and saw his eyes radiate sadness, but she was unaffected.

Softly, Darius said, "I kinda figured that. I just, uh…I just wanted to see you one more time, you know. I've been thinking about you." He paused for a moment, then took a deep breath. "Well, I…I hope he treats you right. I hope he knows what he's got."

Suddenly, reaching out and enveloping her before she was able to pull away, and ignoring the immense pain that shot through his side from the exertion he put forth with his action, he whispered in her ear, "Take care of yourself, all right?" Letting her go, he bravely turned to leave the apartment.

Jamilah had been standing just outside the living room, listening. When he started toward the door, she entered the room. "Darius."

Veering back to her with a courageous smile, he said, "Take care of yourself, Jamilah."

She stepped right up to him and looked into his eyes. "Are you okay?"

"I'll be fine." He kissed her on her forehead and said, "Thank you," then turned and left the apartment.

Jamilah, crying unashamedly, made no effort to hide her tears. After a few seconds, she turned to Sabrina, giving her a menacing stare. A bounty of loathsome thoughts flying through her mind, Jamilah wanted to yell at her; to scream out how wrong Sabrina had been and how much she detested what Sabrina had done to Darius, but she couldn't say a word. She simply ran to her bedroom, where she fell down on her bed and sobbed uncontrollably.

Jamilah's tears were not just for Darius, though. Finally acknowledging that she was in love with him, she knew she would never see him again.

✱✱✱

Later that evening, Jamilah was in the apartment alone. Sabrina had left a couple of hours earlier without a word to her about where she was going or when she would be back. Truthfully, Jamilah did not care where Sabrina had gone, although she would bet that Sabrina was with Quenten.

*So now what? I wanted Sabrina to tell Darius the truth and she has. I knew it would hurt him, but he's better off without her. But what about me? I'll never see him again.* Jamilah missed Darius already. She almost wished that he was still in the hospital. At least then she would be able to visit him. Now she had no way to get in touch with him.

In the next instant, the telephone rang. The loud braying of the phone invaded her joyless solitude; she really didn't care to speak with anyone. The answering machine clicked into action after the third insistent ring.

"Hi, Jamilah, it's Mommy. I was just calling to see how you were since I haven't spoken to you all weekend. Give me a call when you get in. I hope everything's all right with you. I love you."

Jamilah reached for the telephone on her nightstand before her mother broke the connection. "Mommy!"

"Hi, baby. What you doin', screening your calls now?" Alexia said good-naturedly.

"No, I just didn't feel like talking to anyone."

Alexia's tone immediately changed to one of concern. "What's the matter, sweetheart? You okay?"

"No."

"What's wrong?"

"Remember I told you that Sabrina's boyfriend, Darius, got shot."

"Yeah, is he all right?"

"No. Well…he's out of the hospital, but…Sabrina cut him off today. He came all the way here to see her and she just told him that it was over 'cause she's seeing somebody else, like it was no big deal. She never even went to visit him in the hospital."

There was a long silence on the line before Alexia asked, "Jamilah, what's going on?" She knew her daughter well, and knew instantly, that Jamilah was holding back on her.

"I didn't tell you this the other night, but Sabrina and I had a fight the night he got shot because she stood him up for this big dinner he had to go to for his job."

"What has that got to do with you, baby?"

She didn't tell her mother that she had volunteered to attend the dinner with Darius. "He's a really nice guy and she just dogged him. Then she met this other guy who's got all this money, so she cut Darius off to be with him. Today when Darius came here to see Sabrina, he could barely walk 'cause he was in so much pain, and she just…she just acted like it was nothing. It's just like she poured salt on his wound."

"Jamilah…"

"Mommy, he didn't deserve that. He never did anything to hurt her and she just dogged him for no good reason." Tears were streaming down Jamilah's face. She wanted to tell her mother how she felt about Darius, but intuitively knew Alexia would disapprove.

Alexia could feel Jamilah's pain but maternal instincts told her there was a deeper truth behind her daughter's words that she was not telling. In a soft but straightforward manner, Alexia asked, "Have you been with this man, Jamilah?"

"*NO!*"

"So what's going on? Tell me the truth."

Jamilah began to cry. "I'm just tired of being by myself. I just want to meet someone that I can love, Mommy, and who'll love me without all the games and lies. I'm just tired of being alone."

"Why did you fight with Sabrina about this man, Jami?" Alexia gently probed, using the nickname she had given Jamilah when she was a little girl.

"Because he loves her and she just uses him."

"No. Why did you really fight with her?" She waited patiently for the next few seconds before Jamilah answered.

"I can't help how I feel," Jamilah moaned.

"Baby, you don't need to be with anyone who's going to be grinning up in your best friend's face one minute, then trying to push up on you in the next," Alexia said, convinced that Darius had made some type of untoward proposition to her daughter.

"He never did that! He would never do anything deceitful to Sabrina or anyone else. He's not like that. He's the sweetest, kindest, most sensitive man I've ever known, and he loves Sabrina," Jamilah said through her tears. "I never meant to fall in love with him, Mommy. I...I just can't help it. I'm never going to see him again, anyway."

"Jamilah, listen to me." Alexia's tone had changed once again, to the stern, yet sensible and caring one of a loving parent. "You and Sabrina have been friends your entire life, practically. You can't let this man come between you. No matter what Sabrina may have done to him, that's not your concern. It has nothing to do with you, and you have no right to say anything to her about it. He's a grown man and if he let her dog him out, like you say, then that's on him. You girls have been inseparable forever. How are you going to let some man get in the middle of what you've been to each other? You owe Sabrina an apology, honey."

"But Mommy..."

"No buts, Jamilah. You're wrong. It's good that Sabrina won't be seeing him anymore if that means you won't either. Why give yourself all this grief and pain over a man who's in love with someone else? Regardless of whether she loves him back or not."

"But it's not right what she did to him," Jamilah pleaded.

"That's not your problem. You're not Sabrina's judge. If she's living foul, it'll come back to her. What goes around, comes around, baby, and if you're living foul, it'll come back to you, too. Let that man go, Jamilah, and get on with your life. Don't tear up your friendship over this man. Real friends are hard to come by, and despite all of Sabrina's faults and her selfishness, you can't undo all that you two have been through together. Men will come and go in your life like birthdays. Real sister-friends are a rarity and you should hold tight to them when you're blessed to have one in your life."

"Even if I don't agree with the way she's living?"

"Then you talk to her and tell her how you feel, but not because of a man, Jamilah. Especially one who's not even thinking about you."

"We're friends, Mommy."

"Who?"

"Me and Darius."

"And how could that have happened, Jamilah, if he's so in love with Sabrina?"

"We talk. I visited him while he was in the hospital."

"And how does that make you friends?"

"That night Sabrina stood him up, I went with him."

"You did what?"

"It's not like you think, Mommy. It was just so he wouldn't get in trouble with his boss. It was strictly business. Besides, I'm well aware of how he feels about Sabrina. He told me. It's just that…I wish I could meet someone like him. He's so easy to talk to and…" Jamilah sighed in resignation. "You don't understand."

"I understand what it's like to be in love with someone who doesn't love you back. The only thing it brings is pain, Jamilah."

"I know," she admitted sadly.

"Honey, this man, Darius, may very well be as nice as you say, but why make yourself miserable over a love that will never be yours? You're such a beautiful and intelligent young woman, Jamilah, and I don't want to see you hurt because you're wasting your time pining over a man you'll never really know. There are plenty of decent men out there and when it's the right time, someone special will come into your life and bring you all the love and joy you deserve, baby. Don't waste your time crying over him. He's obviously not the one for you," Alexia said with as much compassion as she could. She could remember what it was like to be young and yearning for a love of her own. And of course, she wanted her only daughter to find a man who was deserving of her good heart.

"Mommy, I'm tired. I'm going to bed. I'll give you a call tomorrow, okay?" Jamilah said softly.

"Are you going to be okay?" Alexia asked with motherly concern.

"Yes."

"Talk to Sabrina. Don't let your friendship die, baby."

"I love you, Mommy."

"I love you, too, sweetheart."

# Chapter 17

Despite the conversation Jamilah had had with her mother, relations between her and Sabrina were quite strained over the next four weeks. In fact, they barely spoke. When Jamilah was at home, she pretty much buried herself in her work. She had two new clients, as well as other jobs that she needed to complete, so she occupied her time with her artwork.

Sabrina saw Quenten basically every day. He was frequently at the apartment when Jamilah came home from work. Sabrina also spent the night with him a number of times throughout those weeks.

On Thursday of the fourth week, Sabrina was in the apartment alone when Jamilah came home from work carrying a number of flattened boxes. She immediately inquired about them.

Jamilah calmly turned to her and said, "I'm moving out on Saturday."

Sabrina was stunned. "Where are you going?"

"I have a place…I'm buying a townhouse in Long Island. I'm going to be renting it initially. I plan to buy it later, but I'm moving into it this weekend."

"Why are you just telling me now? I didn't even know you were trying to move."

"What difference does it make? I mean, do you really care?" Jamilah asked wearily. "This will give you plenty of space and privacy so you can be with Quenten. Besides, I need my own space. I don't want to live here anymore, Sabrina."

"And what am I supposed to do about the rent?" Sabrina asked with her hands on her hips.

"I gave you my half of the rent for this month, and I'll give you half of it next month. But past that, I really don't care what you do with this apartment. You can keep it. You can get another roommate. You can move out. I don't care. I just can't live here anymore," Jamilah stated calmly.

"Why?"

"Look, I'm tired. I have a lot of packing to do. I really, really don't want to go into it right now, if you don't mind," Jamilah said with a sigh. She started back to her room.

"Well, I do mind!" Sabrina called after her. "You come in here and drop this bomb on me and you don't expect me to have anything to say about it? We've been living together for over three years, and just like that," she said, snapping her fingers, "you come in here and tell me you're moving out. You don't have the decency to even give me advance notice or anything?"

Pivoting to face Sabrina, with a resolved calm, Jamilah tersely responded, "You know what? I'm tired of living with you. I don't like you anymore, Sabrina. I don't like the way you treat people. I don't like the way you just walk all over them. You have no regard for anyone's feelings but your own and I am so sick of watching you use person after person. I've been watching it for years. You've always done it and I've always turned my back or made excuses for you because I couldn't stand it, but I can't do that anymore. I won't sit by and watch you do that anymore."

"This is because of Darius," Sabrina declared with certainty.

"No! It's not about Darius," Jamilah insisted loudly, as tears welled in her eyes. "It's about you and it's about me! You haven't changed, Sabrina, in all these years, but I have. *I have!* I can't work like this. I can't live like this. I'm always… There's too much negativity here. I can't live like this." Jamilah was practically pleading, trying to make Sabrina understand her feelings. "And it still hasn't changed. Now you're seeing this guy Quenten. He's got all this money, granted, but you don't care about him, and he may very well not care about you either. For all I know, you could be using each other. I don't know. But I do know that you don't care about him. You don't give a damn about this man past what his bank account represents to you. One day, you're going to run into somebody who's not going to appreciate your selfish ways, and they're going to hurt you and you're going to see what it's like to be on the receiving end of the things that you do. I hope it won't... I don't want to see you get hurt, Sabrina. I love you, but if you keep going the way you're going, you'll get hurt, and I don't want to be around when that happens 'cause I never want to see that.

"I know you're not hearing what I'm saying because I can't tell you anything. You think I'm some lonely misfit who doesn't know anything about anything, so I know you don't want to hear anything I have to say." Jamilah sighed heavily. She was tired. "I just need...I need a place of my own."

Sabrina stood there, frozen in place by Jamilah's words. Remaining composed as she listened to the cruel things Jamilah had said to her, she didn't utter a sound, although her insides were churning with pain. She was hurt that her best friend was actually leaving her. They had been best friends since they were children. Jamilah had always been there for her and now she was turning her back on her.

Feeling salty droplets filling her eyes, Sabrina refused to let Jamilah see her cry, so she turned and walked into her own bedroom, slamming the door behind her. She stood in front of her bedroom mirror and gazed at her reflection as the tears rolled down her face. *I'm not like that*, she thought. *You've got it all wrong, Jamilah. That's not me.*

Jamilah stood outside Sabrina's door for a few seconds before she proceeded into her own room. She dropped the boxes she had been carrying on the floor, as if they suddenly weighed a ton. She sat on her bed and stared at the flattened boxes lying in the middle of the floor. Her sobs seemed to travel from the pit of her stomach until they escaped through her lips in an agonized wail. She folded her arms across her torso, doubling over as she cried out her pain.

They had been best friends for as long as she could remember. She and Sabrina had shared all of the milestones young girls experience growing up: their first periods, their first dates, their first kisses, the loss of their virginity. Neither of them had sisters; they had been sisters to one another. Jamilah's mother, Alexia, used to tease them, saying she was going to claim Sabrina as a dependent on her income taxes because she spent so much time at her house. It seemed there had never been a time when they were not together.

Jamilah's heart broke at the thought of their friendship actually coming to an end, but she could no longer sit by and watch Sabrina's careless disregard for other people's feelings. She had watched her play with too many people's emotions;

callously break too many men's hearts. She felt genuine fear for Sabrina—afraid of what she had become; and of what might become of her, but she couldn't be Sabrina's safety net any longer. She had made hundreds of excuses for Sabrina's behavior over the years. Now was the time for Sabrina to reap what she sowed just as much as it was time for Jamilah to stand on her own.

# Chapter 18

The movers were at the apartment early on Saturday morning. Jamilah had packed everything she could and tried to assist them in getting her things out of the apartment. She had hoped to see Sabrina before she left because she wanted to tell her good-bye. After she had informed Sabrina on Thursday that she was moving out, Sabrina packed a bag and, presumably, went to stay with Quenten. She had stayed over last night also.

Although Jamilah knew she had no choice but to do what she was doing, it still saddened her that her oldest and dearest friendship had come to an end. Praying that Sabrina would understand that the things she had told her were not said maliciously, she hoped Sabrina would take a long and honest look at herself.

Jamilah did not entirely fault Sabrina for her selfish ways. She had, after all, been raised to believe that because of her lighter skin tone, she was better than other folks. Jamilah had always known that Sabrina's parents, the elder Richardsons, had grudgingly accepted her as a lifelong friend of Sabrina's, especially her mother. On more than one occasion, as a young girl, Jamilah had overheard Mrs. Richardson ask Sabrina in her regard, "Can't you find someone a little lighter to play with? That child always looks so dirty."

The first time she had heard it, they were in elementary school and Jamilah had never experienced prejudice. She had innocently asked Sabrina what her mother meant, and Sabrina, innocently enough, had told her, "She thinks your skin is too dark."

Not knowing the connotation behind Mrs. Richardson's cruel words, neither girl paid the remarks any heed. It was not until they were both older that the truth of what Mrs. Richardson had been saying hit home. Sabrina rallied against her mother and declared that Jamilah was her best friend and would always be her best friend, "whether you like it or not!" Knowing how headstrong Sabrina had always been, Mrs. Richardson acquiesced, but she made it perfectly clear that Sabrina should steer clear of those "other" dark-skinned kids at school. She wanted her children only associating with "the best."

Also, being the only girl in the family, and the youngest, Sabrina was spoiled. Her parents and her older brothers had doted on her all of her life, giving her whatever she wanted, whenever she wanted. As a child, Sabrina had been known to throw tantrums to get her way. It had always amazed Jamilah whenever she witnessed one of Sabrina's performances. She could laugh about it now, but Jamilah remembered the first and only time she had tried that tactic on her own mother. Alexia had torn her backside up. Message delivered. Jamilah knew she would never try that again.

When her bedroom was empty, Jamilah went out to the living room to see if there was anything that she might have forgotten. She was surprised to see Sabrina sitting on the sofa, legs stretched out across the length of it, looking as if she didn't have a care in the world.

"I didn't know you'd come in," Jamilah told her.

Sabrina did not respond.

Jamilah sighed, then picked up her pocketbook from the coffee table. She opened it and removed a check, which she promptly handed to Sabrina. "That's for my half of next month's rent and your half of what we paid for the easy-chair. I'm taking it with me."

"How nice of you to ask me," Sabrina sneered as she snatched the check out of Jamilah's hand.

"It's the only piece of furniture I'm taking besides my bedroom set and my office furniture," Jamilah countered.

"I couldn't care less." Sabrina swung her long legs off the couch and rose quickly. She tucked the check in the back pocket of the skintight jeans.

"This is my address and phone number," Jamilah said as she handed a slip of paper to Sabrina.

Sabrina looked down at the paper in Jamilah's outstretched hand, but did not reach for it. "You don't really expect me to be calling you, do you?"

Jamilah felt a lump in her throat. "I just thought...in case you needed anything..."

"You'll be the last person I call," Sabrina remarked before Jamilah could finish.

Without another word, Jamilah placed the slip of paper on the coffee table before she closed her pocketbook and threw the shoulder strap over her head and across her torso. She bent over to pick up her portfolio and the tote bag that contained a few personal items she did not trust the movers to transport. She turned toward the door to leave without another word.

Jamilah had her hand on the doorknob when Sabrina said, "Aren't you taking this?"

Jamilah turned. Sabrina was holding a black wooden carving of two little girls with pigtails, holding hands. The words, BEST FRIENDS, were carved into the base. Sabrina had given the figurine to Jamilah when she returned from a trip to Paradise Island in the Bahamas five years ago.

Jamilah smiled. "Oh yeah. Thanks."

She put down the tote bag and portfolio and started back to Sabrina. Just as she put her hand out to take it from her, Sabrina, reverting to her vindictive manner, let the carving drop to the floor. Ironically, it broke down the middle of the base and just above the wrist of one of the little girls. Jamilah stared at the broken carving on the floor until tears blurred her vision. She then looked up at Sabrina, only to find a sinister smirk on her face.

"Bye," Sabrina spat, then turned and walked away from Jamilah toward the back of the apartment.

As Jamilah bent over to pick up the pieces of the carving, salty water spilled from her eyes and splashed against the fine black wood. Then turning back to the door, she dropped the broken figurine into her tote bag, picked it and her portfolio up, and headed out the door.

# PART TWO

A year later. . .

# Chapter 19

The bright sunlight streaming through the window brought Sabrina out of her troubled sleep at seven forty-five that Saturday morning in early May. She turned over and saw that Quenten was still deep in his sleep. She lay there and stared at him as he snored softly with his mouth propped open and a prominent frown creasing his forehead.

Her eyes began to water as her memory took her back to last night and his cruel treatment of her. She had wanted to leave and return to her own apartment after his attack, but she had been too afraid.

He had never struck her in public before, but she attributed his behavior to the bad day he'd had at work, compounded by his drinking at the affair they had attended last night.

It was only just two days ago that Quenten had informed her that the co-owner of his brokerage company had been embezzling money and stealing from their customers. When his partner's deceptive actions were discovered, instead of facing the music and paying for what he had done, he had taken the coward's way out and committed suicide, leaving Quenten in a position where he was responsible for assisting the authorities in getting to the bottom of the situation. Although Quenten swore he was completely innocent of any wrongdoing, the authorities had been treating him like a criminal. His customers were pulling their accounts like wild fire, and his reputation was on the brink of being permanently destroyed.

Already in a foul mood when he picked Sabrina up after work, his demeanor became downright ugly when he thought she was flirting with a business associate at the affair. When she tried to refute his allegations in front of his colleagues, he hit her and knocked her into the pointed corner of a table. The pain immediately traveled through her hip, but the embarrassment she felt due to his actions was far worse.

When they left the affair, Quenten was quite drunk. Sabrina was terrified of riding with him and when she suggested that he let her drive, he immediately accused her of questioning his manhood.

When they had finally arrived at his house, he became quite amorous, feeling her breasts and callously fondling her. Sabrina, however, had been in no mood to have sex with him after what he had done to her. Besides, she hated it when he got drunk. But Quenten had not been in the right frame of mind to handle her rejection, so he had forced himself on her, and she had been powerless to fight him. When he had satisfied his lust for her after his brutal assault, he had passed out. Sabrina had lain beside him and cried herself to sleep.

She knew when he awoke he would apologize profusely and probably buy her some exorbitantly expensive trinket to make it up to her, like he always did.

Throwing the covers off and rising slowly from the bed, she lumbered into the bathroom because her hip was still sore from when she had bumped it last night. Spying her reflection in the bathroom mirror, she gasped in horror. Aside from the nasty blue, green and purple bruise that marked her slender and previously unblemished thigh, her cheek was swollen and bruised where Quenten had struck her.

As she stood there staring at the hideous mark on her face, she cried. *How could he do this to me? How could he tell me he loves me and do this to me?* Quenten had proclaimed his love for her many times, telling her that she was everything he had ever wanted in a woman: beauty, brains and refinement. He would take her out and show her off to his friends and colleagues, proudly boasting that they were a match made in heaven. They did have many of the same ideals, and their personalities were quite suited to each other. They would have their occasional arguments, but he only became violent when he was drinking.

As she stood in front of the mirror on this particular morning, however, Sabrina questioned her own intelligence for staying with him. She did love him; she loved what he represented, and she loved the way he doted on her, buying her whatever her heart desired, taking her on week-long excursions overseas or to the Caribbean on a moment's notice. He had even convinced her that she did not need her job. He had promised to take care of her and he had. It was not often that he hit her, she reasoned, and she always garnered the most beautiful gifts when he apologized. Diamonds and other fine jewels had become a staple in her life since she had been with him.

"Sabrina," she heard him call from the bed.

Quickly stifling her tears and wiping her face, she called in a shaky voice, "Coming." She took a deep breath and opened the bathroom door. A feeble smile crossed her face as she made her way back to the bed. "Hi."

Frowning as he noticed the bruise on her face, Quenten reached out to her and gently beckoned, "Come here, baby." Sabrina climbed back into the bed and he immediately wrapped her in a tender embrace. "I'm sorry, sweetheart; I'm so sorry. You know I didn't mean to do this, don't you?"

"I know," she said as tears came to her eyes.

He kissed her face softly. "Does it hurt?"

"No," she lied.

"Damn." He sighed. "You know I'll make this up to you, Sabrina."

"I know."

"Do you still love me?" he asked apprehensively.

She looked into his eyes before she answered. The sob caught in her throat as she cried, "Yes."

# Chapter 20

T he weather was beautiful that following Friday. Two of Jamilah's co-workers, Grace Foster and Lilly Hernandez, had planned to have dinner that evening at Blackberry's, a nightclub that had recently opened downtown. Grace and Lilly had both been to Blackberry's twice and each time they'd gone, they had tried to get Jamilah to come along. Both times, she had made excuses. Jamilah, put off by the recent failures she had encountered with the men in her life, was giving herself a break from dating. Grace and Lilly swore, however, that the black male population at the club consisted of good-looking, professional types and not all stuffed shirts.

Earlier that year, Jamilah had dated a fellow named Norman Everett for a little over two months. He was a contractor and they became acquainted during a visit to one of her freelance clients. Norman had been working in the building, repairing an air conditioning unit. He was extremely handsome, with "pretty boy" good looks, and was quite the charmer.

Jamilah had greatly enjoyed his company, initially, because his great sense of humor often kept her in stitches. Also enjoying what she had originally thought was his sense of class and style, it had come as a complete shock to learn the truth about him—that he had been putting up a front until he thought she was comfortable with him. He was nothing more than a pimp, although not in the conventional sense of the word. He did not take money from whores; he took money, or at least tried to take money, from the women he dated.

The first incident that set the warning bells off in Jamilah's brain was the wedding.

One of his best friends was getting married and he was to be the best man. He had asked Jamilah for the money to rent his tuxedo for the affair. He claimed that he had not gotten paid for a job he had done and that he was trying to get the money from his client. Until he could, would she lend him the money? Not suspecting his true character at the time, she had loaned it to him. Or so she thought. She never saw that money again.

She then began to notice that every chance he got, he took it upon himself to spend the night with her. Since Jamilah had been so attracted to him from the start, she had allowed him to seduce her after only three dates, and because the sex had been so good, her judgment became somewhat clouded. He had begun to leave some of his personal effects each time he visited. She started to find things that belonged to him all over her house. When she found his dirty clothes in her laundry bag, she knew it was time to reassess the situation.

The final straw was when he invited her to dinner at an elegant restaurant that she had previously told him she was curious to try. The evening had started off perfect. He had picked her up in his car, a rusty ten-year-old BMW 325i, but he was dressed to kill. When they arrived at the restaurant, he escorted her inside like she was his most precious possession. Dinner was excellent. Neither of them had given any thought to the prices on the menu when they ordered their meal. He had told her to order whatever she wanted. When the one hundred and twenty-seven-dollar check arrived at their table, Norman actually went through the motions of looking through his clothes for his wallet. "I must have left it at home," he had stated not too apologetically. Jamilah had been stuck with the bill. She also had been forced to pay eighteen dollars to get his car out of the garage where he had parked when they arrived in the city. He had driven her home that night with the very real expectation of sleeping over. Jamilah quickly suggested that he go home and find his wallet.

She was completely flabbergasted, however, when he called her the next day and asked if he could borrow two hundred dollars, since his wallet was nowhere to be found. She immediately reminded him that he still owed her one hundred and twenty dollars for the tuxedo she had rented for his friend's wedding, plus what she had paid for dinner and parking his car last night. When she was finished telling him off, she slammed the phone down in his ear.

She had been so embarrassed that she had allowed him to make such a complete fool of her that she basically buried herself in her work and hid from the world. The last thing she wanted was to get caught up with another jerk, and that seemed to be the only type of man she had been running into lately.

As she looked out of her office window at the spectacular view of Central Park, she figured, *what the hell. I'm not doing anything else, and I sure don't feel like going straight home to my empty house on a gorgeous night like this.* She picked up her phone and dialed Grace's extension.

"Grace Foster."

"Hey, Grace. What time are you and Lilly going to Blackberry's?"

***

Jamilah's independent business was doing quite well. Fairly certain she would soon be able to go into business for herself, that fund-raising dinner she had attended with Darius Thornton last year had turned out to be quite a boon for her business. After completing the jobs for the first two clients she had garnered from that affair, they had referred her to their friends, thus affording her a great deal of extra income. That, in turn, allowed her to take a much-needed two-week vacation in the Caribbean at the end of last year.

Grace and Lilly were both ad execs at her firm. Grace was a beautiful brown-skinned woman in her early thirties and of Jamaican descent. She was the divorced mother of twin seven-year-old daughters. She was short, about five feet, three inches tall and despite being a bit chubby, had quite a nice figure. She wore her dark brown hair in a short cap of tight curls. Lilly, a slender, twenty-nine-year-old Hispanic woman, was just an inch or so shorter than Jamilah. She was very shapely, with large breasts that she made a point of accentuating, it seemed, in every outfit she wore. Her long brown hair was curly and sometimes looked a bit wild but, somehow, always looked great on her.

When the ladies walked into the restaurant/nightclub, there was a half-hour wait to be seated for dinner, so they strolled over to the already crowded bar and ordered a round of drinks.

"Look at that fine brotha over there," Grace said and gestured with her head to the left of where they stood.

"Chile, there are plenty of good-looking men in this place," Lilly responded.

"That's why I like coming here. You can look in any direction and see some fine specimens of maleness."

The girls laughed.

"Y'all are crazy. I hope I don't get myself into anything hangin' out with y'all," Jamilah said good-naturedly.

"You mean, you hope you do, right?" Grace questioned, then elbowed Lilly conspiratorially.

The three of them laughed and giggled and flirted until they were seated for dinner.

Their waitress had just taken their dinner orders when Lilly gasped and covered her mouth with her hands.

"What?" Jamilah asked in alarm when she noticed Lilly's eyes bulge.

"That's him, Grace. That's Denzel Washington."

"Where?" Grace and Jamilah both immediately turned to see.

"I told you I saw him in here the last time we were here but you didn't believe me. Well, he's back," Lilly continued.

"Where?" Jamilah asked again.

"He just went into the bar area," Lilly said.

"Maybe he's here for dinner," Grace suggested.

"Well, when you see him again, let me know," Jamilah said, turning back around in her seat. "I'll go and say 'hi' for y'all."

"Humph, you don't have to say nothing for me, girlfriend. I'll do that myself," Lilly said with a brisk shake of her head.

They forgot about Denzel Washington after a couple of minutes and continued with their dinner conversation while awaiting their meals. Laughing and chatting about some of their fellow co-workers for a while, Grace then spoke about her twins and her "no-count" ex-husband. That opened the door for a few minutes' worth of male bashing. Each of the women had their own stories to tell, so they took turns doing so.

"There he is," Lilly said in a hushed tone, looking covertly at the man she thought was Denzel Washington as he took a seat at a table across the room.

Grace turned slightly in her seat to see for herself. "That's not Denzel Washington! You are so silly," she said as she turned back to Lilly.

"It's not?"

"No! He kinda looks like him, but that's not him. I don't think Denzel's that tall. Besides, that brother looks better than Denzel, if you ask me," Grace added.

"Where?" Jamilah asked, turning to see as she looked across the restaurant for the man they were speaking of.

"The brother in the light gray suit," Grace indicated.

Jamilah continued to peruse the crowd, looking for the man they spoke of. After a while, when she still hadn't spotted the man, she gave up, but as she started to turn back to her friends, she suddenly did a double-take.

"Darius!"

# Chapter 21

The past year had been a good one for Darius, all things considered.

Completely recovered from his bullet wound and broken heart (seemingly concurrently), he returned to work and got on with his life. His wound kept him out of work for two weeks after he was released from the hospital, so he used the time to reflect on his failed relationship with Sabrina.

Realizing that no matter what he might have done, she never would have been happy with him, he finally acknowledged that their personalities were just too completely different for any kind of long-term relationship to have endured. His recuperation time was also a period of reflection on the things that Jamilah had tried to tell him and the things his sister had emphatically hammered home.

He knew both women had only been looking out for his best interests, but when you're in love, or infatuated, as he later acknowledged he had been, you see only what you want to see.

He had missed Jamilah, though. So many times he had wished that he could call her, just to talk. He had come to value their budding friendship and was sorry that it was lost when his relationship with Sabrina foundered. Never really having a female companion whom he could relate to so well before or after her, he missed her laughter, her honesty and her humble self-assurance.

Five months after returning to work, Darius was offered a partnership at his law firm. He was only the second African-American to be offered that status in the firm's sixty-year history. The other was still a member of the firm and had been a mentor to Darius from the day he had started, ten years earlier.

As a part of his new responsibility and commitment to the firm, he traveled more and was being groomed to handle many of the firm's international banking clients. It was just two days ago that he had returned from a trip to Paris to close a deal with one of the firm's longer standing clients there.

His friend and former law associate, Will Chambers, had called him that beautiful May afternoon and asked if he would meet him for drinks and dinner at Blackberry's that night. He had not seen Will in a few months and since he had no other plans for the evening, he readily agreed to do so.

Darius had dated a number of women over the past year, but none seriously. After his sham of a relationship with Sabrina, he decided to just enjoy his bachelorhood for as long as he could. He wanted to get married and have kids one day, but he figured when the time was right, *she* would come along.

Blackberry's was crowded when they arrived. Although the crowd was a majority of black professionals, there was a smattering of white and Hispanic men and women present, as well. He and Will each had a beer at the bar along with a couple of other guys they knew in attendance while waiting for a table.

Although Darius had met a number of women in Blackberry's on previous occasions, he never pursued any of them. Dispassionate about the club scene, he thought it was the worst place to meet women who would be considered as marriage prospects. Everyone just seemed so desperate, so "hungry" to him. Sometimes he felt as though he was under inspection, as he was sure many of the other patrons there did, too, from time to time.

When the hostess came to get him and Will when a table became available for them to eat, Darius slowly made his way through the crowd. He did not miss the "come hither" look from a woman standing at the end of the bar. He simply smiled and continued to his table.

"Damn, some of the women in here are a little too forward for me," Darius said to Will when they were seated.

"Hey, those are the easy ones," Will commented. "They say come and get it, so I oblige them."

Darius chuckled and shook his head. "You'd better be careful thinking like that."

"Hey, man, I'm not stupid. I keep rubbers on me, 'cause you never know."

Darius chuckled again.

"Darius!"

He turned when he heard his name. He couldn't tell which direction the woman's voice had come from because the noise level in the restaurant was pretty high. When he didn't immediately see anyone he recognized, he shrugged his shoulders and figured whoever it was must have been calling someone else. He went back to studying his menu.

"Darius!"

He looked up again and was shocked to see Jamilah Parsons coming toward him.

"Jamilah!" His face broke into a wide grin, and he rose so quickly from his chair that it tipped over. He started to bend over to pick it up, but quickly changed his mind and started toward her.

"Hi!"

"My girl! Hey!" They embraced tightly, each clearly delighted at seeing the other.

"Oh my God, I can't believe it," Jamilah said as she leaned back to look at him.

He kissed her on her mouth and responded, "Damn, girl, it's good to see you. How've you been?"

Trying to ignore the charge of electricity that coursed through her body with his kiss, she answered, "I've been fine. How've you been? Are you all healed?" Feeling the strength of his long, lean frame in her arms, she answered the question herself. He felt incredible.

"One hundred percent."

"Good. I'm glad to hear that."

They stood in each other's embrace, smiling into one another's eyes for what seemed like minutes until Darius pulled her close once more.

"I'm so glad to see you, Jamilah," he said softly in an emotion-filled voice. "I've missed the hell out of you."

"I've missed you, too."

"So many times I've wanted to call you, but I figured..."

"I know, Darius." She looked up into his eyes with understanding.

"You look good, J," Darius said, as they finally released each other, but he gently caressed her face.

"So do you. I'm happy to see you're back on your feet. You didn't look too good last time I saw you." Jamilah laughed.

Darius joined her. "Yeah, how 'bout that, but I'm fine now. All that's left are a couple of scars."

Delighted that they had fallen right back into the comfortable manner of being together they had briefly shared a year ago, she remarked, "Good."

"Oh yeah, they caught the guys that did it, too," Darius added.

"Good!"

"So how's everything with you? How's business?"

"Business is good. I've got quite a number of regular clients and a few long-term contracts under my belt. And remember the women I met at the dinner last year?"

"Yeah."

"Well, they both liked my work so well, they've sent their friends to me."

"Excellent!"

"Yeah. I'm really starting to look into going independent, but my job is going really well, too. I almost hate to leave it."

"Well, that's good, though. As long as you don't become overwhelmed, don't rush it. Take your time. And remember I told you I'd work up a business plan for you, if you like. The offer still stands."

"Thanks, Darius. I'll let you know when I'm ready. As a matter of fact," Jamilah quickly added, "give me your number right now. I don't want it to be another year before I see you again."

"Yeah, right." Reaching into the breast pocket of his jacket, he removed one of his business cards. "Here. Call me anytime."

"I will and I'll give you one of my cards, too." Rushing over to her table to grab her pocketbook, Jamilah hurried back to Darius' side, completely ignoring the wide-eyed looks on Grace's and Lilly's faces. Instead she asked Darius, "So how're things going on your job? Have you made partner yet?"

"Yes, I did."

Letting out a shriek of joy, she hugged him once again. "Oh, congratulations, Darius! That's wonderful. I'm so happy for you. When?"

"About seven months ago," he said, laughing at Jamilah's reaction.

"That's great. I'm so proud of you."

"Thanks."

"How's Bob?" she asked suddenly of his former boss and now colleague.

"Bob's good. He used to ask me about you all the time. I finally told him the truth about that night." Darius didn't tell her that Bob thought he'd fallen in love with the wrong woman.

"You did?"

"Yeah, he was cool about it, though."

"That's good. He seemed like a nice guy."

"Yeah, he is." Finally, the inevitable question was asked. "So how's Sabrina?"

Lowering her head a moment before she answered, she finally murmured, "I don't know."

"You don't know?"

"No. We don't talk anymore."

"Aw, man, Jamilah, what happened?"

She shrugged. "A lot of things. I moved out a while ago and we just never kept in touch."

"But you've been friends for so long."

"I know, but this is how she wanted it."

"I'm sorry to hear that, Jamilah. I really am."

"Yeah, me, too, but I'm sure she's doing fine. You know how resourceful Sabrina can be. I'm sure she's doing just fine," Jamilah said with a certainty she did not completely feel.

"Yeah, probably."

Conversing enthusiastically for a few more minutes during which each of them inquired about the other's family until Darius noticed that Jamilah's dinner had been served, he asked, "Hey, are you cutting out right after you eat?"

"I don't know."

"Why don't you hang around for a while? We could have a drink and do some more catching up."

"Okay."

Smiling and hugging her once again, Darius said, "I am so happy to see you, Jamilah. You've just made my day."

Jamilah beamed at him. "Likewise."

***

When Jamilah finally returned to the table with her friends, Lilly asked in awe, "You know him, Jamilah?" as she surreptitiously glanced across the room at Darius.

Her smile was still as broad as when she was speaking with Darius. "Yeah, that's my buddy. I haven't seen him in a year. Actually, I never thought I would see him again."

Wanting clarification, Grace asked, "What do you mean when you say 'buddy'?"

"Just what I said. We're friends. Just friends."

"Are you crazy?" Lilly asked. "That man is gorgeous. How come nothing ever happened between you two?"

As Jamilah commenced to tell them about Sabrina, she had to agree with Lilly; Darius *was* gorgeous. Even more enchanting than he was a year ago, she realized suddenly, that he had grown a mustache. The small bit of facial hair only made him that much more alluring.

As their conversation momentarily ceased so they could enjoy their dinner, Jamilah's thoughts began to wander. Traveling back a few minutes to when he had planted that kiss on her mouth, she'd thought her knees would buckle right out from under her. If she hadn't known better, she would have thought there was something more to the buss than what she was sure had merely been a display of affection for an old friend.

There were so many times in the past, though, when she had dreamt of him kissing her, imagined him wrapping his strong arms around her body and pulling her close so she could feel the exquisite contours of his sublime, seductive mas-culinity. Suddenly, her face flushed with heat. *If Darius knew what I was thinking…*

Pondering his reaction if he knew that she had been in love with him then, she wondered if it would affect their friendship. Would he resent her feelings, especially since she knew knew how he'd felt about Sabrina?

"Well, Jamilah, aren't you glad you decided to come with us now?" Grace suddenly asked with a mouth full of food, cutting into her reverie.

"Yes, I am. You said you saw him in here before, Lilly?" Jamilah asked.

"Twice," Lilly said as she held up two fingers.

"Damn. He's the sweetest guy you'd ever want to know, too," Jamilah dreamily muttered.

Grace studied Jamilah's face for a long moment before she spoke. "You like him, don't you?"

"What?"

"You like him."

"Of course, I like him. He's my friend."

"I don't mean like that, Jamilah. You should see your face right now. I've never seen you look so happy. You appear to have found your long lost love."

Jamilah couldn't help blushing. Grateful that her dark skin prevented her from visibly flushing with color, she stammered, "I...I don't know what you're talking about."

Lilly began to giggle. "You're right, Grace. She's in love."

"I am not! I told you he used to date my best friend."

"But I believe you said you're not best friends anymore," Grace said.

"Look, Darius and I are just friends. Nothing more. He's not even interested in me."

"He looked pretty interested to me," Lilly said teasingly as she nudged Grace.

"To me, too," Grace agreed.

"Well, you're both wrong. I told y'all not to be starting anything tonight," Jamilah scolded.

"We're not starting anything. You're the one who's getting all the attention. He's been looking over here since you sat down," Lilly added.

Jamilah shifted in her seat reflexively and met Darius' smiling eyes. She returned his smile but with a mixture of uncertainty and embarrassment.

"See, I told you," Lilly said sweetly.

"Oh shut up."

Lilly and Grace burst into good-natured laughter.

✱✱✱

Darius couldn't believe it. He thought he'd never see her again. She looked better than ever, too. Her beautiful dark brown skin was as smooth and clear as always, but she seemed to glow with a newfound happiness and self-assurance. Her locks, which she had always kept neatly styled, had grown down past her shoulders and she wore them pinned back on one side, but falling free on the other. He wondered briefly if she was seeing anyone.

Savoring her scent, he noticed that she smelled of flowers, clean and fresh.

Although he had never looked at Jamilah with any physical longing before the night of his assault, something changed when he saw her in that red gown. Then, during his hospitalization, he came to know her in a way he would have never thought he could. Seeing her now only solidified his earlier opinion that she was the essence of black womanhood—proud, confident, beautiful, sensitive and loving.

When he had finally gotten over Sabrina and taken a look back at what he had allowed her to do to him, his memory had always found its way to Jamilah. Having been something of a buffer between them, he vividly recalled the hurt look in her eyes when he'd asked her not to interfere in their relationship. She had probably gone home that night after the fund-raiser and reamed Sabrina for standing him up. She had gallantly tried to protect his heart, but he had been so blinded by what he'd thought was love, that he was oblivious to anything else.

Jamilah had been his ally. She had offered her friendship freely, and with no demands. Knowing that she had missed him, too, buoyed his heart. Numerous times after his and Sabrina's breakup he had actually picked up the phone to reach out to her, but stopped because of the likelihood that Sabrina might intercept the call. After her accusation of interest in Jamilah, he'd known that she would've taken it the wrong way, and he had no desire to go through anything else with her if he could avoid it. Scolding himself many times for not having the foresight to have given Jamilah his number, there had been numerous occasions over the past year when he needed the unbridled companionship of a woman, and he knew if he could have contacted Jamilah, that was what he would have gotten.

She had really impressed him that night when she stepped in and accompanied him to his client's fund-raiser. Seeing Jamilah now, looking more beautiful than ever, Darius realized his fascination—there was still a lot he wanted to know about her. He made a promise to himself that he would never let her out of his life again.

# Chapter 22

Jamilah awoke Saturday morning feeling exhilarated. After she, Lilly and Grace had finished eating last night, they accompanied Darius and his friend to another nightclub in the area for drinks and dancing. She'd had the time of her life.

The loud music in the club prevented her and Darius from conversing like they wanted to, but they made the most of their time together and danced all night. She didn't get home until after three o'clock in the morning, but was wide awake five hours later. There were no words to describe the happiness she felt knowing that she and Darius could resume their budding friendship of a year ago.

At nine-fifteen her telephone rang and she answered it with a cheerful, "Good morning."

"Well, good morning to you, too. You sound quite chipper this morning."

"Hi, Mommy! How are you?"

"I'm doing just fine. How are you?"

"I'm great! How's Frank?"

"Frank is Frank. What's got you so excited this early on a Saturday morning?" Alexia asked.

"Remember that guy Darius Thornton that Sabrina used to date last year? The one who got shot?"

"Yes," Alexia said in a questioning tone.

"Well, I ran into him last night. I haven't seen him since that time he came to the house to see Sabrina when she cut him off."

"Jamilah…"

"Mommy, before you say anything, we're friends. We were friends then, and we still are. We just lost touch, that's all. There's nothing more to it than that," Jamilah assured her.

"Yes, but I know how you felt about him then. And don't forget, he *was* Sabrina's boyfriend."

"How could I forget that?"

"Sabrina was your friend, too."

"Sabrina's still my friend. I just haven't talked to her in a year," Jamilah sadly intoned.

"So why don't you call her?"

"She doesn't want to talk to me, Mommy. She made that perfectly clear when I moved out."

"Well, you might have handled that differently, you know."

"Mommy, I did what I had to do for my own peace of mind. Would you rather we still be living together and I be miserable?"

"No, baby, but… I know how you are, and I know how you felt about this… what's his name?"

"Darius."

"Darius. And I don't want you to get hurt."

"I won't. We just have…we have a special connection that I can't explain. It's like we understand each other. He doesn't expect anything from me but honesty, and I don't expect anything other than that from him, either. We've always been straight with each other, and it's never been difficult for me to talk to him and vice versa."

Alexia sighed into the mouthpiece. "I hope you're right."

"I am. You'll see. You'll meet him one day and when you do, you'll understand what I'm talking about."

"Just be careful, please, Jamilah."

"I will, Mommy. You worry too much."

"That's just because you're my only daughter, and I love you and want only the best for you," Alexia said sincerely.

"I love you, too, Mommy, but I also love me and I won't settle for anything but the best. Darius is my buddy and I missed not having him to talk to. And since he and Sabrina are past history, I can get to know him now in a way I couldn't before. And that's all I want, Mommy. I just want to get to know him."

Alexia didn't know how to respond. She worried about her daughter and prayed she wouldn't do anything foolish because of her feelings for this man, Darius Thornton.

# Chapter 23

Jamilah and Darius had lunch on Monday, Wednesday and Friday of the week following their reunion and every day of the following week. Both were amazed to learn they had been working in such close proximity to one another all this time since Darius' office was only three blocks east of Jamilah's. They talked on the telephone daily, without fail, covering a wide variety of subjects, and sometimes just laughing and poking fun at each other. As a year ago, the two had an easy rapport which they fell right back into as if separated for only a day or two.

On Thursday of the second week, Darius called Jamilah at her office just after nine that morning. "Hey, Miss Thing," he said when she came on the line.

"Hi, Darius. How you doin'?"

"I'm great. How're you?"

"Good. A little busy already, but I'm hangin' in there."

"Well, I'm not going to hold you. I just called to see if you'd be interested in catching a game at the Garden with me tonight."

"Oh, who are the Knicks playing?"

"The Sixers."

"Ooh yeah. I'd love to see Allen Iverson play." Pausing with excitement, she asked, "Isn't this a playoff game?"

"Yeah, the Eastern Conference Finals."

"How'd you get tickets to the playoffs?"

"I have season tickets. As long as the Knicks are winning, I'll be at the games."

"You're sure none of your friends will mind getting bumped for this seat? I know how hot these tickets must be."

"These are my tickets, Jamilah. Not mine and everyone else's. I give my extra ticket to whomever I choose," Darius pointed out.

"But haven't any of your fellas put in bids for your spare?"

"Yeah, a few of them, but I'm asking you."

Jamilah's face lit with a smile. "I'd love to go, Darius. What time?"

"The game starts at eight o'clock. I'll pick you up and we can grab a bite to eat before it starts."

"All right."

"So, I'll see you tonight."

"Definitely. Thank you, Darius."

"Anytime, J."

The Eastern Conference Finals game between the New York Knicks and the Philadelphia Seventy-Sixers had been fast and furious from the first to the fourth quarter. That being the case, no one was surprised that the game had gone into overtime. Although they had played a great game, the Knicks lost this one, leaving their standing in this best of seven series at one win, three losses. One more loss by the Knicks and they would be out of it.

When Darius and Jamilah reached the lobby of Madison Square Garden at the game's conclusion, she asked him to walk her into Penn Station so she could catch the train home, despite the late hour. Darius looked at her incredulously.

"You don't really think I'm going to leave you to take the train home by yourself at this time of night, do you? Please don't insult me like that," he scolded.

"I'm not trying to insult you, Darius. I'll be okay. I always take the train from the city. My car is parked at the station at home. There are plenty of people on the train at this time of night."

"I don't care who's on the train at this time of night; I'm not going to let you take the train when I can drive you home."

"But my car..."

"I'll drive you to your car, then," he insisted.

Smiling, she shook her head. "You don't have to."

"Yes, I do and we're not going to argue about this, either," he said firmly.

She gazed into his brown eyes with love and surrendered. "All right, Darius. I won't argue."

Forty-five minutes later, Darius pulled into the parking lot at Jamilah's train stop.

"My car's over there," she said as she pointed to the far corner of the lot.

"Oh, yeah, you'd be really safe out here all alone walking half the distance of this lot to your car," Darius sarcastically stated.

"A lot of people get off here," she told him.

"I don't see that many cars still here."

Jamilah looked at her watch. "A train just left a few minutes ago. I would have been on that train."

"Yeah, well, whatever."

He pulled up his BMW alongside her Honda Civic.

"Thanks, Darius, for inviting me to the game. I've always wondered why they called Allen Iverson 'The Answer.' Now I know. Lord, that man was shaking the Knicks up somethin' fierce."

Their seats had been mid-court, seven rows from the playing floor.

"Yeah, AI's killer cross-over gets 'em every time. It's damn near unstoppable," Darius added.

"I noticed. Too bad for the Knicks."

"I'm glad you had a good time, J. Since you enjoyed yourself so much tonight, next season, you get first dibs on my spare."

"Really?"

"Really."

Leaning over in her seat, she planted a grateful kiss on his cheek. "Thank you."

He blushed as he softly said, "You're welcome."

"Do you want to do lunch tomorrow?" she asked as she opened the car door to get out.

"Sure."

"My treat."

"Okay. Are you going to be okay from here?"

"Yup. I'll be fine. I'm just five minutes away."

"Okay. I'll see you tomorrow."

"Good night."

Darius waited until she had cleared the parking lot before he headed back to the highway for his drive home.

Enjoying himself immensely tonight, despite how much he enjoyed hanging out with his fellas at a game, he couldn't recall having a better time than he had with Jamilah. Each time he was with her, she surprised him.

Although Jamilah had been every bit a lady when they were together at dinner, her more down-to-earth side appeared once they were in the arena and the game had begun. Following the tournament like a true sports enthusiast, she was calling out fouls, walks and other violations right along with the referees, and when one made a call she didn't agree with, she was on her feet letting them know through her own brand of trash talk.

Darius knew some men might have been embarrassed by Jamilah's boisterousness, but he found it quite endearing. He was enamored with the way she took life by the horns and ran with it, not caring what anyone thought of her actions so long as no one was hurt and she had a good time.

When he thought about it, he realized that it was her pragmatic and totally honest personality that was endearing, for she was like a breath of fresh air.

Acknowledging that he had always been attracted to women who had an outward appearance similar to Sabrina's—that being fair and long-haired, slim and vainglorious—Jamilah, the physical opposite of everything he had always looked for in a woman, was far more interesting than any of the "glamour-girls" he'd known in the past—Sabrina included.

He guessed what attracted him the most was her pragmatism, for she didn't put on airs for anyone. But then, she didn't have to. Jamilah was an intelligent woman with a confidence that was neither faked nor forced, and truthfully, until the night she had stood in for Sabrina and accompanied him to the fund-raiser last year, he had never recognized how physically beautiful she was.

Ashamed to admit that he had never even given a dark-skinned woman a second look, when he considered his own complexion, his prejudice was that much more disparaging. His mother was a beautiful ebony-toned woman; so was his sister. What would they think if they knew he had been perpetuating the same bias he despised in other African-Americans?

Upon arrival at his home that night, the first thing Darius did was call Jamilah to make sure she had gotten in safely. Once that had been established, he began making preparations for bed.

He took a quick shower before climbing into his incredibly comfortable king-sized bed, and although he was physically exhausted, he barely slept. Lying awake for over an hour thinking about Jamilah, he replayed every minute of their evening together in his head.

A beautiful woman, inside and out, he noticed, too, that whenever he talked to his mother now, she always asked about Jamilah. On one occasion, she had even gone so far as to ask him why he didn't hook up with her. Darius had to admit to himself that ever since she had walked back into his life, he'd often asked himself that same question.

Involuntarily, his thoughts returned to that evening when they'd run into each other in Blackberry's. In actuality, his memory often returned to those few seconds when he'd held her in his arms and kissed her luscious lips. The action had been purely automatic because he'd been so happy to see her, but his reaction had been just as natural.

In the instant that her body was pressed against his and his arms were around her, he'd felt every single sensuous, seductive curve of her totally feminine physique. A shock had passed through him immediately, and he'd had to will his body to behave for fear of completely embarrassing himself.

As he remembered that moment now, however, as always, he became erect and his thoughts of her transformed into much more than the platonic reality in which the two of them were currently embroiled.

It unnerved him to a small degree, these lustful thoughts he had of her. She was his friend, after all—one of his most cherished friends and the last thing he wanted to do was anything that would jeopardize the special bond they had between them.

Besides, she had never given him any indication that she wanted anything more than what they currently shared, and, truthfully, he didn't expect her to. He had dated her best friend. Although he and Sabrina had never been intimate, he was fairly positive that the simple fact that they had at one time been an item would be deterrent enough for her to steer clear of him.

But he couldn't help what he felt. She was a beautiful, vibrant and seductive woman who made him laugh and with whom he loved spending time.

"Chill out, D," he said to himself in the darkness of his bedroom. "She's out of your reach."

When Darius finally fell asleep, it was the idea of snuggling close to Jamilah's ample bosom that sent him into that blissful state.

# Chapter 24

Memorial Day weekend was upon them and one of Darius' friends was throwing a barbecue at his home that Sunday. Eli and Anne Foster lived in a sprawling ranch home with a large backyard equipped with a kidney-shaped, in-ground pool in the small town of Baldwin, Long Island. Once the weather broke, the couple threw a cookout/pool party each month, into summer, to which they invited friends and family to come and share in their generosity.

Eli and Darius had been friends since college, and although they kept in touch by telephone on a fairly regular basis, they saw each other only a couple of times a year. Whenever Eli and Anne threw one of their fantastic barbecues, Darius made a point of attending, if his schedule allowed.

Darius had thought about inviting Jamilah to the cookout, but hesitated to do so. They had been spending a lot of time together over the past few weeks since their reunion. He thoroughly enjoyed every moment he spent with her, but while feelings were getting somewhat jumbled up in the process, he didn't want to make a fool of himself by accidentally letting on that his interest in her was more than simply platonic, as he was sure hers was for him. He figured, with time, that his feelings for her would dissipate if he kept his distance as much as possible, but that was difficult because he loved being with her.

It struck him as odd that they never talked about their personal lives, as far as romance was concerned, especially since they easily talked about everything else. He was sure, however, that she occasionally dated. He had noticed many times when they were together that she turned more than a few men's heads upon entering a room or strolling by them. *She is beautiful, after all.*

It was ten-thirty that Sunday morning when his telephone rang. He had been up for over an hour doing his daily workout—sit-ups, push-ups and curls—in his weight room. He grabbed the hand towel off the caddy that held his weights and wiped his perspiration-soaked face as he reached for the cordless wall phone.

"Hello," he said, somewhat breathlessly.

"Hi. Did I wake you?"

Recognizing the smooth melodic tone of Jamilah's voice caused an involuntary shiver to course through him. "Hi, babe. No, you didn't wake me. I was just working out. How are you?"

"I'm okay. How are you?" she asked cheerfully.

"I'm good."

"Whatcha doin' today?"

"Oh, I was, uh… A friend of mine is having a backyard barbecue. I was gonna go by and check him out."

"Oh. Where's it going to be?"

"On Long Island."

"Where?"

"In Baldwin."

"I know where that is. That's not too far from here, I think."

Darius didn't immediately respond. Finally he asked, "What are you doing today?"

"Oh, I don't know. I was thinking about going to the movies. There are a couple of new ones I'm interested in seeing. I want to see that new Laurence Fishburne flick that started yesterday."

"Who're you going with?" he asked.

"By myself."

"Why?"

"What do you mean, why?"

"You can't get anyone to go with you?"

"I didn't ask anyone to go with me."

"Do you always go to the movies alone?" he was curious to know.

"Pretty much."

"How come you don't get one of the hundreds of guys who I'm sure are knocking down your door to get next to you, to take you?"

Jamilah laughed as she said, "You saw someone trying to knock my door down to get next to me?"

He had to laugh, too. "Come on, Jamilah; don't be modest. You can't tell me there's no one in your life that you go out with every now and then."

Grateful that they were on the telephone and he couldn't see her face, Jamilah was embarrassed by his comment. Since that jerk Norman, she hadn't dated anyone. *He'll think I'm pathetic when I tell him I haven't been out with a man in over three months.* She swallowed the lump in her throat and said softly, "I'm not dating anybody, Darius."

"Why not?"

"No prospects," she simply stated.

"I find that hard to believe."

"Why?"

"Because you're a beautiful woman," he answered without hesitation.

That remark made her heart swell with love for him. "Thank you for the compliment, but not everyone has the same tastes. There aren't many guys who are interested in a five-foot, ten and a half-inch, dark-brown, full-figured woman these days. Didn't you know, thin is in? I don't exactly fit the mold."

"You don't believe that. I've seen you when you're out, having a good time. You exude confidence and pride. You light up a room, Jamilah, when you enter it," he said.

Her heart skipped a beat as she smiled at his beautiful words. *God, how I love this man. Why can't he see that?* "You're sweet to say that."

"I mean every word."

"I don't mind going to the movies by myself. That way I don't have to listen to anyone talking to me while I'm trying to watch the film."

"Hey, why don't you come with me to this barbecue?"

Although her mind screamed yes, her lips said, "No, that's okay, Darius. I'm not really in the mood for a big party." She wanted to spend the day with him but not with hundreds of other people, too.

"You're sure?" he asked.

"Yeah."

"Well, what time are you going out?"

"I guess about one o'clock or so."

"Would you mind if I stopped by on the way to my friend's house?"

"Of course not. Do you know how to get here?"

"No, but you can give me directions."

***

It was eight thirty-five that evening when Darius arrived at Jamilah's house. Since he hadn't left Brooklyn until a little after one o'clock that afternoon, he decided to stop by and see Jamilah on his way home from his friend's place. He figured since she had been planning to go to the movies, she would probably be long gone by the time he finally made it out to Long Island.

When she opened the door for him, he immediately surmised that she was not in a good mood. She didn't greet him with her usual vibrant smile, but instead with a scowl.

"Hey, J. What's up?"

"I thought you would have been here earlier," she answered solemnly.

"I didn't leave home until late, but I figured you'd be back from the movies by now."

"I didn't go to the movies," she said as she walked into the living room.

"Why not?" he asked as he closed the door before following her into the room.

She sat down on the couch and put her feet up on the glass-topped coffee table in front of her. "Because I thought you were coming over. I was waiting for you."

Darius stood speechless for a moment. Finally... "But you said you were going out at about one o'clock. I didn't think you'd be here."

"Well, I was."

"You didn't go out all day?" he asked as he took a seat sat on the edge of the sofa beside her.

"No."

"Aw, Jamilah. I'm sorry. I was sure you wouldn't be here."

"Why would I leave if I knew you were coming over?" she asked as she looked over at him.

"Because you had already made plans. When I wasn't here by one o'clock..."

"It wasn't like I was going with anyone else. I would've waited. I did wait. I didn't want you to come by and I wasn't here."

"Damn, Jamilah. I'm really sorry. If I had known, I would've been here. You know that, don't you? You know I wouldn't have left you hanging like this. You could've been hanging out with me this afternoon."

"It doesn't matter," she said sadly.

"Yes, it does. You're far too important to me to be neglected that way. I'm truly sorry we got our signals crossed like this," Darius said sincerely. "I'll make it up to you."

"You don't have to."

"Yes, I do. I don't want you to be angry with me." His hand instinctively moved to brush one of her locks out of her face.

"I'm not angry."

"You're disappointed in me," he said softly. "I don't want you to feel that way either."

Jamilah just shrugged.

They sat together in silence for the next few minutes. Darius was about to ask her if she was all right when she asked, "How was the barbecue?"

"It was okay. I wish you had been there. You'd have had a good time. I was telling Eli that you lived nearby. He's only about ten minutes from here."

"Were there a lot of people?"

"Yeah. They've got a pretty big place and they always have a big turnout," he told her.

"Why'd you leave so early?"

"Because I wanted to see you. I didn't want to wait until you were in bed."

Jamilah blushed slightly. "Well, thanks for coming by."

"You're welcome," he answered as he reached over and put his arm around her shoulder. He pulled her close and placed a tender kiss on her forehead.

His embrace comforted Jamilah. She had been upset when he hadn't shown up at her house that afternoon. The last thing she wanted to do was equate him with all of the other men she'd known who had let her down. She'd had plenty of men lie to her. Darius gave her a glimmer of hope that there were still some good men out in the world to be had.

And oh, how she wished she could reveal to him what she felt deep inside. She had never been consumed by such an intense love that she couldn't express freely, but they were just friends and she was fairly certain he didn't want anything more. She certainly didn't want to do anything that would jeopardize their bond. She was prepared to accept the fact that friendship might be all they ever shared, but, she reasoned, at least she would still have him in her life.

In the next seconds, Jamilah rested her head on Darius' shoulder and settled into the comfort of his embrace. This was a slice of heaven for her.

"What are you doing tomorrow?" Darius asked suddenly without moving.

"Nothing."

"Wanna go to the movies?"

Jamilah raised her head and looked into his handsome face. "Sure."

"What time do you want to go?"

"If we catch the early show, we won't have to pay full price."

"Well, that doesn't really matter. I think I can still afford to treat a lady to a movie at full price."

"You don't have to treat."

"Yeah, I do. We're going to hang out all day tomorrow. I owe you for standing you up."

"Well, you didn't really stand me up. I mean, you're here."

"But not when I was supposed to be and I ruined your day."

"No, you didn't."

"Well, anyway, we'll hang out tomorrow and it'll all be on me."

*This man is too sweet for me.* "Darius, can I ask you something?"

"Sure, J. What?"

"How come you're not seeing anyone?"

Darius sat up straight and pulled his arm from across Jamilah's shoulder. She sat up also and turned to face him as she awaited his answer.

"I don't know. I haven't really met anyone I want to get involved with." *Except you.*

"I can't believe that with all the single black women out there looking for a good black man, you haven't been snatched up yet."

Darius smiled at her. "Thank you."

"For what?"

"For referring to me as a 'good man.'"

"Well, you are. You're kind, sensitive, unselfish and gorgeous."

Darius blushed involuntarily as she continued. "I don't mean to embarrass you, Darius. It's just that there are so many guys out there who don't care how they treat a woman as long as they get what they want. That's why I haven't been seeing anyone. The only thing the guys I meet want to do is have sex. They figure if they've bought you dinner a couple of times, they're automatically entitled to it. I'm so tired of men not seeing anything else when they look at me. Just because I'm amply proportioned doesn't mean that's all I'm about." There were tears of frustration in her eyes as she spoke.

Jamilah started to rise from the couch as she said, "I'm so tired of being..."

But Darius halted her movement. "Come here," he whispered, wrapping her in a tender embrace, and trying to comfort her. "Don't cry, Jamilah. I know how hard it is. Believe me I do."

"I'm sorry," she said while trying to pull away from him. "God, I feel so stupid."

"Don't," he said, continuing to hold her gently.

"I don't know what's the matter with me. I must be PMS-ing. I didn't mean to..."

"Jamilah. It's okay. That's what I'm here for. I want you to feel like you can be totally honest with me all the time and if that means breaking down and crying every now and then, then so be it. You're one of my very best friends and I love you and I'll always be here for you. Okay?"

"I love you, too, Darius." She wished he knew exactly how much she loved him.

They sat in silence for a few minutes, each taking comfort in their closeness.

"You know, Jamilah," Darius started softly, "Some men are intimidated by a woman who knows what she wants and isn't afraid to ask for it, and who won't settle for less. You know, who's self-sufficient. Some guys feel compelled to assert their masculinity in an effort to prove their superiority. They'll try anything that will bring a woman down to their level because they're unsure of themselves."

"Seems that way," Jamilah murmured.

"Personally, I want a woman who's got her own. So many women I meet figure because I'm a partner in a big law firm and drive a nice car and don't have any kids, I've got plenty of money to spend on them. But I want someone who's got something of her own to bring to the table, too. You know what I mean?"

"Yes."

Darius could tell that Jamilah was still a little disheartened.

"You'll meet someone special, Jamilah. Someone who will recognize what a special person you are and who will do the right thing by you."

She wanted to ask him why it couldn't be him.

Darius yawned suddenly, although he tried to stifle it.

"You're tired, huh?" she asked.

"Yeah, a little. I'd better cut out before it gets too late."

She sat up, breaking their embrace reluctantly. "Are you going to be all right to drive?"

"Oh, yeah. I'll be okay."

"'Cause I have a spare bedroom. You're welcome to stay over."

Darius smiled as he rose from the couch. "Thanks, J. I appreciate the offer but I'll be all right. I'll take a rain check, though."

"Okay," she said with a smile as she, too, rose from the couch.

Darius reached for her hand. "Come on, lock the door."

Taking his hand, she walked with him to her front door. As he pulled it open, he said, "I'll be here tomorrow at twelve, okay?"

"Okay."

"You're going to be stuck with me for the entire day," he said good-naturedly.

"That's okay. I can think of worse punishments."

They laughed together.

Darius paused a moment, looking deeply into Jamilah's eyes. "Are you okay?" he asked with genuine concern.

She simply nodded.

"Come here. Give me a hug."

As he pulled her close and held her tightly, Jamilah wrapped her arms around him, not wanting to let go ever.

"I'm always here for you, J. Don't ever forget that."

She looked up into his eyes with love. "Likewise."

"I know."

He kissed her gently on her forehead before he released her. "I'll see you tomorrow," he said as he started toward his car.

"Be careful," she called.

He turned back. "I will."

Jamilah stood in the doorway and watched as he drove away, silently counting her blessings. On the one hand, she was sad that they would never be lovers, but on the other, she thanked God that she had a friend like Darius in her life.

# Chapter 25

S abrina was bored out of her mind. She hated these high-society functions she was forced to attend with Quenten. Everyone was so plastic, so phony. The women were all overdressed and trying to outdo one another by telling stories of their children's accomplishments since they had none of their own to boast. *"Barrington was accepted into the advanced program at the Millington School of Excellence." "Well, my Sara will be performing the lead role in her ballet class' performance of 'Sleeping Beauty.'"*

Nauseated by the tedium, she wanted to puke.

The men were just as bad. They stood around discussing stock prices, mergers and acquisitions and hostile takeovers, that is, when wandering eyes weren't ogling each other's wives or mistresses.

Looking at the diamond-encrusted watch on her slender wrist while sighing, she knew Quenten would not even entertain the thought of leaving before ten o'clock, and it was only eight-thirty. She had started to tell him that she didn't want to attend tonight's gala. One of her former co-workers had thrown a cook-out in celebration of her thirty-fifth birthday, and she'd really wanted to attend. It seemed like eons since she'd attended a function where everyone wasn't a snob, but he had sent the RSVP for two, and it would have been too embarrassing for him to show up at one of these gatherings alone.

Besides, the way some of these women carried on when they thought no one were watching was disgusting. If he came to one of these functions stag, he would be like premier goods on an auction block.

Sabrina knew there were plenty of women in the place who envied, or more to the point, were downright jealous of her relationship with Quenten, but she was really getting sick of him.

Sure, the jewels, the furs and the designer dresses were all lovely and she loved being the object of so powerful a man's desires, but when the other side of him surfaced—the mean, domineering and utterly insecure side—she yearned to be free of him.

She was happy that the investigation into his former partner's embezzling had cleared Quenten of any wrongdoing. During the past month and a half before he'd been cleared, life with him had been unbearable to the point that he seemed to have taken all of his hostilities out on her. Her mouth was still sore from when he had hit her three weeks ago, causing her to bite the inside of her mouth. She'd needed three stitches to repair it.

Pulling a pack of cigarettes from her pocketbook, she eased one out of the pack. As she placed the slender stick of tobacco between her ruby red lips, a gentleman standing near her at the bar produced a lighter, from out of nowhere it seemed.

She lit the cigarette and took a long drag before smiling seductively and mouthing, "Thank you."

It was only in the past three months that she had begun smoking to calm her nerves. Sometimes Quenten unnerved her so much that she would smoke a cigarette for lack of anything else to do. He hated it when she smoked, too, although he occasionally smoked cigars.

The man who'd lit her cigarette hadn't moved and Sabrina noticed that he seemed to be searching for something to say to her. Smiling to herself, she recalled seeing him before at one of these functions. A man as attractive as this one wasn't easy to forget. His skin color was a smooth dark brown with undertones of red, giving one the impression that he had Native American blood flowing through his veins. With jet-black hair cut close to his scalp, a set of very sensuous lips peeked out from the close-cut dark hair on his face. An aquiline nose and close-set, almond-shaped eyes trimmed with long silky lashes and hooded by thick black brows completed his strikingly handsome countenance. Despite the magnificence of this extremely gorgeous tuxedo-clad hunk, he appeared to be quite uncomfortable in this setting.

"You look as bored as I feel," she suddenly said to him.

His already attractive face came alive with his smile, revealing a perfect row of gleaming white teeth. "Yeah, this really isn't my scene," he said in a deep and surprisingly sexy drawl that sent shivers straight down her spine.

"I didn't think so," she said with a slight chuckle.

"Avery Williams," he said, extending his hand.

"Sabrina Richardson," she responded with a bright smile, as she took the extra large extremity he offered. As her tiny mitt seemingly disappeared in his, she noticed the rough texture of his skin, as though he regularly worked with his hands.

"My pleasure," he said without releasing her. "Are you unescorted tonight?"

"No, she's not!" Quenten appeared behind Sabrina at that instant, catching her totally off guard. Quickly severing their handshake, her heart raced in fear and her stomach knotted in anxious anticipation of his next words.

Looking back at him with a nervous smile, she sputtered, "Oh…honey…this is…Avery Williams. Mr. Williams, this is my fiancé, Quenten Blanchard."

"Yes, I'm quite familiar with Mr. Blanchard's reputation," Avery said with a mocking grin that did not touch his dark eyes.

"Is that right?" Quenten said coldly, his face twisted in an antagonistic frown. "Then you should know I don't like anyone getting too familiar with anything that belongs to me."

Although he raised an eyebrow at that remark, Avery refrained from commenting. Instead, he picked his drink up off the bar and nodded to Sabrina before walking away. "It was a pleasure meeting you, Miss Richardson."

"You, too." She smiled uneasily.

Quenten pounced immediately. "I can't leave you alone for a minute without you coming on to some guy, can I?"

"I wasn't coming on to him, Quenten. He lit my cigarette and introduced himself, that's all," she said nervously.

"Put that damn thing out. You know I don't like you smoking." Sabrina immediately crushed the cigarette in the ashtray on the bar. "I have some business that I need to take care of. I want you to go home. I'll meet you at the house later," he abruptly ordered.

"Quenten, I was thinking that I'd go back to my place tonight," Sabrina said cautiously.

"Why?"

"Well, I haven't been there in a few days. I wanted to check my mail and..."

"You can check your mail tomorrow," he said, cutting her off. "Go to the house tonight. I'll be there at about two o'clock and you'd better be there," he said, leaving no room for further discussion.

She had been dying to leave this place, but suddenly a feeling of trepidation crept up her spine. Knowing that when he came home, he would have something more to say about the few seconds of innocent conversation she had shared with Avery Williams, she was pretty sure, too, that he would be drunk by the time he arrived.

As she looked into his eyes, she wondered why she had thought he was so handsome when they first met. "Do you want me to take the car?" she asked timidly.

"No, I'm taking the car. You can get a cab. I'll see you later," he said and immediately walked away from her.

Ten minutes later, Sabrina was standing on the street in front of the hotel she had just exited, waiting for a taxi. The temperature was still quite warm on this late June night despite it being just after nine. She pulled a cigarette from her pocketbook and was about to light it when, once again, Avery Williams appeared and lit it for her. Looking up in surprise to find him standing there, her heartbeat quickened almost immediately. Her smile now apprehensive, she was embarrassed that he had witnessed her with Quenten.

"Where you headed?" he asked, easily.

"The East Side."

"Can I give you a lift?"

"No, thank you," Sabrina quickly answered with a shake of her head as she took a pull on her cigarette. She wouldn't look at him.

"I hope I wasn't the cause of any...trouble back there," he said with a tilt of his head.

"No, of course not," was her hasty response. When she looked up into his dark eyes, they seemed to be boring through her, so she quickly turned away.

It appeared as though minutes had passed before their next verbal exchange. She could feel him staring at her, but she was too ashamed to meet his gaze.

"Does he hit you?" he asked suddenly in a caressing tone.

Her head snapped around, and she knew her face revealed what her mouth couldn't say. Her heart began to pound in her chest harder than it already was from being near him.

"Why do you stay with him?" he asked.

At that moment, the hotel's doorman hailed down a taxi for her and opened the car's door.

"It was nice meeting you," she said as she dropped her cigarette into the street, stamping it out as she stepped off the curb and started toward the cab.

"Sabrina." Avery stepped behind her as he reached into the breast pocket of his tuxedo jacket and removed a business card. He offered it to her as he asked, "Call me?"

She stared down at the card for a few seconds, afraid to take it from his hand.

"I won't hurt you," he said softly.

Sabrina's tear-filled eyes met his tender gaze. Taking the card from his outstretched hand, she quickly got into the cab. As the driver pulled off, she looked out of the rear window to find him standing where she had left him.

***

Avery Williams lit a cigarette as he stood on the curb and watched the yellow cab pull away. *What a beautiful woman*, he thought sadly. Wondering what she was doing with a creep like Blanchard, she had to be at least twenty years his junior, he thought, but knew that was what Blanchard was in to.

Knowing he had overstepped his bounds by giving Sabrina his phone number, especially while he was on assignment, something in her eyes seemed to call out to him for help. Recalling the look of terror in her eyes when Blanchard approached them, he thought she was too good to be subjected to his abuse.

As he took a pull on his cigarette, his forehead creased in a frown as he thought, *no woman should be subjected to the brutality of any man*. As far as he was concerned, any man who would hit a woman was the lowest form of scum, in addition to being a straight-up punk.

Loosening the cumbersome bow tie strangling his neck, Avery stepped over to the parking attendant and handed him the ticket for his car. He would be glad when this assignment was completed. Feeling disdain for the tuxedo he wore, he was much too laid-back for these stuffy functions he was forced to attend since this assignment was dropped in his lap two weeks ago. He hoped Sabrina would call him. He didn't know why he felt this sense of urgency with regard to her. After all, he knew nothing about her other than her name and that she was Blanchard's woman. The man's words came back to him—*I don't like anyone getting too familiar with anything that belongs to me*—and left a bad taste in his mouth.

As the attendant pulled his car up, Avery stepped off the curb and around to the driver's seat. He tipped the guy and flicked the butt into the street before getting into his Range Rover. As he pulled off, he thought, *first things first. Once Blanchard's behind bars where he should be, I'll deal with Sabrina Richardson.*

**\*\*\***

Sabrina was grateful that when Quenten got home he didn't awaken her, although she was faking slumber. When she heard him open and close the door upon his arrival at two-thirty that morning, she ducked under the covers and tried to be as still as possible as she prayed for him to simply go to sleep, which he did.

When he left for his office that morning, Sabrina once again feigned sleep. Although he "woke" her when he left, she hadn't been subjected to his advances. She waited a few minutes after he left, just to be sure he was gone, then quickly jumped out of the bed and went straight to the shower, completing the task in little over five minutes. Hurriedly dressing in a free-flowing cotton sheath, she slipped her feet into a pair of flat sandals, grabbed her pocketbook and left.

For the duration of the drive back to her apartment across town, Sabrina thought of the man she had met at last night's gala. Avery Williams. She could remember having seen him once or twice before, but last night was the first time they had ever exchanged words. Embarrassed and humiliated when Quenten came up on them, literally calling her his property, she was surprised and a little disappointed that Avery had been so easily intimidated by Quenten, leaving her immediately to fend for herself. With his imposing stature, she had figured he would be more apt to challenge Quenten since he towered over him and appeared to be quite powerfully built.

Guessing he was somewhere around six feet, three or four inches tall, he was quite broad and his tuxedo fit him perfectly, but she was sure it had been tailor-made to fit his expansive chest. His thighs seemed to bulge beneath the fabric of his pants, but despite his massive frame, she got the impression that he was a very gentle person. *Maybe that was why he walked away so quickly.* That Quenten had frightened him was unconscionable to her. After all, Quenten was old and out of shape, surely no match for a man like Avery.

When she arrived at her apartment, she went straight to her stereo and put on her favorite disc, the *CD101.9 Kids' Fund Hard to Find Sampler.* The soothing cool jazz tunes flowing from her stereo speakers calmed her and eased the loneliness she was suddenly feeling.

Sabrina kicked off her sandals and sat on the sofa with her feet tucked under her. She grabbed her pocketbook from the other end of the sofa where she had dropped it and reached into the side zipper and pulled out his card. AVERY WILLIAMS, SPECIAL INVESTIGATOR. *What kind of investigator*, she wondered. His generic-looking card gave no insight into what he did. The three telephone numbers listed were not identified as home or business or pager numbers. Sabrina sat where she was and stared at his card for nearly five minutes, debating with herself about calling him. *What would I say to him? What will he think?* She had never entertained the idea of stepping out on Quenten. With the reaction she got from talking to Avery for the few insignificant minutes that she had last night, she knew if he ever found out that she had actually called him, he would go ballistic.

*I won't hurt you.* Avery's words continuously echoed in her brain. Somehow she knew he wouldn't. Call it female intuition, but Sabrina felt certain that she would always be safe with Avery Williams. Where once she would have never considered giving a man the time of day if she didn't know his credentials, i.e., job title, monetary worth, etc., her criteria had gradually changed. After all, Quenten had all the right credentials, materially surpassing any man she had ever been with, but she had never been so completely miserable in her life. Suddenly, money was no longer that important to her. *What could I possibly say to him, though?* He had known that Quenten was abusive to her without her even confirming it. *What must he think of me for staying with him?* How could she tell him she didn't have anywhere else to turn? Her only friend had abandoned her a year ago. Her mother thought the sun rose and set on Quenten. "He's every woman's dream," Dolly Richardson believed. *What would she think if she knew the way he treated me?* Sabrina had been too ashamed to even tell her mother the truth about him.

Once again, her attention was drawn to the business card she held in her hand. *Avery Williams, Special Investigator.* She suddenly remembered the other times she had seen him; he had been alone then, too, and seemed to keep pretty much to himself. If he hadn't been there for the purpose of networking, like most of the attendees at these functions did, then why had he been there? *Was he on the job? If so, who was he investigating?* She suddenly wondered, too, about his almost magical appearance at her side after she had left the hotel last night. He seemed to have come from out of nowhere. *He must have been watching me*, she surmised. His presence had been a comfort to her, though. *Could he be my knight in shining armor?* She giggled lightly. She didn't believe in fairy tales, but he had appeared at a moment when she felt quite alone. Once again his words echoed in her mind. *I won't hurt you.* Sabrina reached for the cordless telephone resting on the cocktail table at the far end of the sofa. Before she had time to consider what she was doing, she dialed the first number on the card. Her heart began to pound insistently in her chest with the first ring in her ear.

**✳✳✳**

Avery sat behind his desk in the little closet his employer called an office. The space had been "generously" loaned to him at this Manhattan site for use while he worked this assignment. Normally, he worked out of a field office in South Jersey. Reclining with the heels of his size thirteen cowboy boots resting on the corner of the desk, and although he'd been there for three hours already, he still had not removed the lightweight windbreaker he wore over his white cotton mock-neck shirt. His legs and hips were snug but comfortable in the black jeans he was used to wearing. The tuxedo he'd been forced to wear last night was totally not him.

He was reviewing the file in his hands for the umpteenth time. Blanchard-Thomas Associates, Inc. was quite the moneymaking organization, he had learned. As he went through the financial records that had been made available to him, he tried to decipher many of the codes and notations beside some of the entries. He marked the ones that totally stumped him, making a note to inquire about them later this evening when he met with The Man to give him his progress report.

Quenten Blanchard was as slick as an eel. How he had managed to doctor these figures was still a puzzle to him and everyone else who was working on this case.

Closing the file and putting it on the desk in front of him, he picked up another and opened it to remove the eight-by-ten black and white photos enclosed. He stared at the photo of the man who had allegedly been embezzling funds from Blanchard-Thomas. The forensics team had taken it at the scene. He ignored the numerous photos he had of Scott Thomas that had been taken while he was still alive. It was common knowledge that Thomas had been the brains behind the organization. His sharp intellect and financial acumen had built Blanchard-Thomas into the financial mecca it currently was. What reason did he have for stealing? He was a success in his own right. His net worth was well in the millions of dollars. He'd had a happy marriage and two kids who were exceptional students at the high-class private school they attended, as well as being quite mannerable and well-behaved. There were no gambling debts, no drinking or drug problems, and no threats of extortion or blackmail. His reputation was squeaky clean, and everyone he had worked with had respected and admired him, from the lowest-level employee to his fellow officers.

Quenten Blanchard, on the other hand, was not too well liked by anyone in the organization. He had a reputation for being condescending toward his subordinates and seemed to get a kick out of pulling rank on the officers of the firm, Avery had been told. A former employee had brought Blanchard before the board of directors on charges of sexual harassment. That incident had been swept under the rug by a large cash settlement paid to the young woman to keep her mouth shut. Everything he had read or been told about Blanchard up to this point had a negative connotation.

This train of thought immediately sent him back in time a few hours to last night and the confrontation while he was speaking to Sabrina. He had wanted nothing more than to slam his fist into Blanchard's face for disrespecting that beautiful woman the way he had, but he'd had no choice but to walk away. He could not blow his cover.

The look of terror in her eyes when she heard Blanchard's voice behind her wrenched his heart. *She must think I'm some sort of coward,* Avery thought. *I could have checked him right there.* Dumbfounded by her allegiance to Quenten, he wondered why she stayed with him. It was evident that she was afraid of him. He'd never been able to understand why a woman would allow herself to be abused that way. With all of his training and education, he knew it had to do with a lack of self-esteem and a form of mental dependency, but in his heart, he found it incomprehensible, absurd. He'd seen the shame on her face last night when he asked her about it. God knows he'd meant no harm, but he wanted to understand. He wanted to protect her. In all honesty, he really wanted to take her in his arms and kiss those ruby lips.

He hoped she would call him. He hoped she knew that she would never have to be afraid of him.

The phone on the desk rang suddenly and interrupted his thoughts. He swung his feet to the floor and sat up straight in the chair as he reached for the instrument.

As the second ring ended, he lifted the receiver and put it to his ear. "Williams, here."

He sounds so different from last night, was her first thought before she became paralyzed with fear. *Oh my goodness; what was I thinking? Why did I call him?*

"Hello," the voice boomed again.

She was speechless.

"Hello," he repeated in an irritated tone.

*Who the hell is playing games with me this early in the morning?* He really was not in the mood for this. There were very few people who had this number. He could count on both hands the people he had given... *Could it be?* "Sabrina? Is that you?"

When he said her name, Sabrina panicked. She gasped loudly, shocked by his accurate assumption, and quickly hung up the telephone. *How did he know it was me?*

Her heart was racing. *Stupid! Stupid! Stupid!* Mentally chiding herself, first, for being stupid enough to call him when she didn't have a clue what to say to him, and second, for being a coward and hanging up. She wondered, *how could he have possibly known it was me?* That was what really got to her. She was glad he didn't have her phone number because he probably would have called her back and yelled at her for being so immature.

Her telephone began to ring. Figuring it was Quenten on the line and not really wanting to talk to him, she reached for the telephone, nevertheless.

"Hello," she said dolefully.

"Why'd you hang up, Sabrina?"

"Avery?"

"Yeah. Why'd you hang up?"

"How'd you get my number?" Sabrina asked in alarm.

"I star-six-nined you."

*Stupid! Stupid! Stupid!*

When she didn't respond, Avery said, "I'm glad you called. I was just thinking about you."

"I shouldn't have called you," she said hurriedly. "And you shouldn't call here anymore."

"Sabrina, don't be afraid of me. I won't hurt you."

Against her will, she began to cry softly.

"Can I see you?" he asked. His voice was like a caress.

"No."

"Please, just to talk. Maybe I can help you."

"No. Please don't call here again."

"Sabrina, don't hang up."

"I have to. Good-bye." She broke the connection and tossed the cordless phone she had been using on the sofa. Almost immediately it began to ring again. "No," she cried. "Don't call me. I can't talk to you."

She refused to answer it this time, certain that Avery was on the other end. *If Quenten ever found out...* Her answering machine clicked on. "Hi. I'm not in right now but if you leave a message I'll get back to you as soon as I can. Bye."

"Sabrina. Sabrina, please pick up." It was the smooth, sexy voice she remembered from last night. "I wish you'd let me help you. You don't have to be afraid of me. I would never hurt you. Please pick up the phone, Sabrina." There was silence for the next few seconds. "All right. I won't call you again, but please keep my number and call me if you ever need me. For anything." Silence again. "Take care of yourself."

She was overwhelmed by her mental anguish as she listened to his soothing voice on her answering machine. She couldn't ignore the sadness in his tone. "Avery."

✳✳✳

He sighed as he hung up the phone. *At least she'd been thinking about me.* He retrieved the picture of Quenten Blanchard from the file that had spilled out on his desk when he reached for the phone. *You no-good son of the devil.* Avery felt a burning hatred for the man growing in the pit of his stomach. From everything he had learned and witnessed about him, he seemed to inflict pain or promote misery wherever he went. The fact that he was able to make that beautiful woman tremble in fear turned his stomach.

Avery turned his chair around and gazed out of the window at the skyscrapers across the street. *I've got to get her away from him. But how? How can I make her trust me if I can't even get her to talk to me?* He knew he shouldn't be thinking about her this way; after all, she was not part of the assignment, and if he let her get under his skin too deeply, he could ruin everything, but he couldn't help it. She needed him and he needed to protect her any way he could.

Avery rose suddenly. He dropped the file back on the desk, grabbed his cell phone off of its charger and shoved it into his pocket, then strode out of the office. He was on a mission.

# Chapter 26

Jamilah's mother, Alexia, and her husband, Frank Witherspoon, had planned a two-week cruise to Bermuda to celebrate their second wedding anniversary. Their ship was scheduled to leave from New York City at four o'clock Sunday afternoon, so they flew in a day early to afford Alexia an opportunity to visit with Jamilah, since they hadn't seen each other since the Christmas holiday.

Jamilah invited Darius to dinner with Alexia and Frank because she wanted her mother to meet him. Still skeptical about Jamilah's relationship with Darius, Alexia was not convinced that he was as good a guy as Jamilah had made him out to be. She had difficulty getting past his former relationship with Sabrina. It didn't matter that a year had passed since he or Jamilah had last had any contact with Sabrina; Alexia was a natural-born skeptic, and she had always had a problem accepting any situation which appeared too good to be true.

Jamilah had never told Darius about her mother's feelings. She was positive that once Alexia met him, she would change her opinion, and Jamilah didn't want him to be anything but his naturally sweet self when he met her mother.

Darius arrived at Jamilah's house at five-thirty that Saturday evening. Alexia immediately looked at her watch when the doorbell rang. *Well, at least he's prompt,* she thought.

Seconds later, Jamilah emerged from the kitchen. "I'll get it."

"Is that your friend, Jami?" Frank asked.

"Probably."

She hurried to the door and opened it without checking to see who was there. "Hi!"

"Hey, J," Darius said as he stepped into the house. He gave Jamilah a warm hug and a kiss on her cheek as he always did when they greeted each other. "How you doin'?"

"I'm great. How are you?"

"I'm good," he replied with a smile.

"Come here and meet my mother and father," Jamilah said as she took his hand and led him into the living room.

Alexia closely watched the interaction between Jamilah and Darius. Her first impression upon witnessing him with her daughter was favorable, although she maintained a poker face so as not to reveal anything about how she felt.

He was very handsome, she noticed, and well-dressed. It was a warm day and the cream-colored slacks and collarless long-sleeve shirt, accented by tan shoes, belt and sport jacket, complemented his long, lean frame. Alexia noticed, too, that his smile, while directed at Jamilah, displayed a touch of tenderness.

"So, what do you think?" Frank asked Alexia in a whisper as they sat together on the sofa. He was well aware of her feelings regarding Jamilah's friendship with this man.

"Hush," Alexia said and lightly smacked his leg.

"Mommy, Frank, this is my friend, Darius Thornton. Darius, this is my mother and father, Alexia and Frank Witherspoon."

Frank rose to his feet to greet Darius, but being the gentleman that he was, Darius addressed Alexia first. "Mrs. Witherspoon, it is such a pleasure to meet you." He reached for her hand and held it in both of his. "Jamilah has told me so much about you."

"Likewise, I'm sure," Alexia said from her seat on the sofa.

"Mr. Witherspoon, how are you?" Darius then asked as he extended his hand to Frank.

"I'm fine, Darius. How are you?"

"I'm fine, sir. How was your flight?"

"It was good."

"I'm sure you're looking forward to your cruise tomorrow," Darius said.

"Oh yeah."

"Oh, and happy anniversary," Darius added.

"Thank you," Alexia and Frank chorused.

"Sit down, Darius," Jamilah said.

"What's that delicious aroma I smell?" Darius asked as he sat in the chair adjacent to where Alexia and Frank were seated.

"I baked an apple pie. I figured after dinner, we could come back here and have coffee and dessert."

"It smells great, J. I love apple pie."

"Good, 'cause I make a mean apple pie."

"I bet you do," Darius said with a subtle smile.

"I'll be right back. I think it's time to take it out. Darius, do you want anything to drink while I'm in there?"

"No thanks, J. I'm fine."

"So, Darius, do you live nearby?" Alexia asked.

"No, ma'am. I live in Brooklyn."

"Is that where you're from?"

"No. I was born and raised in Norfolk, Virginia. I moved to New York when I finished law school."

"That's right. Jamilah told us you were an attorney. Do you have your own practice?" Frank asked.

"No, I'm a partner with a large firm in the city."

"A partner?" Alexia was impressed. One of her closest friends had been a legal secretary for most of her career before her retirement. Through her, Alexia had been made aware of the scarcity of African-American partners in the profession who were not in business for themselves.

"Yes, ma'am."

"Is your family still in Norfolk?" she asked.

"My parents are. My younger sister lives in Detroit with her family."

"Do you have children, Darius?" Frank asked.

"Not yet. Hopefully, one day before I'm old and gray, I'll meet a nice woman I can settle down with and start a family."

The fact that he had no children out of wedlock impressed Alexia, too.

"Jamilah tells me you'll be in Bermuda for two weeks. Have you ever been there before?" Darius asked them.

"I have, but only for a couple of days," Alexia answered. "It was one of the ports-of-call on a cruise I took a few years back with a couple of my girlfriends. What I saw of it, though, was beautiful."

"I've heard that. I've been to a few of the islands in the Caribbean, but I haven't made it to Bermuda yet," Darius admitted.

Jamilah then emerged from the kitchen. "Okay, the pie's cooling. We can leave whenever y'all are ready."

"That pie smells great, Jamilah. Do I have to ask whether or not you have ice cream?" Darius said with a grin.

With a smirk she answered, "You know you don't have to ask me that."

"I made a reservation at Michael's Too in Queens for six-thirty. My friend, Warren, is preparing a special treat for us," Darius said.

"Is this the same guy who owns Michaels in the city?" Jamilah asked him.

"Yes. This place is a bit larger, though. He has a dance hall on the lower level."

"Oh yeah? We have to check that out one night," Jamilah said as they prepared to leave for dinner.

"Say the word," Darius told her.

"You know the owner of the restaurant?" Frank asked.

"Yes, we met on a flight from L.A. a few years back that turned out to be the flight from Hell."

"What happened?" Alexia asked.

"Turbulence like you never want to experience. That flight almost made me swear off flying for good."

"That bad, huh?" Frank commented.

"That bad."

They rode to Queens in Darius' BMW. Frank rode shotgun, while Jamilah and Alexia sat in the back seat.

Jamilah noticed that, although Alexia never said so, her mother seemed to be warming up to Darius. She had always known that if given the chance to get to know him, there was no way her mother could not like him.

On the drive to the restaurant, Darius and Frank conversed about the NBA

Finals like old friends. The Seventy-Sixers and the Lakers were in a dead heat in the series—three wins apiece—with the deciding game scheduled for tomorrow afternoon. Darius was a die-hard Sixers fan, while Frank was rooting for the Lakers. The men's friendly bickering about which was the better team reminded the women of two young boys, and since they were basically excluded from the male bonding episode, every now and then, Darius would call into the back seat just to let them know they were not forgotten. No surprise to Jamilah. Darius was his usually considerate self.

As much as she wanted to, she refused to ask her mother what she thought of him. Jamilah figured she would wait until the end of the evening to get the full report.

When they arrived at Michael's Too, Darius parked in the restaurant's private lot. Upon emerging from the vehicle, Alexia and Jamilah started to the restaurant's entrance ahead of the men.

"Hey, lady, can ya help me get somethin' ta eat?" a filthily clad homeless man begged as he suddenly stepped in front of Jamilah with his hand out.

Darius, seeing the look of surprise and disgust on Alexia's face, protectively stepped between Jamilah and the well-aged man and asked, "Can I help you?"

"I just wanna get somethin' ta eat, fella. Can you help a man get somethin' ta eat?"

"Sure, just let me take these ladies inside and get them seated, and I'll be right back, okay?" Darius said.

The homeless man frowned cynically at Darius. "Yeah, right," he grumbled as he turned and moved back to the curb where a broken-down shopping cart with everything he owned was parked.

Upon entering the restaurant, they were immediately seated. Darius, to everyone's surprise—even Jamilah's—said, "Excuse me a minute. I'm going to get a takeout order for that old guy outside." He moved away from the table before anyone could respond.

Alexia looked over at Frank, then at Jamilah and said, "Is he serious?"

"I guess so."

Darius was gone for about ten minutes and when he returned to the table, he sat down and picked up his menu as if nothing out of the ordinary had taken place.

Alexia couldn't resist asking, "Darius, did you really take that man a plate of food?"

"Yeah, I just ordered a chicken dinner with some greens and macaroni n' cheese, and a soda," he said humbly and shrugged. "He looked like he hadn't had a good meal in quite a while. I hate to see old people like that begging for food, 'cause the next thing you know, they're going through the garbage, and that really messes me up. It makes me wonder what happened to their families, you know, and how come there's no one to take care of them. I mean, I know circumstances come up that could put any one of us right in that guy's shoes, but the difference is, I have a family who I know I could lean on if that ever happened, just like you do. It just kinda makes me sad, so I try to do what I can."

Listening to Darius and watching his generosity first-hand gave Alexia new insight into why her daughter was so smitten with this man. She was ashamed to admit that even with her medical training and nursing skills, she had been put off by the dirty old man who'd approached them outside, and couldn't imagine doing anything as selfless as Darius had done. She knew she was more likely to come inside and have her meal without giving the beggar another thought.

Seconds later, a bottle of champagne was sent to their table, compliments of the house, to toast Alexia and Frank's anniversary. Alexia was again surprised and quite delighted. Frank, who had already given Darius his unspoken stamp of approval, said, "I like your style, Darius."

Jamilah simply beamed.

When they had completed their specially prepared dinner of blackened catfish, collard greens and spicy rice and peas, their host, Warren Michaels, came to their table to greet them.

Darius rose from the table when he noticed his friend approaching. "Warren, you've outdone yourself," Darius said as he extended his hand. The men embraced warmly.

"I take it everything was satisfactory?" Warren asked.

"Everything was excellent. How are you?"

"I'm well, Darius. How have you been?"

"Good. How's the family?" Darius asked.

"They're very well, thanks. My wife and I are expecting our second child in a couple of months."

"Congratulations! That's great." Darius shook Warren's hand a second time. "Here, let me introduce you to everyone." He placed his hand on Jamilah's shoulder as he said, "This is my dear friend, Jamilah Parsons, and her parents, Mr. and

Mrs. Witherspoon. Everyone, this is Warren Michaels, our chef and owner of the restaurant."

"Good evening, folks. It's a pleasure to meet you all," Warren said as he shook each of their hands in turn. "I hope you've enjoyed everything."

"Everything was delicious," Jamilah said.

"Yes, it was," Alexia agreed.

"Thank you for the champagne," Frank added.

"You're very welcome, and happy anniversary to you. I understand you'll be cruising to the islands tomorrow."

"Yes," Alexia said with a smile.

"Well, I wish you a wonderful trip."

"Thank you," Frank and Alexia said in unison.

"Would you folks care for dessert? I have an incredible array of treats to finish off your meal."

Darius answered, "We're going to pass on dessert, Warren. Jamilah has a fresh-baked apple pie cooling at home for us."

"Oh, well then, I should leave with you," Warren quipped.

Everyone laughed.

The maitre d' approached Warren. "Excuse me, Warren. Alexandra's on the phone for you."

"Thank you, Rick." To Darius and company, Warren said, "My better half's on the phone, so I have to run. It was a pleasure meeting you, Mr. and Mrs. Witherspoon, and once again, have a wonderful trip."

"Thank you. It was good meeting you, too. I'm going to let the folks back home know where to come for dinner when they're in New York," Frank said.

Warren shook his hand and said, "Thank you, sir. I appreciate that. Jamilah, it was a pleasure meeting you, finally. You're every bit as beautiful as my man said you are."

Jamilah blushed. "Thank you, Warren. It was a pleasure meeting you, too."

"Darius, it was great to see you, man. Keep in touch, hear?"

"I will, Warren. Thanks for everything."

When their check arrived a few minutes later, Frank reached for it, but Darius stopped him. "Please, Mr. Witherspoon. Dinner is on me."

"Darius, that's not necessary."

"I'd like to, though. Consider it an anniversary present."

Frank smiled and shook his head.

"Thank you, Darius. This was very nice," Alexia said.

"It was my pleasure, Mrs. Witherspoon. I'm glad you enjoyed it."

"I really did," she said with a warm smile.

"See, Mommy, I told you he was sweet," Jamilah said as she put her arm around Darius' shoulder and kissed his cheek.

Alexia was tickled when she noticed Darius blush.

**\*\*\***

"So, now what do you think?" Frank asked Alexia as they prepared for bed later that night.

Alexia looked over at her husband and smiled. "I like him. He's got a lot of class about him."

"He's in love with her, you know."

"I know. Now I can see why she's so crazy about him."

"So are you going to tell her that, or are you going to keep giving her a hard time?"

"Listen, Frank, I had to know for sure. Jamilah can be gullible sometimes, you know that. I didn't want to see her get hurt. But yes, for your information, I'll tell her."

# Chapter 27

The upcoming weekend was July Fourth. As they sat in a Chinese restaurant one evening having dinner, Jamilah asked Darius, "So what do you have planned for the long holiday weekend?"

"Oh," he answered excitedly, "I'm driving down to Virginia on Saturday to see my parents. Sunday is their fortieth wedding anniversary, and Brianne and I are giving them a big party to celebrate. She and her husband are flying in from Detroit with their kids."

"Wow, forty years! That's great."

"Yeah, it is pretty cool."

"How are your parents?" she asked.

"They're fine. You know my mother always asks me about you."

"She does?"

"Yup. I've been meaning to tell you that. But anyway, they don't know we're giving them this party. They know we're coming down, but they don't have a clue about the party."

"So how are you planning to pull this off without your parents' knowledge? Where's it going to be?"

"At their house."

"Huh?"

"You heard right. We're doing it under the guise of a cookout. Just on a grand scale. We've invited our relatives from all over, but my parents' house is pretty big, so there'll be plenty of room for everyone," Darius explained. "Besides, there'll only be Brianne's family and me staying at the house. Everyone else has reservations to stay in one of the hotels in town."

Jamilah smiled as she said, "That sounds like it should be a lot of fun."

"Yeah, it will be."

"How is Brianne?"

"She's fine. Damn, I must be getting old 'cause I forgot to tell you that she asked about you the other day, too."

"Well, tell her I said hi."

He surprised her when he said, "Why don't you come down with me? Then you can tell her yourself."

She was putting a forkful of her shrimp with chili sauce in her mouth at the time, and she froze with her mouth open. "What?" She lowered her fork.

"Come with me."

Stunned into speechlessness for a moment, Jamilah's mind began working overtime. *Why'd he ask me to come with him to his parents' home in Virginia? Why would he want me to be a part of what was obviously a big family celebration? What does this mean?*

When Jamilah did not answer right away, Darius asked, "What's wrong?"

"I…I'm just…you caught me a little off guard." She lowered her head quickly to quell the surfacing warmth flowing through her body that she was sure showed on her face.

"Why? My parents would love to see you. You know, you really won them over by being with me at that hospital every day last year. And Brianne would love to see you, too."

"I don't know, Darius. I just feel like… Where would I stay?" she asked suddenly.

"What do you mean, where would you stay? You'll stay at my parents' house with Brianne and me."

"Oh, I couldn't do that. That would be such an intrusion."

"Are you kidding? There's plenty of space, and you could never be an intrusion. You're family, Jamilah," Darius said as he reached across the table and took her hand.

"But this is such a special occasion," Jamilah protested.

"Which is exactly why you should be there. You know, my parents and Brianne were just as excited as I was when I told them that you were back in my life."

*Back in your life,* she questioned in her mind. *What does that mean?* Although there was no doubt about the depth of her feelings for Darius, Jamilah was still exploring the depths of his reciprocation.

Before she could answer, he spoke again in a tone as gentle as a caress. "Jamilah, I would really love it if you came with me. I promise, you'll have the time of your life and my family will be thrilled to have you there. Please, come with me?"

A frown suddenly darkened his handsome face when he realized that he'd never even considered that she might have other plans for the weekend. He wanted to kick himself when he realized how selfish he must sound to her. "I'm sorry. I didn't even ask you if you were doing anything else. Do you have plans for the weekend?"

"No," was all she could manage.

His face brightened immediately. "Good! So you can come with me. Please? I could really use the company on the drive down."

As Jamilah sat across from him in the restaurant, she couldn't help but marvel at the sudden and almost boyish level of excitement that completely outshined his usual totally suave and debonair manner. She had noticed that a few times, Darius had caught the attention of a number of women who entered the restaurant after them. She wondered if he had noticed them. He appeared to be totally oblivious to everything that was going on around them. His attention seemed to be directed at her alone. *Gee, how I'd love to be the center of his attention permanently,* Jamilah thought.

His handsome cocoa brown face with the ever-smiling brown eyes was a sight to behold, one she knew she would never tire of looking at. And his smile—her heart swelled each time he flashed those pearly whites her way.

Jamilah had never been a quick study in interpersonal relationships with the opposite sex, but she was certainly no fool. Her dark brown face broke into a genuine smile as she said, "All right, Darius. I'll go with you."

✳✳✳

Darius picked Jamilah up at seven a.m. Saturday morning, although she had offered to drive into the city to meet him since his apartment, in relation to her house, was in the general direction they were headed.

She had packed fairly light, just one tote bag with her toiletries and underwear, pajamas, T-shirts, shorts, a pair of dress shoes and a garment bag which held two dresses, just in case they decided to go somewhere that she might need to get dressed up for. For the drive South, she had thrown on a pair of denim shorts; a lightweight, sleeveless denim blouse; and a pair of brown leather sandals. Her locks were pulled back in a ponytail and tied with a leather lace. A pair of dangling cowry shell earrings was the only jewelry she wore aside from the wristwatch on her left arm. Since they would be driving for more than seven hours, she wanted to be as comfortable as possible, and she was prepared to help Darius with the driving if he wanted her to.

Although Jamilah had not gone to any great lengths to beautify herself for their trip, Darius thought she looked great in her denim outfit with her hair pulled back, exposing her ebony beauty to the world. This was the essence of her, he thought—proud, natural and unencumbered by a bunch of superficial accessories.

Darius had thrown on a pair of the oldest and most comfortable jeans he owned. The fabric was completely intact but he'd worn them so often and for so many years, that the denim was smooth to the touch and practically molded to his form—a detail Jamilah hadn't missed. The weather was warm, although it was still early in the day, and the close-fitting sleeveless shirt he wore, combined with the form-fitting jeans, gave Jamilah an excellent view of his exquisite masculine form.

Fully aware that Darius drove a BMW, Jamilah was quite surprised when she stepped out of her house that morning and saw the dark-green convertible Mercedes SLK320, with tan leather interior, parked in front. "Is that yours?" she asked as her eyes bulged.

Darius was behind her, carrying her bags. She stopped before she reached her bottom step, but he continued past her. "Yeah. Do you like it?"

"Yes! It's gorgeous. Are we driving down in it?"

"Uh-huh." He was at the trunk, loading her bags.

"When'd you get it?" She stepped alongside the car and ran her hand slowly along the body.

"Well, I haven't actually bought it yet. I have a friend who owns a dealership, and he knows I've been thinking about buying one, so he's letting me use it for the weekend so I can feel it out, in case I decide to go ahead with the purchase," Darius explained.

"He's letting you hold it?" Jamilah asked, unable to conceal her amazement.

"Yeah, but I'll more than likely buy it. I picked it up from him last night, and I've already fallen in love."

Jamilah laughed. "I bet you have."

"Do you wanna drive it?" Darius asked as he stepped up to the driver's side.

"Yeah, but not right now. I just want to sit in it right now. I love this car and I've always wanted to ride in one." She opened the passenger door and climbed in. "I never imagined I'd have an opportunity to actually drive one, too."

"Well, just let me know when you want to get behind the wheel," Darius said as he climbed into the car. "Ready to roll?"

"Yup, let's do it."

Darius and Jamilah arrived at his parents' home at approximately two-thirty that afternoon. They had made two stops along the way; the first to have breakfast, the second to take pictures on the Chesapeake Bay Bridge-Tunnel. He pulled into their driveway at the same instant his brother-in-law, Jason, stepped out of the house to retrieve his family's bags from the trunk of Mr. Thornton's Cadillac.

"Hey, what's up, D? Long time, no see, man," Jason called as he stepped off the porch and over to Darius' car. "Damn, that's a fly ride. When'd you get this?"

"What's up, Jason?" The two men embraced warmly as Jamilah stepped from the car. "It's on loan," Darius said in response to Jason's last question.

"On loan? Damn, it's good to know people, huh?" Jason said with a smug smile.

"Hey, what can I say?" Darius shrugged and laughed. "Jason, this is my friend, Jamilah. Jamilah, this is Brianne's husband."

"Hi, Jason. Nice to meet you," Jamilah responded.

"Nice to meet you, too, Jamilah. I've heard a lot about you."

"Me?" she questioned, genuinely surprised.

"Yeah. You're the young lady who was nursing my man back to health last year when he got shot, right?" Jason asked.

Before she could answer, Darius jumped in. "The one and only." He looked at her with an affectionate smile on his lips.

Jamilah could not help but blush.

"Jamilah! Hi!" Brianne came running off the porch and straight to her with open arms.

"Hi, Brianne," Jamilah said happily. She returned Brianne's warm embrace.

"Darius didn't tell me you were coming with him." Brianne turned to Darius and asked, "How come you didn't tell me she was coming with you?"

"I'm fine, thanks, sis. How you doin'?"

Brianne playfully punched him in the arm. "Hi, Darius." She went up on her toes and he bent down so she could kiss his cheek. "I'm fine, but how come you didn't tell me Jamilah was coming with you?"

"Because it was kind of a last-minute thing."

Brianne suddenly noticed the car. "Wow! When'd you get this car?"

"He borrowed it," Jason informed her.

"From who?"

"You mean, from whom," Darius corrected her facetiously.

"Oh, shut up. Who let you hold their brand-new Mercedes? This is brand-new, isn't it?"

"Yes, it is. I'm thinking about buying it so a dealer friend of mine let me use it for the weekend."

"You mean, you drove it all the way down here, and you haven't made up your mind whether you're going to buy it or not?" Brianne asked incredulously.

"Yeah, I'll probably buy it."

"Damn, this is fly," Brianne said as she stepped closer to the car.

"It is beautiful, isn't it?" Jamilah agreed.

"Yes." She stared at the car in awe for a few seconds longer before she turned her attention back to Jamilah. "So how are you, Jamilah? I'm so glad you came down."

"I'm all right," Jamilah answered with a sincere smile. "How have you been?"

"I've been okay. My kids are driving me crazy." As she lowered her voice and pointed at Jason, she added, "Especially the big one over there," (resuming her normal tone) "but I'm doing good," she answered with a big smile.

"That's good."

"Where were you heading, Jason?" Darius asked.

"Oh, I was just coming to get our bags out of Daddy's trunk. We just got here a little while ago ourselves," Jason answered.

"Where're the kids?"

"They're inside with Mommy. She's stuffing them with cookies and milk, already," Brianne said. She grabbed Jamilah's arm in hers and said, "Come on in, Jamilah. Mommy's gonna be so happy to see you."

The girls went inside as Darius moved to his trunk and opened it to remove his and Jamilah's bags.

"She's pretty, D."

"I know."

"So you finally took Brianne's advice, huh?"

"What advice?"

"You know, to hook up with her," Jason clarified.

Darius was slow in comprehending, then responded, "Oh, no. It's not like that. We're just friends, man. There's nothing happenin' like that between us."

"Why not? I'm assuming you're not seeing anyone else since you brought her with you. So why not?"

"Because we're friends." He closed the trunk of the car and moved away with their bags in tow.

"Yeah, and…"

"And, nothing."

Jason stared at Darius for a long moment before he spoke again.

"What?" Darius asked when he noticed the way Jason was looking at him.

"You know, D, you should really think about settling down. You're getting kinda old."

"Maybe, but I'll never be as old as you are," Darius said, laughing. Jason was a year older than he was.

"Don't you wanna have kids?" Jason then asked as he stepped over to his father-in-law's car and opened the trunk.

"Yeah, and I plan to get married one day, too."

"So what's wrong with Jamilah? I think she's a beautiful sister, man, and from what I hear, you two are pretty tight."

"There's nothing wrong with Jamilah. We just…we're…friends, that's all."

"You've never thought about the possibility of anything more with her. I mean friends make the best lovers. Look at Brianne and me. We were best friends for a long time before we hooked up, and I don't mind telling you, I'm sorry I waited as long as I did. Even though your sister can get on my last nerve sometimes, I wouldn't trade her for all the money in the world. And just like you, I was scared that if we hooked up, things would change between us but they didn't. It just got better, man."

"Jason, that's all well and good for you. I'm not worried about anything changing between Jamilah and me. We just... She's not interested in me like that," Darius said as he helped Jason remove a suitcase from the car's trunk.

"But you're interested in her, I take it."

"I didn't say that."

"You didn't say you weren't, either."

"Look, Jason, Jamilah and I are friends. Let's just leave it at that. I didn't come down here to be hooked up or anything like that and neither did she. We're happy with our relationship just the way it is, thank you."

"All right," Jason said with a shrug of his shoulders as he closed the trunk and picked up his bags.

The two men started toward the house without another word on the subject.

# Chapter 28

It was just before sunset that Saturday evening and Jamilah was sitting on the front porch with Brianne, enjoying the serene tranquility of rural life. Darius and Jason had gone out earlier that afternoon to greet some of the out-of-town relatives who were staying at a hotel in the city, and had not yet returned. Brianne and Jason's two children, Brandon and Tara, were playing with some of the neighborhood children in the yard next door.

"You know, Brianne, even though it's real quiet where I live, this is so much more peaceful."

"Yeah, I think because it's just a slower pace down here overall," Brianne responded.

"Probably."

"Even where we are in Detroit, it's not this peaceful. There are a lot of private homes where Jason and I live, but there's still a lot going on all the time."

"You girls mind the company of an old lady," Mrs. Thornton suddenly asked them as she stepped out of the screened door and onto the porch.

"No, we don't mind. Do you see one coming?" Brianne asked.

"I was gonna say," Jamilah added with a chuckle.

"Oh, now, y'all don't have to try and humor me. Ain't no shame in my game," Mrs. Thornton quipped.

Both women laughed.

Mrs. Thornton sat down in the rocker next to Jamilah. "It sure is a beautiful night tonight," she said.

"It sure is," agreed Jamilah.

"I'm really glad you decided to come down with Darius, Jamilah. Did he tell you that I always ask about you when he calls?"

"Yes, he did," she answered with a smile.

"I'm so happy that you two are in touch again. He really missed having you to talk to."

Jamilah blushed at Mrs. Thornton's revelation but added, "I missed him, too. You know what's funny is that my girlfriend had seen him a couple of times before that night we ran into each other, and she thought he was Denzel Washington."

"Denzel Washington?" Brianne hollered. "Oh, please!"

Mrs. Thornton laughed. "Is that right?"

"Yup. Brianne, he kinda favors Denzel."

"In his dreams. Hmph, Darius wished he looked that good," Brianne replied.

"Well, personally, I think your brother looks better than Denzel," Jamilah stated.

"That's 'cause you're in love with him."

Jamilah's mouth fell open with Brianne's last remark. Feeling her face heat up in embarrassment and wanting to deny what Brianne had just said, the words would not come.

"Don't look so shocked, Jamilah. Did you think I couldn't tell? It's written all over your face every time you look at him."

"It is?"

"Yes."

Jamilah's shoulders slumped at this bit of information. She had no idea that her feelings for him were so transparent.

Brianne reached over and took Jamilah's hand. "Honey, I'm not trying to embarrass you. I think it's wonderful. I can't think of anyone I'd rather have as my sister-in-law."

"I don't think that'll ever happen," Jamilah said sadly.

"Why? You think he doesn't feel the same way? He does—even if he hasn't told you yet, even if he hasn't admitted it to himself."

"I think you're wrong, Brianne."

"Mommy, would you tell her."

Mrs. Thornton smiled knowingly but it was a few seconds before she actually spoke. "He cares about you very much, sweetheart," she finally said in a soft voice.

"I don't know."

"I do," she continued. "He wouldn't have brought you here if he didn't. That I know for a fact."

"That's right," Brianne agreed.

Jamilah sighed. "I know he loves me, but it's as a friend."

"I don't know. I think it's a little more. Have you ever told him how you feel?" Brianne asked.

"No!"

"Why not?"

"I couldn't do that."

"I think you should. I think he needs to know."

"Brianne, don't say anything to him," Jamilah begged.

"I won't."

"Promise me."

"I promise, Jamilah. I won't say anything."

"Isn't that Jimmy?" Mrs. Thornton suddenly said.

A dark blue Lexus had just pulled into the driveway behind Mr. Thornton's car. An extremely handsome brown-skinned man stepped out of the vehicle. He was wearing a white T-shirt with the words PROUD TO BE BLACK emblazoned in black letters across the front. His long legs were enclosed in a pair of white denim jeans and spotless white sneakers were on his feet.

"Hey, Aunt Mary!" he called as he stepped up to the porch, taking the six steps two at a time. "How you doin', lovely?"

"Hi, baby," Mrs. Thornton said with a broad smile as her nephew leaned over and kissed her cheek.

"Hey, Jimmy."

"What's up, baby girl?" he said as he stepped over to Brianne's chair. She rose and gave him a big hug and kiss, which he readily reciprocated as he lifted her off her feet. "How you doin', sweetheart? It's good to see you."

"You, too," Brianne said brightly. "How you doin'?"

"I'm fine."

"You sure are," Brianne teased.

"Hello, lovely," he addressed Jamilah.

"Hello," she said with a shy smile.

"Jamilah, this is my cousin, James. Jimmy, this is Darius' friend, Jamilah."

He extended his hand as he said, "My pleasure, Jamilah. You know Darius and I have always been a bit competitive with one another. I can't believe he didn't tell me that he had such a beautiful woman in his life. I'm jealous."

Jamilah blushed and said, "Thank you, but Darius and I are just friends," as she shook his hand.

"Is that right?" James said as his left eyebrow rose slightly. "Then my cousin's not as smart as I thought he was."

"Watch out, Jamilah. My cousin can be very charming when he wants to be," Brianne said with a chuckle.

He turned to her, although he still had not released Jamilah's hand, and said, "I like to think I'm always charming."

"You know, Jamilah, if he wasn't so sweet, I'd tell you to watch out for his swelling head, but he really is quite humble. Most of the time," Brianne said good-naturedly.

Jamilah laughed.

"So where is my cousin?" James asked as he finally released her hand and leaned against the porch rail.

"He and Jason went out a while ago," Mrs. Thornton volunteered. "I thought they would've been back by now."

"You mean to tell me, Jamilah, that he brought you all the way down here from New York City, and then ran off and left you. I'm gonna have to talk to him about that," James said with a sly smile.

"It's okay," Jamilah said.

"No, I taught him better than that."

She laughed.

James Thornton was the oldest son of Mr. Thornton's youngest brother. He and Darius were the same age and from the time he was fourteen years old, after his father had died, James had lived with Darius' family.

James' mother had died when he was a baby and when his father remarried five years later, his stepmother, grudgingly, became his guardian. Due to the extremely strained relationship he had with his stepmother, through no fault of his own, when his father died, James begged his uncle Fredrick to let him stay with his family until he could move out on his own. Fredrick and Mary Thornton had been more than happy to take James in. James had always been a pleasant, well-behaved child, and they knew about the unfair treatment he received from his stepmother.

Currently, James was an African-American History professor at Norfolk State University. Since he was not married, he was also one of the most eligible bachelors in town.

When Darius and Jason returned a little over an hour later, they and James greeted each other enthusiastically. The three men, along with Darius' father, sat in the den talking while Jamilah helped Brianne get her children ready for bed.

An hour into the conversation, James asked, "So how come you never told me about Jamilah, Darius?"

"What should I have told you about her?" Darius responded.

"You know," James said as he hit Jason on his knee, conspiratorially, and winked at his Uncle Fred. "That you were seeing such a fine sister."

Jason smiled knowingly and Mr. Thornton looked over at Darius, awaiting a response.

"I'm not seeing her."

"Why not?"

"What do you mean, 'why not'?"

"I mean, why not? You're single. She's single, she's intelligent, she's fine and baby's got back and front. Y'all are obviously tight. I mean, you brought her all the way down here…"

"And she helped nurse you back to health when you got shot," Jason chimed.

"Oh yeah?" James asked, turning to Jason.

"She sure did. She was at that hospital with him every day he was in there," Mr. Thornton added.

"Well, there you go. She obviously cares about you, too. So how come you two aren't…you know," James said, smiling deviously.

Darius huffed agitatedly. "Look, Jamilah and I are friends and that's the way we like it."

"That's not what I hear," Jason said.

"What do you hear?" Darius challenged.

"I hear that she'd like to be more than your friend."

"Oh, yeah? And where'd you hear that?"

"Brianne told me."

"She told me the same thing," Mr. Thornton said.

"Brianne doesn't know what Jamilah wants. They don't talk. Today's the first time she's seen Brianne since they met last year. What would Brianne know?"

"Come on, Darius, you know how women talk amongst themselves. Brianne's your sister. She's the most likely person Jamilah would talk to about something like that," James stated.

"Yeah, but you don't know Jamilah. She's not your typical woman. She's very private. And besides, if that was what she wanted, she would've told me. We're like this," Darius said as he held up his hand with his index and middle fingers crossed.

"Exactly the point. As close as you are, she'd be the perfect woman for you to hook up with," Jason said.

"Look, y'all, we're fine the way we are."

"You're not attracted to her?" James asked.

"What?"

"You heard what I said."

"Not like you think," Darius lied.

James chuckled. "You know, Cuz, I'll tell you what. Since you're not interested in her, I'm gonna ask her if we can get to know each other 'cause I like her. I'm sure I don't have to tell you how awesome she is. I think she's beautiful, man..." (Mr. Thornton nodded his head in agreement.) "...and I'd really like to get to know her. I talked to her for a little while before y'all came back and I like where her head is."

Darius stared at his cousin for a long moment before he responded. Eventually, he shrugged his shoulders and said, "Hey, go for it." Inside, however, his stomach tightened anxiously. Had anyone else told him what his cousin just had, Darius wouldn't have given it any merit, but with James he had reason to worry. He knew the caliber of man his cousin was and from the conversation that he and Jamilah had had a while back, Darius knew that James was the type of man she could love and he knew, too, that his cousin would cherish her for being the special woman she was.

*Why don't you just admit what your feelings are for her*, he asked himself.

Jamilah was a beautiful woman, like James said, and she deserved to be treated as such. Darius knew if he had the chance, he would do anything for her, anything that he thought would make her happy. Unfortunately for him, however, he knew that James would, too. Now it looked as though he would lose his chance.

James noticed that Darius had suddenly become quite pensive. He was sure his uncle had noticed the change, too. James and Darius were like two heads of the same coin, and he had a feeling that Darius was not being completely honest with him about his feelings for Jamilah.

"Yo, D, are you all right with that?" James asked.

"Yeah," Darius answered too quickly. He rose suddenly from his seat.

"Where you goin'?" James asked.

"I'll be back."

Darius headed out of the den. As he started up the stairs, his mother called to him from the kitchen. "Darius, honey, are you going to church with us in the morning?"

"Yeah, Mom."

He continued up the stairs. Jamilah was staying in his old room. From the quiet he encountered, he surmised that she, Brianne and the kids were already in bed. The half-inch crack under the bedroom door, however, let him know that the light was still on in Jamilah's room. He tapped lightly on the door.

"Come in," she called from the other side.

He opened the door slowly and stuck his head inside. "Hey."

"Hi. Come on in." She was wearing a pink satin robe over a matching nightgown.

"I see you're ready to turn in," he said as he entered the room.

"Yeah, just about."

"I was gonna ask if you felt like going out for a while, but I guess not."

"No, I'm kind of tired."

Darius stood across the room with his hands tucked into the pockets of his jeans. Jamilah sensed a bit of apprehension.

"I hope my old bed is comfortable enough for you," Darius said as he stepped over to the bed and patted the mattress.

"I'm sure it will be," she said with a smile.

Jamilah moved to the bed and sat down at the end. Darius stood in front of her. It was unmistakable; there was tension emanating from him that had never been there before.

After a few seconds, Darius said, "I'm really glad that you decided to come down here with me."

Her smile brightened as she answered, "I am, too, Darius. Thank you for inviting me. I love being here with your family. They're so nice to me."

"That's because they all like you so much."

"Well, the feeling is mutual."

His next words were so unexpected that she was nearly floored by them. "As a matter of fact, I was just downstairs talking to my cousin. He likes you, too. He told me that he'd like to get to know you. I remember when we were talking a few weeks ago, you were saying you'd like to meet someone who would respect you as a person, and he would. He's a good guy. I think if you got to know him, you'd really like him, too," Darius said quickly.

Jamilah didn't know how to respond. She looked down at her hands in her lap in an attempt to hide the dismay she was feeling in her heart. He was basically pushing her toward James. *Doesn't he know it's him I want to be with?*

"I just thought I'd warn you. He'll probably try to hit on you tomorrow," Darius continued in a matter-of-fact manner.

She had to force a smile when she said, "Thanks. To be forewarned is to be forearmed."

"Yeah."

"So, how are you and Brianne going to pull this off tomorrow?" Jamilah asked to change the subject.

"I'm going to call James when we're on our way to church. He and his sister are going to come by and set everything up and get my other relatives here before we get back from church. When we're on our way back, I'll call him and let him know."

"Did you get a cake?"

"Oh, my Aunt Teresa is bringing the cake. This woman can bake, Jamilah. We're always telling her she should open a bakery. I don't even know what the cake is going to look like, but I can guarantee it will be beautiful and it'll taste awesome," Darius said enthusiastically.

"Who's doing the cooking, though?"

"My other cousins and my aunts who live here. I have a huge family, Jamilah. You'll only be meeting part of it tomorrow, and you'll probably be overwhelmed by them."

"It sounds like it should be fun."

"That it will." Once again, there was a weighted silence between them for a few seconds. "Well, I'ma let you go to bed," Darius finally said, although he made no move toward the door. "You're coming with us to church tomorrow, right?"

"Yes."

"Good. Okay, so I'll see you in the morning."

"Okay." She stood in front of him.

Darius leaned closer and kissed her cheek. "Good night, Jamilah."

"Good night."

He was at the door when he turned back and said, "I'm really glad you're here."

She smiled, although she wanted to cry.

Once he was gone, Jamilah removed her robe and laid it on the foot of the bed, then walked alongside it and turned off the lamp on the nightstand. Climbing into bed and pulling the sheet up to her neck, she lay in the darkness thinking of what Darius had told her about James. Granted, he was very handsome. He and Darius actually looked more like brothers than cousins, and he seemed like a genuinely nice person. Brianne said he was, but she wasn't interested in James. Darius, however, seemed to think he would be good for her. *Why doesn't he think he's good for me?* Tears slid from her eyes down the sides of her face as she stared up at the ceiling. She was in love with Darius but it was obvious to her now that the feeling was not mutual.

She was sorry that she had agreed to come here with him.

# Chapter 29

Jamilah awoke Sunday morning to the smell of bacon frying and homemade biscuits baking in the oven downstairs.

Sometime during the night she'd resigned herself to the fact that she and Darius would never be anything more than friends. She was content to settle for that—for the time being, anyway.

She climbed out of the extremely comfortable bed and reached for her bathrobe. Gathering her underwear and toiletries from her overnight bag, she grabbed the towel and washcloth Brianne had given her last night and headed for the bathroom across the hall. She didn't hear the kids, so she assumed that they were either downstairs or still asleep. *Maybe I can sneak into the bathroom before everyone else gets up.*

As she stood under the spray of the shower minutes later, Jamilah reflected on her relationship with Darius from the time they first met when he was dating Sabrina, up to now. She reasoned that if they were really meant to be more than friends, it would happen naturally. There was no sense in her trying to force the issue, although she had never tried to do any such thing. On the contrary, maybe the reason Darius didn't show any interest in her was because she had never really shown him that she was interested in him. Brianne had asked her if she'd told Darius how she felt. She still couldn't fathom actually doing so. Despite how close they were and how comfortable she felt around him, when it came to baring her soul to him—with regard to him—she just didn't have the guts.

Darius told her last night that James was interested in her. Should she settle for second best? Granted, James did appear to be a genuinely sweet man and he had a great sense of humor, aside from being just as handsome as Darius. Jamilah was sure that if he wasn't well intentioned, Darius would have never mentioned it to her or, if anything, he would have warned her off, but he seemed to encourage her getting to know James. Would it be fair to James, though, to appear receptive to any advances he might make without being honest with him about her feelings for Darius? Seeing as how he and Darius were so close, could she really consider James as a likely candidate for dating, knowing that her true feelings were for his cousin?

When Jamilah stepped out of the bathroom and into the hall after her shower, she almost collided with Darius. He grabbed her to steady her. She was surprised to see that he was fully dressed. His white shirt and gray silk tie handsomely accentuated his navy blue slacks that she was sure were half of one of the many custom-tailored suits he owned.

"Oh, sorry," he said quickly. "I was just coming up to wake you. Breakfast is ready."

"Is everyone up already?" Jamilah asked in astonishment.

"Yup."

"Oh, my God. I thought I was the first one up."

Darius laughed. "No. Kind of the other way around."

"Oh, no."

Placing a comforting hand on her shoulder, he said, "Hey, don't worry about it, J. You're a guest and you were obviously sleeping very well. I'm glad my old bed was so comfortable."

"It was very comfortable. Let me go in here and get dressed. I'll be down in a minute."

"Take your time, Jamilah. Don't rush. I'll save you some food," he said with a smile.

Smiling back, "Make sure you do."

She hurried into the bedroom and closed the door. As she pulled her off-white sleeveless dress from the closet, she smiled, acknowledging how grateful she was to have a friend like Darius in her life. He was someone who loved and respected her for who she was, and whom she could count on in good times and in bad. In this day and age, she reasoned, that was quite a lot to be thankful for.

\*\*\*

Slightly embarrassed as she entered the dining room and saw everyone seated around the table, Jamilah said, "Good morning, everybody. I'm sorry I slept so late."

"Don't apologize, Jamilah. I'm glad you felt cozy enough here that you could rest. Some people just can't sleep in a strange bed," Mrs. Thornton replied.

"Well, that bed felt like home," Jamilah remarked as she took the empty seat next to Darius.

"Whenever Darius comes home and sleeps in there, it's usually twelve o'clock before he can drag himself out of that bed. I think that's the most comfortable bed in the house," Mr. Thornton added.

"See how privileged you are, Jamilah? You got the best bed in the house," Darius teased.

She chuckled before she said, "Well, I do feel privileged. I just want you to know, Mr. and Mrs. Thornton, I really appreciate your having me here."

"You're always welcome here, Jamilah," Mrs. Thornton warmly assured her.

"Thank you. And, by the way, Happy Anniversary."

"Thank you, dear," Darius' parents responded.

Jamilah didn't miss the look of love that passed between Mr. and Mrs. Thornton. It warmed her heart to be with his family at such a special time in their lives.

\*\*\*

The family left for church not long after breakfast at twenty minutes to eleven. Brianne and Jason piled into Mr. Thornton's 1989 Cadillac Eldorado along with their children and Mrs. Thornton. Darius and Jamilah followed in his Mercedes. As they were en route to the church that Brianne and Darius had attended as children, Darius reached for his car phone.

"Who're you calling?" Jamilah asked.

"James, to let him know the coast is clear."

"Oh, yeah."

"Hey, dude," Darius said brightly. "The coast is clear. We're on our way to church now." Listening for a moment, he then continued, "Yeah, go by the hotel and pick up Aunt Jean and them before you head over. I'll give you a call at the house when we're ready to head back." He listened again for a few seconds. "All right. See you later."

As Darius replaced the receiver in its holder just below the dashboard, he said to Jamilah, "James said hi."

Noticing that he kept his eyes on the road when he spoke, once again, like last night, she felt tension between them. She got the feeling that Darius was uneasy with his cousin's interest in her, but she wasn't sure if that was just her imagination or, in fact, the real case. If that was the case though, why would he encourage her to talk to him?

✳✳✳

The church service lasted for a little over two hours. Since Mr. and Mrs. Thornton had been members of the church for almost as long as they had been married, the pastor made an announcement to the congregation that it was their fortieth wedding anniversary. His sermon had to do with the sanctity of the institution of marriage and honoring God's laws.

Although the service ended just after one o'clock, because of the occasion of Mr. and Mrs. Thornton's anniversary, combined with the popularity of the Thornton family and Darius' and Brianne's visit, it was almost an hour before the family was able to get away from the church. It was five minutes to two when everyone started back to the house.

Darius picked up his car phone and dialed his parents' number. "Hey, who's this?" he said when the call was answered. He listened for the response. "Hey, Aunt Tee. How you doin', sweetheart? I'm fine. We're on our way back. We'll be there in about fifteen minutes. Is everything set up? Good. Okay, see you in a few."

"Everything's set," Darius said, looking over at Jamilah with a bright smile. "They're going to be so surprised."

"They really don't suspect anything, do they?"

"Nope. I can't believe we pulled this off. I was sure someone at church would have let it slip."

"Does the pastor know about it?"

"Oh, yeah. He'll be there; so will a good portion of the congregation."

"Wow. This is going to be great," Jamilah said with a bright smile.

"Yeah, it is." He looked over at Jamilah with satisfaction. Then, reaching over, he caressed her face. "I'm really glad you're going to be a part of it."

*See, there he goes again, doing something to make me fall deeper in love with him.* She was so choked up at that moment that she couldn't even speak.

Darius and Jamilah arrived back at the house two minutes before his parents. As soon as he was parked, Darius rushed inside to make sure everything was as it should be.

His Aunt Teresa greeted them. "Hey, baby. Where are they?"

Darius stepped up to his aunt and hugged her as he kissed her cheek. "Right behind me, Aunt Tee."

"Hello, sweetheart. You must be Jamilah. I've heard so much about you from Darius and James that I feel like I know you already."

"Hello," Jamilah said, smiling anxiously. Her eyes darted back and forth from Darius to his aunt. She noticed that he suddenly seemed a bit uncomfortable.

Aunt Teresa was a big woman. She stood just a couple of inches shorter than Jamilah and was quite round. She was the youngest of Mrs. Thornton's four living siblings, all of whom, Darius informed her, would be present today. Aunt Teresa was dark-skinned with a round, cherubic face and a beautiful, bright smile. Jamilah could understand Aunt Tee having heard about her from Darius, but she wondered what James had told her. Just then, the front door opened and in ran Brianne's children.

"Hi, Aunt Tee!" Brandon and Tara screamed as they ran straight into the arms of their great-aunt.

"Hi, babies. How're my sugarplums? My goodness, you've both grown so much."

Mrs. Thornton was right behind the children. "Tee, what are you doin' here?" she said to her sister.

"Hi, Mary. Oh, I just thought I'd come by for a while to visit," Aunt Tee said as she openly winked at Darius and Jamilah.

They both laughed.

"What you winking at them for?" Mrs. Thornton asked with a frown as she put her pocketbook on the foyer mantle.

Aunt Tee ignored her sister's query and asked, "Where's Fred?"

"He's coming in."

"How was the service?"

"It was good. How come you weren't there this morning?" Mrs. Thornton asked as she moved to the living room. The French-doors that opened to the living room were closed. "How come these doors are closed?" she asked as she reached and pushed them open.

"SURPRISE!!"

Mrs. Thornton stood in the door with her hand on her hip and looked around the room. Her other sister, Jean, and her husband, Tom; and her two brothers, Willie and Robert, and their wives were all present, along with James and a few other relatives.

"What's all this commotion I hear?" Mr. Thornton said as he came into the house. "Mary, who's making all that noise? Hey, Tee, what you doin' here?"

"It's good to see you, too, Fred," Aunt Tee said with her hand on her hip.

Meanwhile, Mrs. Thornton was still standing in the doorway. "What y'all trying to do? Give somebody a heart attack with all that noise."

"Happy Anniversary, Mom and Dad," Darius said from behind his mother as he put his arms around her waist and kissed her cheek.

"Thank you, baby," she said as she turned and smiled at him. "Freddie, ain't this nice. The kids done thrown us a surprise party."

"Yeah, it is nice, even though it wasn't no surprise," Mr. Thornton answered.

Brianne came up behind him and said, "What you mean, it's no surprise? You didn't know about it, did you, Daddy?"

Mr. Thornton put his arm around Brianne's shoulder and kissed her on her temple as he said, "Yeah, we did, baby. But it's nice that y'all did this anyway."

"Who told you?" Darius wanted to know.

"It don't matter none, baby," Mrs. Thornton said with a wave of her hand. "This is real nice of you. Thank you, babies." She reached for Brianne and hugged her and Darius. "You both make us very proud."

Jamilah was becoming so emotional at witnessing this scene that her eyes began to water and her cheek muscles began to throb from smiling so hard.

Darius then hugged his father and kissed his cheek. "We're pretty darn proud of you, too."

When Darius released his father and turned to Jamilah, he noticed the tears in her eyes. "Are you crying?" he asked as he stepped over to her.

"Yeah. This is so nice," she said with a big smile.

He chuckled as he wrapped her in a warm hug. "You are just too sweet, you know." She looked up at him and blushed.

Mr. and Mrs. Thornton went into the living room to greet their guests as Darius put an arm around Jamilah's shoulder and said to Brianne, "Let's go out here and make sure they did everything I asked them to before Mom and Dad come out."

Jamilah was nearly flabbergasted when she stepped into the kitchen with Darius and Brianne. There seemed to be food everywhere.

Their paternal Aunt Millie was busy carving an abnormally large roasted turkey that was stuffed with a delicious-looking dressing. It seemed as if his aunts and cousins had cooked everything under the sun. The menu consisted of baked macaroni and cheese, collard greens cooked with ham-hocks, black-eyed peas with okra, fried chicken, barbecue baby-back ribs, barbecue chicken, corn pudding, candied yams, cornbread and homemade dinner rolls just to name a few. An incredibly sweet-smelling peach cobbler sat in the middle of the dining room table simply begging Jamilah to eat it.

After being introduced to Darius and Brianne's aunt and conversing with her for a few minutes, Darius and Jamilah proceeded out the back door to the yard. One of his cousins was already at the grill turning a slab of ribs.

# Chapter 30

J amilah was having a wonderful time. Darius' family was warm, welcoming and funny, despite steadily trying to make her and Darius' relationship more than it was. She took it all in stride, however, actually hoping that their persistence in goading Darius about her would, in fact, give him a nudge in her direction. Nonetheless, she didn't take it too seriously. She was convinced that whatever was meant for her and Darius would come to fruition.

About two hours into the festivities and just as she was about to go upstairs and change from the dress she had worn to church into something more casual, Jamilah encountered a sight that caused her heart to crumble like shards of broken glass. Darius stood just inside the front door of the house in a very familiar and seemingly comfortable embrace with a woman she had never seen before. The two of them gazed into each other's eyes the way lovers do, their faces reflecting the mutual joy of being together, obviously, once again.

Jamilah was halted in her tracks by the observation. Although she tried to will herself to continue on her original course, she was rooted in place. Her left hand rested on the balustrade and her right foot was planted lightly on the first step leading to the second floor. *Is this why you have no room for me in your heart, Darius?* The woman reminded her of Sabrina. Not that she looked like her, but her stature and physical style, from what Jamilah could see, were so like Sabrina's.

The woman was not really that tall, at least not as tall as Sabrina, but she wore heels that had to be at least four inches high, which made it much easier to reach Darius' luscious lips with her own. The dress she wore clung to her body and her ample bosom was pressed close to Darius, as was the rest of her frontal form. Tendrils of long, light brown curls flowed softly down her back. Her skin was fair and her face was lightly made up, although her lips sparkled with the red color plastered there.

Unconscious that she had been staring at them, Jamilah was startled when the woman turned to her with a look of annoyance. Suddenly overwhelmed with embarrassment, Jamilah quickly started up the stairs, but was stopped on the third step by Darius' call. Turning reluctantly, she watched as Darius started toward her with the woman holding tight to his hand. She was beautiful, Jamilah noticed, and definitely what she had concluded was Darius' type.

"Jamilah, I want you to meet my friend, Lauren Taylor. Lauren, this is Jamilah Parsons. She rode down with me from New York," Darius said in a matter-of-fact tone.

"Hi," Jamilah said with a nervous smile.

"Hello, Jamilah," Lauren said, full of righteous indignation as she smirked at her. "I didn't know Darius had brought his girlfriend down with him. I hope you didn't get the wrong idea about what you just witnessed between us. It's just that we haven't seen each other in so long, and it's always so good to see him." She looked up at him with a sweet smile.

"I'm not his girlfriend. We're just friends," Jamilah quickly explained.

"Oh, how fortunate for me," she purred as she turned to Darius and put her free arm around his waist.

Darius, slightly embarrassed by Lauren's flirtatious manner, glanced up at Jamilah and added, "We used to be joined at the hip."

Jamilah tried to smile, but she felt it was probably more a grimace of pain. Hurriedly excusing herself, she muttered, "Well, I was just going upstairs to change. It was nice meeting you." She didn't wait for either of them to respond, but quickly ascended the stairs, seeking the comfort of Darius' old bedroom.

Falling on the bed as tears she couldn't contain flowed from her eyes, jealousy raged in Jamilah's heart and a feeling of self-pity overcame her so strongly, she felt as if she would just die. *Why do I love him so much? Why can't I just accept that he doesn't want me? You're not his type, Jamilah. When are you going to wake up and realize that?* Mentally beating herself up for the next few minutes, she felt so dejected that she didn't even want to return to the party. Unable to face Darius, the thought of seeing him with the woman, Lauren, again would be unbearable. She figured Lauren had picked up on her distress and would probably do anything she could to mock her.

After about twenty minutes, there was a knock on the bedroom door. Not wanting to see anyone, she figured if she didn't answer, whoever was knocking might just walk in, assuming the room was empty. It could be Mr. or Mrs. Thornton, after all.

"Come in," she called listlessly.

"Oh, there you are. What're you doing up here? The party's downstairs," Brianne said brightly as she entered the room and closed the door behind her.

"I just came up to change," Jamilah said truthfully, although she made no move to rise from the bed to get the clothes she had planned to change into.

"Are you okay?" Brianne asked worriedly.

Jamilah nodded her head without looking at Brianne.

She immediately sat down on the bed next to Jamilah. "What's wrong, honey?"

"Nothing," Jamilah answered with a shake of her head.

"Jamilah, talk to me," Brianne urged as she took one of her hands in both of hers. "What's wrong?"

Jamilah tried to smile despite the pools of tears in her eyes and the pain in her heart. "I'm just...I'm feeling a little sorry for myself right now, that's all." She chuckled mirthlessly.

"Why?"

"I don't know. I've got nothing better to do."

Finally, she rose from the bed and moved to her overnight bag. Pulling a pair of khaki shorts and a white polo shirt from the bag, she tossed them carelessly on the bed, then turned her back to Brianne. "Would you unzip me, please?"

Brianne stood and pulled the zipper down on her dress.

In a melancholy tone, Jamilah stated, "I met Darius' friend, Lauren. They used to go out, huh?"

"They were engaged."

That bit of information only added insult to her mental injury.

"What happened?" Jamilah wanted to know.

"They couldn't get along. They used to fight like cats and dogs. They went to law school together and even though they dated for close to three years, they just couldn't get along. They used to have some of the worst arguments, it was ridiculous. When Darius told us that they were planning to get married, Mommy and Daddy lit into him like you wouldn't believe. They told him he needed to have his head examined if he seriously planned to marry her."

"They must have really loved each other," Jamilah surmised.

"I don't know what was up with them. One minute they were all over each other; the next minute, they weren't speaking. It was so stupid. I think it was the lawyer thing, or something. Their points of view have always been so different; then with that argumentative nature they both have, it was like...oil and water."

"Well, he sure looked happy to see her," Jamilah pointed out.

"They're always like that when they haven't seen each other in a long time, but they can't spend any real time together."

"Do you think he might want to try again?"

"No," Brianne quickly answered with a wave of her hand. "Is that what you're worried about?"

"No!"

"Jamilah, Lauren is history. There's nothing between them anymore and hasn't been for years. Believe me."

"I'm not worried about that," she lied.

# Chapter 31

After nearly an hour, Jamilah had finally returned from her safe haven in the house. Brianne had spent nearly fifteen minutes trying to convince her that she had nothing to fear from Lauren, and she wanted desperately to believe her. When she finally stepped out of the house and onto the back porch, she saw that Darius and Lauren were seated together. *Probably catching up on old times,* Jamilah figured. Seeing them together did nothing to assure her that Brianne's words were true, but she tried hard to ignore them as she descended into the yard.

She moved to one of the many buffet tables and fixed herself a plate of light fare, then found a seat on the far side of the yard near some of Darius' relatives. As she ate, she made small talk with them for a while until they were called away for various reasons. Despite the displeasure at having witnessed Darius with the woman who, quite possibly, was his first true love and probably still a very special person in his life, Jamilah could not deny the overall feeling of happiness she felt being around the Thornton family on such a special occasion. They all made her feel so welcome and very much at home.

The children were all running around and having a wonderful time. The teenagers and young adults sat around in groups, laughing and joking and probably making fun of the older adults who were dancing around like teenagers to the music flowing from the large speakers set up on opposite sides of the yard. There had to be at least seventy-odd people present, aside from those inside.

"Hello, gorgeous."

She looked up and was surprised to see James standing over her. She hadn't even noticed his approach.

"Hi," she said with a smile.

"Having fun yet?" he asked.

"Oh, yes. Definitely."

"Do you mind if I join you?" he asked.

"No, of course not."

James stepped away from her and over to where a group of his younger cousins were shooting the breeze. She overheard him when he said to one young man, "Mikey, be a sport and let an old man have your chair."

She was surprised that the young man relinquished his chair without a moment's pause. When he placed the chair next to hers and sat down, Jamilah asked him, "Does he owe you something?"

"Huh?"

"I was wondering if he owed you something. He gave up the chair so easily."

"Oh, Mikey's my nephew and we're pretty tight. He does anything I tell him to do."

"That's nice."

"Well, I look out for him and he knows that. I'd do anything for him," James confessed.

She smiled in admiration.

"So how're you feeling, Miss Jamilah?" he asked playfully.

"I'm fine."

"I didn't ask you how you looked; I asked you how you were feeling."

She blushed and shook her head. "I feel...good."

"Well, I'm glad to hear that. I'm glad you're enjoying yourself."

"I really am. You have a great family."

"Yeah, they're all right. You know, I told Darius that I was jealous because he has such a beautiful lady like you in his life. I told you we've always been competitive. We even took it so far as to tease each other about who was going to get married first and so forth. He almost won, too."

"Yeah, I met his, uh, ex," Jamilah said dolefully.

"Lauren? Yeah, they were a real funny couple. It would have never worked. Of course, everyone saw that except him. But then my cousin has always been a little slow when it comes to affairs of the heart. He has a tendency to not see what's right in front of him, you know, what's obvious to everyone else," James said unpretentiously.

"Really?" She should have known that from his history with Sabrina.

"Yeah, that's why I wasn't really surprised—well, I was, but I wasn't—when he told me that you two aren't...well, you know, an item. I figured since he'd brought you down here, you two were, uh..."

"No, we're not," Jamilah cut him off. There was a touch of sadness to her words.

James noticed, but decided to play his hand regardless. "You know, I'm going to be in New York City in two weeks. Do you think it would be possible for us to get together while I'm in town? I'd really like to get to know you, Jamilah. I have a feeling we could be very good friends, given the chance. I figure since Darius isn't smart enough to recognize what a privilege it would be to have a special woman like you, it's my duty as a single black man to do what I can to give you the praise and attention a beautiful sister like you deserves."

Jamilah regarded him thoughtfully, not quite knowing what to say. His words amazed her, and she had no doubt they were sincere, but how could she take him up on his offer without being honest with him? She had a feeling he was a man of high moral fiber, one who would be a prize for any sensible woman to latch on to, but her heart belonged to his cousin. *Why couldn't it have been Darius who offered me what James was offering?*

"James, I'd like for us to be friends, too. You seem to be a very good person and I know from what Darius and Brianne have told me about you that you're honest and loyal; everything I'm looking for in a man, really."

"But..."

Lowering her head briefly, she continued, "But...I have to be honest with you. You may think I'm foolish for holding out for a dream but, I'm..." She paused, trying to think of how to tell him that she was in love with Darius.

"You're in love with him, aren't you?" he said softly.

Her head snapped up in surprise.

His smile was as soft as a caress and his eyes were filled with a quiet understanding. "I know. I've always known, well, at least since I met you and especially once I saw you with him." Chuckling, he shook his head. "I told you he was slow. You've never told him, have you?"

"No."

"Why?"

"Because I don't want to lose him. His friendship, I mean. I cherish it deeply. If I tell him, and he doesn't feel the same way, I don't want him to be uncomfortable around me because he knows how I feel."

"What makes you think he doesn't feel the same way?"

"He doesn't."

"How do you know?"

"Because last night he told me that you were going to try to talk to me, and he thought you would be good for me. If he felt the same way about me, why would he try to encourage me to talk to you?"

"Because he doesn't have good sense, that's why. Oh, Darius." James sighed. "He's crazy about you, Jamilah. First of all, he wouldn't have brought you down here if he weren't. Second, I wish you could have seen his face when I told him that I was going to make a move on you. He tried to play it off like he didn't care, but he wanted to kill me; I could tell," he said with a laugh. "Jamilah, look at him." James tipped his head in Darius' direction. He was still sitting on the porch, but Lauren was nowhere in sight. He appeared to be looking in their direction but because he was so far away she really couldn't tell. "He's sitting up there stewing, wondering what I'm saying to you. Darius is funny. He's very honorable, really. If you... Say you'd gone along with my proposal—now I knew you wouldn't have anyway, but I had to try," James added with a mischievous smile, "...but say you'd gone along with it, he would never say anything to you about how he felt. He wouldn't say anything to me either. If it made you happy to be with me, he'd live with that. But his feelings wouldn't change for you. He'd still love you just the same."

"I know he cares about me, James, but it's not like you think."

"Jamilah, believe me, it's not like *you* think. Listen, do you want me to talk to him?"

"No!"

"Why not?"

"Please, James, don't say anything to him. Promise me."

"Are you sure?"

"Yes. Promise me you won't say anything to him."

"All right, I promise."

***

Much later that night, after all of the out-of-town relatives and most of the ones who lived in Virginia were gone and the clean-up was nearly completed, a light rain began to fall. Darius sat alone on the darkened back porch. The only light was coming from the kitchen window just behind him. James joined him after a while.

"Hey, dude," James said as he slapped Darius on his shoulder and pulled one of the many folding chairs on the porch closer to the rocker that Darius was seated in. "What's up?"

Darius shook his head. "Nothing."

"Lauren looks great."

"Yeah, she does."

"When's the last time you saw her?"

"About a year ago. When I came home last year after I got shot."

"So is she married yet?"

"She's engaged."

"Again, huh?" James said with a chuckle.

Darius laughed, too. "Yeah, maybe they'll get along better than we did."

"Well, that should be easy."

Darius nodded his head in agreement.

They sat pensively for a few minutes. "The party came off really well, didn't it?" James said, breaking their silence.

"Yeah," Darius agreed. "Did you see what Brianne and I gave them?"

"No. What'd you give them?"

"A trip to Bermuda. A cruise."

"Oh, yeah? That's great! I'm sure they'll love that."

"Yeah, they were psyched about it."

"That's great. They deserve it. I wish you had told me. I would have gone in with you on that."

"That's all right. No big deal."

Silence engulfed them again.

James was thinking about Jamilah. Feeling empathy for her, knowing how she felt about Darius and knowing that he was either blind or just plain dumb for not admitting his inner passion, he leaned over in his chair and rested his elbows on his knees to afford him a better view of Darius' face. "I spoke to Jamilah this afternoon," James finally said.

"Yeah, I know. I saw you."

"We're going to keep in touch," James said as he looked directly at Darius, waiting for a reaction.

Darius' face remained unreadable. "Oh, yeah?"

"Yeah. You know, I'm going to be up in New York in a couple of weeks. We're going to get together then."

James didn't miss the clenching of Darius' jaw at his words. "That's nice."

"I hope you'll be around. We could all hang out."

"Three's a crowd, Jimmy."

James leaned back in his seat, and in a voice dripping with sarcasm, said, "Is that right?" He stared at his cousin until he couldn't stand it anymore. "What the hell is wrong with you, Darius?"

Darius looked over at James in surprise. "What do you mean?"

"You know good and damn well what I mean. You're sitting there acting like you don't care that I'm going to see her when I come up there, but I know you do. I *know* you do!"

"Why should I care? Jamilah's a grown woman. She's entitled to see anyone she wants to see. It has nothing to do with me."

Shaking his head in exasperation, James challenged, "You're going to sit there and tell me that you don't care about that woman?"

"Of course, I care about her. She's one of my best friends," Darius admitted.

"That's not what I mean and you know it."

"Well, what do you mean?"

James sighed. "Darius, why don't you just admit that you're in love with her?

Why sit here with me, of all people, acting like she makes no difference to you? I know you don't want me to be with her. I know how you feel about her, whether you'll admit it or not. She's a beautiful woman, man, and I'm not just talking about on the outside, but you know that."

Darius rose from his seat and took a few steps away before he responded, "Look, what do you want me to do, James? You just told me you're going to see her. I'm not going to fight you over her. Besides, I don't think she would see me, anyway, if I tried to talk to her like that. I used to date her roommate, man. She's not going to go out with me, but I'm all right with that 'cause we're friends and I don't want to lose that. Our friendship means a lot to me, whether you believe that or not."

James shook his head and couldn't help chuckling. "You two are funny. Neither of you wants to lose this precious friendship you have, but both of you are dying inside because you're so certain the other is going to reject you. If your friendship is all that, hasn't it ever occurred to you that it would only get stronger if you admitted to each other that you were in love?"

"I never said I was in love with her."

"You don't have to say it! It's written all over your face—both of you. Man, I know your feelings for her are more than mere friendship, simply by the fact that she's here with you. Everyone knows that. You're not fooling anyone, Darius, except maybe Jamilah, because she's sure you're not interested in her." James suddenly sucked his teeth and swore under his breath before exhaling loudly. "Aw man, I promised her I wouldn't say anything to you."

"What?"

"She turned me down, Darius, when I asked her if we could be...friends. I mean, she said we could be friends, but that was it. She's in love with *you*, but she's so sure you don't want her. Do you know how happy she was when you asked her to come down here with you? She told me you two had a heart-to-heart talk a few weeks ago about what you were both looking for in a mate. She thought you'd pick up on the fact that she was describing you. I told her you were slow."

Darius was silent for the next few seconds as he tried to digest what his cousin had just revealed. "She really said that?"

"I've never lied to you, Darius, you know that."

Darius sighed. "I just thought…"

"That's the problem! Stop thinking so damn much and take a look at her; pay attention to what she says to you, how she responds to you. It's right there in front of you, man." James shook his head. "The woman is in love with you, Darius."

Staring at his cousin for a long moment before lowering his head, Darius couldn't contain the smile that suddenly emerged. "I've always been kinda slow, huh?"

"Like a damn turtle," James said.

"I'm going inside," Darius said after a moment.

"D, I promised her I wouldn't say anything to you."

"I won't say anything," he assured James. He moved to the back door, but when his hand touched the knob, he turned back to his cousin. "Thanks, Jimmy."

"You owe me," James said good-naturedly.

# Chapter 32

Upon entering the house after his talk with James, Darius found Jamilah in the den with his mother, Aunt Tee and Brianne. His niece, Tara, was asleep on Jamilah's lap and his nephew, Brandon, was stretched out snoring lightly on the chaise lounge.

"Is this a ladies-only conversation or can a brother participate?"

"No, brothers are welcome," Jamilah said with a smile.

Darius stepped over to the loveseat where Jamilah was seated and joined her. Taking his niece's legs and placing them on his lap, he said, "You look very comfortable like this."

Unconsciously playing in Tara's hair, she softly responded, "I am."

She looked so maternal and beautiful in that instant that he just wanted to kiss her. There were no words to express how overjoyed he was by James' revelation.

"Where's Jimmy, Darius?" Mrs. Thornton asked.

"I left him on the back porch."

"Is it still raining?" Aunt Tee asked.

"Yeah. Where's Daddy?"

"He passed out," Brianne said with a laugh.

Darius joined her. "I knew he was feeling no pain."

Mrs. Thornton was laughing when she said, "No, he certainly wasn't."

Darius gazed at his mother lovingly. "Did you have a good time, Mommy?"

"Your father and I had a wonderful time, sweetheart. I don't know how we can ever thank you two," she said, looking from him to Brianne.

"You don't have to thank us, Mommy. You deserved this after putting up with us for all these years," Brianne said.

"That's right," Darius agreed. "I just wish I knew who squealed."

"It doesn't matter who told us. It was still a surprise. I certainly wasn't expecting anything as elaborate as this," Mrs. Thornton said.

"This *was* really great, y'all," Jamilah added. "Especially since y'all weren't even here when you planned it."

"Ain't that the truth," Aunt Tee said.

"Yeah, but we couldn't have pulled this off without you, Aunt Tee," Darius noted.

"Well, I'll tell you, I think you children are something else. Your Daddy and I are very proud of you both and we really appreciate this celebration. And Jamilah, I'm so happy that you came down with Darius and was able to share in our special day," Mrs. Thornton said sincerely.

"Thank you, Mrs. T," Jamilah said with a big smile. "I'm glad I was, too."

James entered the room. "Hey, y'all. Looks like these two are out for the count, huh?" he said, referring to Brandon and Tara.

Brianne said, "Yeah, they've had a pretty full day."

Jason entered the room right behind James.

"Hey, where you been, man?" Darius asked.

"I was turning down the beds for the kids. Come on, Brie; let's get them upstairs."

"Okay." Brianne rose from her seat and moved over to Jamilah as Jason lifted Brandon into his arms.

"What time is your flight, sis?" Darius asked as Brianne lifted Tara off his and Jamilah's laps.

She turned to Jason. "Ten thirty-five, right, baby?"

"Yeah."

"Hey, y'all turning in?" James asked Jason and Brianne.

"Yeah, it's been a long day," Jason answered.

"That it has," James agreed.

Jason stepped over to where Aunt Tee was sitting and kissed her cheek. Brianne followed suit. "Bye, Aunt Tee."

"Bye, babies. Y'all have a safe trip home."

James patted Jason on the back and kissed Brianne on the cheek as they started out of the room with their children. "It was good seeing you, Brie."

Brianne stopped. "You know, you can come to Detroit and visit us sometime," she said.

"I will. I promise."

"All right. Good night, everyone," Jason said.

"Good night," they all chorused.

"Aunt Tee, you about ready to hit the road?" James asked.

"Yes, baby. I'm 'bout done in for one day," Aunt Tee answered as she lifted herself out of the chair with great effort.

Darius rose and stepped over to his aunt. He put his arms around her and said, "Thanks for everything, Aunt Tee. We couldn't have done this without you." He kissed her cheek.

"You're welcome, baby. When you told me what you wanted to do, there was no way I couldn't put in my own two cents. You know that."

Darius laughed. "I'll see you on my next trip down."

"All right, baby. You be careful driving back tomorrow."

"I will."

"And Jamilah, it was so nice to meet you, sweetheart. You come on back down here with Darius the next time he comes, all right?"

"I will, Aunt Tee," Jamilah said as she rose and gave Darius' aunt a big hug. "It was nice meeting you, too."

"All right, now, Darius, you take care of this young lady," Aunt Tee added.

"I will." Darius blushed after being captured by Jamilah's smiling eyes.

"Hey, D, what time y'all pulling out tomorrow?" James asked.

"Probably about one o'clock, something like that."

"I'll try to make it back here tomorrow morning before Brianne and Jason leave, but in case I don't, I'll definitely be here before one, so I'll see you tomorrow," James said as he extended his hand to Darius.

Darius clasped his hand and embraced James with his left arm as he responded, "All right, man."

"Open your eyes," James whispered in Darius' ear.

Darius grinned at his cousin and nodded his head, but remained silent.

"Jamilah, sweetheart, I'll see you tomorrow," James said as he stepped over to her and gave her a hug and kiss on her cheek.

"Okay, James. Good night."

Immediately after Aunt Tee and James departed, Mrs. Thornton said good night and went upstairs to bed.

Darius was standing near the door of the den. Earlier in the afternoon, he had changed from the suit he'd worn to church to a pair of jeans and a polo shirt. He had kicked his sneakers off almost immediately upon joining Jamilah, Brianne, Aunt Tee and Mrs. Thornton in the den minutes earlier.

"You guys really outdid yourselves today," Jamilah said to Darius from her seat on the chaise where Brandon had been sleeping.

"Yeah, it turned out pretty good, huh?"

"What are you talking about? It was great!"

He smiled and said, "Yeah, they enjoyed themselves. I'm glad."

"Did you?" she asked him.

Darius walked over to the chaise and sat beside her. "I had a great time," he said softly. "How 'bout you?"

"I had a wonderful time, Darius. Thank you for inviting me."

He nudged her playfully when he said, "It wouldn't have been the same without you, Jamilah."

She blushed at this tribute and they shared an easy silence for the next couple of minutes.

"What time did your friend Lauren leave?" Jamilah finally asked. She had wanted to ask him about her all day.

"Oh, she didn't stay very long. She just, uh…she heard I was home so she came by to say hello. That's all."

"She didn't know about the party?"

"No."

"Brianne told me that you two were once engaged."

"Yeah. That was a long time ago, though."

"What happened?"

Darius chuckled lightly. "We couldn't get along. We were like…oil and water. You know, you shake it up and it comes together for a while but then it quickly separates. That was me and Lauren."

Jamilah couldn't help but mention, "You sure looked pretty cozy when I saw you." Immediately realizing that she sounded like a jealous girlfriend, she wanted to bite her tongue off the moment the words were out of her mouth.

Darius smiled, though. "Lauren has always been a bit…overzealous, especially after we broke up. I mean, I was happy to see her, but she's history—a long time past. As a matter of fact, she's engaged to someone else, so she's not my problem anymore, I'm relieved to say. I wish the man all the luck in the world, too. She's quite headstrong."

"I thought you like a woman with her own mind?"

"I do, but Lauren is the type of person who will try to impose her views upon you. She's somewhat megalomaniacal. If you don't agree with her point of view, you're just wrong—plain and simple. I mean, she's good people, but like I said, she's past history."

Staring at each other for a long moment after his pronouncement, Jamilah was actually quite relieved to know that Darius was no longer interested in Lauren, and Darius was somewhat tickled at witnessing that little bit of jealousy on Jamilah's part.

He couldn't believe how blind he'd been all this time; finding out today that she felt for him the way he'd been feeling for so long, it seemed. The pleasant revelation making him anxious to return home, he didn't feel this was the appropriate time to spring his views on her about the new direction that their relationship should take.

Suddenly, Jamilah yawned and stretched her arms up over her head. "I think I'm going to take my butt to bed, too."

"Yeah, it has been a pretty long day," Darius agreed. "I'm going to go on up, too."

They turned out all of the lights in the living room and den, then started up the stairs together.

"Do you want me to drive back tomorrow?" Jamilah asked as they ascended the flight to the second floor.

"No, I'll drive."

"But I never got a chance to drive the Mercedes," she playfully groaned. Then, excitedly, she said, "I'll tell you what. I'll start out tomorrow, then you can take the second leg of the ride back."

"Okay."

Darius stopped outside of Jamilah's bedroom. Taking her hand, he stood with her for a long moment, motionless and speechless. Jamilah's heart was now racing, hoping he would kiss her, and not like he had the night before, but a passionate, tongue-swapping, lip-latch. But that was probably asking too much, she figured. Knowing that her feelings were not reciprocated, she hoped against hope that maybe James would slip and break his promise, and Darius would realize that no one else could love him the way she did.

Suddenly Darius said, "You know I've never really been crazy about that place Blackberry's, but I'm so glad I went there that night, 'cause I thought I'd never see you again, Jamilah. So many times, I wanted to call you, just to see how you were, but…I didn't want to take a chance on encountering your friend, you know."

Jamilah nodded her head in agreement. "I know, Darius. I started not to go that night either. As a matter of fact, Lilly had seen you in there a couple of times before. She thought you were Denzel Washington."

Darius' laughter rang out in the otherwise quiet house. "Denzel Washington?"

"Yeah." He sighed.

"That's real funny."

"Why?"

"Denzel Washington, Jamilah?"

"You kind of favor him."

Pausing for a moment and trying to figure out if she was being facetious or not, he noticed that she looked quite sincere. "You've certainly caught me off guard with that one."

"But you do. I've always thought so. You look better than him, though."

"Well…thank you."

"I'm glad I decided to go with them, too."

"Yeah," he sighed. "I can't believe a whole year passed."

"I know."

"That's okay, 'cause that'll never happen again."

"Not if I have anything to do with it," Jamilah said definitively.

"Likewise."

Standing only inches away from her, staring into her eyes and marveling again, as he had done so many times before, Darius was in awe at the wonder that was before him. It wasn't Jamilah's outer beauty, either, but being the person she was, the beauty that she projected from deep within made her glow. He suddenly took a step closer to her and wrapped her in a tender embrace.

Jamilah, with sparkling, glistening, joyful eyes, inhaled and exhaled deeply as she held him.

Without warning, Darius took her face in his hands and gazed into her beautiful jewel-like pupils as he whispered, "I'm really glad I have you in my life." Then, after gently pressing his lips to hers for a few seconds, he released her.

In a caressing tone he said, "Good night, Jamilah. See you in the morning."

"Good night, Darius."

When Jamilah entered her bedroom, she closed the door and stood there with her back against it for a moment, trying to comprehend what had just occurred. Tears formed in her eyes, but her face was covered with a huge smile. She folded her arms across her middle and gave herself a big hug for him. *He loves me.*

# Chapter 33

Darius and Jamilah began the drive back to New York at about one-thirty in the afternoon on the following day. Jamilah drove to the far side of the Chesapeake Bay Bridge-Tunnel, at which point Darius took over for the remainder of their trip.

Jamilah delighted in being behind the wheel of Darius' Mercedes. It was a beautiful day so, of course, they had the top down. Darius took pictures of her as she sped across the miles-long bridge with what he called her "movie star" shades and her long locks blowing freely in the wind.

Other than their stop to change places and refresh themselves, they drove straight into New York, arriving at Jamilah's house a few minutes after eight. They were both quite hungry.

There had been a good deal of food left over from the Thorntons' anniversary party, so Darius and Jamilah had packed a tidy portion of it to take with them. Famished, they made a beeline for the kitchen to warm up some of that delicious food as soon as they arrived at Jamilah's house. Their fare included roasted turkey and stuffing, candied yams, corn pudding, collard greens, honey roasted ham, fried okra and a few of Aunt Tee's homemade biscuits, not to mention a slice apiece of sweet potato pie, which Darius had cut and hidden early on. He knew from experience that there would be nothing left of the many cakes and pies prepared for the party when it was over.

Appetites now satisfied, they returned to Jamilah's living room and plopped down on the sofa, both so full they could barely move.

"Wow, Darius, that was so delicious."

"That was good, wasn't it?"

"Oh, God, it was better than yesterday," Jamilah groaned. "I can't believe I ate so much. I'm going on a diet."

"Why?"

"*Because!* With all the food I ate this weekend and today, I know I must have put on about twenty pounds."

"Don't go on a diet, Jamilah," he pleaded.

"Darius, please. I think I can afford to lose a couple of pounds."

"I don't think you should do anything that would affect your figure."

"What?"

"Jamilah, you have a great figure."

"Oh, please."

"I mean it. You know, I personally—you probably don't know this from my history...I mean, Sabrina and Lauren—but I like a healthy woman, you know. I like a woman with some meat on her bones."

"I've got plenty of meat on my bones, Darius."

"Yes, I know. But see, with your height, too, it looks great. It really does. I mean you've got all the right...curves...in all the right places."

"Yeah, right. I've got enough curves for a few people."

"Jamilah, just stop it, okay. You have a great figure. Your whole..." He stopped talking and gestured with his hands as though framing a woman's body.

Jamilah couldn't help blushing from his words and actions. *Is he flirting with me? Does he really think I'm that beautiful?* Wondering if she'd misinterpreted his words of last night, presuming he was trying to tell her that he loved her, maybe all he'd meant was that he was glad they were friends. She really didn't want to get her hopes up too high to be let down, but she couldn't help the wave of love tugging at her heart. She'd been so sure last night that he loved her the way she loved him.

Darius tried to stifle a yawn.

"Are you going to work tomorrow?" she asked him.

"Yeah," he grumbled. "Actually, there's a brief that I was supposed to look over this weekend. I took it all the way down to Virginia and didn't open my briefcase once to look at it. I've got to go over it tonight before I turn in."

"Are you going to be okay to drive?"

"Yeah, I'll be fine."

"You sure?"

He chuckled. "Yeah, I'll be fine, Jamilah. Don't worry. Are you going in tomorrow?"

"Yeah, I'm going in."

"Well, I'ma start on out so you can get some rest." Rising from the sofa, he stretched as another yawn escaped him.

"Are you sure you're going to be okay?" She really didn't want him to leave.

"Yeah, I'll be fine. Don't worry. I'll give you a call tomorrow. We can get together for lunch."

"No! You give me a call tonight, so I know that you made it home all right."

He smiled. "All right, J, I'll call you tonight. As soon as I get in."

"Don't forget, Darius."

"I won't."

She walked him to the door and as they stood there, he took her hand and said, "You know, you are the sweetest woman I have ever known in my life."

"Are you trying to make me blush?"

He laughed. "No. I'm being honest with you, Jamilah. I mean that." His tone softened. "You're my best friend, too."

"You're my best friend."

"No matter what happens, from now until…forever, I hope you'll always be my best friend."

"I hope so, too."

"Where's my hug?"

She put her arms around him and held him tight. He squeezed her, too, and gave her a soft kiss on her ear before leaning back and gazing into her eyes. Then, gently brushing her locks back over her left ear, he said, "I love you, you know."

"I love you, too, Darius."

He gently pressed his mouth to hers before letting her go, with seeming reluctance. He then opened the door, turned and walked out without another word.

Jamilah stood in the doorway and watched him until he drove away. When he was no longer in sight, she closed the door and sighed. Although saddened by his departure, she was determined not to cry.

Her emotions mired in ambiguity, Jamilah's life felt like a great big rollercoaster ride, going up and down, up and down, twisting and turning, over and over again. She wasn't sure what she should feel. She knew she had to get over this man, though. Somehow or another she had to get him out of her system. She couldn't go on like this much longer. If they weren't going to be together the way she wanted, she needed to come to grips with the fact that they were just going to be friends and accept that.

*Might as well go to bed.* She went back to the kitchen and turned out the lights, before turning out the lights in her living room and starting upstairs.

As Darius drove off, he could still feel the impression of her breasts pressed against his chest. Feeling the softness of her body in his arms, she was still with him.

*What the hell is wrong with you, man?*

Jamilah was everything he wanted his woman to be—everything! And now he knew she felt the same way he did. *What are you waiting for?*

He was five blocks away from her house when he turned his car around and headed back. When he pulled into her driveway, he noticed that the lights were out. Knowing she was not asleep that quickly, he took the steps in front of her house, two at a time, and urgently rang the bell. He'd never wanted anything or anyone so much in his life as he wanted her at that moment.

Jamilah was alarmed when she heard her doorbell ring so she cautiously headed back downstairs to see who was there. "Who is it?"

"Darius."

Her surprise was evident when she opened the door. "Hi. Did you forget something?"

Darius stepped into the house, closing the door behind him. "Yes, I did. I forgot this."

He reached for her and gently pulled her into his arms, planting a kiss on her mouth that was so heated, so intense, so full of passion that Jamilah initially resisted—but only for a split second. Quickly succumbing to his tender, but urgent kiss, they squeezed one another as if their lives depended on it. Tongues wrestling frantically, they were completely consumed by the fire that burned inside of them for each other. Jamilah was so overjoyed and relieved that she couldn't help but cry, but she never pulled her lips away from his. Feeling his hard body against hers, her hands involuntarily moved up and down his back as did his along the length of her body, gently caressing her backside, and squeezing her tighter as if trying to meld her body with his.

Their lips parted only a millimeter as Darius sighed. "I love you, Jamilah. I love you so much. I can't believe how blind I've been all this time."

Jamilah couldn't even speak. Overwhelmed and overjoyed, her euphoria was accompanied by tears because he was finally hers. After what seemed an eternity, she finally had the man of her dreams in her arms.

"I've been so blind. All this time, I've been looking for you, and you were right here in front of me and I didn't even see you. I was so sure you wouldn't want me after Sabrina."

"Darius, I've loved you for so long, but I didn't want to lose you, either. I thought you just wanted us to be friends, and I was so afraid that if I told you how I felt, you'd push me away."

"When James told me…"

"He told you?"

Darius chuckled. "He didn't mean to. It kind of slipped."

"Well, I'm not angry with him, if that's what you think," she said with a bright smile. "I mean—I'm glad he doesn't keep promises well."

Laughing again, Darius explained, "He actually is very trustworthy, Jamilah. He just… well, he pretty much knocked me upside my head because he saw how much I was hurting you."

"You weren't hurting me, Darius. I would have been content to be just your friend, if that was all you wanted."

"That's not all I want." He breathed. "I realized that after I saw you at Blackberry's that night."

"You did?"

"Yes, I did. I just didn't know how to tell you."

Eager, exhilarated mouths came together again in a kiss filled with love and hope and the promise of what their new life together would bring for them.

"I didn't want another day to pass without letting you know how much I love you, Jamilah," Darius panted. "You've waited long enough. I don't want you to have to wait any longer."

Sighing with pure happiness, Jamilah stood snug in her man's embrace for the next few minutes reveling in the joy that now surrounded them. Darius, feeling as though a weight had been lifted from his shoulders, sensed that Jamilah felt as if God had finally answered her prayers.

"Come upstairs," she softly murmured.

"No, baby, I'ma go on home."

Her disappointment showed on her face.

Reassuring her, Darius stated, "It's not that I don't want to, Jamilah. I do, more than anything, but I *have* to go over this brief. I'm having a meeting on it first thing tomorrow morning. Tomorrow night, I'm all yours, though. Pack an overnight bag in the morning. I want you to stay with me tomorrow night, okay?"

Starry eyes filled with Jamilah's love and adoration gazed into unwavering brown ones, overjoyed to see identical feelings reflected there. "Okay, Darius," she tenderly acquiesced.

"It's going to be hard enough, tonight, to do this without you there. I know it won't get done if I stay here. Tomorrow, you won't be able to keep me away."

"I don't want to."

He kissed her lips softly. "I love you."

"I love you."

Gently caressing her cheek, he gazed lovingly into her eyes one final time before he opened the door, once again, and walked out.

"Be careful," she called after him.

Turning back, he smiled as he said, "I will. I have too much to look forward to."

Grinning from ear to ear, Jamilah's face could have illuminated the entire block. When she closed the door this time, tears streamed down her face, but now they traveled in the creases formed by her smile.

# Chapter 34

Extremely lighthearted after her unforgettable weekend with Darius and his family, Jamilah walked on clouds into her office that Tuesday morning to find a breathtaking bouquet of wildflowers resting in the center of her desk that only added to the joy that filled her heart. Her secretary, Mattie Delvecchio, followed her in with her phone messages.

"The flowers came just a few minutes before you got here. Any idea who they're from?" Mattie asked with good-natured curiosity as she placed Jamilah's telephone messages and a file in her in-box.

Jamilah's mischievous smile brightened her eyes as she said, "I have a pretty good idea," and she stepped behind her desk to remove the card attached. *Sometimes the very thing you're looking for is the one thing you can't see. I can see clearly now. Darius.*

Her smile brightened upon reading his sweet words.

Mattie had been Jamilah's secretary for almost a year, but she had never seen her boss in such a jubilant mood, and was dying to know who the flowers were from. The love in Jamilah's heart was clearly evident on her face.

"You're killing me with the suspense," Mattie said as she stood before Jamilah with one hand on her hip.

Jamilah laughed exuberantly. "They're from Darius, Mattie," she said as she moved the bouquet to the credenza behind her.

"Darius? Your friend, Darius Thornton?"

"Yes," she said with a nod of her head.

"The one that calls all the time?"

"Yes."

"What's the occasion? It's not your birthday, is it?" Mattie asked with a frown, hoping she hadn't forgotten her boss' date of birth.

"No, it's not my birthday," Jamilah said with a mischievous grin as she sat down at her desk. "It's just that things have…changed between us."

Mattie took a seat in front of Jamilah's desk and leaned forward with her elbows on the desk in anticipation. "I want details."

Jamilah chuckled. She got a kick out of the energetic twenty-three-year-old Italian girl who, from what she'd told Jamilah, had grown up in a predominantly black neighborhood. On many previous occasions, she had told Jamilah some of the funniest stories about some of her and her friends' escapades with the opposite sex, and had confided in her many times about her personal life.

Jamilah liked her optimistic attitude and aside from her tendency to be a bit loud on occasion, she was quite an efficient secretary.

"Close the door," Jamilah said.

Mattie didn't hesitate. She jumped up and pushed the door closed with a loud crash. "Sorry," she said with a grimace when the door slammed.

Jamilah simply shook her head.

"So, what happened?" Mattie asked anxiously as she returned to the chair in front of Jamilah's desk.

"Well, we went down to Norfolk, Virginia for his parents' fortieth wedding anniversary—he and his sister threw them a party—and then we came home."

Mattie waited for the rest of the story. When Jamilah was not immediately forthcoming, Mattie said, "And…"

"And, yesterday we decided that we want to be more than just friends."

Mattie couldn't understand why Jamilah suddenly seemed so nonchalant. Just a few seconds ago she had been simply bursting with effervescent joy. Mattie had always suspected there was something more to their friendship than Jamilah had previously let on, but Jamilah had always insisted that their relationship was purely platonic.

"You guys weren't dating before?" Mattie asked for the umpteenth time.

"I've told you, we were just really good friends."

"So why the sudden change?"

"Well, I've always wanted it to be more, but I guess it wasn't our time. This weekend was something of an awakening for both of us, I think."

"I always knew there was something, at least on your part. You would get so happy whenever I told you he was on the line and no matter what you were doing, you always took his calls," Mattie pointed out.

"I've been in love with him for a long time." Jamilah smiled reflectively before she said, "It's like a dream's come true for me."

Mattie was moved by Jamilah's sentiment. "That's great, Jamilah. I'm really happy for you. He always seemed like a really nice guy."

"He's the best."

"So are you guys going to get married or anything?" Mattie asked.

"Well, we haven't talked about anything like that yet, but I'll tell you, if he asked me, I would in a heartbeat," Jamilah confessed.

"I know that's right. I can't wait to meet him, Jamilah. You've never had such a glow on your face before. You look so happy."

Jamilah's smile radiated warmth in the room. "I am."

As soon as Mattie left her office, Jamilah got up from her desk and closed her office door again. She immediately picked up the telephone and dialed her mother's number.

"Hello."

Jamilah smiled when she heard her mother's voice on the line. "Hi, Mommy."

"Hi, baby. How you doin'?"

"I'm wonderful," Jamilah answered as she sighed with happiness.

"When did you get back?"

"Last night."

"How was your trip?"

"It was great, Mom. Darius and his sister threw this big cookout to celebrate their parents' anniversary. Forty years. It was really nice. He has such a nice family."

"Well, that really doesn't surprise me, seeing the type of man he is. How is Darius?"

Jamilah's smile brightened. "He's wonderful," she said in a singsong tone.

Alexia sensed that Jamilah was itching to tell her something. "What happened?"

"We're a couple now, Mommy. He told me he loves me. Well, he's told me that before, but now it's different. He said he's wanted it this way for a while but figured I wouldn't because of Sabrina."

"Well, I can understand that. Are you sure you're all right with that, Jami?"

"They were never intimate, Mommy. Sabrina was trying to milk him and he wasn't anteing up enough, so she never went there with him," Jamilah said happily.

"Is that what he told you?"

"No, that's what she told me when they were dating."

"Well, that's good."

"I'm so happy, Mommy."

"I know, baby. I can hear it in your voice. I'm happy for you. He's a wonderful person and I know he cares about you, so you have my blessings, honey. I know you'll be very happy with him."

"Thank you, Mommy. That means a lot to me that you said that. I finally feel like I've found my soul mate."

"That's a wonderful feeling, isn't it?" Alexia said. She knew from personal experience.

***

Darius and Jamilah didn't meet for lunch like they usually did because Darius was tied up in meetings most of the afternoon. She was surprised, however, when, at ten minutes to five, Mattie buzzed her and told her she had a visitor.

"Who is it?" Jamilah asked over the intercom system.

"Darius."

Jamilah immediately rose from her desk and headed out of her office to greet him. "Hi!"

Darius was standing near Mattie's desk when he heard her voice. He turned, smiling at the sight of her. "Hi, gorgeous." He reached out his hand to her.

"I wasn't expecting you," she said as she took the hand he offered.

"When I got out of this last meeting, I figured if I went back to my office I'd never get out, and I promised this night to you, so here I am," he said in his smooth baritone voice.

Darius' back was to Mattie so he couldn't see the smile plastered on her face, but Jamilah couldn't ignore it. "Darius, did you meet my assistant, Mattie?"

He turned to her and said, "Not formally."

"Well, this is the person you speak to when I'm not around. Mattie Delvecchio, meet Darius Thornton."

"Hi, Darius. It's so nice to meet you, finally," Mattie said with unusual vibrancy.

"It's nice to meet you, too, Mattie. And thank you for making sure Jamilah gets all of my messages."

"Oh, it's my pleasure."

"Come on inside," Jamilah said to Darius.

Once they were behind closed doors, Darius pulled her into his arms and planted an eager kiss on her lips. "I've been waiting all day to do that," he said when they separated.

"Me, too, and thank you for the flowers. They're beautiful."

"You're welcome, sweetheart. How was your day today?"

"Pretty good. How was yours?"

"Busy, but the best part is about to begin, the part I've been looking forward to with eager anticipation. You about ready to get out of here?"

"Give me ten minutes. I just have to make one quick call."

Darius took a seat opposite her desk as she flipped through her Rolodex file looking for the desired telephone number. "You've got a nice office here," he said.

"Thanks. I like it," she said with a smile.

As she dialed the number, she asked him, "Where do you feel like eating tonight?"

"At home. I'm cooking tonight."

"You are?"

"That's right."

"Hello," she said into the receiver.

As Jamilah conversed with whom Darius assumed was a client, he sat across from her admiring her natural beauty in the midst of her professionalism. He enjoyed watching her like this; she was in her element. He figured the person she was speaking to was a man from the slightly flirtatious tone of voice she used, although it was clear that it was strictly business. She was playing this person like a piano.

Suddenly, turning her attention to him, she winked at him but never skipped a beat in her conversation. "Okay, Mr. Siegel, I will get that draft out to you tomorrow morning, and I look forward to seeing you on Friday. I'll have my secretary call you tomorrow to confirm the time. You have a wonderful evening. Good-bye," she said, then hung up the phone. To Darius, she stated, "I'm ready to go."

"Is that how you handle all of your clients?" he asked as he rose from the chair.

"No, just the stubborn ones," she said with an easy smile.

He chuckled. "I'm glad I'm on your side."

"I'm glad you're on my side, too," she said as she came around the desk to join him. She leaned up to kiss him.

Arriving at Darius' duplex apartment forty minutes later, he gave her a quick tour. On the first floor was the living room and a large den which he called his "vegetation room" that was furnished with a fifty-two-inch television, an entertainment center that housed VCR and DVD machines, a turntable, a tape deck and a CD player. Adjacent to this was a wall rack filled to capacity with VHS tapes, CDs and DVDs. There was also a full-size arcade game in one corner. The dimly lit dining room was relatively small with a cream-colored lacquer table with four straight-back, upholstered chairs covered in a black and beige ethnic design. The table was set with matching mudcloth placemats and napkins. Next was the eat-in kitchen, which Jamilah noticed was immaculate. On the second level were four bedrooms: one was used as an office; two were guest bedrooms with queen-sized beds in each and an adjoining bathroom between them. Last but not least, was the master bedroom with a private bathroom, neither of which would Darius let her see. With a mischievous grin, he told her, "You'll be in there soon enough and you'll have plenty of time to check it out."

When they returned to the main floor, he told her, "Okay, now you sit down and make yourself comfortable. Relax and rest up while I fix dinner."

"Do you want me to help you?"

"Nope. I want you to rest. You're going to need your energy later," he said in a seductive manner.

She smiled. "Weren't you up late last night going over that brief?"

"Yes, I was."

"How much sleep did you get?"

"About four hours."

"Then I think you should rest."

"Oh, no, baby, see, I've got my second wind. I'm wide awake; you can believe that."

"Is there something that I should do to prepare myself?" she asked as she stepped closer to him and put her arms up and around his neck.

Seductively pecking her lips, he softly said, "Just be prepared to spend the most sensuously, enjoyable night of your life with a man who's dying to show you how much you're loved."

"I think I can do that," she whispered.

Darius prepared a dinner of broiled chicken breast cutlets that had been marinating in Italian dressing since the night before with which he served steamed asparagus tips in lemon butter and yellow seasoned rice. Jamilah was delighted because she'd had no idea he was such a good cook. Everything was delicious.

"This is really good, baby. Did your mother teach you how to cook like this?" she asked halfway through their meal.

"No, actually, I have to give the credit to Lauren."

"Your ex?"

"Yup. Lauren is a fantastic cook. When we were in school, we studied together, usually into the wee hours of the morning. Take-out became quite expensive, as I'm sure you can imagine, so she started cooking for us and a few of our classmates. She would sell plates of food for three dollars apiece. After a while, it got to be a bit much for her, with the studying and all, so I offered to help. When I started out, I could barely boil water. After a couple of months, we'd take turns with me doing all of the cooking by myself."

"If you guys couldn't get along, how'd you manage to work together like that?"

"Well, our breakdown really didn't start until after we'd stopped our little business venture. Initially, we were joined at the hip."

"Yeah, you said that before. What happened?"

Taking a moment to consider her question, he answered, "I think we started to grow apart, but neither of us wanted to let go. We were comfortable together and I think the idea of us not being together was a little scary. For both of us."

Jamilah let that sink in.

"She was only the second woman I'd ever been with," he admitted moments later. "Not many people know this, but I didn't lose my virginity until I was twenty-one."

"I was twenty-three," Jamilah said softly.

Smiling, Darius peered across the table with an affectionate gaze. "Slow starters, huh?"

"Yeah."

"Wanna play catch-up tonight?"

Smiling seductively, Jamilah cooed, "Most definitely."

A galvanizing chill wended down his spine with her accommodating tone, causing Darius' body to harden in anticipation of being with her.

They stared into each other's eyes for the next few seconds, but no words passed between them. By this time, Darius had cleaned his plate. He slowly rose from the table and walked over to Jamilah's place. As she boldly looked up at him, he leaned over her, placing two fingers under her chin, bringing his head down to peck the pliant petals she possessed. At first, their mouths touched softly, almost tentatively, but the yearning passion that raged in Darius' heart usurped the moment, and he pushed his tongue into her willing mouth and their dance of love began.

Although her kiss was sweet, it was not enough, he quickly decided. Wanting to feel her body pressed against his, their eyes locked as he pulled the brim of his face away from hers only long enough to slide her chair out and help her to her feet. Then suddenly, simultaneously, they reached for one another, and their lips came together again.

This was his heaven. As their oral tribute continued, Darius tried to pull her through him, although they were already as close as they could be fully clothed. Pressing his maleness to her, slowly and sensuously rubbing against her femininity, he could feel the contours of her ample breasts against his broad chest, and the sensation was mind-blowing. His hands traveled slowly down the length of her back until they found her full, round backside. Cupping her cheeks in his large hands and squeezing them, he pulled her closer still until a moan of pure pleasure escaped her lips. Jamilah ground her hips in rhythm with his, eager to feel the maximum effects of his manhood.

As she continued to rub against him, Darius gently took her face in his hands. As their mouths parted, he looked into her eyes and could see that her carnal desire mirrored his own.

"Are you ready for dessert?" he asked in a soothing, caressing tone.

"I'm starving for it," she panted.

"Do you like bubble baths?"

"Yes."

"Good. I'm going to fix you a nice warm tub of bubbles, then I'm going to slowly wash you from head to toe—every inch of your beautiful five-foot, ten-and-a-half-inch frame. Then I'm going to dry you off and slowly massage some of the sweetest oil into your beautiful black skin with my fingers, tongue and other parts of my anatomy, before I bury myself in your warm, wet love canal," he softly growled.

An anticipatory shiver of delight ran through her at hearing what he had in store for her.

"Are you ready to be loved, Jamilah?"

"Yes, Darius," she murmured weakly.

"Because I want to love you like no one ever has. I want to show you how beautiful you are to me. I want to make you feel like the most loved woman in this world. Will you let me do that?"

"Yes, Darius," she whimpered through her panting.

"When you fall off to sleep tonight, I want you to have a smile on your face from remembering the endless love we're going to share tonight and a smile in your heart from knowing that you have a man who loves you for the beautiful woman you are."

Jamilah was so moved by the power and intensity of his words of love that she could not speak.

He then released her, but took her hand as he said, "Come on, baby. Now I'll show you my bedroom."

# Chapter 35

A week and a half after their return from Virginia, Darius received a call from his cousin James.

It was a quarter to nine and he had just arrived at his apartment after a late evening at the office. If he'd had his preference, he would have gone to Long Island to spend the night with Jamilah. Before leaving the office, he had placed a call to her house, but got only her answering machine. He then took a chance and tried her at her office. She was there and told him she had no idea what time she would be leaving because she and her staff were working fiercely to beat a deadline. He suggested that she come to his place when she left the office instead of going to Long Island after she told him it would be really late and balked about waking him up to let her in. He confessed how much he wanted her and that he probably wouldn't be able to get a good night's sleep without a dose of her sweet loving.

"Well, when you put it that way," she had replied in a flirtatious manner, "how could I possibly refuse you? I'll call you when I'm on my way."

When the telephone rang at ten-fifteen, Darius was certain that Jamilah was on the other end. Regardless of how much he enjoyed talking to his cousin, Darius could not hide his disappointment when he recognized James' voice.

"Oh, what's up, Jimmy?"

"Well, damn, you don't have to sound so happy to hear from me," James responded sarcastically.

"No, it's just that I thought you were Jamilah."

"How is she?"

"She's great."

"So, did you talk to her?"

"Oh, yeah." Darius' tone brightened immediately. "Yeah, as soon as we got back. Well, almost, but we're together now."

"Congratulations."

"Thanks, Jimmy. I mean really—thank you. I don't know what I was waiting for." Darius had to laugh to himself. "When I... Well, when I finally *acted* on my feelings, she just...her response was so awesome. I had no idea that she felt the way she does. I mean, I have never felt so loved in my life, man, and it feels good. It feels really good."

"Hey, man, that's great. I'm real happy for you. You deserve it. Are you going to marry her?"

"Yes."

"Have you spoken to her about that yet?"

"No, but I will. She's my soul mate. I've been looking for her for so long, there's no way I'm about to let her get away from me."

"Well, I'm just happy I was able to be of some kind of help."

"Hey, man, if it wasn't for you, I'd probably still be walking around with my head in the clouds. I owe you, Jimmy. Anytime I can return the favor, let me know."

"Well, now that you mention it, I'm going to be in town for a few days next week, and I need a place to stay. Can you hook me up with a hotel?"

"What are you talking about? You'll stay here with me. I've got plenty of room," Darius insisted.

"No, I don't want to stay with you. You and Jamilah are just starting a brand-new relationship, and I'm not trying to get in the way of anything the two of you might want to get into. If you could just suggest a hotel, or book a room for me somewhere, that'll be fine."

"Jimmy, don't be silly. You'll stay here. If it comes down to Jamilah and I wanting some privacy like that, we can stay at her place. But we only do the swinging from the chandelier thing once a month, and we've already covered this month." Darius laughed.

James joined him. "Oh, it's like that, huh?"

"Yeah." Darius chuckled. "So how long are you going to be in town?"

"Just four days. I'm participating in this seminar that's taking place at LIU's Brooklyn campus. Are you far from there?"

"No, LIU is less than a mile from me."

"Oh, cool. Listen, I'd like to take you and Jamilah out to dinner or something while I'm there, so don't make any plans for Sunday night. I'm flying in that morning. The seminar is Monday and Tuesday, and I figured I'd spend a day doing the tourist thing before I fly out Thursday."

"Hey, that's cool. I can take Wednesday off and we can hang out in the city."

"You sure?"

"Yeah. I need a day off, anyway."

\*\*\*

James arrived at Darius' house on Sunday, just after noon. Jamilah was in the den watching a video when the doorbell rang. Darius was upstairs working in his office.

"Baby, would you get that?" Darius called down to her. "It's probably Jimmy."

"Got it," she called back as she stopped the tape and rose from the couch. Jamilah had been looking forward to James' visit because she wanted to thank him for the part he played in her and Darius' new relationship.

When she got to the door, she looked through the peephole, and a broad smile broke across her face. "Hi, James!" she cried cheerfully, as she hurriedly opened the door.

James was tickled by Jamilah's greeting. Aside from being happy to see her, he was delighted that her whole countenance now seemed to be surrounded by a preternatural glow. "Hey, Jamilah. My, don't you look happy," he said with a big smile.

"I am, thanks to you."

When he came through the door and placed his bag at his feet, Jamilah put her arms around him and gave him a big hug, which he readily reciprocated. "Thank you, James."

"You're welcome. It was a slip, you know. I hope you don't think that I can't be trusted with a secret."

"No, I don't think that at all. I'm actually very happy you let it slip. The last two weeks have been the best of my life," Jamilah freely admitted.

"I'm glad to hear that. I hope you know that you make him really happy, too."

"I hope so, 'cause that's all I want to do."

"Is that Cupid?" Darius called out as he started down the stairs.

Jamilah and James laughed. "The one and only," James replied.

"What's up, Jimmy?" Darius smiled warmly at the sight of his cousin. The two men embraced when he reached the bottom of the landing.

"You, dude. It's good to see you. Both of you," James said as his gaze passed back and forth between Jamilah and Darius. "Together."

Darius put his arm around Jamilah's waist and kissed her on the side of her head. "It's good to be together."

"Amen," Jamilah said softly.

"Come on in and make yourself at home," Darius offered.

"Are you hungry, James?" Jamilah asked.

"No, I grabbed a little something before I got on the plane. It'll hold me for a couple more hours."

The three of them moved into the living room and sat down. Darius and Jamilah sat together on the sofa, and James sat across from them in a big wing-backed chair.

"How was your flight?" Jamilah asked.

"It was good."

Jamilah and Darius were snuggled close together, naturally so, and as they conversed with James for the next fifteen minutes, he studied them closely. Having never seen Darius look so completely happy, he couldn't help but smile.

When Darius noticed the look of amusement on James' face, he asked, "What's so funny?"

Caught off guard, James was slow in responding. "Huh? Oh, nothing."

"So why are you sitting there with that silly grin on your face?"

"Oh, it's just...well, I just can't get over you two. You look so...happy. I mean, like you've both finally found the secret of life or something."

Jamilah and Darius grinned at each other before Darius said, "I think we have."

"I envy you."

"Your day will come, Jimmy. Hopefully, it won't take you as long to recognize that special one as it did me," Darius said.

"Yeah, I hope not either." They all chuckled. "But you know what?" James added with a tinge of excitement. "The day after you guys left, I ran into an old friend of mine. I'd met this young lady over five years ago, and our personalities just clicked right from the start. I mean, she was smart, funny, beautiful…everything…but she was married. We used to talk, anyway. She'd told me then about how things weren't going well in her marriage, but how she really wanted to make it work and all. I remember thinking of how much I admired that about her, you know, that she wasn't willing to just give up because they'd hit a snag. But in the few months that we were communicating, she'd lit a fire in me that took a long time to extinguish. That's why I had to stop talking to her. My feelings were getting out of hand. It was like that Carl Thomas song. When I ran into her the other day, I realized that the fire hadn't really gone out at all. She and her husband divorced each other two years ago. We've been spending a lot of time together in the last couple of weeks, and it's like we were never even apart."

"Hey, that's great, man. It sounds heavy."

"Yeah, it is. I really…I really care about her," James said softly.

"That's wonderful, James. I hope it works out the way you want it to," Jamilah said.

"Thanks, Jamilah. Me, too."

"Well, we've got to take a trip down to Norfolk to meet her," Darius said as he looked to Jamilah for agreement.

"Well, actually," James broke in, "you'll get to meet her on Wednesday. She's flying up and we're going to spend the day together before I head back home. Darius, I know you said you were going to take off so we could hang, but I hope you don't mind…"

"Of course, I don't mind. That's great!"

"What's her name?" Jamilah asked.

"Veronica Jefferson."

"What does she do?" Darius asked.

"She owns an employment agency. She works closely with government programs, you know, job-training programs, getting people jobs who've been on welfare or unwed mothers just out of high school, and the like. Actually, she has two offices, one of which deals exclusively with the underprivileged community and one that, to use her words, 'really brings the money in.' She's pretty amazing."

Jamilah smiled at James and said, "She sounds like it. I can't wait to meet her."

"I can't wait for you to meet her either. She kinda reminds me of you, Jamilah. She has the same down-to-earth quality that you have, you know? She's totally aware of who she is and what she wants and...I'm just crazy about her," James said with a shrug of his shoulders.

# Chapter 36

On Thursday of the week following James' visit to New York, Jamilah decided to go shopping during her lunch hour. She and Darius were planning to attend a party that weekend and Jamilah wanted to buy a new dress to wear. She usually spent her lunch hour with Darius, if their schedules allowed, but on this day he had a lunch meeting at his office, so they made plans to get together for dinner.

Jamilah was in the designer dress department at Bloomingdale's and had her hand on a beautiful silk and sequined gown when she looked across the floor and spotted her estranged friend, Sabrina Richardson.

Jamilah's heartbeat quickened in her chest. Suddenly all of the horrible things she had said to Sabrina came back in her memory, as if it had only been yesterday. *She probably hates me.* Jamilah stood where she was for the next minute or so trying to decide what to do. *Should I say something to her?* Sabrina was wearing a simple white cotton tank dress with a pale yellow sweater draped across her shoulders, and her hair was pulled back in a ponytail. *She still looks great,* Jamilah thought, but she honestly didn't expect anything less than perfection when it came to her old friend. Jamilah had missed her, too. Despite Sabrina's selfishness, they had been friends for most of their lives, and Jamilah genuinely missed their camaraderie. Weighing her options quickly, she decided, *What the heck.* Inhaling deeply, she moved toward her. When she was a couple of feet away, Sabrina started to walk away. Jamilah nervously called out to her. "Sabrina, hi!"

Sabrina stopped, turned and looked right at Jamilah but didn't speak.

Jamilah stepped up to her. An apprehensive smile was on her face as she nervously asked, "How are you?"

Hesitating before she responded, Sabrina answered, "I'm fine."

"It's so good to see you. You look great."

"Thank you."

"How is everything?"

"Fine."

"Are you still in the apartment?"

Continuing with curt, one-word answers, Sabrina said, "Yes."

Jamilah suddenly felt as if she was standing in a freezer, but she couldn't walk away. "How's your job?"

"I'm not working."

Trying to think of something else to say, she was hoping to get some help from Sabrina, but instead they stood in silence for what seemed to Jamilah to be hours, although it was only a matter of seconds.

"Look, I have to go," Sabrina suddenly said.

Jamilah fought to keep the smile on her face as she said, "Well, it was great seeing you."

Sabrina turned away without another word, but Jamilah stood rooted in place. *She does hate me.* Lowering her head and fighting to control painful tears of regret trying to surface, she was no longer in the mood to shop. She turned slowly and lumbered out of the dress department toward the escalator and back to work.

When Jamilah got off work that evening, Darius was waiting for her in the lobby of her building, and a vibrant smile lit his countenance when he spotted her. That smile of his never failed to warm her heart. He opened his arms to receive her. "Hi, beautiful."

Stepping into his welcoming embrace, she immediately placed her arms around him. She sighed happily. "Hi."

Their lips came together in a soft, sensuous kiss.

"I don't see any bags. No luck shopping today?"

His comment immediately sent her back in time to her lunch hour. "No," she said softly.

Picking up on her melancholy mood instantly, he asked, "What's wrong, sweetheart?"

Looking into his eyes, she murmured, "I saw Sabrina today."

"Oh, yeah? How's she doing?"

"All right, I guess."

"You didn't say anything to her?"

"Yeah, I did, but I got the feeling that I was the last person in the world she wanted to see." Jamilah was truly hurt by Sabrina's reaction to her and with Darius, she felt like she could finally let her feelings out.

"What did she say? Was she mean to you?"

"No, she barely spoke. I think she hates me. I can't blame her, though; all those things I said to her."

"Look, honey, I know you," he said softly, "and I know that whatever you might have said to her was the simple truth."

"It doesn't matter. We were friends for so long and I miss her. I never wanted to stop being her friend."

"Jamilah, don't be too upset. Maybe she just wasn't ready to see you."

"She'll probably never be ready to see me."

Darius tried to assure her. "I'm sure she misses you, baby. We both know how selfish Sabrina could be, but she cared about you. That much I'm sure of. She was probably just as hurt by your breakup as you were. Give it a little time. Everything will work out."

❊❊❊

Unable to sleep that night, Jamilah tossed and turned for nearly an hour. Although she and Darius had made love that evening until they could barely move, and by rights she should've been snoring like him, she was wide awake. Her thoughts had once again returned to Sabrina. Wishing she could talk to her and apologize for hurting her feelings, she wondered, momentarily, if she should call her. *She probably had the number changed.* Besides, Jamilah reasoned, if she did call, Sabrina would most likely hang up on her.

She turned over onto her back for the umpteenth time, trying to get comfortable in Darius' normally comfortable bed. Her constant moving about awakened him. He turned onto his side to face her. "Honey, you okay?" Darius questioned in a sleep-filled voice.

"Yeah."

"Can't you sleep?"

"No."

"What's wrong?"

Jamilah didn't immediately answer. A tear slid from her eye and rolled into her ear. The light from the street lamp outside afforded Darius a view of the glistening drop.

"You're thinking about Sabrina, aren't you?"

She was so choked up she couldn't speak, so she just nodded her head.

Darius pulled her closer to him. "Why don't you give her a call tomorrow?"

"I'm going to go see her after work. I don't know if she'll let me in, but I'm going to try to talk to her."

He kissed her softly on her temple. "Don't worry, sweetheart. It'll be all right."

She turned to him. "I'm sorry I woke you."

"That's all right, baby. I really want you to stop worrying. I'm sure if you go by her place, she'll give you the time. I'm sure she misses you, too."

Jamilah looked into his eyes through the darkness in the room and could see his love for her. "I love you, Darius."

"I love you, too, sweetheart."

## Chapter 37

As Sabrina lounged around in the comfort of her apartment that Friday evening, her thoughts returned to the previous day's encounter. She had been quite surprised to see Jamilah yesterday, but even more surprised by the way Jamilah had greeted her. Sabrina had always assumed that since her voluntary move, Jamilah wouldn't want anything to do with her. But yesterday, Jamilah had actually looked happy to see her. Sabrina could not deny that she'd been happy to see her old friend, too, but the hurt of Jamilah's lambasting before she moved still lingered.

Jamilah had been the one person who Sabrina had always been able to rely on. Jamilah had always been on, as well as by, her side. She was happy to see that Jamilah looked so good. Assuming her new job with the ad agency was profitable; besides that, Sabrina knew Jamilah would keep her freelance business going strong. She had always had the ambitious attitude Sabrina envied.

She really hadn't meant to be so cold to Jamilah, but the shock of seeing her had not been easy to overcome. Sabrina was ashamed to admit, too, that after all of the cruel things she had said to Jamilah about her inability to get a man, Sabrina had actually lost out when she decided to give her life over to Quenten Blanchard.

Sighing, she reflected on her negative course—Sabrina had given up her job and her independence to be with a man whom she had been positive would supply all of her material, as well as physical and emotional needs. Granted, in the beginning everything was exactly the way she wanted it to be with him. Quenten had doted on her, giving her expensive gifts for absolutely no reason at all other than to show her how much he cared about her. He took her places—quick weekend excursions to Martha's Vineyard, Cape May or the Caribbean, to name a few—and he had taken her to Monte Carlo during the Christmas holiday. He had even bought her a car to get around in. Although it was only a Hyundai Sonata, it was brand-new. What a rude awakening she had received when he showed his true colors that first time he hit her.

It had happened five months into their relationship, and Sabrina had made the unforgivable mistake of talking back to him in front of one of his colleagues. Although Quenten hadn't said a word at the time, when he got her home that night, he'd literally slapped her across the room and forbade her to ever speak to him in public in that manner again.

When Sabrina threatened to leave him because of his cruel treatment, he apologized profusely, swearing that he hadn't meant to hit her, but she had embarrassed him. The next day, Quenten gave her a two-carat diamond tennis bracelet to make amends. Sabrina had been blinded by the brilliance of the bracelet and immediately forgave him. Lately, however, she had noticed that he'd become crueler toward her, and the beatings came much more frequently and were much harsher, especially since the problems with his brokerage company had come to light.

Sabrina was angry with him now because he had beaten her last night like she was some wayward child. Quenten had actually taken off his belt and held her across his lap as he applied the lash mercilessly to her legs and backside. He had accused her of making eyes at a man seated across from them in the restaurant where they'd had dinner.

*How could a man as powerful as him be so insecure?* Quenten's fits of jealousy had flattered and humored her at first, but his reactions to her imagined flirtations had become increasingly violent, and were always unfounded.

As soon as Quenten had left home for his office that morning, Sabrina had immediately gotten dressed and returned to the safety of her own apartment. The first thing she'd done when she got there was call the nearest locksmith and had her door locks changed. Quenten had the keys to her apartment since he paid her rent every month, but last night's beating was the last straw. Her legs still stung from the many welts that covered them, and her backside was very tender to the touch.

While Sabrina sat on her plush leather sofa, smoking cigarette number six for the day, she asked herself, *What am I doing with a monster like him, anyway? I don't need any man this bad.* She knew if she broke off her relationship with Quenten, she would have to find a job. Having become accustomed to living in the lap of luxury, she wasn't eager to go back to her former lifestyle of sitting behind a desk from nine to five. She had to ask herself, however, if the material things he gave her were really worth all the pain and heartache she had to endure?

Sighing heavily, Sabrina wished Jamilah were here now. She really didn't want to be alone, and despite the fact that she had kept the number Jamilah had given her when she moved out, Sabrina's obstinacy prevented her from calling Jamilah for anything. After all, she had made it perfectly clear that she would never call Jamilah. Besides, how could she ever tell Jamilah that her dream come true— Quenten Blanchard—was more like a nightmare gone awry? It made her sad to acknowledge that she had no other friends she could trust enough to call now, or whom she felt comfortable with like she always had with Jamilah. Avery Williams suddenly slipped into her consciousness, but she couldn't call him either, despite how he insisted he could help her. Besides, she knew nothing about him. Why would she reach out to him? She wished she hadn't alienated everyone she had been close to when she became involved with Quenten. She had never felt so alone in her life.

It was just past six-thirty when Sabrina became aware that someone was at her front door. Her heart seemed to stop beating when she realized it was Quenten unsuccessfully trying to open the door with his key. Suddenly, her telephone rang. She picked it up before the first ring was completed and hoped that he hadn't heard it from the other side of the door.

"Hello," she said in a whisper so he wouldn't hear her voice through the door.

"Open the door, Sabrina!"

She dropped the receiver as though she had been burned. She never had considered that he might call her from his cell phone. Panic rose quickly in her chest, and she suddenly had difficulty catching her breath.

"Oh, God," she moaned. *What am I going to do?*

Immediately, Quenten began banging on the door. "Open the damn door, Sabrina! Now!"

"What am I going to tell him?" she cried softly. She frantically searched her brain for viable reasons for changing the locks. Suddenly afraid for her life, all she could think about, however, was that if she opened that door, he would hit her.

Shivering uncontrollably, the nervous trembling of her hands caused the ashes on the tip of her cigarette to drop to the floor unnoticed. She curled herself up in the corner of her sofa, willing him to go away, but neither the banging nor his yelling ceased.

She was too afraid to call the police. What would she tell them? The apartment was in her name, but he had paid her rent there for the past year. Besides, Sabrina was positive that with his money and connections, the police would align with him, anyway.

It seemed like the banging had been going on forever when her intercom suddenly rang. She hesitated before answering it, believing initially, that it was Quenten, but that couldn't be. He was still outside her door. Instantly, the person ringing her intercom had become her savior. She would let in whomever it was. *Maybe they can protect me from him.* She hurried across the room to answer the ring.

"Who is it?" she asked frantically.

"It's Jamilah."

Sabrina pressed the button to release the lobby door without pause. *Jamilah. She's always been there when I needed her, and here she is again.* Like an angel sent down from heaven.

Sabrina had been on Jamilah's mind all day. *What am I going to tell her when I show up at her apartment, uninvited?* Possessing no misconceptions about Sabrina's eagerness to see her, Jamilah was sure she wouldn't be welcomed with open arms, but she hoped that Sabrina would, at least, give her an opportunity to apologize and try to make amends.

Unable to stop second-guessing herself, Jamilah had left her office a little later than usual. *Should I go see her? Should I just forget about her and get on with my new life with Darius?*

That was another thing. How would Sabrina react when she learned that Jamilah and Darius were now more than friends? Granted, when Sabrina had him, she hadn't wanted him. She had preferred the dynamic and wealthy Quenten Blanchard to the humble, soft-spoken and compassionate Darius. Sabrina had always suspected that Jamilah was in love with Darius even then, despite that it was perfectly clear which of them he wanted. *Would she believe that they had only been intimate friends for three weeks?* He was her friend, too. Darius, in the past few months, had become Jamilah's new best friend. Despite all of that, she still missed the bond she had always shared with Sabrina.

Jamilah left her office at six-ten and caught a cab uptown. During the ride, she decided that the first thing she would do when she arrived was apologize. Then, depending upon Sabrina's reaction, she would decide what to do next. Jamilah was going to offer her old friend an olive branch. If Sabrina chose not to accept it, Jamilah would not force the issue.

She arrived at the apartment building at six-forty. A knot suddenly formed in the pit of her stomach. *Please give me a chance, Sabrina.*

Jamilah half-expected that Sabrina would not buzz her in. *She'll probably tell me to go away when she realizes it's me.* She unconsciously held her breath when she pressed the intercom for Sabrina's apartment. A few seconds passed before she heard Sabrina's voice, but after she identified herself, Jamilah's heart actually leapt when the buzzer that unlocked the lobby door immediately went off and allowed her access into the building. *Could she be as excited about seeing me as I am about seeing her?*

She stepped onto the elevator and pressed five. *I should have brought her a gift or something.* Jamilah was nervous, but a smile was on her face and in her heart.

When the elevator door opened on the fifth floor and Jamilah stepped from the car, a loud crashing sound bounced off the walls from the end of the hall where Sabrina's apartment was located. Jamilah's heart began to flutter with uncertainty. When she turned in the direction of her old apartment, she was shocked to see Quenten Blanchard standing in the hall outside Sabrina's door. "Sabrina, if you don't open this gotdamn door right now, I'm going to break it down!"

*Oh, my God. What have I walked into?* She stood where she was for a moment, frozen, afraid to move. Recalling the refined, sophisticated man she'd met a year ago, this man's face was contorted with rage. Suddenly, he turned toward her. Jamilah's breath caught in her chest. Quenten's hardened eyes pierced her to the core as he stared at her for a few seconds until recognition settled on his face. It seemed as if he was suddenly trying to compose himself on her behalf. The anger melted away from his countenance, and an embarrassed smile formed on his lips.

"Jamilah, right?" he said lightly.

"Yes."

He chuckled insincerely as he said, "I know what this must look like to you. My girl changed the locks on me."

Jamilah cautiously moved toward the door. "I'm sure she must have had a good reason for doing that," she said with a hint of antagonism.

Jamilah had never really liked Quenten, and seeing him now reminded her of that fact. She stepped in front of him and rapped on the door with her knuckles. "Sabrina? Sabrina, it's Jamilah."

After a few seconds, Jamilah heard the lock disengage. Sabrina opened the door slowly. Jamilah noticed immediately that she had been crying, although she tried to hide it. Sabrina smiled at Jamilah, but her fear-filled eyes darted back and forth between Quenten and her friend.

"Hi, Jamilah!" Sabrina said in an unnaturally high-pitched tone.

Jamilah stepped into the apartment, with Quenten right on her heels. Sabrina surprised her when she wrapped her arms around her and squeezed her tightly. "I'm so glad to see you."

"You okay?" Jamilah whispered for Sabrina's ears only.

A nervous smile crossed Sabrina's face as she looked past Jamilah at Quenten and said, "Hi, baby," in an overly cheerful tone.

"Why'd you change the locks, Sabrina?" he asked without circumstance.

Jamilah stepped further into the apartment, but turned to face Quenten. She could see the anger rising in his eyes once again.

"Someone tried to break in. When I came home the lock was messed up, and I couldn't get my key to work so I had to have a locksmith come so that I could get in," Sabrina hurriedly explained.

Jamilah knew she was lying. She knew that Quenten knew Sabrina was lying, too. "Give me the key."

"Oh, uh, I only have the one set. I wasn't able to get a copy made yet."

"So give it here. I'll have a copy made," he said as he held out his hand.

Jamilah stood by and watched this scene with mounting skepticism.

Suddenly, Quenten started toward the back of the apartment. "Come here a minute. I want to talk to you." He didn't wait for a response from her.

"Oh, baby, but Jamilah's here. We haven't seen each other in a year. I don't want to be rude and just leave her out here by herself," Sabrina nearly whined as she reached for Jamilah's hand.

He stopped and turned back to her. "It won't take long." He looked at Jamilah. "Make yourself at home. We'll be just a moment."

He held his hand out to Sabrina and smiled at her, but the smile didn't touch his eyes. Jamilah noticed that they, in fact, seemed to dare her to refuse him again.

Sabrina took a deep breath and released Jamilah's hand as she looked at her pleadingly. *Please don't leave me,* her eyes seemed to say.

"I'll be right here," Jamilah said firmly, letting Quenten know that she wasn't going anywhere.

Sabrina unwillingly followed Quenten into Jamilah's old bedroom, which she had moved into when Jamilah moved out. It was the larger of the two bedrooms. He stood at the door, and as Sabrina passed through, he gently closed it behind her. She hesitantly turned to him, only to find him staring at her in a sinister manner. "What the hell's going on?"

She was paralyzed by her fear of him. He had to ask the question a second time before she could find her voice. "What do you mean?" she asked nervously.

He moved over to the bed and sat at the foot. "Don't play dumb, Sabrina. It really doesn't become you, and I have no patience for dummies."

She turned to him and explained, "When I got home this morning, the lock was messed up..."

He cut her off. "Come here."

She moved closer to him but was still out of his reach.

"Come here!"

When she stepped over to him, he reached out to touch her and she flinched. Quenten looked at her strangely, but didn't comment. He pulled her down on his lap. His arm went around her waist and although his hold on her was not one of restraint, it was firm enough that she knew she could not get away from him, unless he wanted her to.

"Now, don't I take care of you?" he asked in a voice as gentle as a caress.

"Yes."

"Don't I give you everything you need and most of what you want?"

"Yes."

"Then why are you lying to me?"

"I'm not," she said in a trembling voice.

"Sabrina."

She held fast to her lie. "Quenten, someone tried to break in."

"Then why didn't you call me?"

She had no ready answer for him.

"Why didn't you open the door for me?"

Her heart was racing and her chest began to heave as her breaths came sharper and quicker. "I thought somebody was trying to break in again."

Quenten shook his head in disbelief. "See, there you go again. You're lying to me."

Tears fell from her eyes.

"Why'd you change the locks, Sabrina?"

She covered her face with her hands as the sobs escaped her. Quenten continued to hold her, but made no effort to comfort her.

"Sabrina?"

"I was angry and afraid," she finally cried.

"Afraid of what?"

"Afraid you were going to hit me again."

"Why did I hit you, Sabrina?"

"I don't know."

"You know why."

"I wasn't looking at that man, Quenten. I swear I wasn't."

"Yeah, okay. But you just lied to me. After everything I've done for you—after everything I do for you—you lied to me. Now, how am I supposed to take that?"

"I didn't mean to."

"If you didn't provoke me, there would be no reason for me to hit you, now would there?"

*THERE IS NO REASON FOR YOU TO HIT ME,* she screamed in her mind, but she was too afraid to give her thoughts a voice. With overwhelming sadness, she nodded her head, indicating agreement with his words.

Being the controlling, manipulative person he was, Quenten facetiously asked, "What was that? I didn't hear you?"

"Yes," she moaned in defeat.

"Now, we're not going to have any more lying, are we?" he asked as if he were speaking to a child.

"No, Quenten," she said through her tears. He stared at her long and hard until she shifted in his lap and looked into his eyes. "I won't lie anymore."

"You've been smoking."

She didn't respond.

"You know how much I hate that, but you do it anyway. Why?"

"I don't know," she groaned.

"So how long is your friend going to be here?"

"Not too long."

"Where are the keys?"

Sabrina rose from his lap and lumbered over to her dresser. She hadn't yet attached them to her key ring so the two keys were loose on her dresser top. She picked them up and walked back to him. Quenten rose before her and took the keys from her hand.

"I'll have them copied. Don't change these locks again without asking me, you understand?"

"Yes." Her head was bowed in submission.

He took her chin in his hand and tilted her head up to look at him. "I'll be back in a couple of hours. Your friend should be gone by then."

He moved to the door and opened it. Before he stepped out, he said, "We'll stay at my place tonight, okay?"

"Okay."

At that moment, a feeling of hatred for him rose in her chest unlike anything she had ever experienced, but she made sure to keep that emotion from her face.

When they returned to the living room, Jamilah was sitting on the sofa facing the back of the apartment. Quenten strolled to the front door and said, "It was nice seeing you again, Jamilah." A phony smile was on his face.

"Yeah, I bet," she mumbled. Her attention was centered on Sabrina as she followed Quenten to the door.

"I'll be back in a bit," he said to her before he leaned in and kissed her lips.

"Okay," she murmured.

She closed and locked the door behind him, but a few seconds passed before she found the courage to turn and face Jamilah.

"Sabrina, are you all right?" Jamilah asked immediately.

Sabrina took a deep breath and turned to her old friend. It was an effort to try and appear cheerful, but she managed a weak smile as she said, "Yeah."

Sabrina slowly walked to the kitchen. She immediately picked up the pack of cigarettes lying on the counter next to a lead crystal ashtray and shook one free. As she put the stick of tobacco in her mouth and prepared to light it, Jamilah asked, "When did you start smoking?"

"A while ago."

"Why?"

Chuckling mirthlessly, she responded, "It calms my nerves."

"Sabrina, what happened?" Jamilah asked as she rose from the couch and moved toward her. Although she knew Sabrina assumed she was referring to the immediate past, Jamilah wanted to know what had happened in the past year to cause such a drastic change in her oldest friend.

Sabrina shrugged and said, "We had a fight. I was mad at him, so I changed the locks. He pays my rent here, you know. I told you I quit my job, right?"

"Yeah. Why?"

"Quenten told me he wanted to take care of me. He said I didn't need a job and I haven't. He takes care of everything for me," she said dolefully.

Jamilah let this sink in for a moment before she asked, "Does he hit you?"

Barely audible, she replied, "Only when I make him mad."

"Why do you let him do that to you?"

"It's no big deal. He always buys me the best gifts to make it up to me," Sabrina said with false pride.

"You're worth more than some little trinket, Sabrina. You shouldn't let him hit you. You don't deserve that."

Sabrina took a long drag on her cigarette, but failed to respond.

"Why don't you leave him?"

"He's not so bad. He loves me and he takes good care of me, Jamilah. Really."

Jamilah wondered if Sabrina was trying to convince her or herself. "If he really loved you, Sabrina, he wouldn't hit you, no matter how angry you make him."

Sabrina didn't want to talk about her pitiful life anymore, so she abruptly changed the subject. "How's your job going? Are you still with that agency?"

Jamilah knew what she was doing. She stared at her, sorrowfully, before she answered, "Yeah, I'm still there. It's going well."

"You're still freelancing, right?"

"Yeah."

They were each silent for the next couple of minutes.

"Sabrina, you know if you need to get away from him, you can come and stay with me. I have plenty of space."

"I'm okay, Jamilah. Really. I can handle it," Sabrina said as she doused out her cigarette in the ashtray in front of her. She immediately picked up a can of air freshener and started spraying the floral-scented spray throughout the kitchen and living room.

When Sabrina noticed that Jamilah was looking at her strangely, she explained, defiantly, "Quenten doesn't like for me to smoke, but I do it anyway." It was the *one* act of defiance that she had been able to get away with without serious repercussions.

Jamilah was confused. She couldn't understand how her friend's self-esteem had sunk so low that she would allow this man to treat her in such brutal fashion. *What had happened to the strong-willed, man-ruling woman she'd known and loved?* Granted, Sabrina had always been the type of person who longed for everyone's approval, but she had never been so down on herself that she would allow anyone to abuse her the way Quenten obviously did.

Jamilah had known from the first time she met Quenten that he would never allow Sabrina to walk all over him the way she usually did with the men she dealt with. By the same token, she never would have imagined that Sabrina would become a slave to the man who had just left there.

She wanted to cry. Despite all that they had been through, all the ups and downs of their twenty-something-year friendship, despite the many times that Sabrina had infuriated her to no end, Jamilah was heartbroken to find that her dear friend had fallen to such depths. She suddenly noticed, as Sabrina moved past her and into the living room, that her tall, confident strut was gone. She now moved with a defeated gait; her shoulders were slumped and her feet dragged.

"I have to get dressed. Quenten will be back soon, and I'm staying at his place tonight," Sabrina said with her back still to Jamilah.

"I was hoping we'd get a chance to talk. I know I probably should have called before I came by, but...after seeing you yesterday...well...I miss you, Sabrina."

Sabrina turned to her and smiled. It was the first genuine smile Jamilah had seen from her since she had arrived. "I've missed you, too."

Jamilah started rummaging through her pocketbook, looking for one of her business cards. "Listen, I'm going to give you my number and address. If you need me for anything, Sabrina, and I mean *anything*, please call me or if you want to come out, please do. You're always welcome."

As Jamilah offered the card, Sabrina said, "Thanks, Jamilah. I have your number and your address. They haven't changed from what you gave me last year, have they?"

"No, they're still the same." Jamilah was warmed by the idea that Sabrina had kept the information she had given her when she moved out.

"This number hasn't changed either," Sabrina said.

The girls stood in silence for the next few seconds, but both were happy that they had taken this first step to repairing their friendship.

Jamilah broke the silence when she said, "I'm sorry for all those things I said to you before I left."

Sabrina put up her hand to stop her. "It's okay. I'd been pushing you around since we were kids. You had every right to say what you did. I'm sorry that I wasn't as good a friend to you as you've always been to me."

Jamilah took a tentative step toward her. "Are you going to be all right with him?"

Sabrina tried to smile as she softly said, "Yeah."

Jamilah sighed. After a few seconds she said, "I guess I'd better go."

She slowly started toward the door and Sabrina followed. When Jamilah's hand was on the knob, she turned back to Sabrina. Taking a step toward her, instinctively, the girls hugged.

When they released one another, Jamilah pleaded, "Please call me if you need me. I promise I won't judge you. I just want to help."

She could see Sabrina's eyes watering through her own teary eyes. "I will."

By the time she reached the elevator to take her back downstairs, Jamilah was crying uncontrollably for her friend.

***

Darius had prepared a special dinner for Jamilah that night. When she arrived at his place, the aroma of curried chicken, one of her favorite foods, met her at the door. Knowing how apprehensive she had been about visiting Sabrina unannounced, he wanted to soften the blow, if necessary, of an unpleasant visit. He knew how much she enjoyed West Indian cuisine, so he'd gone all out to make her favorites, including peas and rice and fried plantains.

"Hi, sweetheart," he greeted her with a warm smile and a big hug.

"Hi," she said somewhat dolefully.

He leaned back to look into her eyes. "How'd it go?"

"Okay."

Jamilah moved out of his embrace and past him, into the living room. Darius followed. She plopped down on the couch. When she was not immediately forthcoming, Darius asked, "Did she talk to you?"

Jamilah simply nodded her head affirmatively.

He sat next to her and asked, "So, why the long face?"

She was silent for a long moment before she answered. "He's beating her," she said barely above a whisper.

Darius frowned. "What? Who's beating her?"

"That bastard, Quenten."

"Who's that? Her boyfriend?"

"Yeah, I guess that's what you'd call him. When I got there, he was standing outside her door banging on it like some lunatic because she'd changed the locks on him."

"He's living with her?"

"No, he pays her rent, though. She quit her job so he could take care of her, and he's beating her. She's afraid of him, but she won't leave him," Jamilah lamented.

"You know this guy?"

"Yeah. She's been seeing him…" Jamilah suddenly remembered that Quenten was the man who Sabrina had dumped Darius for. She looked up into his eyes with her sad ones. "She met him when you were still dating her. She came home one night telling me about this wonderful guy she'd met. His name is Quenten Blanchard. She was with him the night you got shot."

"Quenten Blanchard? Of Blanchard-Thomas?" Darius asked in shock.

"Yeah, you know him?" Jamilah asked, equally shocked.

"Not personally, but I know who he is. She dumped me for him, huh?"

"Yeah."

"You know, we were just talking about him today in my office. He's under investigation for embezzlement, insider trading and suspicion of murder," Darius informed.

"What?" Jamilah asked in alarm. "Who'd he kill?"

"Well, the thing is this. My firm is representing a number of people who have been duped by his firm. Supposedly, his partner, Scott Thomas, was embezzling money and when he was caught, he killed himself. But Thomas's wife doesn't buy that, nor does anyone else who knew him. They think Blanchard killed Thomas when Thomas found out that *he* was embezzling. The Feds have a special investigator on the case trying to get to the bottom of the whole thing. He was in my office today. We were trading notes on Quenten Blanchard and his organization. Blanchard thinks the investigation has been dropped, but they told him that so he'd relax his guard. They've been watching him now for a couple of months. You know, now that I think about it, this agent seemed to really have it in for Blanchard. It almost seemed like it was personal with him."

"Maybe it is."

"But he said he'd only met him recently. As a matter of fact, he said something about the way he treats his woman, like she's his property," Darius remembered.

"Sabrina."

"I guess."

"She's started smoking, Darius. To calm her nerves, she said. She told me that she had changed the locks on her apartment because they had a fight, but when she let him in after I got there, she told him that someone had tried to break in. I knew he knew she was lying, and when he told her that he wanted to talk to her alone in the back of the apartment, she was terrified. He was looking at her as if he dared her to tell him no. I told her she could come and stay with me if she needed to get away from him, but she said he always buys her such nice things to make up after he hits her."

Darius shook his head in sadness and disbelief. *What happened to the sophisticated, proud and defiant Sabrina Richardson I knew?* He could hardly believe the things Jamilah was telling him. He had always known that Sabrina was materialistically driven, but he could not believe that she would tolerate physical abuse to satisfy an expensive obsession.

"I'm scared for her."

Darius reached over and pulled her into his arms. "I know. But she knows that you're here for her now, Jamilah. Maybe she'll take you up on your offer and leave him." He shook his head. "I can't believe she's letting him do this to her. I can't believe she'd let anyone do this to her."

"She's always been insecure, but I never…I never thought like this," Jamilah said.

"Well, maybe this guy Avery Williams will be able to get to the bottom of this whole thing and get him away from her. My man is determined to see Quenten Blanchard behind bars, J. I don't think he'll rest until he is."

"I hope he can get Quenten away from her before he really hurts her."

"Yeah, me, too."

The telephone rang. Darius had made no move to answer it by the second ring so Jamilah asked, "Aren't you going to get that?"

"Yeah, I guess." He was still slow to move. Sabrina's situation had also made him sad, and Darius just figured whoever was calling could wait.

"You want me to get it?" she finally asked.

"No, I'll get it." Darius rose and quickly moved to grab the phone before the answering machine clicked into action. "Hello."

"Darius?"

"Yes. Who's calling?"

"This is Alexia, Jamilah's mom."

"Oh, hello, Mrs. Witherspoon. How are you?"

"I'm fine, thank you, honey. How are you?"

"I'm pretty good. Here's your girl," Darius said as he handed the telephone to Jamilah.

"Hi, Mommy. What's the matter?" Jamilah immediately presumed the worst since her mother had called her at Darius' house.

"Hi, baby. Are you okay?"

"Yeah, I'm fine. Why?" Jamilah countered.

"Because for some reason, you've been on my mind all day. I just needed to make sure you were okay."

Jamilah chuckled mirthlessly.

"What's the matter?" Alexia immediately picked up on Jamilah's melancholy mood.

"I ran into Sabrina yesterday."

"Oh. How is she?"

"She's not doing too good, Mommy. She's seeing this jerk who's abusing her."

"What? How do you know?"

"Because I went by her place to see her when I got off work, and he was standing outside her door trying to break it down 'cause she changed the locks on him."

"Oh my goodness. Are you sure he's hitting her?"

"Yeah. She told me he only does it when she makes him angry."

"Oh God, she sounds just like her mother," Alexia said sadly.

"What do you mean?"

"Her father used to hit her mother, too. That's what Dolly said to me once when I asked her about a bruise she had on her arm."

Jamilah was amazed. "Dr. Richardson used to beat up Mrs. Richardson?"

"Yup. They say it's a cycle."

"But Sabrina never told me that."

"She may not have known. Dolly tried very hard to cover it up. And Martin never hit her in her face, so unless you saw her with her clothes off, you'd never know," Alexia explained.

"But why would she stay with him if he was doing that? Why would she want to be with a man like that?" Jamilah asked, trying to understand.

"Well, I know Dolly didn't want to lose that money. Martin was pretty well off, you know, and Dolly would've had to start from scratch if she'd left him. She hadn't worked since they got married because he took care of her. He was a good provider, too, but...I don't know, baby. I never could understand why she stayed with him, either. Money's just not that important to me."

"Me, either. Sabrina said this guy always buys her nice things to make it up to her after he's hit her. I told her she was worth more than that, but I don't think she heard me."

"That doesn't surprise me. Abused women seem to have selective hearing. Did you tell her about you and Darius?"

"No. We didn't really get to talk like I would've liked. She kind of rushed me out 'cause he was coming back later. He probably told her to get rid of me because he knew I wasn't happy about him being there. I didn't make any effort to hide my dislike for him."

"How do you think she'll take the news that you two are going together?"

"I don't know, Mommy. I was worried about that before I got there, but when I realized what was going on, I didn't even think about that anymore. But honestly, I don't care how she feels about it. I'm not about to give Darius up for anyone."

"I hope not," Darius mumbled softly.

Jamilah glanced over at him and smiled.

"I understand, but what if that means you won't be friends anymore?"

"I truly hope it doesn't come to that, Mommy, but if it does...well, she'll lose."

Alexia did not respond.

Jamilah quickly added, "I told her she could come and stay with me, though, to get away from him. I know she won't, but I did let her know that I'm here for her."

"Well, that's good, baby. That's really all you can do. That's a situation she has to want to get out of before anyone can help her."

"I know."

"I'll say a prayer for her, Jami. Hopefully she'll come to her senses and leave him."

"I hope so, Mommy. I'm really scared for her."

# Chapter 38

I t was a beautiful cloudless night in mid-August. The temperature was in the low eighties, but there was a rare cool breeze that blew steadily, and made the warmth of the night quite comfortable.

As Sabrina stood on the expansive terrace that overlooked the Hudson River and the twinkling lights of New Jersey, she tried to ignore the pounding in her temples. She was in attendance at yet another boring dinner party with Quenten.

Sighing deeply as she closed her eyes in an attempt to block out the party sounds that flowed from the ballroom, despite the obvious virtuosity of the band onstage, the music, combined with the constant chatter of the patrons in attendance, only enhanced the pain that seemed to ricochet in her head.

Quenten knew how miserable she was feeling, too, but exhibited apathy toward her malady. Over an hour ago, when she pleaded with him to take her home because she wasn't feeling well, he'd told her to go somewhere and sit down until he was ready to leave. She had been tempted to walk out without him, but her fear of him kept her there. She hated him for that.

*Think calming thoughts*, she mused, although her efforts to shut out the music and the voices coming through the open door of the terrace proved futile. The pain was so intense that she felt as if she would throw up at any minute. She didn't even realize she was crying until she felt the tears rolling down her face. *Why am I letting him do this to me? Why can't I just walk away?* She had come to despise everything about Quenten Blanchard in the past few weeks. Many times she had considered taking Jamilah up on her offer to stay with her, but how could she without acknowledging that everything Jamilah had told her would come to pass, had come to pass. She knew her friend was not a malicious person, nor would Jamilah ever tell her, "I told you so." *Why is it that all of a sudden my pride is such that I can't turn to the one person I know would have my back, unconditionally?* Sabrina had actually driven out to Jamilah's house last week to see her, but she had been unable to will herself from the car to ring the bell. Possessing an overwhelming need to see and talk to her friend, something, possibly Quenten's hold on her, kept her from reaching out to Jamilah. Sabrina hated that she had allowed Quenten to use and abuse her the way she had, but she was unable to tear herself away from him. After yesterday's altercation, however, Sabrina was finally coming to realize that if she didn't get away from him soon, he would really hurt her.

During an argument, she had told Quenten that she deserved better than he was giving her. She had been angry and her pent-up fury had given her the courage to speak her mind. By the same token, however, her words had only fueled Quenten's already volatile temper, and he struck her, causing her head to hit the wall from the force of his blow. Fortunately, due to her long hair, she was able to conceal the terrible knot she now had on her head as evidence of his abuse.

"Sabrina?"

She heard the smooth sexy drawl over her shoulder and immediately turned to him.

When Avery saw her tears, he rushed to her side and put a comforting hand on her arm. "Are you all right?"

She could only shake her head to indicate that she wasn't. Even that slight movement seemed to accentuate her pain.

"What's wrong?" he asked softly.

"I have an unbearable headache," she said in a whisper. To speak any louder, she believed, would have been too painful.

"Why don't you go home?"

She lowered her head in shame. "Quenten's not ready to go."

"Did you tell him you're not feeling well?"

"Yes."

Avery's blood now boiling, he released her suddenly and stepped away, then started back toward the ballroom on a path to rearrange Blanchard's face.

"Avery." Sabrina's voice brought him back to the moment, and he pivoted back to face her. "Would you take me home, please?"

"Of course." Retracing the steps he had taken away from her seconds before and placing his arm gently around her waist, Avery led her back into the ballroom and toward the exit.

Quenten was embroiled in a debate with some of his colleagues when he spotted Sabrina out of the corner of his eye with a man at the ballroom's exit. "Excuse me," he quickly said to his colleagues and moved away from them before they could even respond. Quenten stepped right up to Avery and grabbed his arm. "What the hell do you think you're doing?"

Avery stopped in his tracks, but he didn't release Sabrina. He looked down at Quenten's hand on his arm, then into Quenten's eyes with undisguised malevolence. "If you know what's good for you, you'll take your hand off of me before I finish this sentence."

Quenten, indeed, had removed his hand before Avery finished speaking, but he stepped right in front of Sabrina. "Where the hell do you think you're going?" he asked her as he tried to ignore the big man who still held her.

"The lady already informed you that she wasn't feeling well. Since you're too preoccupied with your *business associates* to take care of her, I'm taking her home," Avery answered before Sabrina could speak.

"Sabrina, I told you we'd be leaving in a little while," Quenten said to her.

"She wants to leave *now*, so go back to your business. She doesn't need you," Avery replied.

Quenten looked up at him with utter disdain and a fierce anger toward Avery grew in his gut. "Since when did you become my woman's spokesperson?"

"The moment you decided that what she needed was not as important as what you want."

Feeling that she should try to diffuse this tense situation before it got out of hand, Sabrina moaned, "Quenten, I don't feel well. Avery's just driving me home." Her headache now doubled in intensity with this confrontation; it seemed as though the music had suddenly stopped. Noticing that everyone in the room appeared to be watching them, too, by now she really didn't care. At this point, the only thing important to her was leaving there as quickly as possible.

"I'll drive you home," Quenten stated authoritatively and tried to move between her and Avery.

"You had your chance, buddy, and you blew it. Now step off," Avery said threateningly.

Quenten stood his ground. "Look, this is my woman, and I'm not about to let her leave here with the likes of you."

Avery released Sabrina and took a step closer to Quenten, despite that they were already on top of each other. Quenten stepped back. "Don't challenge me, Blanchard, because there's nothing I'd like to do more right now than rearrange your face. All you need to do is give me a reason. Now, I'm going to take this lady home because she asked me to. If you've got a problem with that, tell someone who cares."

Quenten looked past Avery to Sabrina, the anger and embarrassment in his eyes clearly visible. Surprisingly, she felt no fear of him at that moment, and was able to straighten herself as she, defiantly, looked back at him. "I'll call you tomorrow." She then looked up at Avery. "Can we leave now?"

"Certainly," Avery said tenderly as he placed his arm around her waist again, and proceeded through the exit without another word or thought directed toward Quenten Blanchard.

Quenten was so livid he couldn't move. *That man doesn't know who he's dealing with.* He tried to remember his name. It suddenly occurred to him that he'd found him with Sabrina once before. *Williams, that was it. Avery Williams. Who the hell is he, anyway?* Quenten realized then that he'd started seeing him at these gatherings just a couple of months ago. He didn't know of any affiliations the guy had with any of his colleagues. As a matter of fact, he had noticed that Williams was aloof, somewhat standoffish. He had never really paid much attention to him before, but when he thought about it now, Quenten realized that on more than one occasion, he'd caught Williams paying him undue attention. *What is he up to?* Quenten's suspicious mind began working overtime.

One of his colleagues stepped up to him at that moment. "Quenten, who was that guy?"

Quenten turned to him and malevolently sneered, "Someone who just fucked with the wrong person." He then turned and left the ballroom.

***

Sabrina sat quietly beside Avery with her eyes closed as they pulled out of the underground garage where he had parked his Range Rover. Since her headache was so intense, he opted to leave the radio off. He looked over at her when they stopped at the traffic light at the end of the block. *What a beautiful woman.* When the signal changed to green, he drove through the intersection but pulled over to the opposite curb and stopped. Reaching over, he gently touched her hand. "Are you okay?" he asked in a voice as tender as his touch.

Sabrina opened her eyes and looked over at him. Smiling weakly, she nodded her head. "I just need some sleep, I think," she said softly.

"Where do you live?"

"I'm not going home. My mother lives in Queens. Would you mind driving me there?"

With a smile meant to comfort her, he said, "Of course not."

"Thank you." Sabrina gave him directions and they started out. They were driving through the Midtown Tunnel when Sabrina spoke again. "Quenten's going to be furious when I see him again."

"Why do you have to see him again?"

She looked over at him sadly. "He is my boyfriend, Avery."

"That's not something that can't be rectified."

"What am I supposed to do? Pack up and move out of town? That's the only way I wouldn't see him anymore. He has the keys to my apartment. He knows where my mother lives."

"Don't you have any friends you can stay with that he doesn't know?"

"I can't run from him forever. Besides, he takes care of me."

"He abuses you, Sabrina."

She was adamant. "He takes care of me! He pays my rent; he buys my food, my clothes, everything." Her head pounding fiercely, the dam of Sabrina's tear ducts broke as the reality of her life came into sharp focus.

Avery reached over and took her hand. "It's all right."

"No, it's not," she cried. "I don't know what to do."

"If you want to move out of your apartment, Sabrina, I'll help you. I'll protect you. I won't let him hurt you anymore."

"I don't want you to get mixed up in this, Avery. He's a very powerful man, and he could hurt you."

"No, he'll get hurt if he messes with me," Avery said with conviction.

Suddenly, the cryptic business card he had given her jumped to the forefront of her memory. "Avery, who are you?"

Looking over at her for a long moment before he answered, he finally offered, "Someone who wants to be your friend."

"No, really. Who are you? Your business card says *Special Investigator*. What kind of investigator?"

Avery drove along the dark, desolate roadway in silence trying to decide how much he should reveal to her. He knew he couldn't tell her that he was investigating Quenten. Despite her obvious fear of him, Avery had no indication that Sabrina could be trusted with that information. He knew if he told her that he simply wanted to protect her, she wouldn't accept that answer. He realized, too, that he had feelings for this woman that transcended a simple need to protect her, but he couldn't let his emotions cloud his reasoning. He had a job to do. His employer depended on him. He had a reputation for being the best at what he did because he always kept his emotions out of his work. He was proud of that rep. After careful consideration, Avery replied, "Sabrina, I do background investigations for corporations that are considering offering employment contracts or other big business dealings." It was a partial truth.

"Are you investigating someone now?"

"Yes."

"Who?"

"I can't tell you that. It's confidential."

"Is that why I always see you by yourself at these functions. I've noticed that you always come stag, and you don't mingle very much," she said with a timid smile. The pounding had eased a bit.

He looked over at her and couldn't contain the chuckle that escaped from his lips. "Not much of a low profile, huh?"

"Well, it's pretty obvious. Those folks are always either talking business or minding someone else's business. That much I've noticed since I've been with Quenten."

"How long have you been with him?"

"A little over a year. He wasn't always like he is now. He's had some trouble with his business in the last couple of months and…well, I think that's why he's been so mean lately."

"That's no excuse for hurting you, Sabrina."

"I know."

He needed to understand, "Why do you stay with him?"

"I don't know. I was in love with him once but…I guess I've gotten used to living the good life a little too much. I always thought that if I found a man who would take care of me, I'd be happy, but…" She couldn't continue.

"You deserve better than him. You know that, don't you?"

"I keep trying to tell myself that," she said sadly. Looking over at him with salty droplets flowing freely, she murmured, "You must think I'm pretty pitiful, huh?"

"No," he said sincerely. "No, I don't. I just think you've gotten yourself into something that you feel you can't control. But you can, Sabrina. All you have to do, if you don't feel strong enough to do it yourself, is ask for help."

She was silent for the next few minutes until she needed to give him directions. When Avery pulled up in front of her mother's darkened house, she looked over at him and tried to smile. "Thank you, Avery."

He reached over and took her hand once again. "Sabrina, I'm here for you. I want you to call me and let me know that you're all right, okay?"

"Yes."

"You can call me at anytime, day or night, all right?"

She nodded her head. Tears rolled down her face as she looked over at him. "Good night, Avery."

Avery reached over and gently wiped away a watery bead with his thumb before he said, "Good night, Sabrina."

# Chapter 39

Sabrina's mother, Dolly Richardson, still lived in the same house where she and her deceased husband, Dr. Martin Richardson III, had raised Sabrina and her brothers. Dr. Richardson had suffered a heart attack and died when Sabrina was nineteen years old.

It was seldom that Sabrina visited her mother and when she did, she never spent the night. Over the years, their relationship had become strained because of Dolly's need to control everything in Sabrina's life. Sabrina's brothers, Martin IV and Brandon, both now lived in California with their families. Sabrina had been heartbroken when they moved away because she had gotten quite used to being the little sister they'd always doted on. She spoke to both of them frequently by telephone, but she now took a backseat to their wives and children, which was understandable. She truly believed, however, that their mother's controlling nature was instrumental in their decisions to move across the country. She missed having them around—especially Brandon—but she hadn't told either of them about Quenten's abuse.

Despite the difficulty she had in trying to relate to her mother, that night when Sabrina walked into the house where she'd grown up, she instantly felt that she had found a safe haven, and the headache that had plagued her all evening began to ease up.

"Who's there?" her mother called from the second floor.

Sabrina could see the light from her mother's open bedroom door, although she didn't have a view of her parent. "It's me, Mother."

"Sabrina?" Dolly Richardson then moved to the top of the landing. "What's wrong, honey?"

"Nothing. I just need to stay here tonight," Sabrina said as she placed her pocketbook on the table at the bottom of the landing, and immediately started up the stairs.

"Where's Quenten?"

"I don't know, and right now, I really don't care," Sabrina answered as she reached the top of the landing. Placing an obligatory kiss on her mother's cheek, she then continued to her bedroom. Dolly followed.

"How'd you get here?"

"A friend dropped me off."

"Does Quenten know you're here?"

"No. And I'd really rather not talk about it right now, if you don't mind. I have a terrible headache, and I just want to take a couple of aspirin and go to sleep."

"Did you two have a fight or something?" Dolly persisted.

With her patience at its end, Sabrina turned to the older woman. "Mother, please, not now. I'll tell you all about it in the morning. All right?"

Dolly stood where she was for the next few seconds and studied her daughter intently before she finally acquiesced. "All right. I'll get you some aspirin."

"Thank you." Sabrina sighed in relief.

Dolly scurried out of the room, but was gone for only a minute before she returned with a Dixie cup filled with water and two aspirin. "Here, honey. Take these. Do you want me to get you anything else?"

"No, this is fine. Thank you." Sabrina took the aspirin, placed them both in her mouth at once and drank down the water before she briefly put her arms around her mother and kissed her cheek once more. "Good night, Mother. We'll talk about it in the morning, okay?"

"All right, dear. Sleep tight."

***

When Sabrina awoke the following morning, it was close to noon and a feeling of relief and weightlessness washed over her. Feeling worry free, albeit momentarily, *if only I could stay safely wrapped in this comforting cocoon*, she thought. It was good being back home, even if it was only a temporary excursion. Quenten didn't know her whereabouts, so she did not have to fret about confronting him, at least for the time being. However, she wasn't naive enough to believe that he wouldn't think to look for her here, but until he found her, she could rest easy without fear of the threat of his retaliation for embarrassing him last night.

An image of the look on Quenten's face when Avery challenged him suddenly pervaded her thoughts. He had been furious, but obviously not so much that he'd been willing to provoke Avery. *How could I have ever thought that Avery was afraid of Quenten?* She remembered that, for a brief moment, she had hoped that Quenten would step out of line. She would have relished watching him pick himself up from the floor. But, truthfully, she didn't want to see them fight. She knew now, with certainty, that Avery would have demolished Quenten, and despite how much he had hurt her, she didn't want to see him hurt that way. She still didn't know where she'd gotten the courage to stand up to Quenten and actually walk out of that ballroom with Avery's arm wrapped protectively around her waist. She figured because she had been in so much pain at the time, the idea of Quenten's fury did not merit serious circumspection. Her only thought had been to get out of there and get home where she could rest.

"Sabrina, are you up?" her mother called as she entered her bedroom.

"I guess." Sabrina sat up in the bed as her mother came and sat next to her.

Dolly Richardson was dressed in form-fitting slacks and a silk T-shirt, accented by a colorful silk scarf. Her hair, not a strand of which was out of place, was pulled back in a bun at the nape of her neck. Her face was expertly made up, too, as though she had plans to go out at any moment. As such, she looked just like an older version of her daughter.

"How are you, sweetheart? You look a bit haggard."

Sabrina rolled her eyes in annoyance. "I haven't even washed my face, Mother."

"I know, but you don't look as radiant as you usually do. Is everything all right between you and Quenten?"

Sabrina sighed. She lowered her head before answering. "No, Mother. Everything's not all right."

"What did you fight about? I'm sure whatever it was can be easily rectified if you just talk it out," Dolly assured her.

"He hits me, Mother, and after last night, I'm sure the last thing he wants to do is talk it out."

Dolly acted as though she hadn't heard a word Sabrina said. "Whatever happened between you two can't be that bad. He's quite a catch, Sabrina, and you don't want to be doing anything that would ruin your chances of becoming his wife. It's not every day a woman gets an opportunity to be with a man like Quenten Blanchard. He's done good by you, and you can't deny that."

"Didn't you hear what I just said? I said he hits me!"

"So what," Dolly said with a wave of her hand. "Your father used to hit me when he'd get angry, but it didn't kill me."

"Daddy never hit you."

"Yes, Sabrina, he did. You and your brothers never knew because we didn't want you to. But he loved me and he provided for us. As long as Quenten provides a good home and keeps you financially stable, you should ignore his shortcomings. Nobody's perfect, baby. Not even you."

Eyebrows arched in bewilderment, Sabrina couldn't believe what she was hearing. *She can't possibly be condoning his behavior.* "Mother, there's no excuse for him hitting me. I don't deserve that, no matter what he's given me or how good a home he provides, and you didn't deserve that, either. And I'll be damned if I'd ever marry a man like Quenten Blanchard. He's mean to me and I'm...I'm afraid of him," Sabrina confessed as tears came to her eyes.

Dolly reached out and put her arms around Sabrina. "Honey, I know sometimes it gets tough, and Quenten might have a bad day at the office, and he'll come home and take it out on you. Your father did the same thing. But he loved me, and he took care of our family and me, just like Quenten loves and takes care of you. I never wanted for anything when your father was alive, and you can't ignore everything Quenten's done for you, already."

"I don't care what he's done for me or given me or anything else! Can't you understand that? There's no reason for him to hit me. I don't care how bad a day he had. There is no way you can justify him abusing me, and if Daddy did that to you, I would think you'd do everything in your power to make sure your daughter wasn't subjected to that, as well!" Sabrina yelled as she pulled away from her mother. She threw the sheet back and jumped from the bed. "Or did you like it when he hit you, because I sure as hell don't!"

"You watch your tone of voice, young lady. I'm still your mother," Dolly admonished. Rising from the bed, she stepped over to her daughter. She continued in a softer tone, "Of course, I didn't like it when he hit me, but when he got angry like that, I'd just do whatever I had to do to calm him, and everything was all right after that. You can do the same thing. You don't want to lose everything you've gained by being with him."

"What have I gained? A few pieces of expensive jewelry? What good will they do me if I'm laid up in the hospital because he had a bad day? See, Mother, you don't know Quenten. He puts on one face for you, and when he's with me, he's different."

"He can't be that bad if you've stayed with him for this long."

Sabrina, sighing, ambled over to the wicker chest of drawers that had been a part of her bedroom furnishings since she was a teenager. Facing her mother, she admitted, "No, he wasn't always like this, but ever since that stuff with his partner stealing and the Feds investigating him, he's changed. Or maybe he hasn't changed. Maybe the man I thought I knew was a disguise. I just know that I have to get away from him. Last night..." Sabrina moved away from her mother as she continued, "I embarrassed him last night. I wasn't trying to, but I didn't feel well and he wouldn't take me home, so I left with someone else. He drove me here. Quenten tried to stop us, but Avery..."

"Who's Avery?" A prominent frown was on Dolly's face as she stepped over to the chest of drawers, and turned Sabrina to face her.

"He's a friend," Sabrina murmured, guiltily lowering her head.

"Why would you leave a party you attended with your fiancé, with another man, Sabrina? How do you expect him to react?"

"First of all, he's not my fiancé, Mother. And secondly..."

"Who is this Avery fellow, anyway?"

Sabrina paused momentarily. What could she tell her mother about Avery? She didn't really know anything about him either. "I told you, he's a friend."

"But what does he do?"

"What difference does it make?" Sabrina answered impatiently. "I told Quenten that I didn't feel well and that I wanted to leave. He told me I had to wait. When Avery saw how bad I felt... I asked him to drive me home and he didn't hesitate."

"But why would you do that?"

"Because I was miserable and I didn't want to be there any longer, and I couldn't wait until Quenten decided he was ready to leave," Sabrina explained. "I know when I see him again he's going to be furious; that's why I came here. If I had gone home or even to his place, he would have hurt me last night. I know that."

"Sabrina, why would you put yourself in a situation like that if you know it's going to upset him?"

"What should I have done, Mother? Sat there and suffered?"

"No, but..."

"Look, it doesn't matter, anyway. I'm going to tell him it's over. I can't do this anymore. I thought I wanted a man like Quenten; someone rich and powerful to take care of me so that I wouldn't have to work another day in my life. But, if being dependent on him means I have to take whatever abuse he decides to subject me to, then I have to draw the line, to protect myself. I don't want to be anyone's punching bag. It's about self-preservation now. And I know I'm not perfect, not by any means, but I deserve better than that. I've done myself a gross disservice by allowing him to treat me this way for this long simply because he'd present me with a beautiful diamond as an apology."

"Maybe you can talk to him, sweetheart," Dolly suggested.

Sabrina moved toward the connecting bathroom. "He's not a talker, Mother. His whole point of reasoning is that he's taken care of me, so I should obey him without pause. He doesn't want a woman with a brain; he wants a mindless puppet. I've been blinded by the material things he's offered and given me, but diamonds lose their brilliance when you're looking at them through tear-filled eyes."

"He loves you, Sabrina."

"No, he doesn't." Jamilah's words came back to her at that moment. "If he really loved me, he wouldn't hit me."

"Oh, honey..."

Sabrina's hand was on the bathroom door. "Look, Mother, I don't want to talk about this anymore. I've already made up my mind. Now if you'll excuse me, I'm going to go in here and take a nice long bubble bath."

Dolly Richardson had suffered physical abuse at the hands of her husband, although until now, none of her children had ever known about it. She had suffered in silence because she didn't want to forfeit the material possessions nor the status she had gained by being married to Dr. Martin Richardson III. Dolly Richardson had a warped sense of values as to what was right and wrong, or what was or wasn't acceptable when it came to the well-being of her only daughter. Only wanting the best for Sabrina, as far as Dolly was concerned, at this stage of her life—being a thirty-three-year-old woman who was not getting any younger—Quenten Blanchard was the best thing that had ever happened to her daughter. As Sabrina walked through the door of the bathroom, Dolly frowned in dismay. *Maybe she'll change her mind when he gets here.*

✳✳✳

As she luxuriated in her warm, lavender-scented bubble bath, Sabrina went over the conversation she'd just had with her mother. She couldn't believe her father had ever hit her mother. Where were the marks and bruises? She'd never seen so much as a blemish on her mother's face. Now that she thought about it, she could barely remember her father ever losing his temper. But even if he had been physically abusive, how could her mother honestly condone that kind of behavior? *Why would any woman want to be with a man who physically abused her?* Ashamed that she had allowed Quenten to get away with mistreating her for all this time, when she reevaluated her own life, she realized, sadly, what a shallow person she had always been. No man had ever struck her before Quenten, and she should have walked out on him after that first time like she said she would. Instead, she'd let him buy her forgiveness with diamonds. As she remembered her own shameful actions, tears welled in her eyes. Her memory transported her back to the day Jamilah informed her that she was moving out of the apartment they had shared for two years. Jamilah's prophetic words echoed in Sabrina's subconscious, for she had predicted that all the hurt and the blatant disregard she had shown others would come back to haunt her, and it had in the personage of Quenten Blanchard. Jamilah, the best friend she had ever had, had finally gotten fed up with the disregard she'd always shown her. *Do I really deserve the cruel treatment Quenten has subjected me to?* Sabrina wondered if maybe all of this was her just dessert.

When she looked back at her life, she sadly acknowledged that she had always been driven by a need to have the finer things in life. Her ambition had been to marry a man with money. The men she dated had to have something to give her. She never considered how nice they were or how much they cared about her, so long as they could buy her what she wanted or take her wherever she wanted to go. Suddenly, she remembered Darius Thornton. He had been a genuinely nice guy who had cared for her, and had been willing to do whatever she wanted, but she had pushed him away because he had been too nice, and did not have the power or financial and social status that Quenten had. She had treated him worse than any of the others, too. *I didn't even visit him in the hospital when he got shot,* she remembered sadly. Wallowing in tears anew when she recalled how he had come to see her after he had been released from the hospital, she could still see the pain he'd been in, but all she had done was pour salt in his wound. *And I accused Jamilah of stabbing me in the back because she'd been there for him when I should have been.* That was the type of person Jamilah was, and had always been. *Even after all the arguments I started with her for no good reason, Jamilah was still on my side. Maybe I do deserve Quenten's cruelty.*

✱✱✱

As Sabrina soaked and reflected on her life, Dolly Richardson was letting her daughter's tormentor in the front door.

"Hello, Dolly." Quenten greeted her with a kiss on her cheek and a quick hug. "You're looking as lovely as ever."

"Thank you, Quenten. How are you?" she asked with a wary smile.

"I'm all right. How's Sabrina?" he asked with seemingly genuine concern.

"She's fine. She's upstairs taking a bath."

"Is she expecting me?"

"No, I didn't tell her you were coming."

"Can I go up?"

"Quenten, she said you hit her."

Quenten looked into his "mother-in-law's" eyes, momentarily, before he bowed his head in a show of remorse. "We had a fight and I lost my temper," he said softly. "I didn't mean to hit her, Dolly, I swear. I tried to apologize to her, but... she took off so fast that I couldn't stop her."

"She's very upset."

"I can understand that, but I want to make it up to her. I love her, Dolly. She's very important to me. I know I messed up, but I'm willing to do whatever I have to do to make it right," Quenten stated with conviction.

Dolly nodded her head in acceptance.

Quenten turned to start up the stairs.

"Quenten."

He turned back to her. "Yeah?"

"I don't mean to sound... What are your intentions toward my daughter?" Dolly asked. She straightened herself to her full height once she decided that she had every right to ask.

A slow smile formed on his handsome face. "I plan to make an honest woman of your daughter. I'm going to ask her to marry me tonight. I've planned a special dinner for her just to pop the question," he said with an engaging grin.

Dolly smiled as she said, "I just wanted to make sure. You know, I only want the best for her."

"So do I, Dolly. So do I."

***

When Sabrina stepped out of the bathtub, she took her time lotioning her body. When she finished that task, she stood in front of the full-length mirror and stared at her reflection. It was then that she made up her mind that she would definitely end her detrimental relationship with Quenten Blanchard. She didn't know how he would take the news; somehow she knew that he wouldn't be happy about her decision, but she had to do what she had to do. It was for her own good. She really didn't look forward to going out and finding a job, either, but truthfully, she missed her independence. She would welcome the idea of once again being able to come and go as she pleased, and having her own money that she could spend however she liked. Now all she had to do was summon the courage to tell him. Sure, she had been brave enough to walk out of that ballroom last night with Avery, but she had known that he would have protected her if Quenten had stepped out of line. Breaking up with him was something she would have to do all by herself.

She decided that she wouldn't even bother to ask him for her keys. Spending the money to have her locks changed again would be worth the peace of mind she knew would come from being free of his domineering and insecure personality. She decided, also, that it was time to change her way of thinking. No longer would she determine the value of a man by the size of his bank account. That had brought her nothing but loneliness and heartache, not to mention an occasional black and blue mark somewhere on her body. From now on, she would look at the person behind the man and determine his value by the strength of his character. *Maybe one day, I'll be lucky enough to meet another man like Darius Thornton.* If so, she would definitely treat him in the manner he deserved.

She sighed loudly as she reached for the hairbrush on the vanity. As she slowly brushed her long tresses, she acknowledged that it would probably be best if she just moved out of that apartment all together. When she thought about it, she reasoned that she had two choices. She could either come back and stay with her mother until she could save enough money to get her own apartment again, or she could take Jamilah up on her offer to stay with her. But to do the latter would be like taking advantage of Jamilah once again, and she truly didn't want to do that. Sabrina decided, too, that from now on, she would be a better friend to Jamilah than she had ever been before. She counted herself fortunate that Jamilah even wanted to have anything to do with her after the way she had taken advantage of her over the many years they had been friends.

*That's it, then. I'll just tell Mother that I have to move in for a while until I can get myself back on my feet.* Sabrina also decided that she would call Jamilah and ask her if she'd like to have dinner with her. It was time for her to make amends. Placing the brush back on the vanity, she braided her hair in one long plait, down her back, then opened the door and stepped back into her bedroom. She moved to the dresser and opened the top drawer. Although she didn't visit her mother frequently, Sabrina still had underwear, clothes and shoes at her mother's house. Actually, her bedroom had not changed much from when she had moved out, five years earlier.

Sabrina pulled a pair of panties and a bra from the drawer and after pushing it closed, bent over to step into the panties.

"What a lovely view."

Straightening quickly, she turned as her heart jumped into her throat. Eyes bulging, a loud gasp escaped her lips as she faced Quenten. He was lounging comfortably in the easy-chair in the corner of her room, looking as though he didn't have a care in the world.

"Quenten!" she exclaimed as she instinctively held the underwear up in an attempt to cover herself.

"Hi, baby. Did you enjoy your bath?" he asked in a caressing tone.

Her heart was racing and she suddenly felt beads of perspiration break through the pores on her face. She felt that her blood pressure must have risen twenty points. "Yes," she murmured. She was frozen to the spot.

"I didn't hear you, baby," he said as he slowly rose from the chair and started toward her.

Her eyes were a story in fear. *What is he doing here? How did he get in? Why did she let him in after everything I told her?* "Yes," she repeated.

Quenten stepped in front of her and placed her in a tender hug, although her hands were still between them. "Are you feeling better, sweetheart?"

"Yes."

"I was worried about you. I'm glad you're feeling better."

She tried to collect herself. *Get a grip, girl. He can't hurt you here.* "I didn't know you were coming." Her attempt to sound cool, calm and collected was feeble, for she could feel her lips tremble with each word she spoke.

"Your mother called me this morning and told me you were here. I figured you'd need a ride home since you didn't have your car."

He was staring straight into her eyes. She felt as though he was looking through her. His hand came up toward her face and she flinched, but he simply ran his hand gently over her hair. He pretended not to notice her movement. "You look so good, baby. You know, I'd like to have you right now, but I'd feel kind of funny making love to you with your mother right downstairs. I mean, she could come up here at any moment, and we'd have quite an awkward situation on our hands, wouldn't we?"

"Yeah, I'd feel kind of funny, too," she said, trying to smile.

Placing his hand under her chin and tilting her head up to him, Quenten leaned in and placed a tender kiss on her lips. "I wish I didn't have to go back to my office. I'd love to just take off and go somewhere with you, and make mad passionate love to you for the rest of the day, into the night, but duty calls," he said with a shrug of his shoulders.

*Yeah I bet. Why is he being so sweet to me?*

"If I didn't have this meeting tomorrow morning, I'd suggest we hop on a plane and fly down to St. Lucia for the weekend, but they'd probably fall apart without me. So instead, I've planned a special dinner for you tonight. I have something very important that I want to talk to you about, sweetheart, and I know you're going to be just as excited about it as I am," he said with a smile that, if she didn't know better, could have been genuine.

"What is it, Quenten?" Sabrina asked, anxious to know what was suddenly so important, that would excite her. *Is he going to give me my freedom along with a big cash settlement?*

"We'll talk about it later. Why don't you get dressed and I'll take you home," he said, gently caressing her face.

*I can't leave here with him.* "I was going to spend the day with my mother, Quenten. She asked me to go shopping with her," Sabrina lied as she eased her arms from between them and placed them loosely around his waist. Figuring that she should probably try to appear at ease with him, even though her heartbeat had not yet slowed its pace, she couldn't quite quell the nervousness she felt in her gut. *Why hasn't he said anything about last night?*

"Your mom knows about my surprise. She's as excited about it as I am, so I know she'll understand if you can't hang out with her today."

"But..."

"Come on, baby. I know you won't be disappointed." He reached down and pinched her on her behind. "Put your panties on. You're making it hard for me to resist you, if you know what I mean," he said with a chuckle. His arousal was, indeed, evident and the last thing she wanted to do was have sex with him, now or ever again.

She tried to laugh along with him when she said, "Yeah, I see." She stepped out of his embrace and once again bent over to put on her panties. She then started to put on her bra.

"Turn around; let me fasten that for you."

Sabrina turned her back to him. Before he fastened her brassiere, however, he reached around and cupped one of her mounds and gently squeezed her nipple until it puckered on its own. "Mmm, you know I love your breasts," he murmured as he kissed her softly on her neck.

She felt his hardened member pressed against her backside and was suddenly repulsed by his touch. She moved away from him quickly, but when she realized what she'd done, she tried to recover with, "Oh, baby, I'd better go tell my mother that I won't be able to go with her today."

Quenten's eyes hardened for a brief moment before he responded with a smile, "Yeah, you do that. I'll be right here."

Sabrina turned and grabbed the robe hanging on the bedroom door, then left the room without hesitation. She pulled the robe on hurriedly as she stormed to her mother's bedroom. She closed the door immediately upon entering. "Mother, why did you call him?" Sabrina cried in agony.

Dolly turned to her daughter and asked, "What's the matter, Sabrina?"

"Why did you call him after what I told you?" Her face was a story in confusion.

"Sabrina, I called him this morning before you told me that, but don't worry, honey." Dolly moved closer to Sabrina. "Listen, everything's going to be all right. He's got great news. I talked to him. I told him what you told me, and he promised he would never hit you again."

Sarcastically, Sabrina answered, "Yeah, of course he's gonna tell you that. What else was he supposed to say? That he's gonna take me home and beat me up?"

"Honey, listen. Stop worrying. He loves you. Everything's going to be okay." In her warped mind, Dolly believed what she was saying.

"But he wants me to leave here with him now, Mother."

"Yes, I know. He has a surprise for you."

Sabrina frowned. "What is this *big* surprise he has for me?"

"Honey, don't... Look, I guarantee you'll be okay. All right? You'll be okay."

She turned away from her mother as she said, "I can't believe you would do this to me."

"Do what, baby? I'm looking out for you. I only want what's best for you."

Sabrina turned back quickly as she asked, "Then how could you possibly want me to be with him?"

Dolly sighed. "Sabrina, I think you're making a lot more out of this than there actually is."

"How can you tell me that?" Sabrina asked in disbelief.

Dolly grabbed her daughter's arms and held her as she insisted, "Listen to me. We all go through things in life. He needs you to stand by him. He's been going through a difficult time, and he needs you to stand by him."

Sabrina shook her head as she murmured, "I can't believe you." She turned away from her mother in disgust and walked back out of the room. Before she re-entered her bedroom, however, she stood outside the door for a moment trying to decide what she should do. She obviously couldn't depend on her mother to protect her. *And what could be this big surprise that he had for her,* she wondered.

After a few minutes, Sabrina re-entered the room. Quenten was sitting on her bed. "Everything all right, baby?"

"Yeah," she said with a phony smile.

He rose and moved toward her. "I'm going to drop you off at your place and run back to the office to take care of this business I need to take care of there. I want you to get dressed. Put on something fabulous, you know, look beautiful, as you always do. I'm going to take you to dinner. We're going to have a very special dinner tonight. There are some things I need to say to you, baby. I know it's been a little rough lately, but I want to make it up to you." He reached out and caressed her face lovingly, as he continued, "You're beautiful and I love you, Sabrina. I just want to do right by you. Will you let me do that?"

She looked into his eyes and although her stomach was knotted in fear, and her heart was doubtful of the sincerity of his words, she nodded and whispered, "Yes."

Quenten dropped Sabrina off at her apartment at approximately two-thirty. He told her he would be back to get her around six o'clock that evening. She was to be dressed and ready to go when he arrived.

When six-thirty rolled around, Sabrina was in the same clothes she had worn from her mother's house that afternoon. She had no intention of going anywhere with him that night or ever again. And this big surprise he had for her, if he couldn't tell her right there in her apartment, then she didn't want to know what it was. She had decided, nonetheless, that she would definitely break off her relationship with him. She called her mother when she first got home that afternoon and told her what she planned to do. Despite Dolly's attempts to dissuade her from her plan of action, Sabrina wouldn't hear of it. She wanted nothing else to do with Quenten Blanchard.

Lounging on the sofa smoking a cigarette when her doorbell rang, she was surprised that he hadn't just walked in with the key, as he usually did. Taking her time getting up from the sofa, she leisurely strolled to the door and looked through the peephole to see who was there, although she knew it was Quenten. She unlocked and opened the door, then stood back for him to enter. Quenten was actually wearing a tuxedo.

When he saw that she was still wearing the clothes he'd brought her home in, his face hardened in a frown. "Why aren't you dressed, Sabrina?" He stepped inside and closed the door behind him.

She casually strolled back across the room. "I don't feel like going anywhere tonight, Quenten."

"I told you I wanted to take you out somewhere special tonight. I told you I wanted to talk to you."

"Whatever you want to talk to me about, you can talk to me about it right here. We don't have to go anywhere for that. I'm not in the mood to go out."

"I made reservations."

"Well, they'll have to be canceled." Despite her underlying fear of him, Sabrina had reached the point where she was simply fed up, and didn't care to do anything to make his life easier. "You said you wanted to make things right. Wining and dining me is not going to make things right."

Quenten took a step closer to her, then halted his movement, staring at her like she had lost her mind. Sabrina tried very hard to appear carefree as she moved over to the counter that separated the kitchen from the dining area. She shook the ashes of her cigarette into the crystal ashtray that rested on the counter, then took another drag.

"Why do you want to make this difficult for me, Sabrina? You know I'm trying to do right by you."

"You're trying to do right by me? Is that why you beat me up?"

Quenten chuckled, but there was no humor in it. "I only hit you when you provoke me."

"When I provoke you?" she shouted. "I've never done anything to justify you hitting me."

He moved closer to her. "What about last night, Sabrina? You embarrassed me in front of my colleagues last night when you walked out of there with that...son of a bitch, Avery Williams. What the fuck is going on there? You screwing him behind my back or something?"

Sabrina took a deep breath. "I was wondering when you were going to bring that up. But for your information, no, I'm not sleeping with Avery. As a matter of fact, last night is only the second time I've ever seen him. I didn't feel well, Quenten. I asked you to take me home. You wouldn't. I asked him. He didn't hesitate."

"So you felt it was necessary to embarrass me?"

"I wasn't trying to embarrass you. To be perfectly honest with you, I wasn't thinking about how you'd feel about it because all I could think about was the pain that *I* was in. I was thinking about myself for a change. Now if I'm wrong for that, then I'll just be wrong. You weren't thinking about me. You didn't care."

Quenten pointed a finger at her as he stated, "That man threatened me last night. He doesn't know who he's fucking with 'cause I will hurt him. Whatever your relationship is with him..."

Cutting him off, she yelled, "How many times do I have to tell you? I don't have a relationship with him."

Quenten didn't hear a word she said. "You made me look like a fool last night, Sabrina. You took that man's back over mine. Was that right? How would you feel if I did that to you? How would you feel if I had walked out of there with another woman, Sabrina, while you stood there and watched?"

"I'm sorry I embarrassed you, but I had to leave. I couldn't stay there any longer."

"Why'd you tell your mother that I hit you?"

"Because you did!"

"What'd you think she was going to do? Huh? What'd you think, Sabrina? What goes on between you and me is our business. You understand me? It's our business. It has nothing to do with anyone else, your mother included. Now why don't you go get dressed so we can get out of here? Go 'head, hurry up."

"I don't want to go."

"Go get dressed, Sabrina."

"I'm not going, Quenten," she stated firmly.

Quenten moved closer until he was standing right in front of her and glared at her for a long moment without a word before shaking his head. "Why you want to piss me off tonight? I had a really special evening planned for you, and you want to piss me off."

"Quenten, I…I think it would be best if we stopped seeing each other." Sabrina had absolutely no idea where she'd gotten the courage to say those words. She could see how angry he already was; it was written all over his face. His eyes were blazing, but she didn't care. She had taken all that she cared to take from him. She didn't want any more diamonds, gold, furs, clothes, trips, anything. She didn't want anything from him except her freedom, except her life back.

Staring at her in disbelief, he asked, "What did you just say to me?"

"I said I don't want to see you anymore."

He yelled, "After everything I've done for you, this is the thanks I get? After everything I've given you, you think you can just push me out? You've done nothing for the past year but sit on your ass and take, take, take everything I gave you! You never offered me anything, you never gave me anything, you never did anything for me and now you want to push me out?"

"I'm tired of you abusing me. Yes, I took—I took your abuse. I don't care what you've done for me, Quenten," she yelled back as tears streamed down her face. "I've never done anything to deserve your abuse."

"You're sleeping with that muthafucka, aren't you?" His face was distorted by his rage.

"No!"

"Don't lie to me, Sabrina."

"I'm not lying to you."

"Why should I believe you? You've lied to me before. You lied when you changed the damn locks on the door, telling me that bullshit about somebody breaking in here. You know good and damn well nobody broke into this fuckin' apartment. What do you think, I'm stupid?"

"Quenten, I'm not lying to you. There's nothing between Avery and me. This has nothing to do with Avery. This is about us. Nothing else. I can't…I can't do this anymore. I don't want your jewels, your clothes…"

"I pay your fuckin' rent, bitch," he said chillingly.

"Quenten…"

"What the fuck would you have without me? You wouldn't have shit!"

"I'd have my self respect," she said in defiance.

Quenten stood for a long moment with a menacing glare. His eyes were like dark pools of emptiness. Suddenly, he turned and took a few steps away from her. It was utterly silent in the apartment for the next few minutes. Sabrina was a bundle of nerves as she waited for his next words.

He stood across the room from her, with his head bowed as if in prayer. "All right, Sabrina. You don't want to be with me anymore, all right," he said just above a whisper. His back was still to her. "But when I walk out that door, it's over. It's over, you understand?"

"Yes," she cried. "That's all I want. I just want it to be over." *He's taking it better than I expected.* A feeling of elation and peaceful calm briefly washed over her.

He turned to her. "I have to tell you, though, Sabrina," he continued in that same soft tone. "I had hoped that I'd see your friend Avery again because he has to pay for what he did to me last night." He paused a moment. A prominent frown creased his forehead as he pressed his index finger to his mouth as if in deep thought. Then, quite unexpectedly, in a light-hearted manner, he said, "Do me a favor. I know you say you're not seeing him or whatever, but I want you to give him something for me, all right?" When she didn't respond immediately, he repeated, "All right?"

"What?" she asked full of skepticism.

Quenten stepped close to her once again, and before Sabrina knew what was happening, he slammed his fist into her face. The blow knocked her into the counter. Her body slammed against the counter's overhang so hard that she not only bruised her back, but also felt as if her whole body had been twisted in some unnatural manner. She cried out in pain and shock at the force of his blow. He had hit her before, yes, but Sabrina had never felt anything like this. Feeling like a sledgehammer had been slammed into her head, his blow stunned her so that she was not immediately able to move. Quenten took two long strides toward her, then grabbed her by her hair and turned her face to him as he pummeled it repeatedly with his fist. She tried to put her arms up to shield herself from his blows, but they kept coming, bruising her arms now, as well. Quenten was ranting all the while, but Sabrina could barely hear through the haze that had suddenly engulfed her. She felt as if her head was submersed in water.

Almost as abruptly as he had attacked her, Quenten released Sabrina. She crumbled to the floor like a rag doll. Her hands covered her face as she cried for her life, for she truly thought he would kill her.

Quenten stormed into the bedroom. She didn't know what he was doing but she could hear crashing sounds like he was smashing her things against the wall. In truth, she didn't care what he was doing. All she knew was that she had to get away from him. Somehow she had to get away. She tried to will her body to rise from the floor, but she couldn't move. She could barely breathe. Her head still felt as if it was underwater. Her eyes were swollen almost completely shut so she could barely see.

Sabrina reached up and tried to get a grip on the counter to pull herself up from the floor. It was the greatest effort she had ever made in her life, and she wasn't having much success. Suddenly, the noise from the other room stopped, and she could hear his footsteps coming back toward her. She screamed in her mind, *Oh God, please don't let him hit me again.* Turning her head in the direction of the sound of his footfalls, she could barely make out his form through her swollen eyes.

"You think I'm gonna let you keep all this shit I gave you. You're out of your fuckin' mind, bitch."

Since all of her furs were in cold storage, Quenten loaded himself down with her leather coats and other articles of clothing. The pockets of his tuxedo bulged with the jewelry he'd given her. She could make out a strand of diamonds—be it a necklace or bracelet, she didn't know—dangling from his pocket. "You're going to be sorry you ever crossed me, bitch," he declared dangerously.

Paying no heed to his words, Sabrina was still trying to pull herself up from the floor. *Please don't let him come any closer*, she prayed silently. *Please don't let him come any closer to me.* Finally, after what seemed like an eternity, Sabrina was on her feet, but she still could not stand on her own. Leaning all of her weight on the counter, she tried to hold herself up and prayed that he would just go. *TAKE EVERYTHING, TAKE WHATEVER YOU WANT, AND JUST GO.*

Suddenly, Quenten started toward her. "You think you can just brush me aside after everything I've done for you. You think I'm just going to turn around and quietly walk out that door, after I've paid your rent here for a year, bought your food, your clothes, everything! What the hell would you be without me? What would you have? Nothing! And you think you can just push me aside. No way, bitch. You've got the wrong one, this time."

Sabrina tried to move away from him as he approached, but her legs were like weights that wouldn't budge. Her head felt as if a ton of bricks were inside her skull. She turned her back to him, trying to hold fast to the counter so she wouldn't lose her footing. As she grappled to keep her balance, a number of the items that were on the countertop were knocked to the floor. In the next second, however, her hand was immersed in cigarette ashes. She had unknowingly pushed her lead crystal ashtray to the edge. At once, she realized she had a weapon. Gripping the ashtray firmly as Quenten continued toward her, when he was right behind her, her will to survive took over—because she truly thought her life would end if she let him touch her again—and she turned and swung in one uncoordinated move. She felt the impact of the heavy crystal hitting his head solidly and heard the sickening crunch of what she believed were bones breaking. Through her limited vision—through the slits that were now her eyes—she saw his body crumble to the floor amongst her things. The ashtray fell from her hand and broke as she stood there in shock. Although she could feel how her lips had swelled, how her entire face had swelled from the pounding he had given her moments earlier, her only thought was that she had killed him.

Suddenly, a new brand of panic filled her mind and sent her heart racing in fear. *I don't want to go to prison.* She didn't want to spend the rest of her life behind bars. She had only been trying to protect herself, but she knew when they found his body on the floor of her apartment, no one would listen to her side of the story. He was, after all, a powerful man, a millionaire, and she had killed him. *I have to get out of here*, was all she could think. *I have to get out of here.*

Stumbling across the room to the sofa where her pocketbook lay, she could barely see, but she forced her eyes open as far as she could. Grabbing her pocketbook, she opened it and rummaged inside, feeling for her car keys. Her head pounded, but she ignored the pain. She had to get away, somewhere, as far away from there as she could get.

Sabrina stumbled to the door and pulled it open with great effort, then clumsily fell into the hallway. Quickly picking herself up, she walked along the wall, holding on to keep from falling. Amazingly, her thoughts were clear enough to realize that if she got on the elevator and there were people in the car, they would ask questions, and she would have to explain that there was a dead man in her apartment, so she moved to the staircase. She opened that door and grabbed the railing tightly because she didn't believe she could negotiate even one flight of stairs, much less five, but knew she had to. Upon taking the first step, she lost her footing and slid halfway down the landing, ending up on her backside. She sat there for the next five minutes and cried. *How could I have let it come to this? How could I have even let it get this far? He tried to kill me. I didn't mean to kill him, but he tried to kill me.*

When Sabrina finally made it to the first floor, she was surprised that she hadn't encountered anyone as she stepped from her building. As she slowly, and with great effort, made her way to her car, she ignored the stares from passersby. Once she reached the vehicle, she unlocked the door with her automatic door opener and got behind the wheel, but she had a difficult time locating the keyhole for the ignition. When she finally did, she inserted the key but didn't start the engine. She sat there and tried to collect herself because she was still quite shaken up.

After a few minutes, she reached up to the visor over her head and pulled it down. Lifting the cover of the lighted makeup mirror to see if she looked as bad as she felt, Sabrina gasped in shock at the horrific sight of her bruised and battered face. Uncontrollable tears poured from her eyes as she cried out her physical and mental anguish. She didn't even recognize herself. Her eyes were almost swollen shut; her jaw was distended so much she appeared to have a wad of cotton in her mouth; her lip was busted and swollen; and blood trickled from the corner of her mouth. As she sat there and cried, she asked herself, *Where can I go? I can't call the police. They'll arrest me.*

After nearly twenty minutes, Sabrina finally turned on the ignition, and slowly eased the vehicle away from the curb. She knew in her heart and mind that with her limited vision, she had no business behind the wheel of a car, but how else was she supposed to get away? What if someone had heard the commotion coming from her apartment and had come to investigate or had even called the police? She remembered then, to her dismay, that she hadn't even bothered to lock the door.

They would walk in and find his dead body in the middle of her floor; then she would be considered a fugitive.

As she drove slowly through the streets of Manhattan toward one of the many highways that would take her off the island, Sabrina reflected on all that had happened in the past two days. If she had just put her foot down yesterday and insisted upon not attending the gala with Quenten, it was probable that she would not be in this situation. However, she didn't delude herself that Quenten would not still be angry if she had told him she wanted to call it quits under different circumstances. But at least the idea of her having some kind of relationship with Avery wouldn't have come up to fuel his already volatile temper.

Wishing she knew where Avery was now, she'd have run straight to him if she could, but it was for the best that she didn't know where he was. What would his reaction be if he could see what Quenten had done to her? She hadn't missed the animosity he had for Quenten. How could she? Avery had made no attempt to hide his disdain for the man.

Although he had said otherwise, Sabrina was fairly certain that he thought very little of her for being with Quenten. The longer she dwelt on that, the sorrier she felt, too, but right now she had to keep her emotions in check. If she began to cry, there was no doubt in her mind that she'd cause a major accident on these busy streets.

Her mind turned to her mother, and the regret and pity she felt for herself quickly turned to anger toward her parent. If Dolly hadn't been so busy trying to run her life like she always did, she wouldn't have even had to deal with Quenten today, at all. But no, her mother figured she knew what was best for her. *What are you going to think of your precious Quenten now?*

Sabrina still wasn't sure if she believed her mother's story that her father used to hit her. She knew, however, that if he did, he had never been so brutal as Quenten had been on this night. Sabrina's memories of her father were all good. She had been his angel and he'd been her hero. Her father had doted on her, as had her mother and older brothers, but Dr. Richardson was the only one who had taken no pains about disciplining her. He was very strict, she remembered fondly, but he was also fair, and his patience with her had been limitless. On this night when she felt completely alone, Sabrina missed her father more than ever before.

She had always hoped she would meet a man just like her father. When she was in college, Sabrina had compared all of the young men she dated to him, and none of them stood up to the comparison. She realized now that it was after her father had died that her mother had become even more controlling than she normally was. Dolly had basically run her brothers off because of her domineering ways and her habit of infusing her ideas on them, despite that they were both grown men by that time. Maybe the reason she held on so tight to Sabrina was because, without her, she was all alone.

Sabrina realized, sadly, that the only way Dolly Richardson knew how to show her love was to step in and take over, but this time she had gone too far. She felt sorry for her mother, but the burning anger in her chest overpowered her other emotions, and right then, Sabrina wanted absolutely nothing to do with her.

# Chapter 40

Darius had arrived at Jamilah's house approximately two hours earlier. It was now seven forty-five, and they had finished eating the simple dinner Jamilah had prepared of fried chicken, mashed potatoes and green peas. Jamilah was dressed in a pair of spandex shorts and an old shirt. Darius still had on the slacks he'd worn to work, but he had removed his shirt and tie, so only his undershirt covered his chest.

They were sitting on the couch in front of the television, but they hadn't been watching the program on the screen for some time. Wrapped in each other's arms and engaged in a passionate tongue wrestle, Jamilah's eyes watered as they often did when she thought of how happy she was, of how happy this beautiful black man in her arms made her.

Ever since their relationship had graduated to this more committed one, Jamilah's life seemed to have taken on dream-like qualities. She walked around in a perpetual state of euphoria.

Darius' hand slowly moved up and down her back under her shirt. Sighing with pleasure at the feel of her skin beneath his hands, as his lips softly caressed her face, he whispered breathlessly, between pecks, "I love you, Jamilah Parsons. I want to spend the rest of my life with you. I want you to have my babies." With his heart overflowing from the love he felt for her in that instant, he asked, "Will you be my wife, Jamilah? Will you share your life with me?" Pulling back slightly so he could gaze into her eyes, he saw her tears and gently kissed each of her lids in turn before he murmured, "I hope those are tears of joy."

Her eyes shined with her smile as she responded softly, "They are."

"Does that mean you'll marry me?"

"Yes, Darius."

He stared lovingly at her a moment longer before pressing his lips to hers once again.

This kiss started softly, reflecting the tenderness and love they felt for one another, but the gentle wrestling of their tongues generated an intense heat inside each of them. In the next instant, the love they felt for one another was conjoined by their mutual lust. Darius slowly eased Jamilah back on the couch until they were both horizontal. Although he was a big man, he was practically weightless on top of her.

Responding to his every touch, his every physical command as if programmed, Jamilah felt the hardness of his manhood pressed against her thigh, causing a sensation so pleasurable that she shifted her body slightly so she could feel him at her core. As she moved her hips in chorus with his, she trembled in euphoric deliverance as a multitude of mini-explosions erupted at her center. Suddenly, as if by magic, the buttons on her shirt were undone. She wondered briefly how he had done that so quickly since she couldn't remember his hands performing the task.

Burying his face in the cleavage of her ample bosom, he grasped one of her mounds firmly, and gently nibbled the dark, swollen nipple until it hardened between his teeth. When Jamilah's satisfied moan reached his ears, he looked up at her and a mischievous smile creased his face before he lowered his head to suckle the other. Wanting to give each mound equal time, his exploration continued. Venturing lower, a stiff tongue blazed its trail along the lines of her abdomen until he reached her navel. Swirling his oral protrusion gently in the crevice caused her body to twitch from the stimulation and a slight, sensuous giggle escaped her lips. "Aah, ticklish." He breathed delightedly. Continuing southward, he soon reached the elastic waistband of her shorts. Kneeling over her, Jamilah raised her bottom up from the couch so he could pull her shorts and panties off easily. Tossing the garments across the room, he continued on his original course at once.

Jamilah was drowning in her pleasure.

He kissed her softly along the line of her inner thigh, then gently bit her there, causing a shriek of surprise and delight to spill from her lips. Slipping a long, thick finger into her secret place and marveling at the warm, moist and abundant nectar he encountered, he asked, "Can I drink my fill, Jamilah?"

"Yes, Darius; yes, please."

His tongue traced the portal of her secret garden slowly, lovingly, until he found the lock that released all of her inhibitions.

Jamilah gasped in marvelous wonder at the scintillating sensations he caused in her. No man had ever loved her so completely. Not that she had much experience; Darius was the fifth man she had been with in the eleven years since she had lost her virginity, but she had never experienced anything like this. His tongue bathed her gently as his hands held her backside firmly in place, despite the fact that she had no intention of moving away. She didn't want his loving to ever stop.

Raising his head, he looked up at her, loving the look of lust that covered her beautiful dark brown countenance. He especially loved that he was directly responsible for it. "You taste good, baby," he said seductively. Continuing his rise from the couch, he muttered, "You know I've got to have you now." Towering above her, his eyes never left her face and his scorching gaze was matched by hers. She writhed impatiently, awaiting his return. He removed his pants and underwear without circumstance, and quickly pulled his undershirt over his head. Momentarily entertaining the idea of removing his socks, he decided that would take up too much time, as he was eager to get inside her.

Jamilah's eyes locked on his stiff, pulsing member. Suddenly, she rose from her prone position to sit up. Her face level with his groin, she unceremoniously reached out and captured his thick protrusion in an eager hand. "I want to taste you," she seductively whispered, peeking up at him.

"Jamilah..." he began to protest.

"Shh," she murmured as luscious lips slowly came in contact with his flesh. Kissing it gently, she shyly stuck her tongue out to taste the bead at its tip.

The sensation that traveled to Darius' nerve endings from the sudden moist warmth of her oral cavern was mind-blowing. Slowly, skillfully, she massaged his length, causing uncommon thrills and shivers that went straight through to his bones. Eyes closed reflexively, Darius' shock was overcome by his pleasure.

"Jamilah," he sighed breathlessly as his hands found her head and assisted her sensual motion.

Drowning in the hedonistic torture she was lasciviously inflicting on him, Darius felt his knees weakening. "Oh, God. Oh…yes… Yes!" he growled lustily. She was killing him and he loved every sweet, sadistic second. Feeling his flow near to eruption in the next instant, he forcefully pulled away from her. "Stop! I can't take anymore," he panted. *Who was this incredibly sexual being before him?* This was a side of Jamilah he'd never had the pleasure of seeing. "Who taught you how to do that?" he breathlessly inquired.

Salacious eyes bore through him. "I thought you knew that I'd love every bit of you, Darius. Every…single…inch," she purred as her tongue slid across luscious lips.

Her words left him speechless, but her pupils spoke volumes. She was starving for him.

Instantly cueing on her impatience, he gently pushed her back down on the sofa and wasted no time joining her. He eased himself on top of her, holding his throbbing tool in hand to better guide it home. Darius entered her immediately, and pushed his entire length into her welcoming depths. "Yes," she moaned soft and low. "Yes. Yes."

A sensuous whisper spilled from his lips. "Is that it, baby? Is that what you want?"

"Yes, Darius. Oh, God, yes!"

"Yeah, it feels good. You feel so-o-o good, baby."

Their lovemaking was slow and purposeful, each trying to give the other their all. With each stroke, Jamilah sighed in delight. Gazing into one another's eyes and, without words communicating their feelings, Darius lowered his head to taste her luscious lips. Jamilah's mouth opened to welcome his. As the fervor of their lovemaking increased, the intensity of their kisses heightened with urgency. Feeling the vibrations of an orgasm building inside her with each powerful thrust, Jamilah's legs went up, encircling his waist and pulling him closer, if that was possible. Her hips came up to meet his as she pulled him deeper into her feminine canyon. Then it happened. An implosion like she'd never experienced catapulted her straight to the zenith of life. She yelled out, squeezing him tighter.

Darius could feel her walls contracting on him. The sensation was indescribable. "Are you there, baby? Are you there?" he questioned breathlessly as he pulled her closer still. But he knew the answer. The feel of her breasts pressed against his unyielding chest was incredibly erotic in concert with her fierce gyrations.

"Yes!" she screamed. "Yes, Darius!"

"Oh you feel good." He sighed. "So-o-o good, so-o-o sweet." His lips seeking hers again, he pressed them to hers once more, crushing her mouth as he prepared to follow her to that physical heaven. In the next instant, his seed burst forth fiercely, coating her insides and mingling with her sweet dew. Unable to stifle it, a satisfied wail escaped his lips before he collapsed in her arms.

They lay together in silence for the next few minutes, each trying to slow the frenetic beating of their hearts.

Darius spoke first. "You're amazing, do you know that?"

"It's not me, Darius; it's you."

He smiled at her affectionately and said, "You're too modest." He kissed her softly on her forehead. "I love that about you. As a matter of fact, I love everything about you."

She returned his smile. "The feeling's mutual."

"You know I'm not finished with you, right?"

"I hope not. I'm just getting warmed up."

Kissing her sensuously, he mouthed, "I noticed. Let's turn off the TV and go upstairs."

"Yes, let's."

Darius rose, but not before licking her lips slowly. "You taste so good."

When she stood before him, he removed her shirt and added it to the pile of clothes already on the floor. He bent and kissed her breasts. "I'm your baby. Will you feed me with these?"

Jamilah laughed as she held his head to her bosom. "Only if you're a good boy."

He responded breathlessly, "I'll be good, Mommy," as his passionate eyes burned through her.

Suddenly, without warning, Darius scooped Jamilah into his arms. She let out a shriek of surprise. "What are you doing? You're going to hurt your back."

"How you figure?" he asked as he headed for the stairs.

"I'm too heavy for you to be carrying like this."

"No, you're not."

"Darius, put me down before you hurt yourself."

"You think I can't handle you?" he asked as he began the climb.

"Do you know how much I weigh?"

"I don't care. I can bench press two hundred and seventy pounds easy, and I know you don't weigh anywhere close to that."

"But Darius..."

"Hush, now. A king must be able to carry his queen."

By now they were in her bedroom, and he gently lowered her to the bed. "I love you, Jamilah."

She enfolded her arms around his neck as she pulled him down, affording her access to his sweet lips. "I love you, Darius."

He loved the undeniably female contours of her body. The abundant orbs that were her breasts, the soft tissue of her stomach, and her ample bottom gave him plenty of woman to love. Besides that, he had always been a sucker for a woman with big legs. In the years since he'd become sexually active, Darius had to acknowledge that the women he'd been with had all been fairly small in size, if not in height. Jamilah was, in fact, the biggest woman he had ever been with, but she was also the sexiest, by far. The softness of her body beneath his hands and in his arms had a very pleasing effect on him. He wished she was not so self-conscious about her weight, but since she was, he was even more determined to let her know exactly how beautiful and erotic he found her.

Turning onto his back and pulling her atop him allowed her to do with him as she pleased, and it afforded him a better view of her luscious body. Hungrily, Jamilah kissed his lips before she began a sensuous journey with her lips and tongue; first at his neck and ears, then onto his chest, stopping at the hardened nipples on his muscular torso. Her hands acted on their own, gently stroking his thighs along the outer perimeter as well as the inside of his well-defined limbs.

She rose up off of him just long enough for him to get a handle on her breasts. "Why don't you have a seat and make yourself at home."

Jamilah giggled but took him up on his offer. She positioned herself so that she was straddling him and immediately enveloped his erect protrusion in her warm, wet garden of love.

As their passions ascended once again, Jamilah's slow grind became more and more erratic. Closing his eyes and savoring the sweetness of her body, Darius loved the torture she was inflicting upon him.

Jamilah was so caught up in their love dance and the splendid unification they had created, that she did not hear the doorbell when it rang, but Darius did. An impatient expletive slipped from his lips.

"What's the matter, baby?" Jamilah purred without slowing the smooth, rhythmic grinding motion of her hips.

"Somebody's at the door."

"I didn't hear the bell," she whispered close to his ear. Then it sounded again, this time more insistently.

"Who the hell is that?" Darius asked in annoyance.

"I don't know, but let's just ignore it. I...can't...move...right...now... an...y... way." Jamilah felt an orgasm rising in her depths, and she wanted to ride the wave without pause, but Darius suddenly had a bad feeling in his gut that was cemented when he heard banging on the door.

"Wait a minute, baby," he said as a frown furrowed his otherwise smooth fore-head. "I've got to go see who this is."

"Oh, Darius," she grumbled.

He sat up and because she was still straddling him, they were now face-to-face. Darius took her face gently in his hands and kissed her lips. "I'll be right back, Jamilah. I just want to get rid of the fool who's banging on the door like they have no sense."

"Hurry up," Jamilah ordered as she got off of him.

"I will."

Since they had both removed their clothing in the living room, Darius trekked down the stairs in the nude. As he stepped into the living room, the pounding on the door resumed, although now with less force. "Wait a minute, dammit!" he yelled. His patience nearing its end, he hurriedly pulled on his slacks, not bothering with his underwear because he intended for the impending confrontation to be short and to the point. He was eager to get back to his African queen.

Darius stepped over to the front door and unlocked it. When he yanked the door open, he was totally unprepared to catch the body that fell into the house. "What the hell...?" He almost missed, but he caught the woman before she hit the floor. As he supported the limp body in his arms, he studied the bruised and swollen face for a few seconds, wondering who this was and why she was here. Seconds later, however, recognition dawned on him as he stared in horror at the badly beaten face.

"JAMILAH!" Darius picked Sabrina up in his arms as if she weighed nothing and hurriedly carried her to the couch. "JAMILAH!" he called again.

He heard her footfalls on the stairs as she hurried down them. She had carelessly thrown on her bathrobe and was tying it around her waist as she entered the living room. "What's wrong, Darius?" His yelling had frightened her, and fear was evident on her face.

"It's Sabrina, J."

"What?" She hurried to his side. Darius was kneeling on the floor next to the sofa where he had just laid her.

"It's Sabrina," he repeated.

Jamilah looked down on the bloodstained and swollen face of her oldest friend. She gasped in horror at the sight and covered her mouth in shock. Tears immediately formed in her eyes. "Oh my God." She sighed. "Look what he did to her, Darius. Look what he did." She was crying uncontrollably now. She fell to her knees beside Darius and reached for Sabrina. Jamilah embraced her as she cried, "Oh Sabrina, I'm sorry. I'm so sorry. Why'd you let him do this to you?"

"We've got to get her to the hospital," Darius said calmly.

"We have to call the police!" Jamilah said vehemently.

Darius rose to his feet. "We will, baby, but right now, she needs a doctor." He reached for Jamilah to help her to her feet. "Come on, honey; go get dressed. I won't leave her."

Jamilah turned to him and embraced him tightly. "Oh, Darius. What kind of man would do this to her?"

"That's just it, J. A real man wouldn't do this." He held onto Jamilah as he looked down at Sabrina. He couldn't believe Sabrina would be with anyone who was capable of such violence. He hated men who physically abused women. To him, they were the biggest cowards of all. Any man who would ball his fists to punch a woman in the face like this guy Blanchard had so obviously done, got no respect from him. "Don't worry, baby. That coward will get his due. Now you go on upstairs and get dressed. Let's get her to the hospital."

While Jamilah was upstairs getting dressed, Darius went around the living room, picking up their carelessly discarded clothing. He then put on the remainder of his own clothes. As he was buttoning his shirt, Sabrina began to stir.

"Jamilah?" Sabrina moaned softly.

Darius returned to her side immediately. "Shh, lay still, Sabrina. You're safe now. Jamilah just went upstairs to get dressed."

Sabrina could barely see through her swollen eyes, but the soft, gentle voice she heard was very familiar. "Darius?"

"Yeah, it's me. Everything's going to be all right now."

"Is she awake?" Jamilah bounded down the stairs and hurried back to the living room. She had thrown on a pair of jeans and a T-shirt.

"Yeah, she was asking for you." Darius rose to his feet and Jamilah moved to Sabrina's side.

"Hi, honey," she said tenderly as tears streamed down her face. "You're gonna be okay. We're going to take you to the hospital."

"No!" Sabrina suddenly cried with a force that belied her weakened condition.

"Baby, you need a doctor."

"No, they'll arrest me," Sabrina managed to get out. She tried to sit up.

Jamilah gently restrained her. "No, Brie, they won't arrest you. You didn't do anything wrong. They're going to find him and arrest him. Now you lie still."

"I killed him," Sabrina cried. "I killed him. I don't want to go to jail."

Jamilah looked up at Darius. He was wearing a frown. "Did I hear her right?"

"Honey, what happened?" Jamilah gently asked, without acknowledging Darius' query.

"I killed him," Sabrina repeated. "They're gonna arrest me."

"No, they won't. If you killed him, it was in self-defense. No one'll punish you for that," Jamilah said with certainty.

Darius remained silent. Curiosity about what really happened was eating him up.

"But he's dead. I hit him with my ashtray," Sabrina moaned through swollen lips.

"Is he at your apartment?" Jamilah asked.

Sabrina nodded.

"J, we need to get her to the hospital," Darius softly said from behind her.

"I know," she responded tightly, without taking her eyes off Sabrina.

Indeed, Jamilah was well aware that Sabrina needed medical attention, but with this new information, she, too, was worried about what might happen to her friend. Rising to her feet after assuring Sabrina, "I'll be right back," she grabbed Darius' arm and said, "Come here a second." Once out of Sabrina's earshot, Jamilah whispered, "Darius, can you do me a favor?" He didn't answer; he just waited for her to continue. "Would you go by Sabrina's apartment and see if he's really dead?"

He gave her an incredulous look as he asked, "And what if he is?"

"Then call the police."

"Jamilah, as soon as they check her in at the hospital, the police will be called. Besides, there's nothing I can do if he is dead."

"Darius, she's afraid and so am I."

He grabbed her upper arms gently. "I know you are, but if I went there and by chance he wasn't dead, I'd be in trouble."

"Why?"

"Because I'd kill him," Darius stated with conviction.

Jamilah chuckled as a surge of love for him swept over her, but Darius had spoken without the slightest trace of humor.

"Listen, baby, remember that guy I told you about. The one who was investigating him?"

"Yeah."

"I'll call him. He's a Fed and I think he can be trusted. Let me call him. I'll tell him what happened. He'll know how to handle this. But right now, let's just get her to the hospital. It looks like her jaw is broken and she might have a concussion, too."

Jamilah sighed heavily. "Okay."

# Chapter 41

A very was tired. His eyes were burning from reading report after report on Blanchard-Thomas' financial history. Looking forward to the drive home because his brand-new Jacuzzi was waiting for him, he couldn't wait to get into it with an ice-cold beer, one of his favorite cigars and the remote control. He didn't want to see, hear or think about Quenten Blanchard anymore today.

Hoping he would have heard from Sabrina, he'd actually contemplated driving back out to her mother's house to see if she was okay, but figured that might be too presumptuous. Besides, he was still on the job and, like it or not, she could be detrimental to his investigation.

His cell phone began to vibrate in his breast pocket just as he opened the door to his Range Rover. He pulled it free, flipped it open and put it to his ear. "Talk to me."

"Avery Williams?"

"Yeah, who's this?"

"Darius Thornton...of Fischer Stevenson."

"Fischer Stevenson?"

"Yeah. You were in a few weeks ago. We spoke about Quenten Blanchard."

"Oh, yeah. What's up?" Avery already didn't want to talk to this guy simply because he'd mentioned Quenten Blanchard.

"I need your help."

"What can I do for you?" Avery asked as he climbed into his vehicle and put the key in the ignition.

"I'm at Long Island Medical Center. My fiancée and I just brought that son of a bitch's girlfriend in. He beat her up really bad."

Avery was immediately energized and in that split second, forgot himself. "Sabrina?"

"Yeah. You know her?"

He had picked up on the incredulity in Darius' voice at once, and recognizing his slip of the tongue, immediately assumed a professional tone and answered, "We've met."

"Yeah, well, she and my fiancée grew up together and an hour ago, she showed up at her house. She passed out in my arms when I opened the door to let her in. I don't even know how she drove all the way out here, but..." Darius paused before continuing in a near whisper. "She said she killed him."

"Is she all right?" Avery couldn't help but ask.

"She's with the doctors now, but I think she'll be okay. I'm pretty sure he broke her jaw, though."

Avery swore vehemently. "Where is he?"

"She said he's at her apartment." Darius gave him the address.

"Are you going to be there with her for a while?" Avery asked.

"Yeah. Jamilah and I won't leave her."

"Is there a number where I can reach you?"

"You can page me at 888-321-6543. I'll call you right back."

"All right, thanks. I'll call you as soon as I know something." Avery broke the connection. His level of fury at hearing this news was off the scale. "Son of a bitch better be dead, 'cause I'll kill him if he's not," he growled as he peeled away from the curb.

Avery was twenty minutes from Sabrina's apartment. *Why did she leave her mother's house?* He couldn't figure that out. He was certain of one thing, however—Quenten Blanchard's days as a free man were numbered. By beating up Sabrina, he had now made this quite personal.

Darius returned to the waiting room to rejoin Jamilah.

"Did you get him?" she asked immediately upon his reentry.

"Yeah, he's going to check it out. He knows her."

"Sabrina?"

"Yeah. When I told him what happened, he called her by name. When I asked him if he knew her, he tried to backpedal. Just said they'd met, but there's more to it than that, I bet."

"Is he coming here?"

"I don't know. I gave him my pager number so he can call and let me know what's happening."

"You know, Darius, as much as I dislike that no-good so-and-so, I hope he's not dead. I don't want Sabrina to get in any trouble over him."

"I doubt if she would. It's clear she was attacked. As long as she's straight with the cops, there shouldn't be any problems. Besides I really think this guy, Avery Williams, can help. I think he wants to help her."

About two and a half hours after they had arrived at the hospital, Dolly Richardson showed up. Jamilah had called her not long after their arrival, but was unable to get through to her until approximately thirty minutes ago.

The doctors had given Sabrina a sedative for her pain. X-rays showed that Quenten had broken her jaw and nose. Her right eye socket was badly bruised, cutting her visual acuity in half. An eye patch had been placed over her eye to reduce the strain. She also needed five stitches on the side of her mouth.

When Dolly arrived, detectives who had been called by hospital staff were interviewing Sabrina. Jamilah and Darius were in the hallway waiting for the officers to finish their questioning.

"Jamilah! Where is she?" Dolly asked without circumstance.

"Hi, Mrs. Richardson. She's in there," Jamilah said and pointed to the closed exam room door. "There are a couple of cops in there with her."

Dolly was dressed to the nines. Darius, who had never met Sabrina's mother before, was amazed at how much Sabrina's mannerisms mirrored her mother's; at least, the Sabrina he remembered. Dolly wore a vibrant lime-green linen pantsuit, tailored to her proportions, lime-green and gold sandals and carried a pocketbook that was color-coordinated to match her shoes. *She looks great*, Darius thought. *More like Sabrina's sister than her mother.* Her hair was pulled back and knotted at the nape of her neck. Not a hair was out of place, and her makeup was flawless.

Dolly opened the door of the exam room and entered without another word to

Jamilah. She didn't even acknowledge Darius, although it was clear they were together.

When the door to the exam room closed, Darius said, "So that's where she gets it, huh?"

Jamilah instinctively knew he was referring to Sabrina's haughty attitude. "Yup. She gets it honest."

"Yeah, I see."

Dolly had been inside for about twenty minutes when the detectives emerged from the room. She was at the door five seconds later. "Jamilah, would you come inside, please?"

"Come on," Jamilah said to Darius.

"No, you go ahead. I'll wait out here."

"You sure?"

He kissed her lips softly and said, "Yeah, go on."

Jamilah turned away from him and followed Dolly back into the room.

***

Although Sabrina's apartment building was accessible only by key or the intercom system, Avery was lucky enough to arrive at the building at the same time someone was leaving. He caught the lobby door before it slammed shut, saving him the trouble of having to involve the building superintendent. He had already decided that if her apartment door was locked, he would use his specially crafted tools to pick the lock to gain entry. He didn't wait for the elevator, but headed straight for the stairs and took the five flights two steps at a time with ease. He reached the fifth floor in no time.

Sabrina's apartment, luckily, happened to be the closest to the stairs. Avery pulled a pair of rubber gloves from the inside pocket of his windbreaker and slipped them on. His good fortune continued when he put his hand on the doorknob and it turned, giving him immediate access to the apartment.

He paused then, however, as his finely honed law enforcement instincts took over. He reached back to retrieve the pistol that was holstered at the small of his back. With the weapon cocked but lowered to his side, Avery slowly eased the door open. A strange perfumy scent assaulted his nostrils immediately. He quietly entered the apartment, stepped out of the doorway and closed the door quickly but silently behind him. He then grabbed his weapon in both hands, prepared to fire, if necessary. Immediately, he checked the closet directly to his right. When it had been established that his back was safe, he looked toward the kitchen area. The light from the kitchen afforded him a view of the living room and dining area, which he carefully perused before he moved away from his position. Slowly, he made his way across the room toward the kitchen to see if anyone was hidden from his view. Once he was certain there was no one in the room with him, Avery headed for the back of the apartment. After a minute or so, he returned to the living room. He reholstered his weapon, then stood in the center of the room and surveyed the damage.

A broken lamp lay on the floor at the far end of the sofa. Pieces of what might have been a crystal ashtray lay at the base of the counter that separated the kitchen from the dining area. In the same area, there was a pile of sequined dresses, a strand of pearls and other pieces of jewelry. There was no sign of Blanchard. *Obviously*, Avery thought, *Blanchard's not dead. What a pity*. Sabrina must have only hit him hard enough to knock him out.

Avery moved over to the pile of dresses and squatted on his haunches. There was evidence of what he assumed had been the result of Blanchard's rage in the bedroom—the broken dresser mirror, clothing strewn all over and smashed perfume bottles—but why were these things here? His eye caught the broken pieces of crystal. He turned his attention to it. Upon closer inspection, he could see the pieces had indeed been an ashtray. Remnants of cigarette ash coated each piece.

"What's this?" he said softly.

He picked up one of the pieces. *Blood*. Traces of blood lingered in the grooves of this chunk. *This must be what she hit him with*. Avery smiled. "That's my girl." He replaced the piece as he'd found it and rose to his feet.

His first thought was to go looking for Blanchard, but he quickly chucked that idea. He needed to check on Sabrina. He figured the cops would be here soon anyway, if Sabrina was at the hospital. Hospital officials would have to report that she'd been assaulted. He'd let them handle this aspect of the investigation. He knew what he had to do.

***

"She won't talk to me," Dolly said.

"I don't think the doctors want her to talk. Her jaw is broken. I think it's wired shut," Jamilah replied.

"I don't mean verbally," Dolly said in annoyance. "She has a pad. She answered those detectives' questions."

Jamilah looked at Sabrina. Sabrina immediately started writing. When she was finished, she turned the pad to her friend.

"Sabrina," Jamilah hesitated, giving Sabrina a look of confusion and embarrassment.

Sabrina jabbed the pencil at the words on the pad for emphasis. Her eyes were filled with anger.

"What does it say?" Dolly wanted to know.

Jamilah, unable to answer, wouldn't even look at Dolly. She continued to stare at Sabrina in confusion.

Sabrina began to write again. When she turned the pad to Jamilah this time, Jamilah gasped. She then turned to Dolly.

"What?" Dolly asked when she saw the look in Jamilah's eyes.

"Why'd you call him?" Jamilah asked incredulously.

Dolly straightened her spine as though preparing for battle. "I didn't know."

Sabrina began writing fiercely. She turned the pad toward her mother this time. The words proclaimed, *I TOLD YOU!!*

"But I had already called him when you told me," Dolly defended herself.

Sabrina was scribbling fiercely. *Why can't you mind your business?*

Dolly broke into tears and hurried from the room.

Jamilah noticed a tear slide down Sabrina's face. She wiped it away. "It'll be okay, hon."

Sabrina began writing again. She turned the pad toward Jamilah. *She wanted me to marry him for $.*

Jamilah made no comment.

Sabrina's tears flowed steadily as she put pencil to paper again. *I'm just like her.*

***

When Avery arrived at the hospital, he flashed his credentials and without pause, walked past the security guard and into the treatment area of the emergency room.

He recognized Darius as the man he'd met with a few weeks earlier. He strode purposely toward him. With an outstretched hand, he addressed Darius. "Thornton, right?"

"Yeah. Darius Thornton. This is my fiancée, Jamilah Parsons."

"Hello, Miss Parsons." Avery offered his hand.

"Call me Jamilah."

Smiling, he said, "You call me Avery."

Jamilah smiled at him in return.

"Where is she?" Avery asked, turning his attention back to Darius.

"She's in there," Darius said and pointed to the exam room opposite them. "The doctors are with her. Is he dead?"

"I doubt it. He wasn't at the apartment."

"You sound disappointed," Darius stated.

"I am. How bad is she?"

"Pretty bad," Jamilah chimed in. "I don't know how she drove all the way out here. Her eyes are so swollen it doesn't took like she can even see."

Avery's chest started to rise and fall noticeably as he took several deep breaths. Trying hard to control his anger, he turned away from them for a few seconds. Jamilah and Darius passed a curious look at one another while his back was turned.

"What I don't understand is why she went back home. I took her to her mother's house last night to get her away from him. Why'd she leave?" Avery asked when he turned back to them.

"You were with her last night?" Jamilah and Darius asked in unison.

"Yeah." Avery went on to explain.

As Darius and Jamilah listened to Avery recall the events of the previous evening and how he and Sabrina had met, Darius studied his face and body language. There was no mistaking the hatred he felt for Quenten Blanchard. It was clear in every word he spoke. By the same token, however, Darius also noticed that Avery Williams' feelings for Sabrina had nothing to do with his investigation of Quenten Blanchard.

The doctors emerged from Sabrina's room and walked directly over to them.

"How is she?" Jamilah and Avery asked simultaneously.

"We're going to keep her overnight for observation, but she can go home tomorrow. This guy really did a number on her. I hope they find him," the younger of the two physicians said.

"Oh, he'll be found. Don't worry," Avery assured him.

"Are you with the police?"

"No. I'm a federal agent. The creep that did this has been under investigation for some time now. As far as I'm concerned, he just sealed his fate." The anger in Avery's eyes was almost tangible.

"We'll be moving her upstairs in about a half-hour."

"Can I see her?" Avery asked.

"Sure, but not for too long. She needs to rest."

"Right." Avery walked away from them without another word and entered the exam room. His first glimpse of Sabrina's face knocked the wind out of him. *This can't be my Sabrina.* This woman looked like a one-eyed monster. Avery stepped closer to the bed. Choking back tears, he also knew that he had to suppress the slightest hint of anger in her presence. He didn't want her to know how upset he was.

At least a minute or two passed before he softly called, "Sabrina?"

She opened her unpatched eye as far as she could. She had recognized his voice immediately. She didn't want him to see her like this. She was embarrassed. She turned her face away from him.

Avery moved to her side. He leaned over and gently caressed her swollen face. "Please don't turn away from me," he whispered softly.

Tears spilled from the corner of her eye.

"It's okay, Sabrina. I'm here now, and I won't let him hurt you ever again."

She turned back to him and lifted her pad to write. *They're going to put me in jail.*

"For what?" he asked as gentle as a caress.

*I killed him.*

"No, Sabrina, you didn't. Darius called me and I went to your apartment. He wasn't there."

*You know Darius?*

Avery explained to her exactly who he was and the circumstances with which he and Darius had met. "I hope you'll forgive me for not telling you sooner, but I couldn't."

*He's still out there.*

"We'll find him, honey. Don't you worry about that. Right now, though, I want you to rest. The doctors said you can go home tomorrow. I'll come and get you and take you back to your mother's."

*No!* she quickly wrote.

"What's wrong?"

*My mother called him.*

Avery couldn't believe his ears. "What?"

Sabrina could not explain why she did it, but in her mother's defense, she quickly wrote, *She didn't know.*

"I don't think you should go back to your place."

*Jamilah.*

"Can you stay with her?"

She nodded.

"Okay, good. I'll come and get you tomorrow. You get some rest now, okay?"

She nodded again.

Avery smiled. Then he softly kissed her forehead. "I'll see you in the morning."

When Avery stepped back into the corridor, he went over to where Jamilah was sitting alone.

"Where's Darius?"

"He went to the men's room."

Avery sat next to her, and then, realizing his presumptuousness, suddenly began to rise as he said, "I'm sorry. Do you mind if I sit with you?"

"Of course not. Are you going to catch this bastard?" she asked with anger and disgust apparent in her tone.

"Most definitely. I just hope I get to him before the police do. He's crossed the line this time."

Jamilah studied Avery's face as he spoke. *He's quite a handsome fellow,* she thought. His dark eyes were captivating. They were an open book to his soul. "You care about her, don't you?"

Avery leaned back in his chair and blushed. "Is it that obvious?"

"Yes." She smiled at him. "Actually, Darius noticed before I did. He doesn't miss much."

"The lawyer in him, huh?"

She laughed. "Exactly."

"Sabrina told me her mother called Blanchard."

Jamilah sighed. "Mrs. Richardson is very controlling and materialistic. If I know her, and believe me I do, she probably called him the minute Sabrina showed up at the house. She only sees Quenten's bank account and she wants Sabrina to be… She wants Sabrina to have the solid standing his name would afford her."

"Well, there won't be much of that soon. He's going down."

"Good. I never liked him. Not even the first time I met him when she first started talking to him. I never trusted him. He's always reminded me of a snake."

"He is a snake, Jamilah. Listen, can you do me a favor?"

"Sure, what?"

"Can Sabrina stay with you, at least until we catch him?"

"Oh, I was going to insist that she come home with me anyway. I knew she wouldn't go back to her mom's. She's not talking to her."

"I can't believe she called him. Sabrina *must* have told her what happened last night."

"She probably did. I'm telling you, Dolly Richardson is a piece of work. I've known her since I was a child. She has always been a piece of work."

"You've known Sabrina that long?"

"Yeah, we were bosom buddies. A year and a half ago, just around the time she started seeing him, we had a major falling-out. We hadn't spoken in almost that long. Last month we ran into each other by accident. I was still upset about our split and wanted to make things right again, so I went by her place to see her. That's when I found out he was beating her. I told her then to come and stay with me, because he doesn't know where I live."

Darius walked up then. "How is she?"

"I think she'll be okay," Avery answered.

"So what happens now?" Darius asked.

"I don't know if the police have put out an APB on him, but I'm going to contact my agency and make sure the manpower is stepped up so we can take him off the streets. I'm sure he hasn't gotten far. Sabrina hurt him."

"What will you do if you find him?" Darius asked, looking Avery squarely in the eye.

"Pray he resists arrest."

Darius grinned.

Avery rose to his feet. "Let me get to work. Can I give you two a lift somewhere?"

"No, thank you. We drove," Jamilah answered.

"I'll be back in the morning to pick Sabrina up. Can you give me your address, Jamilah?"

She did. "I want to see her again before we go, Darius."

"All right, baby. I'll be right here."

"It was nice meeting you, Avery." Jamilah offered her hand.

"The pleasure was all mine, Jamilah," he said as he shook her hand and smiled. "She's a nice lady," Avery said to Darius as Jamilah walked away.

"She's the best."

Avery smiled at Darius. "Do you know Sabrina?"

"I used to date her. That's how I met Jamilah."

Avery looked at Darius with a bit of skepticism.

"It's a long story. I'll tell you about it one day, but it's not what you think. She dropped me for Blanchard."

"Really?"

"Yeah, but Sabrina and I would have never worked, anyway. I'm just surprised she would put up with his shit. The Sabrina I knew never would have."

Avery wanted to question Darius more, but reasoned that he had plenty of time for that later. Right now, he had to find Blanchard. "Well, I'm out. I'll keep you and Jamilah posted."

# Chapter 42

Avery arrived at Jamilah's house with Sabrina at eleven-thirty Wednesday morning.

"Hi, Avery; hi, Brie," Jamilah said as she gave Sabrina a warm embrace. "I'm so glad you're here. Come on in."

Avery helped Sabrina to the sofa.

"Sabrina, I know you can't really eat anything yet, but I made some chicken soup that has plenty of broth so if you want some, just let me know, okay?"

Sabrina nodded.

"Avery, can I get you anything?"

"No thanks, Jamilah."

"I have the spare room made up for you, Brie, so anytime you want to rest, let me know and I'll help you upstairs."

"I think that would be a good idea, Sabrina," Avery said. "You probably should stay in bed for a couple of days and just take it easy."

"Yeah, I'll be home for the rest of the week, so anything you need, just let me know."

Sabrina touched Avery's arm and pointed toward the staircase.

"You want to lie down?" he asked.

She nodded.

"Come on, let me show you your room," Jamilah said as she reached for Sabrina's hand to help her up from the couch.

"I've got her, Jamilah," Avery said, rising to his feet. He leaned over and picked Sabrina up, cradling her in his arms. "Lead the way."

Jamilah smiled at him and headed for the stairs. She liked Avery, especially for Sabrina. She thought he was exactly what she needed.

"This is your room, Brie."

Jamilah's spare bedroom was bright and airy. The full-size bed was covered with a vibrant print comforter and several plush pillows covered in the same fabric rested at the head of the bed.

An antique cherry dresser with a large oval mirror was directly across from the bed, and a comfortable-looking rocker with cushioned seat and back sat opposite the television stand that held a 19-inch TV set. The night tables on both sides of the bed held matching lamps, and the remote control for the TV rested on one, along with a clock/radio.

Avery laid Sabrina gently on the bed and positioned the pillows behind her head and back so she could sit up.

"I know it's not much, but it's yours for as long as you want it, Sabrina."

Sabrina smiled at Jamilah as best she could and nodded her appreciation.

"The bathroom is right across the hall. Oh yeah, and there's a pad and pencil right here." Jamilah went to the night table and opened the drawer to remove the pad and pencil, as well as a bicycle bell. "I got this so you could call me if you need anything."

Sabrina took the pad and pencil and started writing. *You'll be sorry.*

Jamilah and Avery laughed.

"Sabrina, would you like some soup or tea?" Jamilah asked.

Sabrina shook her head.

"You're sure I can't get you anything, Avery?"

"No, thank you, Jamilah. I'm fine."

"Yes, I see. Well, I'll leave you two. If you need anything, just ring the bell."

"Thank you, Jamilah," Avery said warmly.

"Anytime." Jamilah closed the door behind her.

"She's a good friend, huh?" Avery said to Sabrina.

She nodded and attempted a smile.

Avery sat on the bed beside Sabrina. He reached over and brushed a strand of hair from her face. "You're going to be all right."

Sabrina began writing. *Will you find him?*

"Yes."

*Told him I didn't want to see him anymore.*

"Good for you."

Sabrina smiled sadly as she held up the pad. *He didn't take it too good.*

Avery returned her sad smile. *At least she's in fairly good spirits.*

She began writing again. *Thank you, Avery.*

"You're welcome," he said softly as he gazed tenderly at her.

*I look terrible, don't I?*

"You'll always be beautiful to me. Besides, your scars will heal. In a week or so, you'll be back to normal."

*What's normal? My life's a wreck.*

"Well, now's the time to take stock and start all over with a clean slate. Remember, there are people who love you and will support you as much as you need. And you can always count on me, Sabrina."

*Thank you.*

"Do you still have my numbers?"

She nodded.

"Good. Feel free to call me anytime for anything."

*Did he kill his partner?* she wrote.

"I think so, but it might be difficult to prove." Avery looked at his watch. "I'd better cut out. I have some leads I want to follow up."

*Will you come back later?*

"If you want me to."

Sabrina nodded.

"Then I'll be back. You get some rest." He pressed his lips to her swollen cheek gently, then rose to his feet. "I'll see you later."

Sabrina waved good-bye as he left the room.

When Avery returned to the first floor, Jamilah was seated on the sofa.

"Is she comfortable?"

"Yeah, she'll be fine. I really appreciate that you're letting her stay here. I think this is the safest place for her right now."

"Sabrina is like my sister. I'd do anything for her if I thought it would keep her safe."

"She's lucky to have a friend like you."

"And you, too."

Avery smiled, sensing he had an ally in Jamilah in regard to his personal feelings for Sabrina. "Would you mind if I came back tonight to check on her?"

"Of course, I don't mind. Besides, I'd like updates on what's happening with that animal."

"Oh, don't worry. I'll keep you posted. Where's Darius?"

"He had to go to work. He'll be by later."

"Well, I'm going to leave. I told Sabrina I have a couple of leads I want to follow up." Avery walked to the door.

"Really?"

"Yeah, I think I know where he might turn up."

"Where?"

"I don't want to say, just yet."

"I understand. Please be careful, Avery." Jamilah opened the door for him.

"I will, Jamilah. I've got to get back to check on my girl," he said with a wink.

"That's right. I think with you around, her recovery will be speedier."

"That's nice of you to say."

"I meant every word."

He smiled. "Darius is a lucky man."

"But not as lucky as I am to have him."

"He told me he dated Sabrina."

"Yeah, but they were never a couple, if you know what I mean."

"I do," Avery said, happy for that bit of information.

Several times that afternoon, Jamilah went to look in on Sabrina but each time she appeared to be resting comfortably, so Jamilah didn't wake her.

Darius returned to the house that afternoon when he got off work, but only stayed for a couple of hours. Avery came by while Darius was there, but since Sabrina was asleep, he opted not to stay but instead get back to his search for Quenten.

# *Chapter 43*

The next morning after her shower, Jamilah went to Sabrina's room. She could hear the television so she figured Sabrina was awake.

"Good morning, Brie," Jamilah said cheerfully upon entering the room.

Sabrina smiled and waved.

"How are you feeling?"

Sabrina raised her hand and flipped it back and forth.

"Are you in pain?"

She shrugged.

"Are you hungry?"

She nodded vigorously.

"Would you like some soup and tea?"

Sabrina reached for her pad and pencil. When she was finished writing, she turned the pad to Jamilah. *I'd like a steak and some eggs.*

When Jamilah looked at Sabrina after she had read what was on the pad, she saw that Sabrina was smiling. Jamilah laughed. Sabrina started writing again. *But I'll have some soup and tea.*

"Okay. I'll be right back."

Fifteen minutes later, Jamilah returned with a tray that held a big bowl of chicken broth with small pieces of soft noodles and finely chopped vegetables.

Sabrina was seated in the rocker.

"I'm glad to see you up. Are you feeling okay?"

Sabrina nodded.

"That's good. There's plenty more soup if you want. I tried to make it as hearty as possible, since you can't really chew anything. The noodles will melt in your mouth, and the vegetables are really fine so you shouldn't have a problem swallowing them."

*THANK YOU*, Sabrina wrote in large letters on her pad.

"You're welcome, honey. Do you feel like company?"

*Yes. Is Avery here?*

"Oh no. I meant me."

Sabrina covered her mouth in embarrassment. She wrote, *Yes. I'm glad you're here but hope you're not losing money babysitting me.*

"Oh, don't worry about that. I have plenty of work to do here. Besides, I needed a break from the office."

Sabrina began eating the soup Jamilah had made her, so a few peaceful minutes passed in silence. Jamilah gave her attention to the program on the television. Once Sabrina had finished her soup, she put down her spoon and picked up her pad and pencil and began to write. *This soup is very good. Can I have some more?*

"Sure!" Jamilah said happily. "I'll be right back." When she returned to Sabrina's room with the bowl refilled, Sabrina turned her pad to Jamilah.

*I had a dream about Darius Thornton.*

Jamilah's heart skipped a beat. Sabrina still didn't know about their relationship. Jamilah tried to act nonchalant. "Really?"

*Yes. Dreamt he carried me to hospital.*

*Oh gosh. How am I going to tell her?* Jamilah was quite apprehensive about what Sabrina's reaction would be when she found out that she and Darius were practically engaged. She decided, however, that she would not lie to her. "Well, now that you mention it, he was here the night you got here."

Sabrina gave her a puzzled look.

Jamilah reluctantly danced around the issue. "We ran into each other in May at this restaurant in the city. We exchanged business cards so we could stay in touch."

Sabrina started writing. *I knew you always liked him. He was nice. He'd be good for you.*

Jamilah was surprised by Sabrina's statement. "You know, Brie, when you were seeing him, I never tried to hit on him, and he never tried to hit on me. He was crazy about you."

*I know he was & I know you wouldn't do that to me.*

"After we ran into each other, we started hanging out."

*I should have stuck w/ him & left Q alone.*

"I never liked Quenten."

*I know.*

After a few minutes, Sabrina asked, *Is D seeing anybody now?*

Jamilah paused momentarily before she answered. "Yes."

*I hope she appreciates him. He's a rare find.*

"I know. I do."

Sabrina's mind was sharp and she picked up on Jamilah's reply instantly. *You?*

Jamilah nodded.

They stared at each other for what seemed to Jamilah like hours without a word passing between them. Finally, Sabrina wrote, *I knew you would.*

"It wasn't something we planned, Sabrina. Just one day we realized that we loved each other more than friends."

While Jamilah was speaking, Sabrina wrote, *You don't have to explain.*

Still nervous despite Sabrina's reassurance, Jamilah continued with her entreaty. "I hope this won't affect our friendship, Sabrina. We've been apart so long, and I really missed having you around. I hope my relationship with him doesn't upset you."

Sabrina didn't look up as Jamilah spoke, which led Jamilah to believe that her news had indeed upset her oldest friend. Sabrina began writing steadily. When she put the pencil down, she held the pad out to Jamilah, who then took it and read what she had written.

*I'm not upset. I love you, J. I'm happy for you. And D. He's a good guy & you deserve someone good like him. I missed you, too, & I'm sorry for all the hurt I caused you over the years. I'm happy you still love me. You're the only friend I have. Don't want to lose you.*

When Jamilah had finished reading Sabrina's words, she looked up at her with teary eyes. As she handed the pad back to her, Jamilah said, "I love you, too, Sabrina."

Tears rolled down Sabrina's face as she stared at her lifelong friend. In the next few seconds of silence between them, Sabrina reflected on all the years Jamilah had put up with her selfish ways and jealousy-driven put-downs. Marveling at how Jamilah had always been able to brush off her snide remarks and remain steadfast through thick and thin, Sabrina sometimes felt she didn't deserve a friend like Jamilah. Sabrina also reflected on her brief relationship with Darius, even though it really couldn't be counted as one. She had never truly put anything into it. All she'd ever done was take, take, take; just like Quenten said. Sabrina was happy Jamilah and Darius had found one another. They were truly two of the most good-hearted and giving people she had ever known.

Sabrina wrote, *Are you happy with him?*

"Yes."

*Good. He deserves you, too.*

"He asked me to marry him the other night."

*I know you said YES.*

"Yes, I did."

*Can I be in the wedding?*

"I'd like you to be my maid of honor."

Sabrina really began to cry. Jamilah moved to her side and knelt next to her chair. She reached up and hugged Sabrina gently. "I missed you, Brie. I'm so glad you're here."

The girls cried together for the next few minutes, each happy they were reunited, but sad about the circumstances that had brought them back together. Finally, Jamilah said, "I'm sorry that Quenten hurt you like this. I hope Avery finds him soon."

Sabrina wrote, *He must think I'm pitiful for being with Q.*

"No, he doesn't."

*He knew Q was violent first time we met. Told me to leave him then. I was too stupid to listen.*

"You weren't stupid. He made you vulnerable, and he took advantage of your weakness. He's a coward."

*Avery wanted to hurt him the other night. I think he was hoping Q would try to hit me.*

"I'm sure he would have wiped the floor with Quenten."

Sabrina nodded in agreement.

"He likes you, you know," Jamilah said.

*Avery?*

"Yes.

*He feels sorry for me.*

"No, Sabrina. He likes you. Darius noticed, too. Besides, he told me he cares about you."

Sabrina studied Jamilah's face.

"Yes, Brie, he really did. At the hospital."

Sabrina wrote, *My life's a mess. Don't know if I'm ready for him.*

"He cares about you. I think he'll wait until you are."

*Is he coming tonight?*

"He said he'd be by today. He came last night but you were sleeping. I'm sure he'll be happy to see you up."

# Chapter 44

Avery had a hunch that Blanchard, in all his audacity, would show up at Sabrina's mother's house looking for Sabrina. That being the case, he staked out Dolly Richardson's home on this day as he had the previous day. Figuring Blanchard would arrive sometime in the middle of the day when he assumed Mrs. Richardson was likely to be out of the house, Avery had gone through a pack of cigarettes in the last two days and lost count of the number of cups of coffee he'd drunk.

Reluctantly, when Avery was forced to go home and sleep, he had one of his colleagues take the watch. He didn't want to take any chances that Blanchard would slip by him. He had given his colleague—a young agent new to the department—specific instructions to contact him the moment Blanchard was sighted and not to apprehend him unless he appeared to be leaving the scene. Avery was happy Blanchard hadn't shown up. The one thing he did not want to miss was Blanchard's apprehension.

Avery had been parked a block away from Dolly Richardson's house for close to five hours when he spotted his suspect. He picked up his binoculars, aimed them in Blanchard's direction and adjusted the focus. Blanchard was dressed in a tuxedo that looked as if it had been slept in. His gait was unsteady, as if he were drunk. The white bloodstained bandage that was tied around his head marked Sabrina's defensive attack.

It was evident to Avery that Blanchard had hit rock bottom. The past few days had seen an amazing amount of activity associated with Blanchard's business. It appeared that his attack on Sabrina had spawned a negative chain reaction. Blanchard had to know that the law was closing in on him. Information had been leaked to the press that Quenten Blanchard was suspected of murder, fraud and embezzlement. As a result, his public relations business, which until then had been unaffected by Blanchard's double-dealing, began to suffer. There were news reports that a number of his more prominent clients had pulled their business upon learning of the accusations against him. With the additional clientele he'd lost from his brokerage company, Avery guessed that the past few days must have been very trying for Blanchard. *Pity. The best is yet to come, creep.*

Avery watched as Blanchard approached Sabrina's mother's house. Blanchard walked past the front door, but looked around suddenly, to see if he was being watched or followed. The street was empty. A lone car had passed through the block moments earlier, but neither slowed down nor stopped.

When Blanchard moved to the side of the house and opened the gate to pass through, Avery sprung into action. Leaping from his vehicle, he pulled his cell phone from the breast pocket of his jacket and pressed the speed dial code that connected him directly to his agency.

After the brief call, he trotted across the street, but when he reached the house, he slowed his pace a bit and reached for his weapon. Once it was cocked and ready to fire, he followed the path Blanchard had taken to the back of the house, but held the gun at his side.

When he reached the corner of the house, Avery paused and grabbed the gun with both hands and held it down in front of him so, if necessary, it could be pointed and fired in a split second. Avery stuck his head quickly around the corner to get a glimpse of Blanchard and see what he was up to. Avery was not surprised to see that Blanchard was trying to break in. He acted at once.

"Freeze, Blanchard! You're under arrest," Avery yelled as he rounded the corner with his gun pointed at Quenten. Avery approached him with caution.

Quenten paused and turned. "You!" His shock at seeing Avery was overwhelming.

"Yeah, me. Now put your hands above your head and back away from the house."

"Who the fuck *are* you?" Quenten asked in an exasperated tone.

"Your worst nightmare. Put your hands up!"

Quenten did as instructed and moved away from the back door. "Where's Sabrina?"

"That's for me to know and you to never find out."

Blanchard appeared to be cooperative, so Avery moved closer to him.

"You're a cop?"

"No, worse. Federal agent."

"What do you want with me? I haven't done anything wrong."

"Oh, you've done plenty, and now it's time to pay the piper."

Quenten stopped in his tracks.

"Turn around and keep your hands where I can see them," Avery ordered.

"Listen, there's been some sort of misunderstanding. What could the Feds want with me?"

"I said, turn around. Don't make me tell you again."

Quenten turned slightly. "If you let me go, I can make it worth your while," he furtively suggested.

"Don't you know it's a federal offense to try and bribe an agent of the government. Should I tack that on to the charges that are already mounting against you?" Avery asked calmly.

"I don't know what you're talking about," Quenten said indignantly, as if his last words had never been uttered.

As Avery moved in closer, Quenten asked over his shoulder, "You're fucking her, aren't you?"

Avery ignored him. He stepped up behind Quenten, but kept the gun lowered in front of him.

"Put your hands behind your back," Avery ordered. He removed one hand from the butt of the gun and reached behind him to remove the handcuffs from the pocket attached to his belt.

In that split second, Quenten acted. He turned and swung his arm in a desperate attempt to strike Avery in the neck, but he was too slow. Avery blocked the swing and grabbed Quenten's arm.

"I was hoping you would do something stupid like that."

Avery twisted Blanchard's arm around his back until he yelled in pain. "Aagh, let me go!"

Avery holstered his gun but never loosened his grip on Quenten's arm.

"You like beating up on women, huh? You punk! Whatcha gonna do now?"

"You talk real big with that gun in your hand!" Quenten yelled.

"The gun's holstered." Avery released him. "You wanna challenge me?"

Quenten faced Avery.

"Is that Sabrina's work?" Avery asked with a taunting smile. He could see that his remark had further enraged Quenten. "How many stitches?"

Blanchard yelled as he lunged at Avery, but Avery's reflexes were sharp. Stopping Quenten's rush with a sharp blow to the head, Quenten staggered back a few steps, but driven by his anger, he made the mistake of trying to swing at Avery again. This time Avery retaliated with an upper cut to the chin which straightened Quenten up, followed by a blow to the mid-section, which doubled him over. Avery then pushed Quenten aside, and he landed on his backside on the ground.

"Had enough?" Avery asked as he stood over the woman-beater.

Sirens were lurking in the background, but Avery's young colleague arrived on the scene seconds before the police. "Williams!"

Avery heard his name and turned away from Quenten long enough for him to draw the pistol he had tucked in an ankle holster.

"Avery, duck!" his colleague yelled as he fired.

Avery dropped to the ground, but as Quenten was hit, he got off a shot and hit his mark.

# Chapter 45

It was just after seven that evening when Darius arrived at Jamilah's house. After greeting her with a hug and tender kiss, he asked, "How's our patient doing?"

"She's doing pretty good. She ate a couple bowls of soup and sat up watching television for a few hours. She said the pain is minimal now, and the swelling in her face has gone down quite a bit," Jamilah replied.

"Have you heard anything from Avery?"

"No, and that's got me worried. Sabrina was asking if I'd heard from him, too. She's asleep right now, but I wish he would call one way or the other, so I can tell her something when she wakes up."

"Yeah," Darius said as he moved into the living room. "I know what you mean. I'd like to know what's up, too."

"Are you hungry, baby?" Jamilah asked.

"Yeah, but I want to talk to you first. Come on, let's sit down a minute." He took her hand and led her to the sofa.

"What's up, honey?"

"I know I asked you this the other day, but I want to do it the right way," he said.

Jamilah was confused. "What?"

Darius dropped to one knee and with his left hand, pulled a ring box from his jacket pocket. With his right hand, he took Jamilah's left as he flipped the box open with his thumb.

Jamilah's eyes immediately lighted on the brilliant two-carat marquise diamond set in platinum that rested in the black velvet case.

"Jamilah Parsons, I love you with all my heart and soul. Would you honor me by becoming my wife?"

Tears of joy sprang to Jamilah's eyes and spilled over as a smile lit her face. Her gaze shifted from the ring box and was filled with the handsome face of the man who had made all of her dreams and fantasies about true love a reality. Her adoration for him overwhelmed her at that moment. She wrapped her arms around his neck and cried, "Yes!"

The elation he felt at hearing the solitary word was evident. Darius gently peeled her arms from around his neck and once again took her left hand in his. He carefully removed the ring from its holder and placed it on Jamilah's ring finger, then looked up into her eyes and smiled. "Thank you," he whispered.

Jamilah couldn't resist the urge to kiss him. Her lips found his, commingling with a passion neither had ever felt for another soul. Delirious in her joy, the love she felt for Darius colored her every thought and action. Finally, everything she had ever wanted in life was hers.

As Darius shared the kiss with the woman who would soon become his wife, his thoughts transported him into the future, and he pictured the two of them with their children, living and loving together as he had always dreamed. To him, his parents were the model couple, one he wanted to emulate. He could imagine celebrating a forty-year wedding anniversary with Jamilah, God-willing, and sending their kids off to college. Darius looked forward to the coming years with Jamilah—sharing, caring and growing.

When their lips parted, Jamilah said, "You've just made me the happiest woman in the world."

"Well, that's good, since I'm the happiest man on the planet."

Darius rose from the floor to sit beside Jamilah on the sofa. His arm went across her shoulder as he pulled her close to him.

"I told Sabrina about us today," Jamilah admitted.

"Oh, yeah? What'd she have to say?"

"She said she was happy for us. She said we deserve each other."

"Well, I agree with her there. I'm glad she didn't give you a hard time about it."

"Yeah, I was kind of nervous about telling her, but I figured she's going to find out anyway, and I'd rather she heard it from me. I didn't want it to seem as though we were trying to keep it from her."

"That's good. Besides, we didn't do anything wrong. It's not like she and I, or you and her, for that matter, were together."

"Right. I told her, too, that I think Avery likes her."

"Oh, he's definitely got a thing for her."

"I think he'd be good for her."

"I do, too. I think this experience with Quenten Blanchard has been something of an eye-opener for her."

"Oh, yeah, most definitely. I'm sorry it took a tragedy like this, though, for her to see that her priorities were in the wrong place."

"I agree, but I think she'll be okay now," Darius said.

"I think so, too."

"Are you okay?" Darius asked tenderly.

"Oh, I'm more than okay. You've made everything wonderful."

"Have you thought about when you want to do this?"

"I was thinking about May of next year. On the twelfth."

"Any particular reason you picked that date?" Darius asked.

"Yes. That's the day we ran into each other at Blackberry's."

"The twelfth it is then."

"Are you going to stay tonight, Darius?" Jamilah asked, hoping he would.

"Of course, I'm staying. We've got to consummate our engagement," Darius said playfully as he stuck his tongue in Jamilah's ear.

With a giggle, she replied, "Ooh, well, then I'd better fix you a plate, because you're going to need all of your energy tonight."

"Yeah, that's right, baby; threaten me."

# Chapter 46

S abrina awoke at twelve-fifteen that morning. Although she was certain they were making every effort to be as quiet as possible, it was the muffled sounds of Darius and Jamilah's love play flowing through the otherwise silent house that awakened her. She grabbed the remote control and turned on the television.

Noticing the time, Sabrina frowned because she figured that Avery must have come and gone again while she was still asleep. *That's twice now that I've missed him.* Sabrina figured he still must not have found Quenten. *Jamilah would have wakened me if he had; she knows how anxious I am that he be found and captured.* It didn't matter that she was hidden at Jamilah's house, and Quenten didn't know where Jamilah lived. Sabrina knew she would never feel completely safe until Quenten was behind bars.

Suddenly, her stomach growled. Sabrina was hungry. She wondered if Jamilah had any more of that delicious soup she had given her earlier. After lying there for another twenty minutes staring at the screen, she decided to get up.

Sabrina was happy the dizziness she had experienced that morning when she first arose did not recur. She put on the bathrobe Jamilah had left for her and went to the bathroom to wash her face. *My God, I look horrible. At least the swelling's gone down some,* she thought, sighing heavily as she stared at her reflection in the bathroom mirror. In the next few minutes, she slowly started down the stairs.

Since she had been bedridden for the past couple of days, Sabrina had not had a chance to check out Jamilah's house. As she passed through the living room with the meager light from the foyer, Sabrina now saw that her friend's home was cozily decorated. She thought the furnishings suited Jamilah's personality well. A matching mauve brocade sofa and chair were adjacent to one another and a glass-topped coffee table was positioned in front of the sofa. The plush beige carpet felt great under foot. There was recessed lighting in the living room ceiling, but a decorative table lamp rested on an end table at the juncture between the sofa and chair. On the wall above the sofa, Sabrina noticed an abstract print in a beautiful gold wooden frame. She recognized the design as one of Jamilah's own. She remembered when Jamilah had completed it. *She must have had it enlarged.* A wall unit opposite the couch was filled with stereo equipment, a twenty-five-inch television, and a generous amount of videotapes and CDs. Two more prints, which Sabrina guessed were Jamilah's designs, adorned another wall.

Against the wall in the hallway between the living room and kitchen was a book-shelf, which aside from Jamilah's extensive collection of books, held various framed photographs and other knick-knacks. Sabrina noticed a picture of Jamilah and Darius and stopped to examine it closer. They were both dressed casually in jeans and white T-shirts. Darius stood behind Jamilah with his arms wrapped loosely around her waist. Jamilah's hands rested on his in front of her. They were both looking directly into the camera, and the happiness in their hearts showed clearly in their eyes.

Sabrina's eyes misted over briefly at the realization that she could have been in the photo with Darius if she had only recognized what a treasure he really was when she dated him before she met Quenten. But it was for the best, she reasoned. Darius and Jamilah were more suited to one another, anyway. She was happy that Jamilah had finally found a good man.

She continued to the kitchen. Sabrina hit the wall switch and headed straight for the refrigerator. The kitchen was spotless and despite being somewhat small, it seemed that Jamilah had made the most of her space. There was a bay window over the sink and on the sill was an array of small plants and flowers. It was almost by accident that Sabrina noticed the little wooden picture frame in the shape of a butterfly. She recognized it from their apartment. The frame held a picture of the two of them when they were teenagers. They had gone on a bus trip to Great Adventure amusement park. They both held the small stuffed toys they'd won at one of the park's numerous games of chance. Their arms were linked, and they appeared not to have a care in the world.

Sabrina smiled as she remembered, *that was a good day.*

She opened the refrigerator door and was happy to see that the container with the soup was right there in front. She removed it and began looking through the cabinets for a bowl. Once she had found one and utensils, she scooped a large bit into the bowl, covered it and placed it in the microwave for a minute and a half.

When the microwave alarm sounded, Sabrina took the bowl to the kitchen table, but let it cool a bit before she tried to eat any. Spooning some of the broth into her mouth, after a while, she was still only able to open her mouth wide enough to slurp the soup off the spoon. *It tastes even better than it did yesterday.*

After she had finished that first bowl, Sabrina realized that her hunger was not completely abated, so she heated a bit more. As she slowly ate the second helping, Sabrina reflected on her life. Once Quenten was behind bars, and her scars were healed, she had to start looking for a job. Sabrina was grateful that she had a marketable skill. She had never planned to be a secretary for the rest of her life, but with the ten years of experience as an executive secretary under her belt, she was certain she would have little difficulty finding a decent job. She decided to look for another apartment as well. Although she had wonderful memories from the years she and Jamilah had shared the place, she would never be comfortable living there again after what had happened with Quenten. In fact, she wanted nothing that reminded her of him. She recalled him taking some of her clothing and jewelry when he'd beaten her up. Good. *It was good riddance to bad rubbish.* If there was anything that he had left, she decided she would either sell it or give it away.

Suddenly, Avery came to mind. Did he really care about her as Jamilah said, or would he be gone from her life when this investigation was over and the case closed? Sabrina admitted to herself that her attraction to him had been there from the first time they had met. He was a strikingly handsome man and something of a gentleman from what she had seen. *But am I ready to be involved with anyone, now?* She really wasn't sure. She wanted a man in her life, certainly. Having no desire to be an old maid, she had always wanted a family of her own. Only now her criteria for suitable mates had changed drastically. Experiencing first-hand that monetary worth was no way to judge a person's character, she promised herself that she would never again start a relationship with a man solely based on his net worth.

Now she wanted a man who was strong but sensitive, confident but humble, ambitious but family-minded. Sabrina wanted a man she could talk to and listen to. Jamilah used to tell her that the man she ended up with had to be her friend. Sabrina had always waved her off as being unrealistic, but Jamilah had always had the right idea. She needed to know that her man, whoever he turned out to be, would respect her and accept her with all of her flaws. Avery seemed like that type of man, but she knew she was getting ahead of herself. After all, he might not want anything further to do with her once Quenten was captured.

When Sabrina had finished her second bowl of soup, she went to the sink and washed the dishes she had used. Turning out the light and starting back to her room, she paused to take another quick look at the picture of Darius and Jamilah and smiled. She wished she were more like her friend.

✱✱✱

Jamilah was sleeping like a baby. Darius had lain in the dark for the past ten minutes just staring at her. *God, how I love her.* His heart was full from the love he felt for Jamilah. She was the best thing that had ever happened in his life. *I have to thank Sabrina someday.*

He was thirsty, but he needed to use the bathroom, too. He pushed the covers off his body and rose from the bed, but not before he kissed his love. He used the private bathroom in Jamilah's bedroom, and once he had washed his face and hands, he reentered the bedroom and pulled on a pair of sweatpants and a T-shirt and headed out of the room.

He was surprised to see the light on in Sabrina's room. He wondered if she was all right. Since the door was open, he decided to look in on her to see if she needed anything.

Sabrina was sitting in the rocking chair, staring into space.

He tapped softly on the door as he stuck his head in the room. "Hey, Sabrina, you okay?"

She was startled at first, because she hadn't heard anyone in the hall. She smiled and waved.

"Can I get you anything?" he asked as he took a step into the room.

Sabrina shook her head. She then rose from the rocker, and put her hand up for him to wait. She walked over to the bed and grabbed her pad and pencil from the nightstand. She sat on the bed and began to write. *Sorry I woke you.*

"You didn't. I was just going down to get something to drink."

*Jamilah sleep?*

"Yes."

*Did Avery come?*

He took a few more steps into the room. "No, we didn't hear from him last night. Jamilah and I were wondering if everything was okay."

Sabrina held up the pad, but a worried expression covered her bruised face. *Do you think he's hurt?*

"I don't think so. He looks like he'd have no problem taking care of himself."

She nodded in agreement.

"How are you feeling?" Darius asked.

*Better. Mouth sore, look a mess but okay.*

Darius smiled. "You'll be back to your glamorous self in no time."

She smiled at him. She wrote, *Sit down,* and patted the bed next to her.

Darius moved to the bed and sat.

*Congratulations.*

"Thank you, Sabrina." He looked at her with a warm smile.

*I'm happy for you & J.*

"Thank you. That means a lot to her, you know." Darius paused a moment before he added, "I'm sorry this happened to you. I hope Avery gives him a taste of his own medicine before he locks him up."

*Me too.*

"Can I ask you a very personal question, Sabrina?"

She hesitated a few seconds before she nodded her head affirmatively.

"Why'd you stay with him after the first time? I mean, I remember you as being such a no-nonsense woman."

She thought a moment before she began to write on her pad. *I don't know. I guess I thought he'd never do it again. He apologized and...* Sabrina paused a moment in her writing, as if she had reconsidered her ready answer. She crossed out her first words and began again. *That's not true. I stayed with him because he bought my forgiveness. My priorities were in wrong place. Jamilah told me it would catch up with me.*

"Jamilah never wanted anything like this to happen to you."

*I know. I owe you apology too.*

"For what?"

*Would you like a list?*

"Oh come on, Sabrina. I know you're not talking about what happened a year ago, because that's past history, long gone and forgotten."

*Still owe you apology. I never gave you anything but a hard time. I stood you up the night you got shot, then poured salt in your wound when I told you about Quenten.*

"Yeah, but you also introduced me to Jamilah. That cancels out everything else," he said as he took her hand and smiled at her.

Sabrina smiled gratefully. She then wrote, *You really love her, don't you?*

"Yes, Sabrina, in a way I've never loved anyone; in a way I never thought I *could* love anyone. You know, I believe everything happens for a reason. You turned out to be the bridge that led me to Jamilah, and I thank you for that. I never even realized what a terrific person she was *until* you stood me up, and she offered to fill in for you. I thought that was pretty generous of her."

*She's always been a very giving soul.*

"Yes, I get that impression."

*She was in love with you then.*

"She never went behind your back, Sabrina."

*I know. She'd never do anything like that. But she knew I didn't truly appreciate goodness in you and that, combined with her feelings for you, pushed her to brink. She really let me have it that night. I know I have a lot of work to do on me, a lot of amends I need to make.*

"The folks who love you, Sabrina, love you still. And if it matters, I want you to know I was never angry with you about Quenten. I knew before I got to your place that day that it was over between us. I care about you, and I'd like us to be friends, if you don't mind."

Darius' kind words were more than she could stand. Sabrina started to cry.

He put an arm around her shoulder and gently soothed her. "It's all going to be okay, Sabrina. Please don't cry."

Comforted by his soothing words, after she had gotten herself together, Sabrina wrote, *Jamilah is blessed to have you in her life and I'm blessed to know you, too. I'd love for us to be friends, too.*

"Is everything all right?" Jamilah stood in the doorway of Sabrina's room.

"Oh yeah, baby. I saw Sabrina's light on, so I thought I'd check in on her, make sure everything's okay. We were just talking about you."

"I hope it was good," she said as she came and joined them. She sat next to Darius.

"What else could it be?" Darius said as he kissed her cheek.

"Sabrina, are you hungry?"

She wrote, *I went down and had two more bowls of soup. It tastes even better than this morning.*

"You could have come and got me. I would have gotten it for you."

*Nope. You were entertaining.*

"Yes, she was," Darius said with a mischievous grin.

Jamilah hit him on his leg. "Behave."

Sabrina reached over Darius for Jamilah's hand. She had noticed her ring.

"Oh yeah, he gave it to me today."

Sabrina wrote, *Beautiful! Congratulations!*

"Thank you."

*Thank you, Jamilah. With friends like you two, I think I'll be okay, after all,* Sabrina wrote.

✴✴✴

The next day was Saturday. Since Jamilah and Darius had been up fairly late talking with Sabrina, they were still in bed when the doorbell rang at ten that morning.

Darius quickly pulled on his sweatpants and shirt to go answer the door. As he was about to step out of the room, Jamilah awoke and asked, "Where you going?"

"Someone's at the door. Maybe it's Avery."

She looked over at the clock as Darius continued out of the room. Jamilah hopped out of bed and headed straight to her bathroom.

Darius, meanwhile, was downstairs opening the front door.

"Hey! What happened to you?"

Avery Williams stood just outside the door with his left arm in a sling. "I took a hit yesterday, but it's nothing serious."

"Did you get him?"

"Yes, we did. I had been staking out Sabrina's mother's house figuring he'd come there looking for Sabrina, and I was right. He actually tried to break into her house."

"You're kidding."

"No, he was in a bad way. You've seen the papers in the past couple of days, right?"

"Yeah."

"And Sabrina must have really put something on him, too, because he was acting like he'd lost his mind."

"So you've arrested him."

"Yeah, but he's in the hospital now, in a coma. My colleague shot him and, truthfully, saved my life."

"The girls were really worried about you when they didn't hear from you yesterday."

"Yeah, I figured they would be; that's why I came by so early. I hope I didn't wake you guys."

"Actually, you did. We were all up late last night talking."

"Who's that, Darius?" Jamilah asked as she came down the stairs.

"Hello, Jamilah," Avery said.

"Oh my goodness, Avery, what happened?" she said when she saw his sling.

"It's not serious. I'm all right."

"Quenten?"

"He's in the hospital. They don't know if he's going to make it."

"So, if he dies, the investigation's over, right?"

"No, my office still wants to get to the bottom of his dirty dealings, if possible. They won't close the file until everything's been proven or disproved. How's Sabrina?"

"She's doing a lot better, but she was really worried about you. I was, too," Jamilah admitted.

"Well, I'm okay."

Just then Avery's cell phone rang. "Excuse me." He answered the call, "Talk to me." He listened for a moment. "All right, I'll be in later."

When he broke the connection, he looked at Darius and Jamilah and said, "He's dead."

Neither of them responded for a few seconds. Finally, Jamilah said, "I'd better let Sabrina know." She started back up the stairs. Midway, she stopped and turned back. "Avery, you're not leaving right away, are you?"

"No, I'd like to see Sabrina first."

"Good. Why don't you stay for breakfast?"

"I don't want to intrude."

Darius said, "You're not intruding. Come on in and sit down."

When Jamilah reached Sabrina's room, Sabrina was sitting on the side of the bed. She held up her pad. *Is that Avery?*

"Yes. They got him."

Sabrina closed her eye as a feeling of relief swept over her.

"He's dead, Brie," Jamilah added softly.

Her eye opened and she looked into the eyes of her best friend and saw a sadness that surprised her. *Why sad? Thought you hated him?* Sabrina had written.

"I didn't hate him; I just didn't like him or what he was doing to you. I think it's a shame and a waste that such a successful Black man was so messed up in the head that this is how he ended up."

*Did Avery kill him?*

"I think so."

*He's all right?*

"Yes, but he got hurt a little. His arm's in a sling."

Sabrina twisted her mouth in anguish. As she rose from the bed, Jamilah got her robe off the rocker and helped her put it on. Sabrina grabbed her pad and pencil, and the two headed out of the room.

Avery saw them on the stairs and rose from the sofa. He walked over to meet Sabrina. "There she is," he said with a warm and amorous smile. "How are you feeling?"

Sabrina reached out to him and gently touched his injured arm. Her face was a story in anxiety.

"I'm fine, Sabrina. I took a bullet in the shoulder, but it passed through, no broken bones or anything. It looks worse than it is. I just have to keep it immobilized," Avery explained as he led Sabrina to the sofa where they sat together.

*He's dead?* she wrote.

"Yes. He died this morning. One of my colleagues shot him when he shot me. He was at your mother's house looking for you."

"You were there?" Jamilah asked. She and Darius stood to the side.

"Yes, I was staking it out. I had a feeling he would go there and I was right."

*So what now?* Sabrina's pad read.

"Well, my office will continue its investigation, but it's over for you, Sabrina. It's all over."

Tears of relief welled in her eye. *Thank you,* she wrote.

Avery put his good arm around Sabrina's shoulder and hugged her gently. "You're welcome."

The two of them stared into each other's eyes for a long moment without a word passing between them. Jamilah and Darius quietly left the room.

Sabrina wrote, *Will I ever see you again?*

Avery turned slightly on the sofa and took her chin gently in his hand. "You can't get rid of me so easily, Missy. When you're ready, I'd like to take you to dinner or something."

Sabrina smiled and nodded.

"I'd like us to be friends, Sabrina. Actually, I'd like us to be more than friends, but I won't rush you. We'll take our time and let nature take its course. Whatever happens then, well... Let me just say, I'll always be around."

# Epilogue

Sabrina was thoroughly relaxed when she stepped out of Avery's Jacuzzi that Wednesday night after a harrowing day at work. As the office manager at a small computer networking firm, she had just overseen a big party that was thrown to celebrate the recent acquisition of a major client to their fold. She had had the unenviable task of putting the entire event together. Although party planning was something she did with great aplomb and skill, it had seemed that with this affair, she had been challenged at every turn. First, the caterers had balked about the menu she requested; then the florist had tried to convince her that the orchids she desired were out of season. Although she had been planning the event for weeks, it wasn't until she walked out of the office that night at ten p.m., leaving the building crew to the clean-up, that she was able to exhale. It helped that she had the rest of this week and all of next week off, too.

Jamilah and Darius were getting married in three days, and she was going to be Jamilah's maid of honor. Although she had a major role in the planning of her best friend's bridal shower, wedding and reception, these were tasks she took on with great joy.

Nearly a year had passed since her nightmarish relationship with Quenten Blanchard had come to an end. Since then, her life had taken a complete one hundred and eighty-degree turn. Aside from Jamilah and Darius, she had Avery Williams to thank for the wonderful new outlook she had on life.

After Quenten's death, Avery had done everything in his power to show Sabrina how special she was to him. He made her believe, for the first time really, how beautiful she was, both inside and out. Convincing her that she was worth more than all the material possessions she owned, Avery had shown her a different side of life. She had become less selfish (although he also made sure she knew that a little bit of selfishness was necessary in order to truly take care of oneself), more confident, generous and forgiving.

It had taken a few months before she had been able to forgive her mother for the betrayal which resulted in Quenten's final attack on her, but with Avery's constant reassurance, Sabrina began to see a therapist who helped her overcome her feelings of inadequacy. Once she began to believe that she was deserving of unconditional love, Sabrina was able to recognize the same self-destructive trait in Dolly, and she did everything she could to bring her mother to the same satisfying realization.

Avery had become an invaluable and cherished friend. Although his feelings for Sabrina had always been very deep, he had never pressured her into anything more than she was willing to offer. Despite his strong physical desire for her, Avery had tried hard to keep his love for her on a platonic level, at least until he felt she was ready to begin another relationship.

It was on New Year's Eve that Sabrina had made his dreams a reality. Avery had made reservations for them to spend the holiday weekend at a ski lodge in Vail, Colorado. He had never been into the black-tie/tuxedo scene and avoided such gatherings as much as possible. Discovering Sabrina's affinity for skiing, which, coincidentally, was one of his favorite outdoor sports, he suggested the trip and made it clear that he would arrange for them to stay in a suite with separate bedrooms.

They had arrived late in the afternoon on Friday, December twenty-ninth and were up early Saturday morning, ready to hit the slopes. Spending the entire day, until nearly five p.m., skiing, stopping only for lunch and the occasional mug of hot chocolate, Sabrina had never had so much fun. That night, the lodge held an informal dance party at which Avery and Sabrina danced the night away. They turned in at a few minutes to two in the morning and were back up and on the slopes again at nine o'clock Sunday morning.

The New Year's Eve celebration that the lodge had planned was a semi-formal affair and began at ten o'clock Sunday night. Avery grudgingly traded in his jeans for a pair of black wool slacks, which he complemented with an off-white silk, mock-neck sweater. A black lambskin blazer and his ever-present black alligator cowboy boots completed his ensemble.

He was waiting in the living room of their suite with two stemmed flutes of champagne when Sabrina emerged from her bedroom, dressed in an ankle-length, A-line, off-white wool skirt. A long-sleeved, silk turtleneck blouse and four-inch leather boots of the same hue completed her outfit. Avery thought she was a vision of loveliness, and he let her know.

"I've told you this a hundred times or more, Sabrina, but you are... You're absolutely beautiful." He had spoken the words almost reverently.

Sabrina had never been shy, nor was she one to be frequently caught at a loss for words. Avery, however, always gave her pause. He was the first man she had ever known, outside of her father, who had never tried to be anything more than he was for her sake. Feeling no need to be impressionable, Avery was confident in who he was and happy with his life. She envied that about him, but more than that, his self-assurance made it easy for him to display his love for her, and she saw it clearly each time she looked into his eyes.

When he complimented her that evening, Sabrina smiled and stepped right up to him. "Do you know how good you are for my ego?"

"Well, not to toot my own horn," Avery began, as he put his arms around her waist and pulled her even closer, "but I can be good for a lot of other things, too."

Sabrina gazed up into his eyes and what she saw there sent shivers to the tips of her toes. It seemed like eons since she had felt the desire to share physical love with anyone, but as she stood in Avery's gentle embrace, she realized how very much she wanted to share her love with him.

"Will you show me?" she had asked softly.

It was a few seconds before Avery moved in response to her words. He had waited for an invitation from her and here it was. Slowly lowering his head, he had gently pressed his lips to hers for a long moment before parting her lips with his tongue and taking the prize he had longed for for months.

They never made it to the New Year's Eve party that night. In fact, they never made it to the bedroom, either. Instead, they shared a quiet night of love, laughter and shared promises in front of a roaring fire on the plushy carpeted living room floor.

Five months later, Sabrina was at a place in her life where she had never been. She was genuinely happy with every aspect of her life, for the first time. Despite the headaches that came with her job, she reveled in the challenge and flourished in the midst of it. She was in love with a man who never let her forget how important she was and who accepted her with all of her bumps and bruises. Her oldest and dearest friend, Jamilah, was back in her life, and their renewed friendship had grown to new heights with her maturity. Even her relationship with her mother was becoming stronger with each new day.

When she stepped into Avery's bedroom that warm May evening, wrapped only in the towel she had used to dry herself, he turned his attention from the television screen where the quarter-final contest between two of his favorite basketball teams was taking place at a furious pace.

"Feel better?" he asked as she stepped up to the bed.

Sabrina removed the towel and let it fall to the floor as she climbed up on the king-sized bed, crawled over to him and placed a sensuous kiss on his eager mouth. "Now, I do."

Avery immediately pressed the POWER button on the remote control, then pressed another button that plunged the enormous room into darkness.

"You think so?" he murmured sensually. "Wait 'til you feel this."

Seconds later, Sabrina giggled. "Ooh, that's nice."

It was perfect weather for an outdoor wedding. The temperature was a comfortable eighty-two degrees, and a light ocean breeze blew steadily across the lawn where the ceremony was to take place.

The wedding banquet was being laid out under a canopied pavilion that was nearly the width and half the length of a football field. The outer edges of the pavilion were ensconced by tables covered with white linen, each of which held a beautiful bouquet of white orchids as a centerpiece. The floor of the pavilion was a freshly polished, but removable, parquet covering, ideal for dancing.

To the left of the pavilion and about twenty yards away, two columns of white folding chairs, ten to a row, were already being filled with the wedding guests. The seating was directly in front of a gazebo.

The wedding and reception were being held on the beautifully landscaped property of a country club in Long Island of which a number of Darius' law partners were members.

Darius and his groomsmen were inside the club in a suite that had been reserved for their exclusive use. Although he was thoroughly excited about the impending ceremony, Darius was still feeling the effects of the bachelor party his best man and cousin, James, had hosted the previous night.

He was lounging on the plush tan suede sofa, with his head resting on the back and his eyes closed. He was dressed in a tuxedo shirt with the bow tie hanging loosely around his collar, his socks and boxer shorts. His tuxedo jacket hung nearby on a wooden valet, and his pants were carefully placed across the back of the adjacent recliner.

"How's your head, dude?" James asked as he sat on the opposite end of the sofa. He was fully dressed.

"I've been better," Darius groaned without opening his eyes.

"Your guests are starting to arrive."

"Good for them."

"Do you think Jamilah will be here on time?"

"I hope not." Darius raised his head and looked at his cousin. "I really hope she'll be fashionably late. I could use a good nap."

"Sorry 'bout last night. I guess we overdid it, huh?"

"Last night was great, man. I just shouldn't have drunk so much. I don't know what I was thinkin' about," Darius stated.

The party had been off the hook. James had hired a couple of exotic dancers, who, although Darius was not into that scene, had been undeniably entertaining. The guys who had attended the party all left with huge smiles of satisfaction and kudos for being invited to such an exciting event. Although only light fare had been served, the food and drink had been of the highest quality, and despite his hangover, Darius had really enjoyed himself and was grateful to his friends for making his last night as a bachelor such a memorable one.

But he was eagerly looking forward to starting his new life as Jamilah Parsons' husband.

The rehearsal dinner had taken place at Michael's, and when he and Jamilah had parted company at the restaurant's entrance, Darius had taken her in his arms and held her close. After a few seconds he softly had said, "Well, this is it, huh?"

She had smiled and nodded. "This is it. Are you sure you want to go through with this?"

His answer was a slow, sensuous kiss. When their lips had parted, he had asked, "Do you want to ask me that again?"

"No. I've got my answer," she had replied as tears formed in her eyes. "I love you, Darius. I can't wait to be your wife. I'm going to do everything I can to keep you happy, too."

"As long as you continue to be the beautiful woman you are, Jamilah Parsons, I'll be happy. But I want you to know something, too. You are the most important person in the world to me, and I will never, ever do anything to make you feel anything other than loved."

"I wish I didn't have to leave you now," Jamilah had said.

"Yeah, me, too. But just think, after tonight..."

"After tonight, we'll have forever."

There was a knock on the door to the suite then that brought Darius back to the present. His brother-in-law answered the door. "Hey, Mr. Witherspoon. How are ya?" Jason asked as he held the door open.

"I'm good, Jason, and call me Frank, will you?"

"Okay."

"Hey, fellas," Frank said, addressing Darius and James.

"Frank, how are you?" Darius asked as he sat up straight on the couch.

"I'm good. You look a little worse for wear. You okay?"

"Yeah, just a little hung over."

"Some party last night, huh?"

"To say the least."

"Is Jamilah here?" James asked Frank.

"No. I left her mother and the rest of the party back at Jamilah's house. You know they've got to do their woman thing. I'm not tryin' to be in the middle of that," Frank replied.

"I heard that," said Jason.

"There's quite a few folks here already," Frank said. "I guess they want to get the best seats in the house."

"Did you see my father out there?" Darius asked.

"Yeah, he's on his way up. We dropped your mother off at Jamilah's."

"Jimmy, did Veronica come up this morning?" Darius asked.

"Yeah. I spoke to her a little earlier. She drove up with her brother. He was driving up to see his girl at Vassar College upstate, so he dropped her off on the way. She got in at about six o'clock this morning."

"Where's she staying?"

"At the Marriott near LaGuardia Airport."

"She could've gone to my place. She didn't have to check into a hotel."

"Yes, she did," James said with a sly smile.

"Oh, okay." Darius nodded in understanding.

There was another knock on the door of the suite. James answered it. "What's up, Uncle Fred?" He then noticed Avery Williams at the other end of the corridor. "Avery! Over here, dude."

Mr. Thornton walked into the suite and Darius rose to greet him. "Hi, Daddy." Fred smiled at his son and the two men embraced. Darius kissed his father's cheek. "Big day, huh?" Mr. Thornton said.

"Yeah."

"You ready?"

"Yeah, Dad. I am."

Mr. Thornton gazed at Darius for a long moment before he smiled and said, "I'm very proud of you, son. I'm sure you'll make Jamilah a fine husband. I wish you as much happiness in your marriage as I've had with your mother, and that's more than I can express to you."

"Thank you, Daddy. I just hope I can be as great a father to my kids as you've been to me."

"Oh, Jamilah, you look so beautiful!" Sabrina sung as tears came to her eyes. Everyone concurred.

The bridal party—which consisted of Sabrina as maid of honor; Brianne as bridesmaid; and her daughter, Tara, as flower girl—was gathered in Jamilah's living room with Darius' mother and the photographer when Jamilah, followed closely by Alexia, came down the stairs in her wedding gown.

"Thank you," she answered with a vibrant smile.

The photographer immediately began snapping pictures of Jamilah as she joined the women in her living room. Jamilah was amazed at how the woman was able to move amongst them without ever getting in anyone's way, but was always right on hand to get the shots that would capture this day for all posterity.

"Your limo is outside," Mrs. Thornton stated.

"I know; I saw it from the window upstairs."

Mrs. Thornton stepped up to her and gave her a warm hug. "You look so beautiful."

"Thank you, Mrs. Thornton."

"We should probably get going," Alexia said. "We don't want to be too, too late."

"Yeah, besides, I wanna get married," Jamilah added.

Everyone laughed.

"Sabrina, you ride with Jamilah. We'll take the other car," Alexia directed.

"Okay. You ready to go, girl?" Sabrina asked Jamilah.

"Yes."

The friends stared at each other for a few seconds before Sabrina said, "I'm so happy for you, Jamilah." She sighed. "We always talked about this day when we were little, remember?"

"Yeah."

"You look so beautiful."

"Will you stop it? You're going to make me cry; then I'll have to do my makeup all over again."

Tears streamed down Sabrina's face but she chuckled. "I know; me, too." She dabbed at her eyes with a handkerchief.

"I'm glad you're here with me," Jamilah told her.

The girls embraced. "You're next, you know. I'm going to throw the bouquet straight to you and make sure that Darius throws my garter to Avery."

"I've got my catcher's mitt under my gown."

✳✳✳

The ceremony was spectacular. Jamilah was simply stunning in her silk and chiffon wedding gown designed by Lena Caldwell, a new up-and-coming designer

Sabrina had met through friends of Avery; and Darius was a vision of male excellence in his Hugo Boss white-on-white tuxedo. The vows they exchanged, which they had written themselves, had the entire audience, male and female alike, in tears. Even Darius and Jamilah shed a few tears during the ceremony.

The reception was simply one big party. After James had saluted the newly-weds with a toast, and Jamilah and Darius had cut the cake, Jamilah took to the floor to toss her bouquet. Although there were quite a number of single women in the audience who had positioned themselves at the edge of the crowd to catch the bouquet, the lucky recipient was somewhere in the middle. When the ladies dispersed and headed back to their seats with grumbles and moans, there stood Sabrina holding the bouquet of white roses and baby's breath.

Jamilah simply beamed. Her eyes scanned the enclosure until she found Avery seated at the table with her and Darius' parents. When their eyes met, Jamilah pointed and mouthed, "You're next."

Avery smiled and winked at her.

Darius then took the floor. A chair was placed in the middle of the pavilion and Jamilah was led there to sit. Darius made a show of removing her garter belt, and the crowd loved it. Jamilah threatened that she would make him pay for his performance later. He made her promise that she would. After that, Darius called all the single men to join him on the floor.

When the men took the floor, Darius found Avery amongst the crowd and when they made eye contact, the corner of Darius' mouth turned up in a mischievous smile. He turned his back to them and tossed the garter. Almost as if it was planned, the crowd scattered from around Avery, which was fine with him because he was not keen on the idea of anyone else placing the garter around his woman's leg. He grabbed the lace accessory and immediately turned to Sabrina.

"Come here, woman," he called to her.

Blushing like a schoolgirl, Sabrina moved back to the center of the floor and took a seat in the chair that Jamilah had occupied only minutes earlier.

Avery entertained the audience for nearly five minutes as he placed the garter around Sabrina's ankle before slowly and seductively sliding it up and under her gown. Before he rose from his knee, however, he called for the deejay to bring him a microphone.

"Thank you, my man," he said into the mike. Then, he added, "I know you folks are probably wondering what's going on here. I just have a little something I'd like to say. It's been a longstanding tradition that the lady and gentleman who catch the bouquet and garter are supposedly the next ones to tie the knot. I don't know if that's always the case because most of the time, personally anyway, I never find out what becomes of that particular man and woman. So, I thought it would be nice to let you all leave here today knowing what's to become of me and this beautiful woman here."

Avery then gave his undivided attention to Sabrina. He spoke softly into the microphone. "Sabrina Richardson, you've known for some time now how special you are to me and how much I love you. At least, I hope you know. But, anyway, I want to take this opportunity, just in case you have any doubts, to let you know that I love you with all my heart and every once of my being, and I'd like to ask you, if you would do me the honor of becoming my wife?"

There was a simultaneous chorus of oohs and aahs as Avery pulled a small box from the pocket of his jacket. Sabrina's mouth stood open in shock. He opened the box to reveal a beautiful one and a half-carat solitaire diamond ring.

"Oh Avery." Sabrina sighed as tears of joy formed in her eyes.

As he placed the ring on her finger, Avery again spoke into the mike, "Will you marry me, Sabrina?"

She was crying softly, and as she looked into his eyes through her tears, she nodded her head and said, "Yes, Avery. I will."

Avery's face broke into a brilliant smile. "She said yes, y'all." The audience broke into a thunderous applause as Avery dropped the microphone to the floor with a thud that reverberated throughout the pavilion. He rose to his feet and pulled Sabrina to hers, then wrapped her in a tender embrace as he covered her mouth with his.

## THE END

# ABOUT THE AUTHOR

*Be Careful What You Wish For* is Cheryl Faye's fifth published novel. Her previous titles, *At First Sight, A Time For Us,* and its sequel, *A Test Of Time,* and *First Love,* as well as the short story, "Second Chance At Love," from the Arabesque collection *Mama Dear* have been well received by readers of modern romance as indicated by numerous Amazon.com reviews, letters and emails she has received. A self-described romantic, she has been writing poems, essays, and tales of love and romance since her early teens and admits to living vicariously through her characters.

Currently residing in Jersey City, New Jersey, she is the proud mother of two sons, Michael and Douglas; grandmother of Mikayla; and an active member of the renowned Abyssinian Baptist Church in her hometown of Harlem, New York. Cheryl is also a legal secretary at one of the largest law firms in the country.

Although she has been putting pen to paper and developing fiction stories for over thirty years, Cheryl's first attempt at writing a full-length novel was spurred by a wager in 1987. Accepting that challenge (and winning the bet), she has embraced the art of storytelling, viewing each of her novels as one of her children. She has developed a loyal following by creating realistic tales about relationships between progressive African-American men and women, with protagonists who struggle to grow and maintain life-affirming bonds by opening their hearts and minds to one another's shortcomings and realizing that any relationship worth its salt takes time, patience, understanding, and dedication.

Having just completed her sixth novel, *Necessary Work,* Cheryl is presently hard at work on her seventh novel.

You can write to Cheryl at CherylFaye@aol.com. Please include the book's title in the subject line. (No attachments, please.)

**Baptiste, Michael**
*Cracked Dreams* 1-59309-035-8

**Bernard, D.V.**
*The Last Dream Before Dawn*
0-9711953-2-3
*God in the Image of Woman*
1-59309-019-6

**Brown, Laurinda D.**
*Fire & Brimstone* 1-59309-015-3
*UnderCover* 1-59309-030-7

**Cheekes, Shonda**
*Another Man's Wife* 1-59309-008-0
*Blackgentlemen.com* 0-9711953-8-2
*In the Midst of it All* (May 2005)
1-59309-038-2

**Cooper, William Fredrick**
*Six Days in January* 1-59309-017-X
*Sistergirls.com* 1-59309-004-8

**Crockett, Mark**
*Turkeystuffer* 0-9711953-3-1

**Daniels, J and Bacon, Shonell**
*Luvalwayz: The Opposite Sex and
Relationships* 0-9711953-1-5
*Draw Me With Your Love*
1-59309-000-5

**Darden, J. Marie**
*Enemy Fields* 1-59309-023-4

**De Leon, Michelle**
*Missed Conceptions* 1-59309-010-2
*Love to the Third* 1-59309-016-1
*Once Upon a Family Tree*
1-59309-028-5

**Faye, Cheryl**
*Be Careful What You Wish For*
1-59309-034-X

**Halima, Shelley**
*Azucar Moreno* 1-59309-032-3

**Handfield, Laurel**
*My Diet Starts Tomorrow*
1-59309-005-6
*Mirror Mirror* 1-59309-014-5

**Hayes, Lee**
*Passion Marks* 1-59309-006-4

**Hobbs, Allison**
*Pandora's Box* 1-59309-011-0
*Insatiable* 1-59309-031-5

**Johnson, Keith Lee**
*Sugar & Spice* 1-59309-013-7
*Pretenses* 1-59309-018-8
*Fate's Redemption* (May 2005)
1-59309-018-8

**Johnson, Rique**
*Love & Justice* 1-59309-002-1
*Whispers from a Troubled Heart*
1-59309-020-X
*Every Woman's Man* 1-59309-036-6
*Sistergirls.com* 1-59309-004-8

**Lee, Darrien**
*All That and a Bag of Chips*
0-9711953-0-7
*Been There, Done That*
1-59309-001-3
*What Goes Around Comes Around*
1-59309-024-2

**Luckett, Jonathan**
*Jasminium* 1-59309-007-2
*How Ya Livin'* 1-59309-025-0

**McKinney, Tina Brooks**
*All That Drama* 1-59309-033-1

**Quartay, Nane**
*Feenin* 0-9711953-7-4
*The Badness* (May 2005)
1-59309-037-4

**Rivers, V. Anthony**
*Daughter by Spirit* 0-9674601-4-X
*Everybody Got Issues* 1-59309-003-X
*Sistergirls.com* 1-59309-004-8

**Roberts, J. Deotis**
*Roots of a Black Future: Family
and Church* 0-9674601-6-6
*Christian Beliefs* 0-9674601-5-8

**Stephens, Sylvester**
*Our Time Has Come* 1-59309-026-9

**Turley II, Harold L.**
*Love's Game* 1-59309-029-3

**Valentine, Michelle**
*Nyagra's Falls* 0-9711953-4-X

**White, A.J.**
*Ballad of a Ghetto Poet*
1-59309-009-9

**White, Franklin**
*Money for Good* 1-59309-012-9
*Potentially Yours* 1-59309-027-7

**Zane (Editor)**
*Breaking the Cycle* 1-59309-021-8
(March 2005)

Printed in the United States
149037LV00005B/8/P